Excavation

BY JAMES ROLLINS

Altar of Eden

The Doomsday Key

The Last Oracle

The Judas Strain

Black Order

Map of Bones

Sandstorm

Ice Hunt

Amazonia

Deep Fathom

Excavation

Subterranean

Coming Soon in Hardcover

The Devil Colony

Excavation

James Rollins

HARPER LUXE

An Imprint of HarperCollinsPublishers

EXCAVATION. Copyright © 2000 by Jim Czajkowski. All rights reserved. Printed in the United States of America. No part of this book may be used or reproduced in any manner whatsoever without written permission except in the case of brief quotations embodied in critical articles and reviews. For information address HarperCollins Publishers, 10 East 53rd Street, New York, NY 10022.

HarperCollins books may be purchased for educational, business, or sales promotional use. For information please write: Special Markets Department, HarperCollins Publishers, 10 East 53rd Street, New York, NY 10022.

FIRST HARPERLUXE EDITION

HarperLuxe™ is a trademark of HarperCollins Publishers

ISBN: 978-0-06-206648-0

11 12 13 14 ID/OPM 10 9 8 7 6 5 4 3 2 1

For the 1985 graduating class of
the University of Missouri Veterinary School,
especially my roommates:
Dave Schmitt, Scott Wells,
Steve Brunnert, and Brad Gengenbach.

Acknowledgments

This novel would not have been possible without the invaluable help of both friends and colleagues. First and foremost, I wish to express my gratitude to Lyssa Keusch, my editor, and Pesha Rubinstein, my literary agent. It was their determination, skill, and labor that helped hone this story into its present form. But I also would be remiss without acknowledging and thanking a group of friends who helped pick apart and polish the first draft: Inger Aasen, Chris Crowe, Michael Gallowglass, Lee Garrett, Dennis Grayson, Debra Nelson, Dave Meek, Chris Smith, Jane O'Riva, Judy and Steve Prey, and Caroline Williams. And the most heartfelt thanks to Carolyn McCray and John Clemens for standing by me through the ups and downs of this past year.

For technical assistance, I must also acknowledge Frank Malaret for his knowledge of Peruvian history and Andie Arthur for her help with the Latin translations. I wish also to thank Eric Drexler, PhD., whose book *Engines of Creation* was the inspiration for the science behind this story.

And the Lord God formed man of the dust of the ground, and breathed into his nostrils the breath of life; and man became a living soul. And the Lord God planted a garden eastward in Eden; and there he put the man whom he had formed.

—GENESIS 2:7

Prologue

Sunrise
Andean Mountains
Peru, 1538

There was no escape.

Crashing through the misty jungle, Francisco de Almagro had long given up all prayer of ever outrunning the hunters who dogged his trail. Panting, he crouched along the thin path and caught his breath. He wiped the sweat from his brow with his sleeve. He still wore his Dominican robe, black wool and silk, but it was stained and torn. His Incan captors had stripped him of all possessions, except for his robe and cross. The tribal shaman had warned the others not to touch these talismans from his "foreign" god, afraid of insulting this stranger's deity.

Though the heavy robes ill suited his flight through the dense, cloud-draped jungle of the upper Andes, the young friar still refused to shed his raiment. They had been blessed by Pope Clement when Francisco had first been ordained, and he would not part with them. But that did not mean he couldn't alter them to suit his situation better.

He grabbed the hem of his garment and ripped it to his thighs.

Once his legs were free, Francisco listened to the sounds of pursuit. Already the call of the Incan hunters grew louder, echoing along the mountain pass behind him. Even the screeching cries of the disturbed monkeys from the jungle canopy overhead could not mask the rising clamor of his captors. They would be upon him soon.

The young friar had only one hope left—a chance at salvation—not for himself, but for the world.

He kissed the torn edge of his robe and let it drop from his fingers. He must hurry.

When he straightened too quickly, his vision darkened for a heartbeat. Francisco grabbed the bole of a jungle sapling, struggling not to fall. He gasped in the thin air. Small sparks danced across his vision. High up in the mountainous Andes, the air failed to fill his lungs adequately, forcing him to rest frequently, but he could not let shortness of breath stop him.

Shoving off the tree, Francisco set off once again down the trail, stumbling and weaving. The sway in his gait was not all due to the altitude. Before his scheduled execution at dawn, he had suffered a ritualistic bloodletting and been forced to consume a draught of a bitter elixir—*chicha*, a fermented drink that had quickly made the ground under his feet wobble. The sudden exertion of running from his captors heightened the drug's effect.

As he ran, the limbs of the jungle seemed to reach for him, trying to trap him. The path seemed to tilt first one way, then the other. His heart hammered in his throat; his ears filled with a growing roar, washing away even the calls of his pursuers. Francisco stumbled out of the jungle and almost toppled over a cliff's edge. Far below, he discovered the source of the thunderous rumbling—frothing white waters crashing over black rocks.

A part of his mind knew this must be one of the many tributaries that fed the mighty Urabamba River, but he could not dwell on topography. Despair filled his chest, squeezing his heart. The chasm lay between him and his goal. Panting, Francisco leaned his hands on his scraped knees. Only then did he notice the thin, woven-grass bridge. It spanned the chasm off to the right.

"*Obrigado, meu Deus!*" he thanked his Lord, slipping into Portuguese. He had not spoken his native language since first taking his vows in Spain. Only now, with tears of frustration and fear flowing down his cheeks, did he fall back upon his childhood tongue.

Pushing up, he crossed to the bridge and ran his hands over the braided lengths of *ichu* grass. A single thick cord stretched across the width of river below, with two smaller ropes, one on each side, to assist in balance. If not for his current state, he might have appreciated the engineering feat of the bridge's construction, but now all his thoughts dwelt on escape—putting one foot in front of the other, maintaining his balance.

All his hopes lay in reaching the altar atop the next peak. As they did many of the mountains of the region, the Incas revered and worshiped this jungle-fringed spire. But to reach his goal, Francisco needed first to cross this chasm, then climb out of the cloud forest to the crag's rocky escarpment above.

Would he have enough time?

Turning to listen once again for the sounds of pursuit, Francisco could hear nothing but the crashing tumble of the river below. He had no idea how far behind the hunters remained, but he imagined they were closing the distance quickly. He dared not tarry or cower from the drop below.

Francisco ran a sweating palm over the stubble of his shaven scalp, then grasped one of the two support ropes of the bridge. He squeezed his eyes closed for a moment and grabbed the other cable. With the Lord's Prayer on his lips, he stepped onto the bridge and set off across the chasm. He refused to look down, instead fixing his eyes on the bridge's end.

After an endless time, he felt his left foot strike stone. Sagging in relief, he clambered off the bridge and onto solid rock. He almost fell to his knees, ready to kiss and bless the earth, but a sharp call barked out behind him. A spear struck deep into the loam near his heel. Its shaft thrummed from the impact.

Francisco froze like a startled rabbit, then another cry shouted forth. Glancing behind him, he saw a single hunter standing on the far side. Their eyes met briefly across the chasm.

Predator and prey.

Under a headdress of azure and red feathers, the man grinned at him. He wore thick chains of gold. At least, Francisco prayed it was gold. He shuddered.

Not hesitating, Francisco slipped a silver dagger from inside his robe. The weapon, stolen from the shaman, had been his means of escape. It must now serve him again. He grabbed one of the bridge's balancing ropes. He would never have time to hack through the main trunk of the span, but if he could sever the side ropes, his pursuers would have difficulty crossing. It might not stop them, but it could gain him some time.

His shoulders protested as he sawed at the dried-grass braid. The ropes seemed to be made of iron. The man called out to him, speaking calmly in his heathen language. The friar understood none of his words, but the menace and promise of pain were clear.

Renewed fear fueled Francisco's muscles. He dug and sliced at the rope while hot tears streaked his muddy face. Suddenly, the rope severed under his blade, snapping away. One end grazed his cheek. Instinctively, he reached a hand to touch the injury. His fingers came back bloody, but he felt nothing.

Swallowing hard, he turned to the second support rope. Another spear struck the rock at the cliff's edge and fell away into the chasm. A third followed. Closer this time.

Francisco glanced up. Four hunters now lined the far side of the chasm. The newest hunter held a fourth spear, while the first hunter deftly strung a bow. Time had run out. Francisco eyed the untouched rope support. It was death to stay there. He would have to hope that severing the one braid would slow them enough.

Turning, he sped back into the jungle on the far side of the chasm. The path climbed steeply, straining his legs and chest. Here the trees were less thick, the canopy less dense. As he struggled, the forest grew thinner with each hard-earned league. While glad to see the jungle begin to thin, he knew the lack of foliage also made him an easier target for the hunters. With each step, he expected an arrow to feather his back.

So close . . . Lord, do not forsake me now.

He refused to look ahead, concentrating on the ground beneath his feet. He fought to place one foot after the other. Suddenly light burst around him, as if the Lord Himself had pushed aside the trees to shine His Glory down upon him. Gasping, he raised his head. Even such a simple movement was difficult. In a single step, the jungle was behind him. Raw sunlight from the dawning sun blazed across the red and black stones of the barren peak.

He was too weak even for a prayer of thanks. Scrambling up through the last of the brush, he used his hands and feet to fight for the summit. It must happen there. At their holy altar.

Crying now, but deaf to his own sobs, he crawled the final distance to the slab of granite. Reaching the stone altar, he collapsed back upon his heels and raised his face to the heavens. He cried out, not in prayer, but in simple acknowledgment that he yet lived, casting his voice for all to hear.

His call was answered. The sharp cries of hunters again echoed up from the pass below. They had crossed the chasm and renewed their pursuit.

Francisco lowered his face from the blue skies. Around him, spreading to all horizons, were the countless peaks of the Andes. Some were snow-tipped, but most were as barren as the one upon which he knelt. For a moment, Francisco could almost understand the Incas' worship of these mountain heights. Here among the clouds and skies, one was closer to God. A sense of timelessness and a promise of eternity seemed to ring forth in the heavy silence. Even the hunters grew hushed—either from respect for the mountain or from a desire to sneak upon their prey unawares.

Francisco was too tired to care.

His gaze settled upon the one other type of peak that shared these heights. Below, to the west, were two smoldering mountains, volcanic caldera, twin craters staring up at the same morning skies. From here, the shadowed pair were like two blasted and cursed eyes.

He spat in their direction and raised a fist with his thumb thrust between his two fingers in a ward against evil.

Francisco knew what lay within those warm valleys. From his mountaintop altar, he christened the twin volcanoes. "*Ojos el de Diablo*," he whispered . . . *the Devil's eyes.*

Shivering at the sight, he turned his back on the view. He could not do what must be done while staring at those eyes. He now faced the east and the rising sun.

Kneeling before the blaze of glory, he reached within his robe and slipped out the cross that hung from around his neck. He touched the warm metal against his forehead. Gold. Here was the reason the Spaniards had struggled through these foreign jungles—the dream of riches and wealth. Now their lust and greed would damn them all.

Francisco turned the crucifix and kissed the golden figure upon its surface. This was why *he* had come here. To bring the word of the Lord to these savages— and now his cross was the only hope for all the world. He brushed a finger along the back of the cross, fingering the etchings he had carefully carved into the soft gold.

May it save us all, he prayed silently, and nestled the cross back into his robes, resting it near his heart.

Francisco raised his eyes to the dawn. He had to be certain the Incas never took the cross from him. Though he had reached one of the Incas' sacred sites—this natural mountaintop altar—one final act was required of him to ensure the cross's safety.

Once again, he slipped free the shaman's silver dagger from his robe.

With a prayer of contrition on his lips, he begged forgiveness for the sin he was about to commit. Whether he damned his soul or not, he had no choice. Tears in his eyes, he raised the knife and slashed the blade across his throat. Lancing pain dropped the dagger from his fingers. He fell to his hands. Blood poured from his throat across the dark stones under him.

In the dawn's light, his red blood glowed brilliantly against the black rock. It was his last sight as he died— his life's blood flowing across the Incan altar, shining as brightly as gold.

DAY ONE

Ruins

Monday, August 20, 11:52 A.M.
Johns Hopkins University
Baltimore, Maryland

Professor Henry Conklin's fingers trembled slightly as he unwrapped the final layer of blankets from around his frozen treasure. He held his breath. How had the mummy fared after the three-thousand-mile trip from the Andes? Back in Peru, he had been so careful to pack and crate the frozen remains in dry ice for the trip to Baltimore, but during such a long journey anything could have gone wrong.

Henry ran a hand through his dark hair, now dusted with a generous amount of grey since passing his sixtieth birthday last year. He prayed his past three decades of research and fieldwork would pay off. He would not have a second chance. Transporting the mummy from South America had almost drained the last of his grant money. And nowadays any new fellowships or grants were awarded to researchers younger than he. He was becoming a dinosaur at Texas A&M. Though still revered, he was now more coddled than taken seriously.

Still, his most recent discovery of the ruins of a small Incan village high in the Andes could change all that—especially if it proved his own controversial theory.

He cautiously tugged free the final linen wrap. Fog from the thawing dry ice momentarily obscured his sight. He waved the mist away as the contorted figure appeared, knees bent to chest, arms wrapped around legs, almost in a fetal position, just as he had discovered the mummy in a small cave near the frozen summit of Mount Arapa.

Henry stared at his discovery. Ancient eye sockets, open and hollow, gazed back at him from under strands of lanky black hair still on its skull. Its lips, dried and shrunken back, revealed yellowed teeth. Frayed remnants of a burial shawl still clung to its leathered skin. It was so well preserved that even the black dyes of the tattered robe shone brightly under the surgical lights of the research lab.

"Oh God!" a voice exclaimed at his shoulder. "This is perfect!"

Henry jumped slightly, so engrossed in his own thoughts he had momentarily forgotten the others in the room. He turned and was blinded by the flash of a camera's strobe. The reporter from the *Baltimore Herald* moved from behind his shoulder to reposition for another shot, never moving the Nikon from her face. Her blond hair was pulled over her ears in a severe and efficient ponytail. She snapped additional photos as she spoke. "What would you estimate its age to be, Professor?"

Blinking away the glare, Henry backed a step away so the others could view the remains. A pair of scientists moved closer, instruments in hand.

"I . . . I'd estimate the mummification dates back to the sixteenth century—some four to five hundred years ago."

The reporter lowered her camera but did not move her eyes from the figure cradled on the CT scanning table. A small trace of disgust pleated her upper lip. "No, I meant how old do you think the mummy was when he died?"

"Oh . . ." He pushed his wire-rimmed glasses higher on his nose. "Around twenty . . . It's hard to be accurate on just gross examination."

One of the two doctors, a petite woman in her late fifties with dark hair that fell in silky strands to the small of her back, glanced back at them. She had been examining the mummy's head, a tongue depressor in hand. "He was thirty-two when he died," she stated matter-of-factly. The speaker, Dr. Joan Engel, was head of forensic pathology at Johns Hopkins University and an old friend of Henry's. Her position there was one of the reasons he had hauled his mummy to Johns Hopkins. She elaborated on her statement, "His third molars are partially impacted, but from the degree of wear on the second molars and the lack of wear on the third, my estimation should be precise to within three years, plus or minus. But the CT scan results should pinpoint the age even more accurately."

Belying her calm demeanor, the doctor's jade eyes shone brightly as she spoke, crinkling slightly at the corners. There was no disgust on her face when she viewed the mummy, even when she handled the desiccated remains with her gloved fingers. Henry sensed her excitement, mirroring his own. It was good to know Joan's enthusiasm for scientific mysteries had not waned from the time he had known her back in her undergraduate years. She returned to the study of the mummy, but not before giving Henry a look of apology for contradicting his previous statement and estimation of age.

Henry's cheeks grew heated, more from embarrassment than irritation. She was as keen and sharp as ever.

Swallowing hard, he tried to redeem himself. He turned to the reporter. "I hope to prove these remains found at this Incan site are not actually Incan, but another tribe of Peruvian Indians."

"What do you mean?"

"It has been long known that the Incas were a warrior tribe that often took over neighboring tribes and literally consumed them. They built their own cities atop these others, swallowing them up. From my study of Machu Picchu and other ruins in the remote highlands of the Andes, I've theorized that the lowland tribes of the Incas did not build these cloud cities but took them over from a tribe that already existed before them, robbing these ancestors of their rightful place in history as the skilled architects of the mountaintop cities." Henry nodded toward the mummy. "I hope this fellow will be able to correct this error in history."

The reporter took another picture, but was then forced back by the pair of doctors who were moving their examination farther down the mummy. "Why do you think this mummy can prove this theory?" she asked.

"The tomb where we discovered it predates the Incan ruins by at least a century, suggesting that here might be one of the true builders of these mountain citadels. Also this mummy stands a good head taller than the average Inca of the region . . . even its facial features are different. I brought the mummy here to prove this is not an Incan tribesman but one of the true architects of these exceptional cities. With genetic mapping available here, I can substantiate any—"

"Professor Conklin," Joan again interrupted him. "You might want to come see this."

The reporter stepped aside to let Henry pass, her Nikon again rising to cover half her face. Henry pushed between the two researchers. They had been fingering the body's torso and belly. Engel's assistant, a sandy-haired young man with large eyes, was bent over the mummy. He was carefully tweezing and extracting a length of cord from a fold around the figure's neck.

Joan pointed. "His throat was slashed," she said, parting the leathery skin to reveal the bones underneath. "I'd need a microscopic exam to be sure, but I'd say the injury was antemortem." She glanced to Henry and the reporter. "Before death," she clarified. "And most likely, the *cause* of death here."

Henry nodded. "The Incas were fond of blood rituals; many involved decapitation and human sacrifice."

The doctor's assistant continued working at the wound, drawing out a length of cord from the wound.

He paused and glanced to his mentor. "I think it's some sort of necklace," he mumbled, and pulled at the cord. Something under the robe shifted with his motion.

Joan raised her eyes to Henry, silently asking permission to continue.

He nodded.

Slowly the assistant tugged and worked the necklace loose from its hiding place. Whatever hung there was carefully dragged along under the robe's ragged cloth. Suddenly the ancient material ripped and the object hanging from the cord dropped free for all to see.

A gasp rose from their four throats. The gold shone brilliantly under the halogen spotlights of the laboratory. A flurry of blinding flashes followed as the reporter snapped a rapid series of photos.

"It's a cross," Joan said, stating the obvious.

Henry groaned and leaned in closer. "Not just a cross. It's a Dominican crucifix."

The reporter spoke with her camera still fixed to her face. "What does that mean?"

Henry straightened and waved a hand over a Latin inscription. "The Dominican missionary order accompanied the Spanish conquistadors during their attack upon the Central and South American Indians."

The reporter lowered her camera. "So this mummy is one of those Spanish priests?"

"Yes."

"Cool!"

Joan tapped at the cross with her tongue depressor. "But the Incas weren't known to mummify any of their Spanish conquerors."

"Until now," Henry commented sourly. "I guess if nothing else the discovery will be worth a footnote in some journal article." His dreams of proving his theory dimmed in the glare of the golden crucifix.

Joan touched his hand with a gloved finger. "Don't despair yet. Perhaps the cross was just stolen from one of the Spaniards. Let's first run the CT scan and see what we can discover about our friend here."

Henry nodded but held no real hope in his heart. He glanced to the pathologist. Her eyes shone with genuine concern. He offered her a small smile, which, surprisingly, she returned. Henry remembered that smile from long ago. They had dated a few times, but both had been too devoted to their studies to pursue more than a casual acquaintance. And when their careers diverged after graduation, they had lost contact with each other, except for the occasional exchange of Christmas cards. But Henry had never forgotten that smile.

She patted his hand, then called to her assistant. "Brent, could you let Dr. Reynolds know we're ready to begin the scan?" She then turned to Henry and the reporter. "I'll have to ask you to join us in the next room. You can view the procedure from behind the leaded glass in the control room."

Before leaving, Henry checked the mummy to ensure it was properly secured on the scanner's table, then slipped the gold crucifix from around the figure's neck. He carried it with him as he followed the others out of the room.

The adjoining cubicle was lined with banks of computers and rows of monitors. The research team planned on using a technique called computer tomography, or CT, to take multiple radiographic images which the computer would then compile into a three-dimensional picture of the mummy's interior, allowing a virtual autopsy to be performed without damaging the mummy itself. Besides the professional contact, this was the reason Henry had hauled his mummy halfway around the world. Johns Hopkins had performed previous analyses on other Peruvian ice mummies in the past and still had backing from the National Geographic organization to continue with others. The facility also had a keen genetics lab to map ancestry and genealogy, ideal for adding concrete data to substantiate his controversial theories. But with the Dominican cross in hand, Henry held out little hope of success.

Once inside the control room, the door, heavy with lead shielding, closed snugly behind them.

Joan introduced them to Dr. Robert Reynolds, who waved them to the chairs while his technician began calibrating for the scan. "Grab a seat, folks."

While the others scooted chairs into a cluster before the viewing window, Henry remained standing to maintain a good view of both the computer monitors and the window that looked out upon the scanner and its current patient. The large white machine filled the back half of the next room. The table bearing the mummy protruded from a narrow tunnel leading into the heart of the unit.

"Here we go," Dr. Reynolds said as he keyed his terminal.

Henry jumped a bit, almost dropping the gold cross, as a sharp clacking erupted from the speakers that monitored the next room. Through the window, he watched the tray holding the contorted figure slowly inch toward the spinning core of the scanner. As the crown of the mummy's head entered the tunnel, the machine's clacking was joined by a chorus of loud thunking as the device began to take pictures.

"Bob," Joan said, "bring up a surface view of the facial bones first. Let's see if we can pinpoint where this fellow came from."

"You can determine that from just the skull?" the reporter asked.

Joan nodded, but did not turn from the computers. "The structure of the zygomatic arch, the brow, and the nasal bone are great markers for ancestry and race."

"Here it comes," Dr. Reynolds announced.

Henry turned from the window to look over Joan's shoulder. A black-and-white image appeared on the monitor's screen, a cross section of the mummy's skull.

Joan slipped on a pair of reading glasses and squeaked her chair closer to the monitor. She leaned forward to study the image. "Bob, can you rotate it about thirty degrees?"

The radiologist nodded, chewing on a pencil. He tapped a few buttons, and the skull twisted slightly until it was staring them full in the face. Joan reached with a small ruler and made some measurements, frowning. She tapped the screen with a fingernail. "That shadow above the right orbit of the eye. Can we get a better look at it?"

A few keys were tapped and the image zoomed in closer. The radiologist removed the pencil from between his teeth. He whistled appreciatively.

"What is it?" Henry asked.

Joan turned and tilted her glasses down to peer over their rims at him. "A hole." She tapped the glass indicating the triangular shadow on the plane of bone. "It's not natural. Someone drilled into his skull. And from the lack of callus formation around the site, I'd guess the procedure was done shortly after his death."

"Trepanning . . . skull drilling," Henry said. "I've seen it before in other old skulls from around the world. But the most extensive and complicated were among the Incas. They were considered the most skilled surgeons at trepanning." Henry allowed himself a glimmer of hope. If the skull had been bored, maybe he *had* uncovered a Peruvian Indian.

Joan must have read his thoughts. "I hate to dash your hopes, but trepanning or not, the mummy is definitely *not* of South American ancestry. It is clearly European."

Henry could not find his voice for a few breaths. "Are . . . are you sure?"

She took off her glasses, settled them back in her pocket, and sighed softly, clearly well accustomed to passing on a dire diagnosis. "Yes. I'd say he came from Western Europe. I'd guess Portugal. And given enough time and more study, I could probably pinpoint even the exact province." She shook her head. "I'm sorry, Henry."

He recognized the sympathy in her eyes. With despair in his heart, he struggled to keep himself composed. He stared down at the Dominican cross in his hand. "He must have been captured by the Incas," he finally said. "And eventually sacrificed to their gods atop Mount Arapa. If his blood was spilled on such a sacred site, European or not, they would have been forced to mummify his remains. It was probably why they left him his cross. Those who died on holy sites were honored, and it was taboo to rob their corpses of any valuables."

The reporter had been hurriedly jotting notes, even though she had a tape recorder also monitoring their conversation. "It'll make a good story."

"Story, maybe . . . even a journal article or two . . ." Henry shrugged, attempting a weak smile.

"But not what you were hoping for," Joan added.

"An intriguing oddity, nothing more. It sheds no new light on the Incas."

"Perhaps your dig back in Peru will produce more intriguing finds," the pathologist offered.

"There is that hope. My nephew and a few other grad students are delving into a temple ruin as we speak. Hopefully, they'll have better news for me."

"And you'll let me know?" Joan asked with a smile. "You know I've been following your discoveries in both the *National Geographic* and *Archaeology* magazines."

"You have?" Henry stood a little straighter.

"Yes, it's all been very exciting."

Henry's smile grew wider. "I'll definitely keep you updated." And he meant it. There was a certain charm to this woman that Henry still found disarming. Add to that a generous figure that could not be completely hidden by her sterile lab coat. Henry found a slight blush heating his cheeks.

"Joan, you'd better come see this," the radiologist said in a hushed voice. "Something's wrong with the CT."

Joan swung back to the monitor. "What is it?"

"I was just fiddling with some mid-sagittal views to judge bone density. But all the interior views just come back blank." As Henry looked on, Dr. Reynolds flipped through a series of images, each a deeper slice through the interior of the skull. But each of the inner images was the same: a white blur on the monitor.

Joan touched the screen as if her fingers could make sense of the pictures. "I don't understand. Let's recalibrate and try again."

The radiologist tapped a button and the constant clacking from the machine died away. But a sharper noise, hidden behind the knock of the scanner's rotating magnets, became apparent. It flowed from the speakers: a high-pitched keening, like air escaping from the stretched neck of a balloon.

All eyes were drawn to the speakers.

"What the hell is that noise?" the radiologist asked. He tapped at a few keys. "The scanner's completely shut down."

The *Herald* reporter sat closest to the window looking into the CT room. She sprang to her feet, knocking her chair over. "My God!"

"What is it?" Joan stood up and joined the reporter at the window.

Henry pushed forward, fearing for his fragile mummy. "What—?" Then he saw it, too. The mummy still lay on the scanning table in full view of the group. Its head and neck convulsed upon the table, rattling against the metal surface. Its mouth stretched wide open, the keening wail issuing from its desiccated throat. Henry's knees weakened.

"My God, it's alive!" the reporter moaned in horror.

"Impossible," Henry sputtered.

The convulsing corpse grew violent. Its lanky black hair whipped furiously around its thrashing head like a thousand snakes. Henry expected at any moment that the head would rip off its neck, but what actually happened was worse. Much worse.

Like a rotten melon, the top of the mummy's skull blew away explosively. Yellow filth splattered out from the cranium, spraying the wall, the CT scanner, and the window.

The reporter stumbled away from the fouled glass, her legs giving way beneath her. Her mouth chanted uncontrollably, "Oh my God oh my God oh my God . . ."

Joan remained calm, professional. She spoke to the stunned radiologist. "Bob, we need a Level Two quarantine of that room. Stat!"

The radiologist just stared, unblinking, as the mummy quieted its convulsions and lay still. "Damn," he finally whispered to the fouled window. "What happened?"

Joan shook her head, still calm. She replaced her glasses and studied the room. "Perhaps a soft eruption of pocketed gas," she mumbled. "Since the mummy was frozen at a high altitude, methane from decomposition could have released abruptly from the sudden thawing." She shrugged.

The reporter finally seemed to have composed herself and tried to take a picture, but Joan blocked her with a palm. Joan shook her head. There would be no further pictures.

Henry had not moved since the eruption. He still stood with one palm pressed to the glass. He stared at the ruins of his mummy and the brilliant splatters sprayed on walls and machine. The debris shone brightly, glowing a deep ruddy yellow under the halogens.

The reporter, her voice still shaky, waved a hand at the fouled lead window. "What the hell is that stuff?"

Clutching the Dominican crucifix in his right fist, Henry answered, his voice dull with shock: "Gold."

5:14 P.M.
Andean Mountains, Peru

"Listen . . . and you could almost hear the dead speak."

The words drew Sam Conklin's nose from the dirt. He eyed the young freelance journalist from the *National Geographic*.

An open laptop computer resting on his knees, Norman Fields sat beside Sam and stared out across the jungle-shrouded ruins. A smear of mud ran from the man's cheek to his neck. Though he wore an Australian bushwacker and matching leather hat, Norman failed to look the part of the rugged adventure photojournalist. He wore thick glasses with lenses that slightly magnified his eyes, making him look perpetually surprised, and though he stood a little over six feet, he was as thin as a pole, all bones and lanky limbs.

Sam rolled up to one elbow on his mat of woven reed. "Sorry, what was that, Norm?" he asked.

"The afternoon is so quiet," his companion whispered, his Boston accent flavoring his words. Norman closed his eyes and breathed deeply. "You can practically hear the ancient voices echoing off the mountains."

Sam carefully laid the tiny paintbrush beside the small stone relic he had been cleaning and sat up. He tapped his muddied cowboy hat back farther on his head and wiped his hands on his Wranglers. Again, like so many times before, after working for hours upon a single stone of the ruins, the overall beauty of the ancient Incan city struck him like a draught of cold beer on a hot Texas afternoon. It was so easy to get lost in the fine ministrations of brush on stone and lose sight of the enormity and breadth of the whole. Sam pushed into a seated position to better appreciate the somber majesty.

He suddenly missed his cutting horse, a painted Appaloosa still back on his uncle's dusty ranch outside Muleshoe, Texas. He itched to ride among the ruins and follow its twisted paths to the mystery of the thick jungle beyond the city. He sat there with the ghost of a smile on his face, soaking up the sight.

"There is something mystical about this place," Norman continued, leaning back upon his hands. "The towering peaks. The streams of mist. The verdant jungle. The very air smells of life, as if some substance in the wind encourages a vitality in the spirit."

Sam patted the journalist's arm in good-natured agreement. The view was a wondrous sight.

Built in a high saddle between two Andean peaks, the newly discovered jungle city spread in terraced plazas across half a square mile. A hundred steps connected the various stonework levels. From Sam's vantage point among the remains of the Sun Plaza, he could survey the entire pre-Columbian ruin below him: from the homes of the lower city outlined in lines of crumbling stone, to the Stairway of the Clouds that led to Sun Plaza on which they perched. Here, like its sister city Machu Picchu, the Incas had displayed all their mastery of architecture, merging form and function to carve a fortress city among the clouds.

Yet, unlike the much-explored Machu Picchu, these ruins were still raw. Discovered by his uncle Hank only a few months back, much still lay hidden under vine and trees. A spark of pride flared with the memory of the discovery.

Uncle Hank had pinpointed its location from old tales passed among the Quechans of the region. Using hand-scrawled maps and pieces of tales, he had led a team out from Machu Picchu along the Urabamba River, and in only ten days, discovered the ruins below Mount Arapa. The discovery had been covered in all the professional journals and popular magazines. Nicknamed the Cloud

Ruins, his uncle's picture beamed from many a front page. And he deserved it—it had been a miraculous demonstration of extrapolation and archaeological skill.

Of course, this sentiment might be clouded by Sam's feelings for his uncle. Hank had raised Sam since his parents had died in a car crash when he was nine years old. Henry's own wife had died of cancer the same year, about four months earlier. Drawn together in grief, they developed a deep bond. The two had become nearly inseparable. So it was to no one's surprise that Sam pursued a career in archaeology at Texas A&M.

"I'd swear if you listen close enough," Norman said, "you can even hear the wail of the warriors calling from high in the peaks, the whispers of hawkers and buyers from the lower city, the songs of the laborers in the terraced fields beyond the walls."

Sam tried to listen, but all he could hear were the occasional snatches of raised voices and the rasping of shovel and pick echoing up from a nearby hole. The noises were not the voices of the Incan dead, but of the workers and his fellow students laboring deep in the heart of the ruins. The gaping hole led to a shaft that dropped thirty feet straight down, ending in a honeycomb of excavated rooms and halls, a subterranean structure of several levels. Sam sat up straighter. "You ought to be a poet, Norman, not a journalist."

Norman sighed. "Just try listening with your heart, Sam."

He thickened his west Texas drawl, knowing how it irritated Norman, who hailed from Boston. "Right now all I kin hear with is my belly. And it ain't saying nothing but complaining about dinnertime."

Norman scowled at him. "You Texans have no poetry in your souls. Just iron and dust."

"And beer. Don't forget the beer."

The laptop computer suddenly chimed the six o'clock hour, drawing their attention.

A rattling groan escaped the narrow confines of Sam's throat. "We'd better wrap up the site before the sun sets. By nightfall, the place will be crawling with looters."

Norman nodded and twisted around to gather his camera packs. "Speaking of grave robbers, I heard gunfire last night," he said.

Sam frowned while storing away his brushes and dental picks. "Guillermo had to scare off a band of *huaqueros*. They were trying to tunnel into our ruins. If Gil hadn't found them, they might have pierced the dig and destroyed months of work."

"It's good your uncle thought to hire security."

Sam nodded, but he heard the trace of distaste in Norman's voice at the mention of Guillermo Sala, the ex-policeman from Cuzco assigned as the security head for the expedition. Sam shared the journalist's sentiment. Black-haired and black-eyed, Gil bore scars that Sam suspected weren't all from the line of duty. Sam also noticed the sidelong glances he shared with his compadres when Maggie passed. The quick snippets of Spanish exchanged with guttural laughs heated Sam's blood.

"Was anyone hurt in the gunfire?" Norman asked.

"No, just warning shots to scare off the thieves."

Norman continued stuffing his gear. "Do you really think we'll find some tomb overflowing with riches?"

Sam smiled. "And discover the Tutankhmen of the New World? No, I don't think so. It's the dream of gold that draws the thieves, but not my uncle. *Knowledge* is what lured him here—and the truth."

"But what is he so doggedly searching for? I know he seeks some proof that another tribe existed before the Incas, but why this stubborn need for secrecy? I need to report to the *Geographic* at some point to update them before the next deadline."

Sam bunched his brows. He had no answer for Norman. The same questions had been echoing in his own mind. Uncle Hank was keeping some snippet of information close to his chest. But this was always like the professor. He was open in all other ways, but when it came to professional matters, he could be extremely tight-lipped.

"I don't know," Sam finally said. "But I trust the professor. If he has his nose into something, we'll just have to wait him out."

A shout suddenly arose from the excavated hole on the neighboring terrace: "Sam! Come look!"

Ralph Isaacson's helmeted head popped from the shaft, excitement bright in his eyes. The large African-American, a fellow grad student, hailed from the University of Alabama. Financed on a football scholarship, he had excelled in his undergraduate years and managed to garner an academic scholarship to complete his master's in archaeology. He was as sharp as he was muscular. "You have to see this!" The carbide lamp of Ralph's mining helmet flashed toward them. "We've reached a sealed door with writing on it!"

"Is the door intact?" Sam called back, getting to his feet excitedly.

"Yes! And Maggie says there's no evidence of tampering."

This could be the breakthrough all of them had been searching for these past months. An intact tomb or royal chamber within the ancient ruins. Sam helped Norman, burdened by his sling of cameras, up the steep steps toward the highest terrace of the Sun Plaza.

"Do you think—?" Norman huffed.

Sam held up a hand. "It may just be a basement level to one of the Incan temples. Let's not get our hopes up."

By the time they had reached the excavated terrace, Norman was wheezing. Ralph frowned in disdain at the photographer's exertion. "Havin' trouble there, Norman? I could ask Maggie to help carry you."

The photographer rolled his eyes and refrained from commenting, too winded to speak.

Sam joined them atop the plaza. He was breathing hard, too. Any exertion at this high altitude taxed lungs and heart. "Leave him alone, Ralph," he scolded. "Show us what you found."

Ralph shook his head and led the way with his helmet lamp. The black man's wide frame filled the three-foot-wide shaft as he mounted the ladder. Unlike Sam, Ralph did not get along with Norman. Ever since the photographer had let his sexual orientation be known, a certain friction had grown between the two. Raised in the Bible Belt, Ralph seemed unable to let go of certain prejudices that had nothing to do with color. But Henry had insisted they all work together. Be a team. So the two had developed a grumbling cooperation.

"Jackass," Norman mumbled under his breath, shifting his camera load.

Sam clapped the photographer on the shoulder and glanced into the excavated hole. The rungs of the ladder descended thirty feet to the warren of chambers and hallways below. "Don't let him get to you," Sam said. He waved toward the ladder. "Go on. I'll follow."

As they descended, Ralph spoke, his words growing in excitement again. "We just got the carbon-dating back on the deepest level this morning. Did you hear, Sam? A.D. 1100. Predating the damn Incas by two damn centuries."

"I heard," Sam said. "But the margin of error on dating still leaves this result questionable."

"Maybe . . . but wait 'til you see the etchings!"

"Are they Incan imagery?" Sam called down.

"It's too soon to say. When we uncovered the door, I rushed up to fetch you two. Maggie is still down there trying to clean up the door. I figured we should all be present."

Sam continued to climb down. Lamplight bloomed from below, casting his shadow up the wall of the shaft. He could imagine Maggie bent with her nose an inch from the door, meticulous with brush and tweezers as she freed the history of these people from centuries of mud and clay. He could also picture her auburn hair pulled back in a long ponytail as she worked, the way her nose crinkled when deep in concentration, the small noises of pleasure she made when she discovered something new. If only he could attract a tenth of the attention the stones of the ruins earned from her.

Sam stumbled on a rung of the ladder and had to catch himself with a quick grab.

After three more steps, his feet touched rock. He stepped from the ladder into the cramped cavern of the first level. The sodium lamps stung his eyes with their brightness while the heavy odor of turned soil and moist clay filled his nostrils. This was not a dusty, dry tomb of Egypt. The continual mist and frequent jungle storms of the high Andes saturated the soil. Rather than sand, the archaeologists battled moldy roots and wet clay to release the trapped secrets of the underground structure. Around Sam, the handiwork of ancient engineers glowed in the light, bricks and stones so skillfully fitted together that not even a knife blade could slide between them. But even such design could not fully withstand the ravages of time. Many areas of the subterranean structure had been weakened by winding roots and centuries of accumulated clay and soil.

Around Sam, the ruins groaned. It was a frequent noise, stressed stones settling after the team had cleared the clay and dirt from the rooms and halls, hollowing them out. The local Quechan workers had installed a latticework of wooden support beams, bolstering the ancient, root-damaged bulwarks and ceilings. But still the underground structure moaned with the weight of earth piled atop it.

"This way," Ralph said, guiding them toward the wooden ladder that descended to the second level of tunnels and rooms. However, that was not their final destination. After climbing down two more ladders, they reached the deepest level, almost fifty feet underground. This section had not been fully cleared or cataloged. Throughout the honeycomb of narrow excavated tunnels and rooms bolstered by wooden frames, shirtless workers hauled sacks of mud and debris. Normally, the tunnels echoed with the workers' native songs, but now the halls were quiet. Even the workers suspected the importance of this discovery.

Silence hung like a wool blanket across the ruins. The garrulous Ralph had finally halted his discourse on the discovery of the sealed chamber. The three proceeded in silence through the last of the tunnels to the deepest room. Once in the wider chamber, the trio, who had been squeezing through the passage single file, spread out. Sam could finally see more than just the bowed back of Norman Fields.

The chamber was no larger than a cramped single-car garage. Yet, in this small room buried fifty feet underground, Sam sensed that history was about to be revealed. The chamber's far side was a wall of quarried stone, again so artfully constructed that the granite pieces fit together like an intricate jigsaw puzzle. Though still covered in many places with layers of clay and mud, the workmanship had obviously withstood the ages and the elements. Yet as amazing as the architecture was, what stood in the center of the wall drew all their eyes: a crude stone arch blocked by a carefully fitted slab of rock. Three horizontal bands of a dull metal, each a handspan wide, crossed the doorway and were bolted to both door and frame.

No one had been through this portal since the ancients had sealed it.

Sam forced himself to breathe. Whatever lay past the locked door was more than just a passage to a subbasement. Whoever had sealed it had intended to protect and preserve something of enormous value to their society. Beyond this portal lay secrets hidden for centuries.

Ralph finally broke the silence. "Damn thing's sealed tighter than Fort Knox!"

His words broke the door's spell on Sam. He finally noticed Maggie seated cross-legged before the portal. She leaned an elbow on one knee and rested a cheek in her palm. Her eyes were fixed on the door, studying it. She did not even acknowledge their presence.

Only Denal, the thirteen-year-old Quechan boy who served as camp translator, greeted them with a small nod as they entered. The youth had been hired off the streets of Cuzco by Sam's uncle. Raised in a Catholic missionary orphanage, Denal was fairly fluent in English. He was also respectful. Slouching against a wooden support to the right, Denal held a cigarette, unlit, between his lips. Smoking had been outlawed in the dig for the sake of preserving what was uncovered and protecting the air quality in the tunnels.

Sam glanced around and noticed someone was missing. "Where's Philip?" he asked. When the professor had left for the States, Philip Sykes, the senior grad student, had been assigned to oversee the dig. He should have been there, too.

"Sykes?" Maggie frowned. A hint of her Irish brogue shone through the tightness in her voice. "He took a break. Left over an hour ago an' hasn't been back."

"His loss," Sam mumbled. No one argued about fetching the Harvard graduate student for the moment. After assuming the title of team leader, Philip's haughty attitude had rubbed everyone raw, even the stoic Quechans. Sam approached the door. "Maggie, Ralph mentioned writing on the doorway. Is it legible?"

"Not yet. I've cleared the mud, but I've been afraid to scrape at the surface and risk damaging the engraving. Denal sent one of the workers to fetch an alcohol wash kit for the final cleaning."

Sam leaned closer to the archway. "I think it's polished hematite," he said as he rubbed the edge of one of the bands. "Notice the lack of rust." He backed away so Norman could take a few photos of the untouched door.

"Hematite?" Norman asked as he measured the room's light.

Ralph answered while the journalist snapped his pictures. "The Incas never discovered the art of smelting iron, but the mountains around here were rich with hematite, a metallic ore from old asteroid impacts. All the Incan tools found to date were either made of plain stone or hematite, which makes the construction of their sophisticated cities all the more amazing."

After Norman had taken his photos, Maggie reached a finger out to the top band of metal, her finger hovering over its surface, as if she feared touching it. With her fingertip, she traced the band where it was fastened to the stone arch. Each bolt was as thick around as a man's thumb. "Whoever built this meant to keep whatever is inside from ever seeing the light of day."

Before anyone could respond, a black-haired worker pushed into the chamber. He bore vials of alcohol and distilled water along with a handful of brushes.

"Maybe the etchings will reveal a clue to what lies within," Sam said.

Sam, Maggie, and Ralph each took brushes and began painting the diluted alcohol solution across the bands. Norman looked on as the students labored. Working on the center band, Sam's nose and eyes burned from the fumes as the alcohol worked upon the dirt caught in the metal's inscriptions. A final dousing with distilled water rinsed the alcohol away, and clean rags were passed to the three students so they could wipe away the loosened debris.

Sam gently rubbed the center of his band in small buffing circles.

Maggie worked on the seal above him, Ralph on the band below. Sam heard a slight gasp from Ralph. Maggie soon echoed his surprise. "Sweet Mary, it's Latin," she said. "But that . . . that's impossible!"

Sam was the only one to remain quiet. Not because his band was blank, but because what he had uncovered shocked him. He stepped away from his half-cleaned band. All he could do was point to its center.

Norman bent closer to where Sam had been working. He, too, didn't say a word, just straightened, his jaw hanging open.

Sam continued to stare at what he had uncovered. In the center of the band was a deeply etched cross on which was mounted the tiny figure of a crucified man.

"Jesus Christ," Sam swore.

Guillermo Sala sat on a stump at the jungle's edge, a rifle leaning against his knee. As the sun crept closer to the horizon behind him, young saplings growing at the ruin's edge spread their thin shadows across the ground, stretching toward the square pit fifteen meters away. From the hole's opening, lamplight glowed out into the twilight, swallowing the shadows as they reached toward the shaft. Even the hungry shadows knew what lay below, Gil thought. Gold.

"We could slit their throats now," Juan said at his elbow. He nodded toward the circle of tents where the scientists had retreated to study the engravings on the tomb's door. "Blame it on grave robbers."

"No. The murder of *gringos* always draws too much fire," Gil said. "We stick to the plan. Wait for night. While they sleep." He sat patiently as Juan fidgeted beside him. Four years in a Chilean prison had taught Gil much about the price of haste.

Juan swore under his breath, while Gil merely listened to the awakening rain forest around him. At night, the jungle came alive in the moonlight. Each evening, games of predator and prey played out among the black shadows. Gil loved this time of the evening, when the forest first awoke, shedding its green innocence, revealing its black heart.

Yes, he could wait, like the jungle, for the night and the moon. He had already waited almost a year. First, by ensuring that he was assigned as security for this team, then putting the right men together. He came to guard the tomb and did so dutifully—not for the sake of preserving the past for these Yankee scientists, but to safeguard the treasures for himself.

These *maricon* Americans galled him with their stupidity and blindness to the poverty around them. To raid a country's tombs for the sake of history when the smallest trinket below could feed a family for years. Gil remembered the treasures discovered in 1988 at Pampa Grande, in an unmolested Moche tomb. A flow of gold and jewels. Peasants, trying to snatch a crumb from the harvest of wealth, had died at the hands of guards just so the treasures could languish in foreign museums.

Such a tragedy will not occur here, he thought. *It was our people's heritage! We should be the ones to profit from our past!*

Gil's hand strayed to the bulge in his vest. It was one of the many gifts from the leftist guerrillas in the mountains who had helped Gil in this venture. Gil patted the grenade in his pocket.

It was meant to erase their tracks after the raid on the tomb, but if these *pelotudo* American scientists tried to interfere . . . well, there were always quicker ways to die than by a knife's blade.

Maggie O'Donnel despised Latin. Not a simple distaste for the dead language, but a heartfelt loathing. Educated in strict Catholic schools in Belfast, she had been forced to study years of Latin, and even after repeated raps across her knuckles from sadistic nuns, none of it had sunk in. She stared now at the charcoal tracings of the door's inscription spread across the table in the main tent.

Sam had a magnifying lens fixed over one of the filigreed etchings from the top band. A lantern swung over his head. He was the best epigrapher of the group of students, skilled at deciphering ancient languages. "I think this says *Nos Christi defenete*, but I wouldn't stake my eyeteeth on it."

The journalist, Norman Fields, hung over Sam's shoulder, his camera ready on his hip.

"And what does that bloody mean?" Maggie asked sourly, feeling useless, unable to contribute to the translation. Ralph Isaacson, who was just as weak in his Latin skills, at least knew how to cook. He was outside the tent struggling to light the campstove and get dinner started.

Ever since the professor had left, the team had struggled to efficiently clear the ruins and catalog as much as possible. Each had their assigned duties. Every evening, Ralph did the cooking, leaving cleanup to Norman and Sam, while Maggie and Philip tediously entered the day's reports into the computer log.

Sam interrupted her reverie. He scrunched up his nose as he tried to read the writing. "I think it says, 'Christ preserve them,' or 'Christ protect them,'" he said. "Something like that."

Philip Sykes, the senior grad student, lay sprawled on a cot, a cold rag across his eyes. His irritation at being left out of the discovery still clearly rankled him. "Wrong," he said bitingly, not moving from where he lay. "It translates, Christ protect *us*. Not *them*." He followed his assessment with a disdainful noise.

Maggie sighed. It was no wonder Philip knew Latin so well. Just another reason to hate the dead language. He was forever a font of trivial knowledge, ready at any instance to correct the other students' errors. But where he excelled in facts, he lagged in on-site experience—hence, the team was burdened with him now. He needed to clock dig hours before he could earn his Ph.D. After that, Maggie suspected the wanker would never leave the ivy halls of Harvard, his alma mater, where his deceased father's chair in archaeology surely awaited him. The Ivy League was still one big boys' club. And Philip, son of an esteemed colleague, had a key.

Stretching her shoulders, she moved closer to Sam. A yawn escaped her before she could stop it. It had been a long day topped by fervid activity: photographing the door, getting a plaster cast of the bands, charcoal etching the writing, logging and documenting everything.

Sam gave her a small smile and shifted aside the etching of the middle band. It contained only the single crucifix carved into the metallic hematite. No other writing. Sam lowered his magnifying glass on the third and final onionskin tracing. "Lots of writing on this one. But the script is much smaller and isn't as well preserved," he said. "I can only make out part of it."

"Well then, what can you read?" Maggie asked, sinking into a folding chair near the table. A seed of a headache had started to grow behind her right temple.

"Give me a few minutes." Sam cocked his head to the side as he squinted through his lens. His Stetson, usually tilted on his head, rested on the table beside him. Professor Conklin had insisted on a bit of common courtesy out here in the jungle. When inside the tents, hats had to come off, and Sam still maintained the protocol, even though his uncle was not present. Sam had been raised well, Maggie thought with a small hidden grin. She stared at the professor's nephew. Sam's dusky blond hair still lay plastered in place from the Stetson's imprint.

Maggie resisted the urge to reach over and tousle his hair back to a loose mop. "So what do you think, Sam? Do you truly think the Spanish conquistadors etched these bands?"

"Who else? The conquistadors must have searched this pyramid and left their mark." Sam raised his head, a deep frown on his face. "And if the Spanish were here, we can kiss good-bye any chance of finding the tomb intact. We can only hope the conquistadors left us a few scraps to confirm Doc's theory."

"But according to the texts, the Spanish never discovered any cities in this region. There is no mention of the conquistadors ever reaching their thieving hands this far from Cuzco."

Sam merely pointed to the table laden with Latin etchings. "There's the proof. We can at least walk away with that. The conquistadors that arrived here must never have made it back to their battalions at Cuzco. The natives must have killed them before they could make it down out of the mountains. The discovery of this city died with them."

"So maybe they didn't get a chance to loot this tomb," Maggie insisted.

"Perhaps . . ."

Maggie knew her words did little to convince anyone. She, too, knew that if the conquistadors had the time to etch the bands, then they had more than enough time to raid the temple. She didn't know what else to say, so she simply slumped in her seat.

Sam spoke up. "Okay. This is the best I'm able to pick out of this mess. *Domine sospitate* something something *hoc sepulcrum caelo relinquemeus.* Then a few lines I couldn't make out at all, followed by *ne peturbetur* at the end. That's it."

"And what does that mean?" Maggie asked.

Sam shrugged and gave her one of his wise-ass smiles. "Do I look like a Roman?"

"Oh my God!" Philip exclaimed, drawing Maggie and Sam's attention. He bolted upright. The rag dropped from his face to his lap.

"What?" Sam lowered his magnifying lens.

"The last part translates, *We leave this tomb to Heaven. May it never be disturbed.*"

Ralph suddenly pushed through into the tent, his hands full with four mugs. "Who wants coffee?" He paused when he saw them all frozen with eyes wide. "What happened?"

Sam was the first one able to speak. "How about we break out the champagne instead? Toast a few ol' conquistadors for protecting our investment here."

"What?" Ralph asked, his face scrunched with confusion.

Philip spoke next, his voice edged with reserved excitement. "Mr. Isaacson, our tomb may still be intact!"

"How do you—?"

Maggie picked up one of the onionskin tracing sheets. She held it toward him. "By Jesus, you gotta love Latin."

Sam could barely contain his excitement as he waited for his computer to connect to the university's internet site via the satellite hookup. He sat in the communication tent with the other students gathered around behind him. The tent was weathertight and insulated against the elements, protecting the delicate equipment from the eternal mists of the jungle heights.

Sam checked his watch for the hundredth time. Two minutes shy of ten o'clock, the time each evening when Sam or Philip updated the professor on their progress on the dig. That night, though, was the first time the team had exciting news for his uncle. Sam jabbed hurriedly at the keys as the connection was made. He initiated the video feed. The small camera fixed to the top of the monitor blinked on its red eye. The video satellite link had been a gift from the National Geographic Society. "Smile everyone," Sam muttered as he finished calling up his uncle's internet address.

The computer whirred through its connections and a small flittering picture of Henry appeared in the upper right-hand corner. Sam tapped a few keys and the picture filled the entire screen. The video feed was jittery. When his uncle waved a hand in greeting, his fingers stuttered across his face.

Sam pulled the microphone closer. "Hi, Doc."

His uncle smiled. "I see everyone is with you tonight. You must have something for me."

Sam's face ached from the wide grin still plastered to his lips, but he wasn't going to give up the team's prize that easily. "First give us the lowdown about the mummy. You said yesterday that the CT was scheduled for this morning. How'd it go?" Sam regretted his question as soon as he saw his uncle's face cloud over. Even from three thousand miles away, Sam could tell the old man didn't have good news. Sam's smile faded away. "What happened?" he asked more soberly.

Henry shook his head; again it was a jittering movement, but the words flowed smoothly through the receiver. "We were correct in judging the mummy as non-Inca," he began, "but unfortunately, it was European."

"What?" Sam's shock was shared by the others.

Henry held up a wavering hand. "As near as I can tell, he was a Dominican priest, probably a friar."

Maggie leaned toward the microphone. "And the Incas mummified one of their hated enemies—a priest of a foreign god?"

"I know. Strange. I plan to do a little research here and see if I can trace this friar's history before returning. It's not what I wanted to prove, but it is still intriguing."

"Especially in the light of our discovery here," Sam added.

"What do you mean?" Henry asked.

Sam explained about their discovery of the sealed door and the Latin inscriptions.

Henry was nodding by the end of Sam's description. "So the conquistadors truly did find the village. Damn." Henry slowly took off his glasses and rubbed at the small indentations on his nose. His next words seemed more like he was thinking aloud. "But what happened here five hundred years ago? The answer must lie behind that door."

Sam could almost hear the gears whirring in his uncle's mind.

Philip grabbed the mike. "Should we open the door tomorrow?"

Sam interrupted before his uncle could answer. "Of course not. I think we should wait until Doc returns. If it's a significant find, I think we'd need his expertise and experience to explore it."

Philip's face grew red. "I can handle anything we discover."

"You couldn't even handle—"

Henry interrupted, his voice stern and tight. "Mr. Sykes is right, Sam. Open the door tomorrow. Whatever lies hidden beyond the sealed portal may aid my research here in the States." His uncle's eyes traveled over the entire group. "And it is not just Philip I trust. I am counting on all of you to proceed as I've taught you—cautiously and meticulously."

Even with these last words, Sam noticed the gloating expression on Philip's face. The Harvard grad would be unbearable from there on out. Sam's fingers gripped the table's edge with anger. But he dare not question his uncle. It would sound so petty.

"Sam," his uncle continued, "I'd like a few words in private." Henry's words were severe and scolding in tone. "The rest of you should hit your pillows. You've a long day tomorrow."

Muttering arose from the others as they said their good-byes and shuffled off.

Henry's voice followed them from the tent. "And good work, folks!"

Sam watched the others leave. Philip was last to slip out of the tent, but not before shining a tight smile of triumph on his lips. Sam's right hand balled into a fist.

"Sam," his uncle said softly, "are they all gone?"

Forcing his hand to relax, Sam faced his uncle again. "Yeah, Uncle Hank," he said, dropping to a more familiar demeanor.

"I know Philip can rankle everyone. But he is also a smart kid. If Philip can grow to be half the archaeologist his father was, he'll be a fine scholar. So cut him some slack."

"If you say so . . ."

"I do." Henry slid his chair closer to the computer. His shaky image grew on the screen. "Now as to the reason I wanted to speak to you in private. Though I voiced my support of Philip, I need you to be my eyes and ears tomorrow. You've had a lot more dig experience, and I'm counting on you to help guide Philip."

Sam could not suppress a groan. "Uncle Hank, he'll never listen. He already thinks he's the big buck at the salt lick."

"Find a way, Sam." Henry replaced his eyeglasses, ending the matter. He stared silently at Sam as if weighing him. "If you are to be my eyes and ears, you'll need to know everything I know, Sam. There are some items I've kept from the others. To properly evaluate what you discover tomorrow, you'll need to be fully informed."

Sam sat straighter. His irritation at Philip vanished in a single heartbeat. "What?"

"Two items. First, something odd happened to the mummy here at Johns Hopkins." Henry explained about the explosion of the mummy's skull and the brilliant golden discharge.

Sam's eyebrows were high on his forehead. "Christ, Uncle Hank, what the hell happened?"

"The pathologist here hypothesized a possible burst of trapped methane from sudden thawing. But after four decades in the field, I've never seen its like before. And that discharge . . . Dr. Engel is researching what it is. I may know more in a few days, but until then, I want you to keep your eyes open. The mystery as to what occurred in this village five centuries ago may be answered when you open that door."

"I'll watch out for any clues and proceed with care, even if I have to force an iron bit and reins on Philip."

His uncle laughed. "But remember, Sam, experienced riders know it's best to control a willful horse with only the lightest touch on the reins. Let Philip think he is leader and all will go well."

Sam frowned. "Still . . . why the secrecy, Uncle Hank?"

Henry sighed, a slight shake of his head. He suddenly seemed much older, his eyes tired. "In the world of research, secrets are important." Henry glanced up at Sam. "Remember the looters. Even in the remote wilds of the Andes, a few loose lips drew the scavengers like flies to horse droppings. The same can occur in the research community. Loose lips can sink grants, fellowships, and tenures. It's a hard lesson I don't like teaching."

"You can trust me."

Henry smiled. "I know, Sam. I trust you completely. I would have been glad to share all I know with you, but I didn't want to burden you with secrets. Not yet. You'll find how it weighs on your heart when you can't speak openly with your own colleagues. But matters now force me to shift my burden onto your shoulders. You must know the last piece of the puzzle, the reason I am sure an older tribe built this city." Henry leaned closer to the screen. "I believe I may even know who it was."

"What are you talking about? Who? This site has the Incas' stamp all over it."

His uncle held up a hand. "I know. I never disputed that the Incas eventually took over this site.

But who was here before them? I've read tales, recorded oral histories spread from ancestor to ancestor, of how the first Incan king went to the sacred
mountains and discovered a bride in a wondrous city.
Returning with her, he started the Incan empire that
would last hundreds of years. So even in their ancient
tales, the Incas admit that a foreign tribe shared their
roots. But who? It's the mystery I've been investigating for decades. My research into this matter led to
the discovery of these ruins. But the answer to the
question—*who built this city?*—*that* I only discovered
last month."

Speechless, Sam's mind spun at the prospect of how
much his uncle had kept hidden. "Y . . . you truly
know who built this city?"

"Let me show you." Henry reached to his own keyboard and mouse and began manipulating files. "I
wish I could claim it was a brilliant piece of research
on my part, but in actuality it was one of those fortuitous events that always seem to push archaeology
forward."

His uncle's image shrank to the corner of the screen
and a three-dimensional schematic of the current dig
appeared. Colored lines marked off the various levels
of the dig. The detail of the computer-generated landscape and surmounting ruins amazed Sam. Using the

mouse, Henry manipulated the pointer, and the screen zoomed into an aerial close-up of the ruins atop the Sun Plaza. A small black square marked the entrance tunnel to the ruins below.

"Here is our site. The tunnel into the underground structure."

"I know," Sam said, "but what does this have to do with—?"

"Patience, my boy." Henry cracked a wry smile from the corner of the screen. "Last month, a bit of luck occurred—I received a CD-ROM from a fellow researcher from Washington University in St. Louis. It contained computer-generated maps of several Moche pyramids currently under excavation at Pampa Grande along the coast. Six hundred miles away."

"Moche sites?" Sam remembered his lessons on this region. Many centuries before the Incan civilization arose, the Moche were a tribe that lived along a two-hundred-mile stretch of Peruvian coast. Pyramid builders and masters of intricate metalwork, their tribes had prospered between A.D. 100 and 700. Then for no known reason, their civilization vanished.

Henry tapped a few more keys, and Sam's computer screen split into two images, side by side. On the left was the aerial map of their ruins. On the right was a new computer schematic of a flat-topped pyramid. His uncle pointed a finger at it. "Here is the pyramid at Pampa Grande." He zeroed the image onto the tip of the Moche structure.

"Oh Lord!" Sam gasped.

"Now you know my little secret." The two images merged together, overlapping one another. It was a perfect match. "The Sun Plaza is actually the tip of a buried Moche pyramid. Our underground ruins are actually the remains of a subterranean pyramid. One of their sacred temples."

"My God, Uncle Hank! Why are you keeping this a secret? You should announce your discovery!"

"No. Not until I have further physical proof. I had hoped the researchers here at Johns Hopkins would be able to correlate genetic markers in the mummy to a Moche lineage, thus substantiating my claims. But . . ." Henry shrugged. "It looks like the mysteries of this jungle ruin just grow with each new piece we add to the puzzle."

"The Moche," Sam said, stunned with too much information. Mummified priests, exploding skulls, buried pyramids, strange warnings scrawled in Latin . . . how would they tie it all together?

As if reading his thoughts, his uncle spoke. "The answers to all these mysteries may lie beyond that door, Sam. I can almost feel it. So be careful."

Guillermo studied the dark camp. Midnight beckoned. The group of young scientists and the Quechan laborers had all retired to their tents. The only lights left were those positioned around the dig.

Raising his rifle, Gil signaled Juan and Miguel.

Juan, his skeletal frame barely discernible under the eaves of the surrounding forest, nudged his companion. Broad of back but squat in height, Miguel stepped out from the jungle's edge, his back bowed with a large canvas bag. It contained the tools they would need to crack through the tomb door. Juan followed, a pickax over his shoulder.

Gil waved them toward the highest terrace. He knew they would have to be quick, but Gil did not complain. Sufficient hours until daybreak still remained, and the news that the tomb had a good chance of being intact had buoyed Gil's hopes for a significant strike.

He joined Juan and Miguel by the entrance to the shaft. "Keep it quiet, you *hijos de putas*," he hissed to them. Gil threw the switch that sped current from the generator in the camp to the lamps below. He nodded for Juan to lead, followed by Miguel.

Gil kept a watch on the camp as they climbed down. The surrounding rain forest, its edges lit up by the four spotlights positioned at the compass points around the ruins, echoed with the hoots and occasional screeches of the night. The jungle noises and the chugging rattle of the camp's generator should mask their efforts.

Satisfied, Gil hooked his rifle over his shoulder and climbed down the ladder to join the others.

"Ai, *Dios mio*, it's a fucking maze down here," Juan whispered sourly.

Miguel just grunted, spitting out a jawful of *hoja de coca*. The coca leaves splattered against the granite stonework.

Neither had been down into the ruins. Only Gil had intimate knowledge of the tunnels and rooms of the buried building. Crouching, he led them through the maze to the last chute that led to the sealed door.

Juan continued to grumble behind him until the thin man stepped fully into the chamber and saw the door. "*Jesu Christo!*"

Gil allowed himself a small grin. The arched doorway set in quarried stone spoke of ancient times and hidden treasures. Its bands glowed in the glare of the single sodium lamp. The writing and crucifix were a dark blemish against the silvery metal.

"We don't have all night," Gil snapped.

They knew what had to be done. Miguel dropped his bag of tools to the floor with a clanking clatter and fished through its contents. Juan swung his pickax in precise swings, loosening the rock around the bolts. Miguel then used his crowbar and hammer to free the bolts. Within minutes, the top band fell to the mud and rock underfoot.

Juan wiped sweat from his brow, his grin wide. Miguel's shirt clung to him like he had just climbed from a river. Even Gil, who did nothing more than oversee the labors, found himself mopping his face with a handkerchief. The eternal dampness of the tombs seemed to cling to them, as if claiming the three as its own.

In short order, the other two bands soon joined the first in the mud. Rock dust sifted through the room, stinging eyes and irritating noses raw. Juan sneezed and swore a stream of vulgarities.

Gil clapped him on the shoulder. "A little respect for our ancestors, *ese*. They are about to make us rich." He wiped a smudge of mud from Juan's cheek with his thumb. "Filthy rich."

With a swing of his arm, Gil waved his two companions aside. He grabbed the crowbar and approached the unfettered block of stone. "Let's see, *mamita*, what you've been hiding for so long."

Gil worked the edge of the crowbar between rock and arch, then leaned his weight against the bar, his shoulder and back muscles straining. The door held firm against his efforts. He dug his toes in and pushed harder. Suddenly a loud grinding crack erupted from the door, and the stone shifted.

Gil stepped back, his face still ruddy from the struggle. He nodded to Juan and Miguel. "Put your backs into it."

The two leaned their shoulders to the loosened stone door and shoved. The block of stone toppled forward. Dust bloomed like a shrouded phantom from the mouth of the burial chamber, and a muffled thud echoed through the room as the stone struck the floor of the tomb's entrance.

Waving the cloud of dust from his face, Gil strode to the door. "Hand me one of those lights," he said, bending by the entrance.

Miguel tossed him a flashlight from his canvas bag. Gil caught its long silver handle.

"Stinks in there," Juan said as he joined Gil and stared over his shoulder.

"It's a grave," Gil said, clicking on the light. "What did you expect from—" Words died in his mouth as the light lanced into the dark depths of the tomb, illuminating the passage ahead. Beyond a short entry hall lay a huge chamber, about thirty meters along each side. Gil had expected to discover piles of bones and scattered pottery, but what his handlamp actually revealed was a sight he could never have imagined—not even in his most drunken dreams.

"*Dios mio!*" he exclaimed in a voice hoarse with awe.

His partners gathered to either side, speechless.

Ahead, the right and left walls of the square chamber were plated with sheets of gold. The beam of Gil's flashlight reflected and sparked off the mirrored surfaces, a brilliance that almost blinded after the dim tunnels of the excavation. But Gil ignored all this, his light still fixed on a single object resting against the far stone wall of the chamber, directly opposite the gathered trio.

"We are all going to be filthy rich, *mis amigos*."

Across the open chamber stood a six-foot golden idol, a figure of an Incan king outfitted in ritual mantle and crown, bearing a staff topped by a stylized sun. The detail work was so lifelike that the figure's stern face seemed ready to shout a warning at any moment. But no word of protest was raised. The Incan king, sculpted of gold, stood silent as Gil led the others into the chamber.

Bending, Gil ducked through the threshold. He did not wait for the others. He pushed forward down the short hallway, the gold drawing him on. Past the doorway, he was able to stand straight again. Gil held his breath at the sight. Both the roof and floor were also covered in precious metals, an intricate pattern of gold and silver tiles, each about a meter wide. The roof's pattern was a mirror image of the floor. At the feet of the idol were piled tools and weapons, also sculpted of precious metals and bejeweled with rubies, sapphires, amethysts, and emeralds. Gil shook his head. The sheer amount of wealth was too large to comprehend.

Juan finally moved forward to stand beside Gil. He shifted uneasily, intimidated by their find. When he spoke, he tried to act undaunted, but his voice cracked. "S . . . so let's get hauling."

Miguel had joined them by now and made the sign of the cross, eyeing the golden king.

"He's not one of your dead relatives, Miguel," Juan jibed at his compadre. "Lighten up."

"This place is cursed," Miguel mumbled, eyes wide as he searched the room. "We should hurry."

"Miguel is right," Gil said. "We must move fast. Grab what we can tonight and store it in the jungle. We'll return before daybreak and take care of the *americanos* and their scrawny Indian laborers. Once they're out of the way, we can call in the additional men, those we can trust, to help clear this lot out."

Juan started across the tiled floor, his bootheels echoing oddly in the hollow chamber. He nodded toward the mound of precious items left at the foot of the idol. "I say we collect all the small stuff. Leave the lugging and toting of the heavier objects to the others. Make them earn their share."

Gil followed, with Miguel hovering at his heels. "When we're done here, there'll be plenty for everyone. A hundred men couldn't spend this wealth in a lifetime."

Juan glanced back, a wide grin on his face. "Oh yeah? Just watch me."

Halfway across the chamber, the trap was sprung. Juan stepped on a silver tile, and the corresponding gold tile in the roof above snapped open. A cascade of silver—thousands of tiny chains—swept over Gil's companion. Gasping, Juan ducked as his form was instantly drenched in the fine chains. Once fallen, the chains draped from the open panel, like a frozen waterfall of silver. They clinked brightly as Juan danced among them, shocked but clearly unharmed. His motions only succeeded to enmesh himself further.

"What the—?" Juan started to say, reaching to shove aside the tangling links of silver. His hand darted back. "Shit, they got hooks all over them."

Gil finally noticed the hundreds of glinting centimeter-long barbs sprouting along the lengths of chain. Their points were all curved upward, hinged, so they caused no harm when they fell from the ceiling.

Gil froze in mid-reach. *Fuck*, he thought as he suddenly realized the danger. A warning rose too late on his lips.

Suddenly the cascade of chains spun viciously around Juan, ripping upward at the same time. The man screamed, an animal's cry of panic and fear. Juan was lifted two meters off the ground by the barbed chains, writhing in their hooked grips, before his weight finally dropped him to the floor.

Juan pushed himself onto his hands and knees. Most of his clothes had been ripped from his body, along with large swaths of skin. He raised his face toward Gil. His left ear was gone; his scalp lay torn and flapped over to one side. Both eyes were bloody ruins. Blind, all Juan could do was howl. Even now, Gil saw Juan's skin begin to blacken where the hooks had dug in.

Poison.

Still Juan wailed in agony, crawling, dragging himself slowly across the floor. He didn't make it far. The poison reached his heart, and he collapsed to the gold and silver tiles. The scream ended in mid-rattle.

Miguel went to check on his friend.

Gil grabbed a fistful of Miguel's shirt and pulled him to a stop. The two men shared a single gold tile on the floor. With their friend's cries echoing away to nothing, Gil now heard the tick and grind of massive gears hidden behind the tiles and walls all around them. They had walked into a massive booby trap.

Gil glanced around. They stood on the single tile that centered the room. He studied the gold under his feet. "It must have been built to activate only after someone fully entered the room." He eyed the tiles that led toward the golden idol and those that led back toward the entrance. The ticking of the gears sounded from all around. He suspected neither path was now safe.

Miguel moaned beside him.

Gil scowled at the enormous wealth around him. Knowing death lurked behind its beauty, the luster faded from the gold. "We're trapped."

Nestled in his sleeping bag atop a camp cot, Sam awoke to the noise of some animal snuffling by his tent door. At night, opossums and other curious nocturnal creatures were always wandering from the rain forest's edge to investigate the camp. But whatever was out there now was large. Its shadow, cast by the camp's spotlights, blotted out a good section of the tent flap. Sam tried to remember if he had snapped the fasteners after zipping up the door against mosquitoes. His first thought was jaguar. A few of the large cats had been spotted along the Urabamba River, which ran through the jungle below the ruins.

As silently as possible, Sam reached for his Winchester rifle, a legacy from his grandfather, passed from father to son through the Conklin family, dating back to 1884. Sam didn't go anywhere without it. The rifle had not been fired for years, more a keepsake and good-luck charm than a weapon. But right now, unloaded, it might serve as a good club.

His fingers slipped over the wooden butt of the rifle.

Whatever was outside rattled the flap near his toes. Damn, he *had* forgotten to fasten the door! Sam sprang up in his sleeping bag and snatched the rifle up in his fist.

As he swung the rifle back, the flap was torn open.

"Sam, are you awake?" Maggie peeked her head under the flap and made a halfhearted effort to knock on the canvas side of the tent.

Sam lowered the rifle to his lap, his heart still pounding in his ears. He swallowed hard to clear his throat and forced his voice into a nonchalant tone. "Yeah, I'm up, Maggie. What's the matter?"

"I couldn't sleep and got to thinking about those etchings. I needed to run something by you."

Sam had some fantasies of Maggie sneaking to his tent in the dead of night, but none of them involved discussing ancient Latin etchings. Still, any nighttime visit from Maggie was welcome. "Okay. Give me a sec'."

Rolling out of his sleeping bag, he slipped his Wranglers over his boxers. With a night this muggy, he wouldn't normally bother with a shirt, but with Maggie out there, modesty more than comfort mattered. Sam pulled a leather vest over his shoulders.

Grabbing his Stetson, he pulled down the zipper to the tent and pushed through into the night. Silver glow from a full moon washed over the camp, paling the four spotlights at the camp's periphery. He swiped his disheveled hair back from his forehead and trapped it under his hat.

Maggie stepped back. She still wore the same khaki pants with a matching vest over a blood-red shirt. The only indication that Maggie had made any effort at relaxing this night was that she had untied her hair from its usual ponytail. Cascades of auburn curls, frosted silver by the night, flowed over her shoulders.

Transfixed by the play of moonlight across Maggie's cheeks and lips, Sam had to search for his voice. "So . . . what's up?"

As usual, her eyes didn't seem to see Sam. "It's that writing on the last band. The bottom one. Those missing words an' lines. Latin's a weird language. A single word can change the entire meaning of the message."

"Yeah?"

"What if we're not reading it right? What if one of those missing words or lines negates our translation?"

"Maybe it might . . . but tomorrow we'll know the truth anyway. When we crack the tomb in the morning, it'll be intact or it won't."

A hint of irritation entered her voice. "Sam, I want to know *before* we open the tomb. Don't you want to know what the conquistadors really meant to communicate on those bands?"

"Sure, but the words are illegible."

"I know, Sam . . . but that was with just alcohol cleaning." She looked at him meaningfully.

Suddenly Sam knew why Maggie had roused him. He kept his lips clamped tight. Two years ago, he had presented a paper on the use of a phosphorescent dye to detect and bring out the faint written images worn by time on rock and metal. He had been uniformly scoffed at for his idea.

"You packed your stuff, didn't you?" Maggie said.

"I don't know what you're talking about," Sam mumbled. He had told no one, not even his uncle, that he had refused to abandon his theory, spending years researching the various viscosities of different dyes and ranges of UV light. He had kept his studies under close wrap, not wanting to humiliate himself until he could test it in the field, try it when no one else was around to ridicule him. Suddenly he realized he was not unlike his uncle in keeping secrets.

Maggie's eyes glowed in the dark. "I read your paper. You found a way to make it work, didn't you, Sam?"

He just stood, unblinking. How had she known? Finally, the shock faded enough for him to speak. "I *think* I solved it. But I haven't had a chance to put it through a field trial."

Maggie pointed toward the ruins. "Then it's about time. The others are already waiting for us by the entrance to the excavation." She turned to leave.

"Others?"

Glancing back over her shoulders, Maggie frowned. "Ah sure, Sam . . . Norman and Ralph. They should be in on this."

"I suppose." Sam rolled his eyes, preparing himself to be humiliated if he should fail. At least, Philip had not been invited. Sam could not have tolerated failing in front of Mr. Harvard. "Let me grab my bottles and UV light."

As Sam reached for his tent flap, the jungle suddenly erupted in a cacophony of screeches and calls. A thousand birds burst from the canopies around the camp and took to the air.

Maggie took a step closer to Sam. "What the hell . . . ?"

Sam glanced around, but the rain forest quickly settled back down. "Something must have spooked them." He listened a bit longer, but only the humming of the generator reached his ears. The jungle lay silent, like a dark stranger staring toward them. Sam studied the forest a moment more, then turned back to his tent. "I'll get my stuff."

He pushed through the flap and collected the satchel that held his dyes and special ultraviolet handlamp. As he was leaving, his eyes settled on the old Winchester. Instinctively, he grabbed it and slung it over his shoulder, but not before quickly loading a few 44/40 cartridges into the rifle's magazine and pocketing a cardboard box of spare shells. After years of overnight camps in the Texas wilderness, Sam had learned to be prepared.

Crawling out of the tent, he found Maggie's back to him. She searched the edges of the jungle. "It's still so bloody quiet," she said. "It's like the forest's holding its breath."

"If we want to test this," Sam said, anxious to be under way, "we'd better hightail it. Dawn is only a few hours away."

Maggie nodded, reluctantly pulling her gaze away from the jungle.

Sam led the way toward the terraced ruins. With the rain forest so subdued, their footsteps on the granite stones seemed unusually loud. Sam found himself walking carefully, afraid of disturbing the silence, as though they were strolling through a graveyard at midnight. He was glad when they finally reached the summit of the Sun Plaza. Light shone up from the excavated shaft.

Limned in the light were two shadowy figures—one thin and one wide. Norman and Ralph. They stood apart from one another.

The ex-linebacker raised a hand in greeting. He pointed toward the shaft. "Who left the lamps on?"

Maggie shook her head as she climbed onto the flat-topped plaza. "I know I switched them off." She surveyed the ruins around them. "That feckin' Guillermo probably turned them on during his rounds and left 'em on. Where is he anyway? I thought he was supposed to be guarding this place."

"He's probably in the forest watching out for those looters from last night. Maybe he was the one who spooked all those birds."

The jungle remained deathly still. Norman eyed the black forest. "I never liked the dark. I get the willies alone in my darkroom at home."

Ralph teased him with a remarkable rendition of the *Twilight Zone* theme. Norman pretended not to hear.

Sam climbed down first while Maggie and the others followed. Once at the bottom of the ladder, he helped Maggie off the rungs.

She turned to him, her head slightly bent, her palm still resting in his. "Did you hear something just then?"

Sam shook his head. All he could hear was his own pounding heart. He found his hand squeezing hers.

Ralph and Norman joined them.

Maggie pulled her hand away, listened for a moment more, then shrugged and took the lead. "Must be those Incan ghosts," she muttered.

"Thanks, Maggie," Norman said sourly. "That's just what I wanted to hear when crawling through the ruins at midnight. I already got a bad enough feeling about this."

Ralph again started his *Twilight Zone* theme.

"Bite me, Isaacson," Norman snapped.

"I don't lean that way, Normie."

"Are you sure? You were a football player, weren't you? What's with all that ass slapping and piling on one another?"

"Shut up."

"Jesus," Maggie exclaimed. "Enough from the both of you. I can't hear a feckin' thing."

Following behind Maggie, Sam ignored them all, lost in appreciating how Maggie moved as she climbed. Through the thin cotton khakis, her legs were muscled and firm and their shapeliness drew his eyes up her curves. Sam swallowed hard and wiped the dampness from his brow with a handkerchief. *She's a colleague,* he had to remind himself. Like the army, his uncle frowned on fraternization while in the field. Unwanted attentions among members could strain a small site.

Still, it never hurt to look.

As they traversed to the second level of the dig, Sam marveled at his uncle's revelation. This was once a Moche pyramid! It was hard to believe. Sam ran a palm along the granite stone walls.

Ahead, Maggie stopped again, pausing with her hand on the ladder that led to the third level. "Now I know I heard something," she whispered. "Words . . . and somethin' knocking . . ."

Sam strained to hear, but he still heard nothing. He glanced to Ralph and Norman. Both men shook their heads. Norman's eyes were huge behind his eyeglasses. Sam swung back to Maggie, ready to dismiss her worry, when a scream burst from below, blowing past them like a frightened bird.

Maggie turned wide eyes toward Sam.

Sam swung the Winchester from his shoulder.

Gil studied the metal tiles all around him. The gears of the hidden mechanism ticked and groaned behind the walls.

Miguel shared the gold square with him, crowding Gil's right side. The squat man's eyes were wide with fear, and words of prayer whispered from his lips.

Gil ignored him. No gods would protect them there. Survival was up to them. But Gil was not only interested in survival. His eyes kept drifting to the wealth at the feet of the golden idol. Counting, Gil noted that fifteen rows of tiles lay between him and the statue of the Incan king, and fifteen rows lay behind him. Fifteen meters either way. Too far to jump.

He scowled at the trap, sensing that there must be some key to crossing this floor. He turned in a slow circle. The tiles' pattern was not that of a checkerboard but a complicated crisscrossing pattern of gold and silver squares. It was not unlike some of the geometric patterns found in the work of Incan tapestries and clothing. There was an order, a clue perhaps, to a safe course. But what was it?

Juan's corpse lay upon a neighboring gold tile, where he had managed to drag himself before dying. Blood pooled under his silent form. No new trap had been triggered when Juan had crawled off the silver tile that had originally sprung the trap. Could that be the answer? Were the gold tiles safe and the silver a danger?

There was only one way to find out.

Gil unslung his short rifle and poked it into Miguel's ribs. "Move," he ordered.

Miguel glanced from the rifle's barrel to Gil's face. "¿Que?"

"Hop over to that gold square," Gil nodded toward a tile beyond the neighboring silver one. The direction led toward the golden idol. If they were to risk their lives, Gil wanted something to show for their efforts.

Miguel still stood frozen, disbelief and horror on his face.

"Go. Or die right here." Gil shoved his rifle harder against Miguel.

His squat companion stumbled back a step, his heels just inside the square. "Please, ese, don't make me do this."

"Do as I say, or I'll use your corpse to test the tiles."

Miguel trembled, gaze swinging between the rifle and Juan's corpse. Finally, his shoulders sagged. He turned to face the deadly pattern, made the sign of the cross, and jumped. His legs were so wobbly from fear that he barely managed to leap the short distance. He landed hard and fell to his hands and knees on the gold tile.

Gil saw that the man's eyelids were squeezed tight as he froze in place, expecting the worse. But nothing happened. Slowly, Miguel opened his eyes and pushed shakily to his feet. He turned toward Gil, a feeble smile on his lips.

Gil called to him, relieved to find his theory proving true. "The gold tiles are safe. Stick to them and we can get in and out of here." Still, Gil was taking no chances on being wrong. He waved his rifle. "Go on to the next, and I'll follow."

Miguel nodded. The next gold tile adjoined the tile he occupied. He merely had to step onto it. He did so slowly. Again nothing happened. The ancient mechanism just continued its constant creaking from beyond the walls and ceiling. Miguel moved onto the next golden tile, again having to leap a silver one. Still safe.

As Gil followed, he saw Miguel's attitude grow more relaxed, though his lips still moved silently in continuous prayer. The pair slowly worked their way across the chamber. Tile by tile, row by row, they neared the golden idol. At last they reached the last tier that stood between them and the treasure. The tiles were all silver. The only gold tile was the one upon which the idol and the treasure rested.

Miguel turned to Gil, his expression clearly asking *what now?*

Gil studied the Incan king. Against the backdrop of black granite, the statue's gold eyes seemed to stare back, mocking him. Gil bristled. He would not be thwarted by a bunch of idol worshipers. Not when he was so close.

He moved beside Miguel, again sharing his tile. Neither dared cross that silver river of tiles to the treasure beyond, but that did not mean he could not pilfer the piled wealth at the statue's feet. Holding his rifle by its butt, Gil reached out with his weapon, stretching his arm across the silver toward the statue.

The tip of his rifle just reached the hoard. Gil nudged a few of the items, searching. He held his breath as he did so. What if there was another booby trap there? His straining ears seemed to pick up a slight change in the cadence of the mechanism's gears. He cringed, but nothing happened.

Gil swore under his breath. The rifle bobbled in his extended grip. He was getting too jumpy. He took a steadying breath, then concentrated on his task, refusing to fail. He ground his teeth and ignored the growing burn from his straining shoulder. Finally, his efforts paid off. A pair of twin goblets was exposed, one gold, one silver, each embedded with rubies and emeralds in a serpent pattern. But the feature that most attracted Gil was the arched handles on the cups.

Something he could hook!

Slipping his rifle's barrel through the handle of one, he lifted it free of the pile. He tilted the weapon, and the silver goblet slid down the barrel to rest against its wooden stock. Gil pulled the weapon back and stood. He shook the treasure off his weapon and passed it to Miguel. "For your bravery, *mi amigo.*"

Miguel held the goblet in trembling fingers. There was enough wealth in that single token to set up the squat man and his family for the rest of their lives. Miguel whispered a prayer of thanks.

Gil frowned and turned away. His companion should be thanking him, not his God. Gil knelt again and stretched his rifle to retrieve the golden cup. The second goblet was soon in his hands. Here was his reward. He knew a dealer in stolen antiquities who would pay triple the price of the gold in the cup for any intact Incan artifacts. Gil shoved the goblet into his jacket and turned his back on the statue.

He plotted what he had to do next. He patted the grenade in his vest. He had to protect the rest of the wealth here until he could bring in a demolitions team to neutralize the booby trap. Once the cursed apparatus was disabled, he and his team could collect the rest of the riches at their leisure. In his mind, he pictured the only other obstacle to his plans: the group of *americanos* sleeping snugly in their tents. He gripped his rifle. They must never see the dawn.

With his plan set, Gil waved Miguel on toward the exit. His companion needed no further coaxing, clearly glad to escape with his single small treasure. Miguel hopped to the next gold square.

It shot up under him with a scream of gears and pulleys. The tile, with Miguel atop it, flew toward the ceiling, borne up by a thick trunk of wood. Overhead, the corresponding silver tile in the ceiling slid back. Silver spikes thrust downward.

Miguel saw his death and tried to roll off the tile, taking his chance on the fall below—but he was not quick enough. His legs, from the knees down, were pinned by the spikes, driven through muscle and bone. Miguel screamed. Bones snapped like broken twigs as he thrashed in the grip of the spikes.

The gold tile then descended, sliding smoothly back to its place in the floor's pattern. Smeared with blood, it was empty. Gil looked up. Miguel still hung by his spiked legs from the roof.

Blood rained down from Miguel's ruined legs. He thrashed, arms pushing against the stakes. He finally won his freedom and fell the two stories to the metal floor. Again the crack of bones sounded with the impact.

Gil had glanced away when Miguel fell. He turned back. Miguel lay broken upon the tiles. Only one limb was still intact. The man tried to push up on his good right arm, but the pain was too much. He collapsed again. Too weak, too shocked to scream, only a low moan escaped his lips. He stared at Gil with begging eyes.

Gil could not save him.

Raising his rifle, Gil whispered, "I'm sorry, ese." He shot Miguel through the forehead, the rifle's blast deafening in the enclosed space. Miguel's moaning stopped. Blood dribbled from the small hole in his forehead.

Gil studied the tiles once again. A gold one had killed Miguel! Why were they no longer safe? Was his theory wrong to begin with—or had the rules changed? He remembered the shift in the mechanism's cadence as he had fished through the treasure. Something had altered. Gil stared. Miguel had landed on a silver square with no repercussion. Were the silver tiles now the safe ones? Gold when one approached, silver as one left. Could it be that easy?

Gil had no other cohort to bully into taking the risk. He would have to test his theory himself. Cautiously, he reached with his rifle and tapped its butt on the next tile—a silver one. Nothing happened. But did that prove anything? Maybe it would take his full weight to spring the trap. Slowly, he reached a booted foot and placed it on the square. Holding his breath, he leaned his weight onto this leg, ready to leap back with any shift in the tile or change in the gear's timbre. Soon he stood with one leg on the new silver tile and one on the gold tile. Still, nothing changed.

Cringing, Gil pulled his other leg over onto the silver. He stood motionless. No harm came to him. Safe.

Sighing out his trapped breath, he wiped the sweat from his eyes. Tears ran down his cheeks. He did not know when they had begun to flow.

He stood on the silver tile. The next one would require jumping a gold square. Before he could lose his nerve, he leaped, rifle in hand, and landed roughly on the silver tile. He froze but remained safe.

Grinning, he straightened and glanced back to the king. "I beat you, you bastard!"

He turned toward the exit and worked his way cautiously, but more rapidly, across the floor. It was his speed that saved his life. He hopped from one silver tile to its neighbor, just leaping off the first as it opened under him. From the shift in his footing as he jumped, he fell hard to the next tile. Overhead, a spray of water jetted from small openings that appeared in the corresponding roof tile. It showered into the newly opened pit behind him. Gil rolled around. A bit of the mist from the spray struck his exposed cheek; it burned with a touch of fire. Gil shoved away. Acid!

He touched his flaming cheek. His skin already lay blistered and oozing.

Gil shivered at the thought of being trapped in that pit below when the shower of acid struck. His death would have been long and painful.

The burning rain ended and the silver tile slid closed over the pit. Death had come within a breath of claiming him. Trembling, he struggled to his feet.

He stared at the traitorous silver tile. Silver! He had been wrong all along. Only pure luck and chance had carried him this far.

With this horrible realization dawning, he swung to face the exit. Escape lay three rows away—about three meters. He now knew he could trust none of the tiles. He would have to risk jumping. If he dived, he might just make it.

Gil stared at his rifle. He could not chance its weight. He dropped it along with the ammunition belt slung over his chest to the floor. Taking out the heavy golden goblet, Gil stared at it a moment, then returned it to inside his vest. He would rather die than lose this treasure. He shrugged out of his boots instead. Besides, if he was barefooted, he had a better grip on the tile's silver surface anyway.

Once ready, he backed to the far edge, giving himself as much of a running start as possible. But he had only two short steps at most. Girding himself, Gil closed his eyes, and for the first time in decades, he prayed to his God for strength and luck. Prepared, he opened his eyes and clenched his fist. "Now or never," he mumbled.

Leaning forward, he dashed two quick steps, then flung himself headfirst with all the strength in his legs. He flew across the rows of tiles and landed hard upon the stone floor, ducking enough to take the brunt of the collision on his left side. Something snapped in his shoulder as he rolled into the short passage and came to rest against the toppled stone door.

With a grimace, Gil shoved to his feet. He ignored the shooting pain in his neck. He had made it! Fingering his shoulder, he realized he had most likely broken his collarbone. Not a big deal. He had once taken three bullets in the chest. In comparison, this was nothing more than a scratch.

Gil pulled free the precious goblet. One of its lips was slightly bent from the weight of his fall. But, like Gil, it had sustained no real harm.

Stepping to the edge of the deadly pattern, Gil raised the chalice and spat toward the distant Incan king, the gold idol bright against the black stone. "I'll come back and rape you yet!" he cursed.

With that promise, he turned on a heel and fled.

Maggie knelt by the top of the ladder that led down to the third level of the ruins. "Someone's coming!" she whispered, pushing Sam back from her shoulder.

An instinct told her they needed to hide. Raised on the streets of Belfast, Maggie knew to listen to that inner voice of hers. Surviving among the constant gunfire and bombings between the warring Irish factions and the British military had taught Maggie O'Donnel the value of a good hiding place.

"C'mon," Maggie urged, pulling Sam with her. Norman and Ralph followed.

Sam resisted, raising his rifle. "Maybe it's looters. We should stop them."

"And get us all killed, you stupid git? You don't know how many are down there, or how well they're armed. Now let's go!"

Norman agreed. "She's right. The leftist guerrillas around here, the Shining Path, are well equipped. Russian AK-47s and the like. We should leave any investigation to the security team."

Sam stared back to the ladder, then shook his head and followed Maggie. She led the group to a side chamber. No sodium lamps lit the room. Darkness swallowed them.

"Stay low," Maggie warned. "But be prepared to run on my signal."

Sam muttered as he hunkered down beside her, "Maggie O'Donnel, combat archaeologist."

Maggie could just make out Sam's form as a darker shadow among the others, but she could imagine his sarcastic smile.

"You know," Ralph added in a whisper, "it's probably just Gil or one of his men."

"And the scream?" Maggie said.

"I'm sure that—"

Maggie reached a hand to his knee to quiet the large man. She could hear the creaking wood as someone mounted the ladder from below. Whoever climbed was in a hurry. She could hear his panting breath and his scrambled flight. Lowering herself closer to the stone floor, Maggie watched the climber's head rise from the shaft.

She recognized the lanky black hair and the spidery white scar on his bronze cheek. Guillermo Sala. The ex-policeman frantically crawled from the ladder, his feet almost slipping. Maggie allowed a breath of relief to escape her throat. Ralph was right. It was just the camp's guard.

She started to stand when she spotted the large burn blistered on his cheek. It cracked and bled. Gil swiped a hand to his wounded face and smeared the blood across his shirt. His eyes were wide, the whites of which almost glowed in the lantern near the ladder. His lips were thin with hatred—but she also sensed fear and shock emanating from him.

Maggie knew that expression. A childhood friend, Patrick Dugan, had worn the same shocked face when caught by a stray bullet during a firefight back in Belfast. He had raised his head too soon from their shared hiding place in a roadside drainage ditch. Maggie had known better. Even as Patrick's body collapsed atop her, she hadn't moved. Danger lay in haste. Having learned her lesson, Maggie stayed hidden and kept the others back with a hand.

What had happened below? What could frighten a man as hard and tough as Gil?

As on that noon day in the streets of Belfast, Maggie knew safety still lay in the shadows. She peered from the room's edge as Gil reached to his vest and fingered an object bulging in a pocket. It seemed to center the panicked man, as a crucifix would reassure an old woman.

Then, from another pocket, he pulled free what looked like a green apple with a handle. It took Maggie a heartbeat to recognize the armament, so out of place in an ancient Incan ruin.

Bloody hell! A grenade!

With a final glance at the shaft, Gil scrabbled to his feet and raced down the tunnel.

Listening to his fading footsteps, Maggie found she could not move. In her mind's eye, the grenade still loomed large—a familiar weapon in the war on the streets of her home. Buried childhood panic swelled, threatening to choke her. Her hands trembled. She clenched her fists, refusing to succumb to the panic attack that verged. Her vision swam slightly as her breath became stilted.

Sam must have sensed her distress. "Maggie . . . ?" He reached to her shoulder.

His touch ignited her. She sprang to her feet. "Och, we need to get out of here," she said, her words rushed. "Now!"

Sam pulled his Stetson firmer on his head. "Why? It's only Guillermo."

Her face fierce, Maggie swung toward Sam. The Texan had not seen the grenade. Sam backed up a step from whatever he saw in her eyes. She did not have time to explain her fears. "Go, you bloody wanker!" she hollered, the panic thickening the Irish brogue on her tongue. She shoved Sam toward the tunnel and waved the others after him.

Sam's long legs ate up the distance. Maggie followed, keeping one eye on their back trail. Ahead, Ralph kept up with Sam, but Norman, burdened with his cameras, had slipped behind.

"Hurry," she urged the journalist.

Norman glanced back. His face was stark white in the glow of the lamps. But he fought for more speed and closed the distance as the two quicker men reached the ladder to the next level of the dig.

Ahead, Sam flew up the wooden rungs with Ralph at his heels. Norman went next. Maggie stood at the foot of the ladder, her ears straining for any danger behind them. Far away, echoing up from below, she thought she could just make out a deep ticking, like a large watch winding down.

"Maggie, c'mon!" Sam whispered urgently to her from above.

Maggie turned to find the ladder clear. For a moment, time had slipped away from her. It was one of the signs of a pending attack. Not now! She flew up the ladder. Sam helped her off the last rung, hauling her up with his arms. The ladder to the surface lay only a handful of meters away. On her feet, Maggie led the way.

She followed the zigzagging line of lanterns, lights flickering past as she ran. As she spotted the ladder's base, she heard a low grunting coming from the shaft to the surface. It was Gil. It sounded like he had almost reached the plaza above.

With her goal in sight and a freshening breeze from above encouraging her, Maggie sped faster.

Suddenly, words echoed down to her: "Swallow this, you *hijo de puta!*"

Maggie froze as a hard object pinged and bounced down the shaft to land at the foot of the ladder. She stared in disbelief at the green metallic cylinder. It rested in the mud beside the wooden beam that acted as the main shaft support. The grenade!

Maggie cartwheeled back toward Sam. He grunted as she fell against his chest. "Back . . . back . . . back . . ." she chanted.

The group tumbled, tangled in each other's arms, away from the ladder.

"What—?" Sam said in her ear.

With adrenaline fierce in her veins, she shoved Sam and the others into a side chamber.

The blast caught them at the entrance. The concussion and explosion of air propelled them all across the room. They struck the far wall and fell to the stone floor in a pile of limbs.

With the lamps flickering around them, Maggie rolled up to her knees. Past her ringing ears, she heard

Ralph groan beside her. Maggie took stock of her own injuries. She seemed to be unscathed, but as she viewed the damage done by the grenade through the settling dust, a moan escaped her throat, too.

They were trapped!

The passage that led to the last ladder was now a tumble of rock and dirt. The grenade had collapsed the tunnel to the surface, taking out a good section of the first level's ceiling. Stones lay in a jumble from the triggered landslide.

Around her, the remainder of the ruins grumbled and groaned with the shift in stresses. Thirty feet of earth pushed to collapse more of the subterranean ruin.

What were they going to do?

Then the lights flickered a final time and died. Blackness swallowed them up.

"Everyone okay?" Sam asked numbly, his voice exaggerated by his deafened ears.

Norman answered, "Fine. I'm buried thirty feet underground . . . in a tomb. But otherwise, I'm fine."

"Okay here, too, Sam," Ralph added, his usual bravado dimmed.

Sam coughed on the thick dust in the air. "Maggie?"

She could no longer answer. She felt her limbs stiffen and begin the first of the characteristic tremors. She fell back upon the stone floor as the seizure grabbed her body and dragged her consciousness away.

The last she heard was Norman's strangled cry. "Sam, something's wrong with Maggie!"

Gil fled from the blast in the pit, the roar ripping through the quiet jungle. Smoke and debris, sweeping up into the night, chased him down the slope to the floor of the camp. Though the loose stones cut his bare feet, he scrambled down the stairs, cursing himself for abandoning his boots below. Why hadn't he tossed his footwear and rifle free of the booby trap before he jumped? But he knew the answer. He had panicked.

Overhead, a flock of frightened parrots scattered across the beam of one of the nearby spotlights. The blaze of blue-and-red plumage across the black night startled him. As the single explosion echoed away, the jungle answered the grenade's challenge with bird screeches and monkey calls.

The jungle had awakened—as had the camp below.

Lights swelled within several of the workers' cheap tents. Shadows already moved inside as the sleepers awakened. Even one of the students' tents blossomed with the warm glow.

Weaponless and with no companions, Gil dared not try to take the camp alone. He would have to gather other men and return quickly to eliminate the *americanos* and their workers. At least the grenade had managed to bring down the only entrance to the subterranean ruins. The bounty below should be protected until he could return with men and construction tools to dig it free. Not concerned about "damaging the fragile site," his team could have the treasure hoard plucked in short order. A day or two at the most.

Yet, before Gil could gather more men, he had one more mission to complete here at the camp. Reaching the cluster of tents, he slipped into the darker shadows between two of the workers' rough shelters. Faces began to peek out of tent flaps. Their eyes were surely on the plume of dirt still smoking from the excavation site.

No one spotted Gil.

As he slipped behind the tents, the whispered squabble in the guttural Quechan tongue could be heard from the neighboring tent. A shrill voice also called from where the students kept their more expensive shelters. "Guillermo! Sam! What happened?" It was the pompous leader of these *maricon* students.

Gil ignored the growing exchange of voices. From a pile of stacked work tools, he silently removed a pickax and shearing knife. Crossing to the rear of one of the shelters, Gil used the knife to slice a new entrance.

His sharp blade hissed through the thick canvas. Slipping through the hole, Gil entered the tent with his pickax.

He studied his quarry—the satellite communication system. Luckily, he did not need to wreak havoc on the entire assembly. It had a weak link. The small computer itself. Much of the other equipment had spare parts, but not the CPU. Without it, the camp would be cut off from sounding the alarm or calling for help.

Gil raised the pickax over his shoulder and waited. His fractured collarbone protested the weight of the iron tool—but he did not have long to pause. Again Philip Sykes's angered voice barked frantic orders from his tent flap, clearly scared to leave the safety of his shelter: "Sala, where the hell are you?"

As the student yelled, Gil drove the ax's spike into the center of the computer. Cobalt sparks bloomed in the shadowed interior of the tent, but they quickly died away. Gil did not bother hauling the pickax free or checking to see if his sabotage had been noticed. He simply ducked back through the sliced rear of the tent and darted away.

With all eyes turned toward the smoking tunnel on the plaza above, Gil slipped into the jungle fringe unseen, knife in hand and revenge in his heart.

He clenched the blade's hilt in a white-knuckled fist.

No one bested Guillermo Sala—especially not an ancient Incan idol!

"Hurry, Sam!" Norman's voice was frantic in the darkness.

In the stygian darkness of the temple ruins, Sam dug through his bag of research tools. None of them had thought to bring a flashlight. He would have to improvise. Blind, his fingers sifted through the clinking bottles. His palm finally settled on his buried Wood's lamp. It was the ultraviolet light source used to illuminate his deciphering dyes. Pulling it free, Sam clicked it on.

Under the glow of ultraviolet light, an eerie tableau appeared. Dust, which still hung in the air from the explosion, fluoresced like snow in the odd purplish light but did little to obscure the others. The teeth, whites of the eyes, and pale clothing of his companions all shone with an unnatural brightness.

Norman Fields knelt beside Maggie. She stared at the ceiling, her back arched off the stone, her heels drumming on the ancient floor. Norman held her shoulders, while Ralph hovered over them like a dark phantom. Norman glanced up at Sam. "She's having some type of seizure."

Sam scooted beside them. "She must have hit her head. Maybe a bad concussion." He lifted his lamp to examine her eyes, but the ultraviolet light did little to illuminate her pupils. Under the glow, her facial muscles twitched and convulsed; her eyelids fluttered. "I can't tell for sure." Sam examined his companions' faces.

None of them knew what to do.

Small noises of strangulation escaped Maggie's throat.

"Aren't you supposed to keep her from swallowing or biting her tongue or something?" Ralph said, uncertain.

Sam nodded. Already Maggie's face had taken on a vaguely purplish hue. "I need a gag."

Norman reached to his back pocket and extracted a small handkerchief. "Will this work?"

Sam had no idea, so he simply took the scrap of cloth and twisted it into a rope. He hesitated as he reached toward Maggie, uncertain what to do. A small sliver of saliva trailed from the corner of her mouth. Though slipping an iron bit in his horse's mouth was second nature to him, this was different. Sam fought back his fear.

Gently he tried to push Maggie's chin down, but her jaw muscles were clenched and quivering. It took extra force to pry her mouth open, more than he would have imagined. Finally, he used a finger to roll the tip of her tongue forward. Her mouth was hot and very wet. He cringed but worked the handkerchief back between her molars, pinning her tongue down and keeping her from gnashing.

"Good job," Norman congratulated him.

Already, Maggie's breathing seemed more even.

"I think it's ending," Ralph said. "Look."

Maggie's heels had stopped their drumming, and her back relaxed to the floor.

"Thank God," Sam muttered.

After a few more seconds, Maggie's trembling stopped. An arm rose to bat weakly at the empty air. She blinked a few times, her eyes glazed and blind. Then her gaze settled on him, and suddenly Sam knew Maggie was back. She stared at him, her anger bright.

Her fingers found Sam's hand, the one holding her gag in place. She shoved him away and spat out the gag. "Wh . . . what are you trying to do?" She rubbed roughly at her lips as she sat up.

Norman saved Sam from having to explain. "You were having a seizure."

Maggie pointed to the saliva-soaked handkerchief. "So you all tried to suffocate me? Next time just roll me on my side." She waved away their explanations. "How long was I out?"

Sam found his voice. "Maybe two minutes."

Maggie frowned. "Damn." She crossed to the wall of tumbled stone and clay that blocked the way out of the buried temple.

From her lack of surprise or concern at the seizure, it dawned on Sam that her attack was not from a blow to the head. He found his voice, his own anger freeing his tongue. "You're an epileptic."

Throwing back her hair, Maggie turned on him. "Idiopathic epilepsy. I've had attacks periodically since I was a teenager."

"You should have told someone. Does Uncle Hank know?"

Maggie looked away. "No. The attacks are so infrequent that I'm not even on medication. And it's been three years since I've had a seizure."

"Still, you should have told my uncle."

Fire edged her words. "And be kicked off this dig? If Professor Conklin knew about my epilepsy, he would never have let me come."

Sam met her heat with his own. "Maybe you shouldn't have. Not only is it unsafe for you, but you've put my uncle at risk. He's both responsible and liable for this dig. He could be sued by your relatives."

Maggie opened her mouth to argue, but Norman interrupted. "If you're done debating medical histories and the finer points of tort law, might I point out that we are now buried under thirty feet of unstable rock?"

As if to emphasize his words, stones groaned overhead, and a slide of dirt hissed from between two large granite slabs and trailed to the floor.

Ralph moved forward. "For once I agree with Norman—let's get our butts out of here."

"My point exactly," Norman added.

Sam frowned at Maggie once more. Emotions warred in his chest. He did not regret his words—Maggie had a responsibility to tell someone—but he wished he could go back and erase the anger from his outburst. He had been frightened for her, his heart squeezed into a tight ball, but he had been unable to voice such a thing aloud. So instead, he found himself snapping at her.

Sam turned away. In truth, a part of him understood her desire to maintain her secret. He, too, would have done anything to remain on this dig—even lie.

He cleared his throat. "Philip and the others must have heard the explosion. When they find our tents empty, they'll know we're down here and come looking. They'll dig us out."

"Hopefully they'll do so before we run out of air," Norman added.

Ralph moved to join the group now huddled before the collapsed section of the tunnel. "I hate putting my life in Philip's hands."

Sam agreed. "And if we survive, we'll never live it down."

In the dead quiet of the tomb, stones could be heard creaking and groaning overhead. Sam glanced up, raising his lamp. Dirt trickled from between several stones. The explosion had clearly destabilized the ruins of the pyramid. Reexcavating this site to rescue them might bring the entire temple down around their ears, and it was up to Philip Sykes to realize this.

Shaking his head, Sam lowered his lamp. He could not imagine a worse situation.

"Did you hear something?" Norman asked. The photographer was staring now, not at the blockage of debris, but back behind them, deeper into the temples.

Sam listened. Then he heard it too and swung around. A soft sliding noise, like something being dragged along the stone floor of the ruins. It came from farther into the maze of tunnels and rooms. Beyond the edge of his light, from the total darkness, the noise seemed to be coming closer.

Maggie touched his arm. "What is it?"

With her words, the noise abruptly stopped.

Sam shook his head. "I don't know," he whispered. "But whatever it is, it now knows we're here."

Philip Sykes was hoarse from yelling. He stood in his bare feet at the flap of his tent, robe snugged tight to his slim figure. Why was no one answering him? Outside the tent, the camp was in turmoil after the explosion. Men ran across the shadowy ruins, some armed with bobbing flashlights, others with work tools. No one seemed to know what had happened. Spats of native Indian dialect were shouted from the top of the Sun Plaza, where the cloud of dust was finally dissipating. But Philip understood only a smattering of Quechan words. Not enough to decipher the frantic calls and answers.

He looked at the luminous dial of his watch. It was after midnight, for Christ's sake. Various scenarios played in his head. The looters from the previous day had returned with better arms, and they were attacking the camp. Or maybe the Quechan laborers themselves, a swarthy and suspicious lot, had mutinied. Or maybe one of the three generators had just exploded.

Philip clutched the collar of his robe tight to his neck. Where were his fellow students? Finally, fear and irritation drove him barefooted from the flap. He took a quick peek around the edge of his tent. Farther back, the three other shelters were dark humps huddled against the night. Why hadn't the others been roused? Were they hiding in the dark?

Stepping back to his own tent, Philip's eyes grew wide. Maybe he should do the same. His own lamp-lit shelter was surely an illuminated target for any aggressor. He darted inside and blew out the lamp. As he turned back to the tent's entrance, a huge black shadow filled the doorway. Philip gasped.

A flashlight blinded him.

"What do you want?" he moaned, his knees weak.

The light shifted to illuminate the face of one of the Quechan workers. Philip could not say which of the many laborers stood at his tent flap. They all looked the same to him. The man garbled some words of Quecha, but Philip understood none of it. Only the wave of the man's hand, indicating Philip should follow, was clear.

Still, Philip hesitated. Did the man here mean him harm or was he trying to help? If only Denal, the filthy urchin from Cuzco who had acted as their translator, were there. Unable to communicate, Philip felt defenseless, isolated, and trapped among these foreigners.

Again the shadowy figure waved for Philip to follow, then stepped back and turned to leave. Philip found himself skittering after the man into the darkness. He did not want to be alone any longer. Barefooted still, he hurried to keep up.

Outside the shelter of his tent, the night wind had grown a crisp edge to it. It sliced through Philip's robe to his bare skin. The man led him to the other students' tents. Once there, he threw back the flap to Sam's tent and flashed the light inside for Philip to see. *Empty!*

Philip backed up a step and surveyed the ruins. If the bastard was out there, why hadn't Conklin answered his calls? His Quechan guide showed him the other tents. They were empty, too. Sam, Maggie, Ralph, even the photographer Norman, had disappeared. Panic, more than the cold breezes from the mountaintops, set Philip's limbs to shaking. Where were they?

The worker turned to him. His eyes were dark shadows. He mumbled something in his native tongue. From his tone, the Indian was just as concerned.

Edging farther away, Philip waved an arm behind him. "We . . . we need to call for help," he mumbled from behind chattering teeth. "We need to let someone know what's going on."

Philip turned and hurried toward the communication tent. The Quechan worker followed with the flashlight. Philip's shadow jittered across the path ahead of him. He needed to alert the authorities. Whatever was happening, Philip could not handle it himself.

At the tent, Philip worked the zipper and snaps with fumbling fingers. Finally the flap was open, and he crawled within. The worker remained at the entrance, pointing the flashlight inside. In the beam of light, Philip stared wide-eyed at their communication equipment. A pickax was embedded in the heart of the central computer.

Philip slid to his knees with a moan. "Oh, God . . . no."

Sam held the Winchester pointed toward the dark corridor that led to the heart of the ruins. A furtive scuffing and shuffling moved toward them through the darkness.

Beside him, Ralph held Sam's ultraviolet lamp out toward the darkness. Its illumination did little to pierce the well of shadows. What lay within the blackness remained a mystery.

Maggie and Norman stood behind the two men. Leaning forward, Maggie whispered in Sam's ear, her breath hot on his neck. "Gil was running from something. Something that scared the hell out of him."

Sam's arms trembled with her words, his grip on the rifle slipping. "I don't need to hear this right now," he hissed back at her, steadying his hand.

Ralph had heard her words, too. The ex-football player swallowed audibly and raised the lamp higher, as if that would spread the glow farther. It didn't.

Sam tired of this game of silences. He cleared his throat, and called out, "Who's there!"

His answer was instant and blinding. Light flared up from the dark corridor, so bright it stung the eye. The group tumbled backward. Sam's finger twitched on the rifle's trigger, but only instinct drilled into him from hunting trips with his uncle kept him from firing off a round: *you never shoot what you can't see.*

Sam kept his rifle pointed, but he eased back on the trigger.

A squeaky voice, timid and frosted with terror, echoed up from behind the blinding light. "It's me!" The light suddenly tilted away from their gathered faces to play across the ceiling. A small figure stepped forward.

Sam lowered his weapon, silently thanking his uncle for his training in restraint. "Denal?" It was the young Indian lad who acted as their translator. The boy's face was ashen, his eyes glowing with fear. Sam shouldered his rifle. "What the hell are you doing down here?"

The boy hurried forward, keeping the flashlight he bore pointed down now. Words in fractured English rushed from him. "I . . . I see Gil sneakin' down here with Juan and Miguel. With bags of stuff. So I follow 'em."

Maggie pushed beside the trembling boy and put an arm around him. "What happened?"

Denal used his free hand to slip a cigarette to his lips. He did not light it, but its familiar presence seemed to calm him. He spoke around the cigarette. "I no know . . . not sure. After they broke the sealed door—"

"What!" Sam gasped out. Even in their dire situation, such a betrayal shocked him.

Denal merely nodded. "I no see much. I stay out of sight. They crawl through door . . . and . . . and . . ." Denal glanced up to Sam, his eyes frightened. "Then I hear screaming. I run. Hide."

Maggie spoke, "Goddamn. The feckin' bastard was going to loot the place right out from under our noses."

"But obviously something went wrong," Norman added tensely, glancing back at the wall of rubble behind them. He turned back around. "What about the other two? Juan and Miguel?"

"I no know." Denal seemed to see the blockage for the first time. He crossed to the cascade of boulders and clay. "Guillermo run out . . . I wait. I scared others might catch me. But no one come out. Then big boom. Stones fall . . . I run." Denal raised a hand toward the tumbled section of the temple. "I should no come down alone. I should tell you instead. I so stupid."

Sam took the Wood's lamp from Ralph and turned off its ultraviolet glow. "Stupid? You at least thought to bring a flashlight."

Maggie moved closer to Sam. "What are we going to do?"

"We'll just have to wait for Philip to realize we're down here."

Norman scowled at Sam's side. "We'll be waiting a long time."

Denal crossed back to them. "Why no call him on walkie-talkie?"

Sam frowned. "Like the flashlight, that's another thing none of us thought to bring."

Denal reached to a back pocket and pulled free a small handheld unit. "Here."

Sam stared at the walkie-talkie. A smile grew on his face. "Denal, don't ever call yourself stupid again." He took the pocket radio. "If you're stupid, what does that make all of us?"

Denal stared gloomily back at the rubble. "Trapped."

Philip still knelt in the communication tent when the camp's radio erupted with static. The loud noise drew a gasp from the startled student. Garbled words flowed between screeches of static: ". . . stones collapsed . . . someone pick up the line . . ."

It was English! Someone he could talk to! Philip scrambled for the receiver. He stabbed at the transmission button and spoke into the receiver. "Base camp here. Is anyone out there? We have an emergency! Over!"

Philip waited for a response. Hopefully whoever was there would be able to send help. Static was his only answer for a few strained heartbeats; then words formed again. "Philip? . . . It's Sam."

Sam? Philip's heart sank. He raised the receiver. "Where are you? Over."

"We're trapped down in the temple ruins. Gil blew the entrance." Sam explained about the security chief's betrayal. "The whole structure is unstable now."

Philip silently thanked whatever angel had been watching over him and kept him from being buried down there with the others.

"You'll need to send an S.O.S. to Machu Picchu," Sam finished. "We'll need heavy equipment."

Eyeing the pickax in the damaged CPU, Philip groaned softly. He clicked the transmit button. "I have no way of reaching anyone, Sam. Someone took out the satellite system. We're cut off."

There was a long pause as Philip waited for a response. He imagined the string of expletives flowing from the Texan's lips. When Sam next spoke, his voice was angered. "Okay, Philip, then at first light send someone out on foot. Someone fast! In the meantime, you'll need to survey the damage on the surface when the sun's up. If you and the workers could begin a cautious excavation—at least get started—then when help arrives you can move quickly. I don't know how long the air will hold out down here."

Philip nodded, even though Sam could not see. His mind dwelt on other concerns—like his own safety. "But what about Gil?" he asked.

"What about him?" Sam's voice had a trace of irritation. "He's surely long gone."

"But what if he comes back?"

Again a long pause. "You're right. If he blew the place and sabotaged the communications, he must be planning to return. You'd better post guards, too."

Philip swallowed hard as the growing danger he faced dawned on him. What if Gil returned with more bandits? They had only a few hunting rifles and a handful of machetes. They would be sitting ducks for any marauders. Philip glanced to the single Quechan Indian who still held the flashlight at the tent's entrance. And who among these swarthy-skinned foreigners could he trust?

A squelch of static drew Philip's attention back to the radio. "I'm gonna sign off now, Philip. I have to conserve this walkie-talkie's battery. I'll check back with you after sunrise to get an update on how things look from above. Okay?"

Philip held the receiver with a hand that now shook slightly. "Okay. I'll try to reach you at six."

"We'll be here. Over and out."

Philip settled the receiver back to the radio unit and stood up. From outside the tent, the worst of the commotion from the riled camp seemed to have died down. Philip crossed to the tent's flap and stood beside the small Quechan Indian.

Barefoot, wearing only his robe, Philip stared out at the black jungle and the smoking ruins. The chill of the night had settled deep into his bones. He hugged the robe tight to his frame. Deep in his heart, a part of him wished he had been trapped down in the temple with the others.

At least he wouldn't be so alone.

DAY TWO

Janan Pacha

Tuesday, August 21, 7:12 A.M.
Regency Hotel
Baltimore, Maryland

As early-morning sunlight pierced the gaps in the heavy hotel curtains, Henry sat at the small walnut desk and stared at the row of artifacts he had recovered from the mummy: a silver ring, a scrap of faded illegible parchment, two Spanish coins, a ceremonial silver dagger, and the heavy Dominican cross. Henry sensed that clues to the priest's fate were locked in these few items, like a stubborn jigsaw puzzle. If only he could put it all together . . .

Shaking his head, Henry stretched a crick from his back and rubbed at his eyes under his glasses. He must look a mess. He still wore his wrinkled grey suit, though he had tossed the jacket on the rumpled bed. He had been up all night studying the items, managing only a short catnap around midnight. The artifacts kept drawing him back to the hotel-room desk and the array of books and periodicals he had borrowed from the library at Johns Hopkins. Henry simply could not quit working at the puzzle, especially after his first discovery.

He picked up the friar's silver ring for the thousandth time. Earlier, he had gently rubbed the tarnish from its surface and uncovered faint lettering around a central heraldic icon. Henry raised his magnifying lens and read the name on the ring: "*de Almagro.*" The surname of the Dominican friar. Just this one piece to the puzzle brought the man to life in Henry's mind. He was no longer just a *mummy.* With a name, he had become flesh and blood again. Someone with a history, a past, even a family. So much power in just a name.

Laying the magnifier down, Henry retrieved his pen and began adding final details to his sketch of the ring's symbol. A part of it was clearly a family crest—surely the de Almagro coat of arms—but a second image was incorporated around the family heraldry: a crucifix with a set of crossed sabers above it. The symbol was vaguely familiar, but Henry could not place it.

"Who were you, Friar de Almagro?" he mumbled as he worked. "What were you doing at that lost city? Why did the Incas mummify you?" Chewing his lower lip in concentration, Henry finished the last flourishes on his drawing, then picked the paper up and stared at it. "This will have to do."

He glanced to his watch. It was almost eight o'clock. He hated to call so early, but he could not wait any longer. He swiveled his chair and reached for the phone, making sure the portable fax unit was hooked in properly. Once satisfied, he dialed the number.

The voice that answered was officious and curt. "Archbishop Kearney's office. How may I help you?"

"This is Professor Henry Conklin. I called yesterday to inquire about gaining access to your order's old records."

"Yes, Professor Conklin. Archbishop Kearney has been awaiting your call. One moment please."

Henry frowned at the receptionist's manner. He had not expected to reach the archbishop himself, but some minor clerk in their records department.

A stern but warm voice picked up the line. "Ah, Professor Conklin, your news about the mummified priest has caused quite a stir here. We're most interested in what you've learned and how we might be of help."

"Thank you, but I didn't think the matter would require disturbing Your Eminence."

"Actually, I am quite intrigued. Before entering the seminary, I did a master's thesis in European history. A chance to participate in such a study is more of an honor than a bother. So, please, tell me how we can be of assistance."

Henry smiled inwardly at his luck in finding a history buff among these men of the cloth. He cleared his throat. "With Your Eminence's help and access to Church archives, I had hoped to piece together the man's past, maybe shed light on what happened to him."

"Most certainly. My offices are fully at your disposal, for if the mummy is truly a friar of the Dominican order, then he deserves to be sanctified and interred as befits a priest. If descendants of this man still survive, I would think it fitting that the remains be returned to the family's parish for proper burial."

"I quite agree. I've tried to glean as much information as I can on my own, but from here, I'll need to access your records. So far, I've been able to determine the fellow's surname—de Almagro. He was most likely a friar in the Spanish chapter of the Dominicans dating back to the 1500s. I also have a copy of the man's family coat of arms that I'd like to fax you."

"Hmm . . . the 1500s . . . for records that old, we might have to search individual abbeys' records. It might take some time."

"I assumed so, but I thought to get started before I headed back to Peru."

"Yes, and that does give me an idea where to start. I'll forward your records to the Vatican, of course, but there is also a very old Dominican enclave in Cuzco, Peru, headed by an Abbot Ruiz, I believe. If this priest was sent on a mission to Peru, the local abbey there might have some record."

Henry sat up straighter in his chair, excitement fueling his tired body. Of course! He should have thought of that himself. "Excellent. Thank you, Archbishop Kearney. I suspect your help will prove invaluable in solving this mystery."

"I hope so. I'll have my secretary give you our fax number. I'll be awaiting your transmission."

"I'll forward it immediately." Henry barely paid attention while he was passed back to the receptionist and given the fax number. His mind spun on the possibilities. If Friar de Almagro had been in Peru long, surely there might even be some of the man's letters and reports at the abbey in Cuzco. Perhaps some clue to the lost city might be contained in such letters.

Henry replaced the receiver with numb fingers and slid his sketch of the ring into the fax machine. He dialed out and listened to the whir and buzz as the fax engaged.

As the drawing was forwarded, Henry forced his mind to the other mystery that surrounded the mummy. He had spent the night pursuing this fellow's past, but with such matters out of his hands, he allowed himself to speculate on the last puzzle concerning the mummy. Something he had not related to the archbishop. Henry pictured the explosion of the mummy's skull and the splatter of gold.

What exactly had happened? What was that substance? Henry knew the archbishop could shed no new light on that matter. Only one person could help him, someone whom he had been looking for an excuse to call anyway. Since meeting her again for the first time in almost three decades, he could not get the woman out of his mind.

The fax machine chimed its completion, and Henry picked up the phone. He dialed a second number. It rang five times before a breathless voice answered. "Hello?"

"Joan?"

A puzzled voice. "Yes?"

Henry pictured the pathologist's slender face framed by a fall of hair the shade of ravens' wings. Time had barely touched her: just a hint of grey highlights, a pair of reading glasses perched on her nose, a few new wrinkles. But her most delightful features remained unchanged: her shadowy smile, her amused eyes. Even her quick intelligence and sharp curiosity had not been dulled by years in academia. Henry suddenly found it difficult to speak. "Th . . . this is Henry. I'm . . . I'm sorry to disturb you so early."

Her voice lost its cold dispassion and warmed considerably. "Early? You just caught me arriving home from the hospital."

"You worked all night?"

"Well, I was reviewing the scans of your mummy, and . . . well . . ."—a small embarrassed pause— "I sort of lost track of time."

Henry glanced down at his own wrinkled clothing and smiled. "I know what you mean."

"So have you learned anything new?"

"I've put together a few things." He quickly related his discovery of the friar's name and his call to the archbishop. "How about yourself? Anything new on your front?"

"Not much. But I'd like to sit down and go over some of my findings. The material in the skull is proving most unusual."

Before Henry could stop himself or weigh such a decision, he pushed forth. "How about lunch today?"

He cringed as the words came out. He had not meant to sound so desperate. His cheeks grew heated with his awkwardness.

A long pause. "I'm afraid I can't do lunch."

Henry kicked himself for being so unprofessional. Surely she saw through his words. Ever since Elizabeth had died, he had forgotten the knack of approaching a woman romantically—not that he'd ever had much of a desire to do so before now.

Joan continued, "But how about dinner? I know a nice Italian place on the river."

Henry swallowed hard, struggling to speak. Dare he hope that she was suggesting more than just a meeting of colleagues? Perhaps a renewal of old feelings? But it had been so long. So much life had passed between their college years and now. Surely whatever tiny spark that had once flared between them had long gone to ash. Hadn't it?

"Henry?"

"Yes . . . yes, that would be great."

"You're staying at the Sheraton, yes? I can pick you up around eight o'clock. That is, if a late dinner is okay with you?"

"Sure, that would be fine. I often eat late, so that's no problem. And . . . and as a matter of fact, um . . ." Henry's nervous blathering was thankfully interrupted by the beep of an incoming call. He awkwardly coughed. "I'm sorry, Joan. I've got another call. I'll be right back."

Henry lowered the receiver, took a long calming breath, then clicked over to the other line. "Yes?"

"Professor Conklin?"

Henry recognized the voice. His brow crinkled. "Archbishop Kearney?"

"Yes, I just wanted to let you know that I received your fax and took a look at it. What I saw came as quite a surprise."

"What do you mean?"

"The emblem of the crossed swords over the crucifix. As a former European historian, it's one I'm quite familiar with."

Henry picked up the friar's silver ring and held it to the light. "I thought it looked familiar myself, but I couldn't place it."

"I'm not surprised. It's a fairly archaic design."

"What is it?"

"It is the mark of the Spanish Inquisition."

Henry's breath caught in his throat. "What?" Images of torture chambers and flesh seared by red-hot irons flashed before his eyes. The black sect of Catholicism had long been disbanded and vilified for the centuries of deaths and tortures it had inflicted in the name of religion.

"Yes, from the ring, it seems our mummified friar was an Inquisitor."

"My God," Henry swore, forgetting for a moment to whom he was speaking.

An amused chuckle arose from the archbishop. "I thought you should know, but I must be going now. I'll forward your information to the Vatican and to Abbot Ruiz in Peru. Hopefully we'll learn more soon."

The archbishop hung up. Henry sat stunned, until the phone rang in his hand, startling him. "Oh, God . . . Joan." Henry clicked back to the pathologist he had left on hold. "I'm sorry that took so long," he said in a rush, "but it was Archbishop Kearney again."

"What did he want?"

Henry related what he had learned, still shaken by the revelation.

Joan was silent for a moment. "An Inquisitor?"

"It would appear so," Henry said, collecting himself. "One more piece to an expanding puzzle."

She replied, "Amazing. It seems we'll have even more to ponder over dinner tonight."

Henry had momentarily forgotten their supper arrangements. "Yes, of course. I'll see you tonight," he said with genuine enthusiasm.

"It's a date." Joan quickly added her good-byes, then hung up.

Henry slowly returned the receiver to its cradle. He did not know what surprised him more—that the mummy was a member of the Spanish Inquisition or that he had a date.

Gil climbed the stairs of the only hotel in the jungle village of Villacuacha. The wooden planks creaked under his weight. Even in the shadowed interior of the inn, the late-morning heat could not be so easily escaped. Already a sweltering warmth wrapped itself around Gil like a heavy blanket. He swiped the dampness from his neck with the cuff of his torn sleeve and swore under his breath. The nightlong flight through the jungle had left him scratched and foul-tempered. He had managed only a short nap after arranging this meeting.

"He had better not be late," Gil grumbled as he climbed to the third landing. After fleeing the campsite of the Americans, Gil had reached a dirt track in the jungle just as the sun finally rose. Luckily, he stumbled upon a local Indian with a mule and a crooked-wheeled wagon. A handful of coins had bought him passage to the village. Once there, Gil had telephoned his contact—the man who had arranged for Gil's infiltration onto the Americans' team. They had agreed to a noon meeting at this hotel.

Gil patted the golden cup secured in his pocket. His contact, a dealer in antiquities, should pay a tidy sum for such a rare find. And this broker in stolen goods had better not balk at Gil's price. If Gil had any hopes of hiring a crew to return to the dig and commandeer the site, he would need quick funding—all in cash.

Gil ran a hand over the long knife at his belt. If it came down to it, he would persuade the fellow to meet his price. He would let nothing stand between him and his treasure, not after how much it had cost him already.

Atop the stairs, Gil pushed the taped bandage covering his burned cheek more firmly in place. He would be rewarded for his scarring. That he swore. Teeth gritted with determination, Gil walked down the narrow corridor. He found the right door and rapped his knuckles on it.

A man's firm voice answered. "Come in."

Gil tried the door. It was unlocked. He pushed his way into the room and was instantly struck by two things. First, the refreshing coolness of the room. Overhead, a ceiling fan turned languidly, creating a gentle stir to the air that seemed to wash away the humidity. A double set of French doors were swung wide open upon a small balcony overlooking the hotel's shaded garden courtyard. From somewhere beyond the steamy warmth of the jungle, a cool breeze flowed through those open doors into the room. White-lace curtains drifted in the gentle breezes, while thin mosquito netting around the single bed billowed softly like the sails of a ship.

But more than the breezes, the room's occupant struck Gil as the source of the room's coolness. It was the first time Gil had ever met his contact in person. The tall man sat in a cushioned rattan chair, facing Gil, his back to the open double doors. Dressed all in black, from shoes to buttoned shirt, the fellow sat with his legs casually crossed, a drink clinking with ice in one hand. From his burnished complexion, he was clearly of Spanish descent. Dark eyes stared at Gil, appraising him from under clipped black hair. A thin mustache also traced the man's upper lip. He did not smile. The only movement was a flick of the man's eyes toward the other chair in the room, indicating Gil should sit.

Still wearing his ripped and sweat-stained clothes, Gil felt like a peasant before royalty. He could not even manage to roil up a bit of righteous anger at the man's attitude. He sensed a vein of hardness in the man that Gil could never match, nor dare challenge. Gil forced his tongue to move. "I . . . I have what we talked about."

The man merely nodded. "Then we need only discuss the price."

Gil lowered himself slowly to the chair. He found himself perched just at the edge of the seat, not comfortable enough to lean back. He suddenly wanted nothing more than to be done with this deal, no matter what the price. He longed to leave the chill of the room for the familiar swelter of the bustling town.

Gil could not even meet the other man's eyes. He found himself staring out the window at the town's church steeple, the thin white cross stark against the blue sky.

"Show me what you found," the man said, his drink still clinking as he gently rocked his glass, drawing back Gil's attention.

"Yes, of course." Swallowing the dry lump in his throat, Gil fished out the dented chalice and placed it on the table between them. Rubies and emeralds flashed brightly against the gold setting. Gil felt a resurgence of his resolve as he eyed the jeweled dragon wrapped around the thick gold cup. "And . . . and there's more," Gil said. "With enough men and the right tools, by week's end, I could have a hundred times as much."

Ignoring Gil's words, the man lowered his drink to the table and reached to the Incan cup. He picked up the chalice, raised it to the sunlight, and examined its surface for an excruciatingly long time.

Gil's hands wrung in his lap as he waited. He stared at the dent along the cup's lip as the man studied the workmanship on the chalice. Gil feared such a blemish might significantly reduce the price. The fellow had insisted any artifacts be brought to him intact.

As the man finally lowered the cup back to the table, Gil dared meet his eyes. He saw only anger there.

"The dent . . . it . . . it was already there," Gil stammered quickly.

The man stood silently and crossed to a small bar behind Gil. Gil listened as the man added more ice to his glass. He then stepped behind Gil.

Gil could not bring himself to twist around. He just stared at the treasure atop the table. "If you don't want it, I . . . I will not hold you to any obligation."

Without turning, Gil knew the man leaned toward him. The small hairs on the nape of his neck quivered with the instinct of his cave-dwelling ancestors. Gil then felt the man's breath at his ear.

"It is only ordinary gold. Worthless."

Sensing the danger too late, Gil's hand snapped toward the knife at his belt. His fingers found only an empty sheath. Before Gil could react, his head was yanked back by the hair; he saw his own knife gripped in the man's hand. He did not even have time to wonder how the blade had been snatched from his side. A flick of the man's wrist, and the dagger sliced open Gil's throat, a line of fire from ear to ear. Gil was tossed forward and fell to the floor as his blood spilled across the whitewashed planks.

Rolling to his back, Gil saw the man return to the bar for his abandoned drink while Gil choked on his own blood. "P . . . Please . . ." he gurgled out, one arm raised in supplication as the light in the room began to dim. The man ignored him.

Eyes filled with tears, Gil again turned to the open window and the bright crucifix in the blue sky. *Please, not like this*, he prayed silently. But he found no salvation there either.

Finished with his drink, the man eyed the still form of Guillermo Sala. The pool of blood appeared almost black against the white floor. He felt no satisfaction in the killing. The Chilean had served his purpose and was now more a risk than a benefit to his cause.

Sighing, he crossed the room, careful not to foul his polished shoes with blood. He retrieved the Incan treasure from the table and weighed it briefly, judging its worth once the gems had been pried free and the cup melted into a brick. It was not the discovery his group had hoped to find, but it would have to do. From Gil's description of the underground vault, there was still a chance of a more significant strike. Stepping back to the room's bed, he collected the small leather satchel and secured the cup inside.

He studied the room. It would be cleaned up by nightfall.

Satchel in hand, he left the room and its cool breezes for the moist heat of the narrow corridor and the stairs. Sweat quickly broke across his forehead. He ignored it. He had grown up in these moist highlands and was well-accustomed to the swelter. Born of mixed blood, Spanish and local Indian, he was a *mestizo*, a half-breed. Neither Spanish nor Quechan. Despite carrying this mark of dishonor among the highland people, he had managed to fight his way to a place of respect.

Once through the hotel's small lobby, he crossed into the midday sunlight. The steps outside were blinding in the bright light. Shading his eyes against the glare, he worked his way down the steps and almost stumbled over an Indian woman and her babe near the foot of the stairs.

The woman, wearing a rough-spun tunic and shawl, was as startled by him as he excused himself. But she fell to her knees before him, snatching at his pant leg and raising her baby, wrapped in a brightly colored alpaca blanket, toward him. She beseeched him in her native Quecha.

He smiled benignly at her and nodded in answer. Placing his bag on the last step, he reached to his throat and slipped out his silver pectoral crucifix. It stood stark against his black raiment. He raised a hand over the babe's head and gave a quick benediction. Once done, he kissed the baby on the forehead, collected his bag, and continued down the village street toward his church, the steeple overhead guiding him home.

The small Indian woman called after him, "*Gracias!* Thank you, Friar Otera!"

In the darkness of the collapsed temple, time stretched. Maggie was sure entire days had passed, but if her watch was accurate, it was only the following morning, close to noon. They had been trapped for less than half a day.

Arms across her chest, Maggie studied the others as she stood a few paces down the main corridor. With his rifle slung over a shoulder, Sam stood by the rockfall, the walkie-talkie glued to his lips. Since dawn, the Texan had been in periodic contact with Philip, conserving the walkie-talkie's battery as much as possible but trying to aid their fellow student in his appraisal of the ruined site.

"No!" Sam yelled into the walkie-talkie. "The debris pile is all that is holding up this level of the dig. If you try to excavate the original shaft, you'll drop the rest on top of us." A long pause while Sam listened to Philip's response. "Shit, Philip! Listen to me! I'm down here. I can see how the support walls are leaning on the blockade of stone. You'll kill us. Find where those looters had been tunneling into the dig. That's the best chance."

Sam shook his head at the walkie-talkie. "The bastard is spooked up there," he told her. "He's looking for the quickest fix as usual."

Maggie offered Sam a wan smile. Personally, she was looking for the quickest fix, too.

Ralph and Norman were huddled around their only light source, Denal's flashlight. Ralph held it for Sam to survey the destruction and the state of their crumbling roof. Norman had snapped a few photographs after the short naps they had managed overnight. He now stood with his camera hanging by a strap, clutched to his belly. If they survived this, Norman was going to produce some award-winning footage of their adventure. Still, from his pale face, Maggie was sure the photographer would gladly trade his Pulitzer for the chance to escape alive.

"Watch out!"

The call from behind startled Maggie. She froze, but a hand suddenly shoved her off her feet. She stumbled a couple steps forward just as a large slab of granite crashed to the stones behind her. The entire temple shook. Dust choked her for a few breaths.

Waving a hand, Maggie turned to see a dusty Denal crawling to his feet. The chunk of loosened rock stood between them. Maggie was dumbstruck by how close she had come to being crushed.

Sam was already beside her. "You need to keep an eye on the ceiling," he admonished her.

"No feckin' kidding, Sam." She turned to the boy as he clambered over the slab. Her voice softened with appreciation. "Thank you, Denal."

He mumbled something in his native tongue, but he could not meet her eyes. If the light were better, Maggie was sure she'd find him blushing. She lifted his chin and kissed him on the cheek. When she pulled away, his eyes had grown wider than saucers.

Maggie turned to spare Denal further embarrassment. "Sam, maybe we should retreat down another level." She waved a hand to the fallen rock. "You're right about the instability of this area. We might be safer a little farther away."

Sam considered her suggestion, taking off his Stetson and finger-combing his hair as he studied the ceiling. "Maybe we'd better."

Ralph stepped forward, raising the light toward the ceiling. "Look how all the roof slabs are out of alignment."

Maggie studied the roof. Ralph had keen eyes. Some of the square stones were tilted a few centimeters askew from the others, displaced by the explosion. As they watched, one of the stones shifted another centimeter.

Sam must have seen it, too. His voice was shaky. "Okay, everybody, down another floor."

Ralph led the way with the flashlight.

Norman followed. "Right now, I'd love a large glass of lemonade, filled to the brim with ice."

Sam nodded his head. "If you're taking orders, Norm, I'll take something with a bit of a head on it. Maybe a tall Corona in a frosted mug with a twist of lime."

Maggie wiped the dust and sweat from her forehead as she followed. "In Ireland, we drink our pints warm . . . but right now, I'm even willin' to bow to your crass American custom of drinkin' it cold."

Ralph laughed as they reached the ladder. "I doubt the Incas left us a cooler down there, but I'm willing to search." Ralph waved his flashlight for Maggie to mount the ladder first while he lit the way.

Maggie's smile faded from her lips as she climbed away from Ralph's light and into the gloom of the next level. Their banter in the face of their predicament did little to fend off the true terror; the darkness beyond the brightness was always there, reminding them how precarious their situation was.

As she awaited the others, she considered Ralph's last words. Just what *had* the Incas left them down there? What lay within the chamber beyond the sealed door, and what had happened to Gil's two companions?

By the time the others had regrouped at the foot of the ladder on the second level, Maggie's curiosity had been piqued. Also by focusing on these mysteries, her fear of being buried under fifty feet of collapsing temple could be somewhat allayed. If the anxiety grew too intense . . .

Maggie shook her head. She would not lose control again. She watched Sam climb down the ladder with a twinge of guilt. After her attack last night, she had not been totally honest with him. She had failed to explain that the onset of her "seizures" had begun after witnessing the death of Patrick Dugan in the roadside ditch in Belfast. Afterward, the doctors had not been able to find any physiological cause for her attacks, though the consensus was the seizures were most likely a form of severe panic. She shoved back the growing guilt. The details were not Sam's business. After the initial entrapment, she had come to grips with their situation. As long as she could keep herself distracted, she would be okay.

Nearby, Sam tried his walkie-talkie. The radio still worked, but the static was a bit worse this much deeper. He let Philip know about their repositioning.

Once he was done, Maggie crossed to Sam. She wet her lips. "I'd like to borrow your ultraviolet lamp."

"What for?"

"I want to go see what damage Gil and the others did to the dig."

"I can't let you go traipsing about on your own. We need to stick together." He began to turn away.

She grabbed his shoulder. "It wasn't a request, Sam. I'm going. It'll only take a few minutes."

Denal stood a few steps away. "I . . . I go with you, Miss Maggie."

Sam faced them and seemed to recognize her determination. "Fine. But don't be gone longer than fifteen minutes. We need to conserve our light sources, and I don't want to be hunting you both down."

Maggie nodded. "Thanks, Sam."

"I'm coming with you two," Norman said, snugging his camera around his shoulder.

Ralph also had a gleam of interest, but Sam squashed it. "The three of you go on. Ralph and I will go through this level with the flashlight and assess the structural integrity." He dug his lamp out of his pocket and held it toward Maggie, but he did not release it without a final word of caution. "Fifteen minutes. Be careful."

She heard the worry in his stern voice, and that dulled the annoyance in her own response. "I know,

Sam," she said softly, taking the Wood's lamp from him. "You needn't worry."

He grinned, then returned to his walkie-talkie and ongoing argument with Philip.

Maggie clicked on the ultraviolet light and signaled for her two companions to follow her to the next ladder. As they abandoned the brighter light, the darkness of the temple wrapped close around them. Ahead, the purplish glow lit up the quartz in the granite blocks, creating a miniature starscape spreading down the passage. Maggie led them onward, the others sticking closer to her side.

As they traversed the series of ladders to the deepest level of the dig, Maggie's heart began thudding louder and louder in her own ears. Soon her heartbeat seemed almost to be coming from beyond her chest.

"What's that noise?" Norman asked as he stepped off the rung of the last ladder.

Denal answered, his voice a whisper. "I hear it before. After Señor Sala crawled through that doorway."

Maggie realized the beating in her ears wasn't her own heart but the external thudding of something deeper in the temple. It even reverberated through the stones under her feet.

"It sounds like a big clock ticking," Norman said.

Maggie raised her light. "Let's keep going." Compared to the sonorous beat from below, her own voice sounded like the squeak of a mouse.

Winding past the last of the tunnels, Maggie soon stood before the violated doorway. Broken bolts marked where the seals had been shattered. In the dirt to the sides of the threshold, the three bands of etched hematite lay discarded, all of them cracked and chipped from the crowbar used to pry them loose. The offending tool still leaned against the wall.

Denal bent and picked up the crowbar, hefting it in his grip. He glanced to Maggie. She did not begrudge him a weapon.

The doorway ahead lay partially blocked by the toppled stone that had once sealed the section of the temple ahead. Norman knelt a couple spaces back from the opening. He nudged his glasses higher on his nose and tried to peer inside. "I can't see anything."

Maggie moved beside him. Neither seemed willing to draw closer to the door. She remembered the terror in Gil's eyes and the bloody blistering across his cheek. What lay ahead?

Norman exchanged a glance with her. She shrugged and stepped forward, the lamp held before her like a pistol. She paused just at the edge of the doorway, then extended her arm through the threshold. The glow stretched down the throat of a short passage. The deep ticking sounded much louder there. Maggie spoke quietly. "There seems to be a large room just ahead. But the light doesn't quite reach it." She glanced over her shoulder back to Norman.

"Maybe we'd better wait for the others," the photographer whispered.

Maggie was about to suggest exactly the same thing, but since Norman suggested it first, she now balked. She could picture Sam's smug expression if she didn't at least take a peek. They had wasted the battery of the Wood's lamp to come this far; they should at least have something to show for the expenditure. "I'm going in," she said, moving forward before fear slowed her. She would not be ruled by the paralyzing terror of her childhood.

"Then we'd better all go," Norman said, closing in to crowd her rear as she began to crawl over the toppled stone door.

Maggie scrabbled over the obstruction and stood in the hall. Norman and Denal joined her. "Look," she said, pointing her lamp. "There's somethin' ahead, reflecting back the glow." Intrigued, she crept ahead slowly.

"Wait," Norman said. "Let's see what's out there first."

Maggie turned to see the photographer raise his camera.

"Don't look at the flash directly," he warned.

She swung back around just as the camera exploded for a briefest second. She gasped. After so long, such brightness stung. But her shocked response wasn't all due to the pain. Blazed for just a fractured second, an image of the room had branded her retinas. "D . . . Did you see that?" she asked.

Denal mumbled something in his native tongue, clearly awed.

Norman coughed to clear his throat. "Gold and silver everywhere."

Maggie raised her own light, its purplish glow now seeming so feeble. "And that statue . . . did you see it? It had to be at least two meters tall."

Norman moved next to her as Maggie edged forward again. Denal kept to their side with his crowbar. Norman whispered, "Two meters. It couldn't have been gold, too. Could it?"

Maggie shrugged. "When the Spanish first arrived here, they described the Temple of the Sun found in Cuzco. The *Coriancha*. The rooms were said to have been plated with thick slabs of gold and, in the innermost temple stood a life-size model of a cornfield. Stalks, leaves, ears, even the dirt itself . . . all of gold."

By now, they had reached the room's entrance. Maggie knelt down and ran a hand gently over the gold plate at her feet. "Amazing . . . we must have uncovered another Sun Temple."

Norman stood still. "What's that out there? Out on the floor."

Maggie pushed back up. "What do you mean?"

He pointed to a dark shadow at the edge of her light's reach. She raised her lamp. Its glow reflected across the gold and silver like moonlight spilling on a still pond. Some dark island lay out there, a ripple on the pond. Maggie began to step closer with her light, one foot on the edge of the metal floor.

Denal stopped her, holding his crowbar across her path. "No, Miss Maggie," he murmured. "Smells wrong here."

"He's right," Norman said. "What's that reek?"

Now brought to her attention, Maggie noticed an underlying stench that penetrated through the cloying scent of wet clay and mold. She nodded to the camera. "Do it again, Norman."

Nodding, the photographer raised his camera as Maggie turned her eyes back to the floor. The flash exploded out into the room. Maggie swore and stumbled away from the tiles. "Sweet Jesus!"

She covered her mouth. She had been staring at the dark island on the room's floor when Norman's flash had burst forth. The tortured face still blazed in her mind's eye. The torn and twisted body, the eyes wide with death, and the blood . . . so much blood. Another body lay beyond the first, close to the far wall.

"Juan and Miguel," Denal mumbled.

There was a long stretch of silence.

"Gil didn't do that to them, did he?" Norman asked. "Murder them for the gold?"

Maggie slowly shook her head. Juan's mutilated form had become just a shadowed lump again. As she stared, the thudding heartbeat of some great beast still echoed across the treasure room. She now recognized it for what it was—the ticking of large gears behind the walls and floor of the room.

The warning etched on the chamber's seals suddenly wormed through Maggie's skull: *We leave this tomb to Heaven. May it never be disturbed.*

"Maggie?"

She turned to Norman. "No. Gil didn't murder them. The room did."

Before Norman could react, the chamber shuddered violently, throwing them all down. Maggie landed hard upon the edge of the plated floor, knocking the wind from her chest. Gulping air, she scrambled back, sensing the danger.

"What was that?" Norman yelled.

Maggie swung her lamp around. Through the entrance to the tomb, a thick cloud of dust rolled toward them. She fought to speak. "Och! Jesus! Up . . . up . . . !" Maggie urged them all.

"What's going on?" Norman pressed, panic edging his voice.

Maggie pushed him toward the exit. "Goddammit! Move, Norman! The bloody temple is collapsing!"

Sam checked on Ralph. The large black man pushed groggily up on his arms. His scalp had been clipped when a section of the roof had given way. Luckily a grinding from above had warned them before the sky came crashing down. "Are you okay?" Sam asked, dusting off his Wranglers.

Ralph rolled to his knees. "Yeah, I think." He gingerly touched a bloody bump on his forehead. "I never been tackled by a slab of granite before."

"Don't move," Sam warned. He collected the flashlight from where it had fallen. "I'm gonna check on what happened."

Ralph scowled and climbed to his feet. "Like hell. We stick together."

Sam nodded. Truthfully, he didn't want to investigate on his own. This level of the temple was now almost a solid cloud of drifting silt and dust. Sam coughed, covering his mouth and nose with the crook of his elbow. "This way," he mumbled. He led them back to the shaft leading up to the first level of the temple.

Ralph groaned as the remains of the shattered ladder came into view ahead. "This can't be good."

And it wasn't. The way up was blocked by a jumbled pile of hewn boulders, like tumbled children's blocks. "The first level must have entirely collapsed," Sam said.

Sam's walkie-talkie squelched static at his waist. He collected it and heard Philip's frantic voice. ". . . okay? Report, goddammit! Over!"

Sam pressed the transmitter. "Philip, Sam here. We're okay." Overhead, the roof moaned ominously; dirt drizzled down. "But I don't know for how long. How're you coming with tunneling in a new entrance from the base of the hill?"

Static . . . then . . . ". . . just found the looter's shaft. It's barely begun . . . at least two days . . . . sent for help, but don't know how long . . . ." Static overwhelmed the tinny voice of their fellow student, but Sam had still heard the panic.

"Shit, two days . . ." Ralph grumbled. "The temple will never last that long."

Sam tried to get more information from Philip, but only snatches of words made it through. "I'll try to reposition for better reception," Sam yelled into the radio. "Stand by!"

He slipped the walkie-talkie away. "Let's find the others. Make sure they're safe."

Ralph nodded. "Maybe it's best if we holed up in the lowest level anyway." Another small groan sounded overhead. "It looks like this place is going to crumble one level at a time."

Sam led the way through the corridors. "Let's just hope we're rescued before we run out of levels."

Ralph had no rebuttal and followed in silence.

Just as they reached the ladder that led down to the third level, Sam saw Norman pop out of the shaft, his eyes wide in the flashlight. The photographer held a hand against the glare. "Thank God, you're okay!" Norman said in a rush. "We didn't know what we'd find."

Denal came next. Sam noted the crowbar in the teenager's hand, but didn't comment on it.

Maggie climbed out last. "What happened?" she asked tersely, clicking off the Wood's lamp.

"The top level collapsed," Sam said, and quickly recounted their narrow escape. "With the upper levels so shaky, we thought it best to shelter in the fifth level. Just in case."

"So we keep our heads as low as we can," Maggie said.

Norman eyed the ladder. "That means back down again."

Sam saw a worried glance pass between Maggie and Norman. "What is it?"

"We found Juan and Miguel down there," Norman said.

Sam knew from his tone and manner that the men were not alive. "What happened to them?"

Maggie answered, "You'd better see for yourself." She turned away.

In silence, the group clambered down the ladders to the deepest level of the temple. Sam soon found himself staring at the scattered seals of the door. "The bastards . . ." he mumbled under his breath as he bent by the doorway.

"They've paid for their crimes, Sam," Maggie said dourly. "Come on." She ushered him into the next room, then followed herself, sticking close to his side.

With his flashlight, Sam quickly took in the scene in the next chamber. He did not let the light's beam linger too long on either broken body. For a moment, he had a sudden flashback to seeing his own parents' bloody bodies being carried away on stretchers. Safely buckled into the backseat of the family Ford, Sam had escaped the fatal crash with only a broken arm. He rubbed his forearm now. "Wh . . . what happened to them?"

"The tomb's booby-trapped," Maggie said, then nodded ahead. "Listen to the winding of winches under the floor. Some bloody contraption meant to catch looters."

"I didn't think the Incas had such technology."

"No, but some of the coastal Indians were fairly advanced in pulley construction for their irrigation systems. If they helped here . . . ?" She shrugged.

Sam's light beam focused on the gold Incan king as it stood against the wall of black granite. "Either way, there's the lure. One look at that prize and who wouldn't rush over." Sam played his light over the pattern of gold and silver tiles. He knew a trap when he saw one. "Here's a game I wouldn't want to play."

The stones rumbled underfoot, and a grinding roar echoed down from the levels above. "We may be forced to," Maggie said. "Buttressed by the trap's machinery, this may be the safest room if the rest of the temple collapses."

Ralph's voice called back to them from the threshold. "Sam, try to reach Sykes again! Light a fire under him! This place is coming apart!"

Sam unhooked the walkie-talkie and switched it back on. Static screeched from the speakers. It was silenced as Sam hit the transmitter. "Philip, if you can hear me, come in. Over."

White noise was his only answer, then a few words came through: ". . . trying to widen the shaft so more workers can dig . . . will work around the clock . . ."

"Speed it up, Philip!" Sam insisted. "This place is a shaky house of cards."

". . . doing the best . . . damn workers don't understand . . ." A long stretch of static followed.

"This is useless," Sam mumbled to himself with a shake of his head. He raised the radio to his lips. "Just keep us informed on the hour!" He switched the walkie-talkie off and turned to Maggie. "We've a long wait ahead of us."

Maggie stood with her head cocked, listening to the moans of the strained temple. "I hope we have a long time," she said with clear worry. Sam tried to put an arm over her shoulders, but she shrugged it off. "I'm okay."

Sam watched Maggie retreat from the room. With a final pass of his light over the deadly chamber, Sam turned to follow, but the pattern of gold and silver fixed in his mind. It was no plain checkerboard, but a complex mix of zigzagging steps with two patches of rectangular gold islands, one at the upper left of the room, and one at the lower right.

Sam stopped, pondering the pattern. It was naggingly familiar. He turned back to the floor, shining his light across it.

"What's wrong?" Maggie called back to him.

"Just a sec," Sam stepped to the edge of the chamber. He stood silently, letting his mind calm. There was a clue hidden here. He just knew it. The two men's corpses had distracted him, shocked him from noticing before. "My god," Sam mumbled.

Maggie had returned cautiously to his side. "What?"

Sam waved his light across the thirty rows of yard-wide tiles. "You were right about other Peruvian Indians being involved here. This isn't Incan."

"What do you mean?" Maggie asked. "That statue sure looks Incan."

"I don't mean the statue. The Incas probably added that later. I meant the floor, the room itself. The booby trap."

"I don't understand."

"Look at the pattern. It's so large that I almost missed it." Sam pointed with his flashlight's beam. "The various tribes in ancient Peru—the Paracas, the Huari, the Nasca, the Moche, even the Incas—none of them had a written language. But their pictographs and ideograms, found in drawings and woven in their textiles, were elaborate and unique to each tribe. Look at this pattern. The two golden rectangles at opposite corners connected by snaking zigzagging lines. Where have you seen that before?"

Maggie took a step closer. "Sweet Jesus, you're right. It's a huge pictograph." She turned to face Sam, eyes bright with excitement. "It is *Moche*, not Inca."

"It's just like Uncle Hank had figured," Sam mumbled, his voice awed. "We're in a Moche pyramid."

"What? When did Professor Conklin mention anything about the Moche?"

Sam realized he had misspoken, letting out his uncle's secret. Sam sighed. Considering their circumstances, any secrets now seemed ludicrous. "Listen, Maggie, there's something my uncle's kept from you all." Sam quickly recounted how the professor had discovered that the Sun Plaza here matched the tip of a Moche pyramid found along the coast. "He made the discovery just before he left with the mummy."

Maggie frowned. "So I wasn't the only one keepin' secrets . . ."

Sam blushed, remembering his own lambasting of Maggie for keeping facts hidden. "I'm sorry."

A long stretch of silence ensued. Maggie finally spoke. "It makes rough sense. Considering the complexity of the room, the Moche were better at metallurgy than the Incas. They also built elaborate canals and irrigation systems for their lands, with crude pumps and gearwork. If any of the tribes was capable of constructing this trap in precious metals, it would be the Moche." Maggie nodded toward the pattern. "You're the expert epigrapher. What does it mean?"

Sam explained, using his flashlight as a pointer. "See how the stair-step pattern connects the two gold rectangles. It depicts the rising of a spirit from this world to the realm of spirits and gods." Sam turned to Maggie. "It basically means this is the gateway to Heaven."

"Jesus . . ."

"But that's not all." Sam shone his light on the ceiling, where an inverted image of the floor's pattern was depicted in tile. "Each gold tile on the floor has a matching silver tile above it and vice versa. The Moche . . . and the Incas for that matter . . . believed in dualism. In the Quechan language, *yanantin* and *yanapaque*. Mirror imagery, light and dark, upper and lower."

"Yin and yang," Maggie mumbled.

"Exactly. Dualism is common in many cultures."

"So what you're saying . . ." Maggie found her eyes drifting to the two mutilated corpses.

Sam finished her statement, "Here also lies the gateway to Hell."

From across the ruins, Philip stared at the collapsed hilltop. The entire roof of the subterranean temple had caved in on itself, leaving a clay- and boulder-strewn declivity ten feet deep. A smoky smudge still hung over the sunken summit like some steaming volcano, silt forever hanging in the moist air.

Philip remained near his post by the communication tent, but he wasn't due to contact Sam for another half hour. Philip hugged his arms around his chest. The Quechan workers were all but useless. Pantomiming and drawing out his instructions were the only ways to communicate with the uneducated lot—and still, they often mistook his orders.

However, Philip was beginning to suspect some of their "misunderstandings" were deliberate, especially after he had insisted the Indians attempt to redig the original shaft, defying Sam's own warnings. The Texan's assessment had quickly proven valid; the temple had collapsed further when some of the laborers attempted to pry loose a particularly large slab of granite. One of the Indians had broken his leg when the roof gave way. Ever since, the Quechans had grown sullen and slow to respond to his orders.

Upon reaching Sam earlier, Philip had deliberately sidestepped mentioning his own culpability for their near tragedy. Luckily, poor communications had saved him from having to explain in detail.

Philip glanced to the jungle's edge. If nothing else, at least the workers had discovered the partially excavated tunnel of the looters near the foot of the jungle-shrouded hill. From his calculations, he estimated another forty feet of tunnel would have to be dug before reaching the temple itself—and at the current pace, it would take closer to four days, rather than the two-day estimate he had given Sam.

"That is, unless help arrives first," he grumbled. If not, the others were doomed. Even if the temple remained standing, which was doubtful, water would become more and more crucial. Even in this humidity, death by dehydration posed a real danger. Help must come. He would not have the deaths of the others on his hands—or his résumé. If such a scandal broke with his name associated with it, he risked losing any chance of a future position at Harvard.

Philip shadowed his eyes against the late-afternoon sun. A pair of workers had left at dawn to seek help, running on long, lean legs. The two young men looked capable of maintaining their pace all day long. If so, they should be reaching the tiny village of Villacuacha and a telephone anytime, and with an expedient response, a rescue operation could be under way within the next two days.

Philip pinned all his plans on this one hope—rescue. With others around, he would be relieved of any direct culpability. Even if the other students died, it would not be his sole responsibility. Shared blame could weaken the blemish on his own record.

But there was one other reason he prayed for the appearance of rescuers. The sun was near setting, and Philip feared another long, black night with the forest screeching around him. Guillermo Sala was out there somewhere, surely waiting for the proper time to attack.

Staring off toward the distant village of Villacuacha, Philip sent a whispered prayer to the two Indian runners. "Hurry, you bastards."

Along a jungle trail, Friar Otera glanced toward the setting sun, then pulled the cowl of his robe higher over his head, shadowing his features. They should be at the ruins by midday tomorrow. "Come," he ordered, and led the way.

Behind, a row of five brown-robed monks kept pace with him. The brush of their robes was the only sound disturbing the twilight forest. The jungle always grew strangely quiet as the sun began to set, hushed as if the creatures of the forest held their breath against the dangers of the approaching night. Soon the dark predators would be loose again for the hunt.

It was this pregnant silence that allowed the black-haired friar to hear the snap of a branch and the ragged huffing breath of someone approaching. He cocked his head. No, two men approached. Friar Otera held up an arm and, without a word, the others stopped. The Church had trained them well.

Soon two bare-chested Indians appeared along the trail ahead. Sweat shone off their sleek bodies as if they were aglow in the last rays of the sun. On closer inspection, it was clear the two, thorn-scratched and shaky of limb, had traveled far and at a hard pace.

Within his cowl, the friar's lips drew to hard lines of satisfaction. Though he hated his poor upbringing here among the Indians, it now proved useful. As a boy, he had been chased and tormented because he was of mixed blood, a half-bred *mestizo*. The shadowy jungle trails became his only sanctuary from the constant ridicule and he knew these jungle trails as well as any. He also knew any attempt to call for help must travel this trail—and he had his orders. Friar Otera raised a palm in greeting.

The first of the Indians seemed wary of the group of strangers. Wisely so, since the jungles were the haunts of many guerrillas and marauders. But soon, recognition of their robed raiments and silver crosses filled the Indian's eyes. He dropped to his knees, chattering his thanks in guttural Quecha.

Friar Otera bowed his head, crossing his wrists within the long folds of his sleeves. One hand reached the dagger's hilt in his hidden wrist sheath. "Fear not, my child. Calm yourself. Tell me what has happened."

"Friar . . . Father, we have run far. Seeking help. We are workers for some *norte americanos* high in the mountains. There was an accident. A horrible accident."

"An accident?"

"An underground tomb has collapsed, trapping some of the *americanos*. They will die unless we hurry."

Friar Otera shook his head sadly. "Horrible indeed," he muttered in his native Quecha, though inwardly it galled him to do so. The old language, a crude derivation of the Incan language called *runa simi*, was so plain and base, the language of the poor. And he hated to be reminded of his own roots by speaking it so fluently. A spark of anger rose in his heart, but he kept it hidden within the shadows of his robe. Friar Otera listened in silence as the frantic Indian finished explaining about the explosion and the damaged satellite phone. He just nodded in understanding.

"So we must hurry, Father, before it's too late."

Friar Otera licked his lips. So only one of the *americanos* was still loose among the ruins. How fortuitous. "Yes, we must hurry," he agreed with the panting Indian. "You have done well bringing us this news, my child."

The Indian lowered his head in thanks and relief.

Friar Otera slipped past the kneeling Indian and approached the second fellow. "You have done well, too, my child."

This other Indian had remained silent during the exchange and had not knelt. His dark eyes had remained wary. He backed up a step now, somehow sensing the danger, but he was too late.

Friar Otera lashed out with the long blade hidden at his wrist, slicing cleanly. The man's hands flew to his slashed throat, trying to stanch the flow of blood. A spraying spurt struck the friar's robe as the Indian fell to his knees. *Too late to pray now, heathen.* With a scowl, Friar Otera used his booted foot to topple the gurgling man backward.

Stepping over the body, Friar Otera continued on his way down the trail. He had not even heard a sound as the other monks dealt with the first Indian. He nodded in satisfaction.

The Church had certainly trained them well.

Joan tried the wine. It was a decent vintage merlot, not too dry, with a sweet bouquet. She nodded, and the waiter filled her glass the rest of the way. "It should accent the porterhouse nicely," she said with a shy smile.

Across the candlelit table, Henry returned her smile. "A forensic pathologist and a wine connoisseur to boot. You've grown to be a woman of many surprises. As I recall, you used to be a beer-and-tequila woman."

She stifled a short laugh. "Time has ways of refining one's taste. As does a stomach that can no longer tolerate such excesses." She eyed Henry. He still filled his dark suit well, a double-breasted charcoal jacket over a crisp white shirt and pale rose tie. The colors accented perfectly the salting of silver-grey in his dark hair. Clean-shaven and impeccably attired, it was hard to believe this fellow had been tromping through the Peruvian jungles just last week. "And I must say you're full of surprises, too, Henry. Your years in the field have done you no harm."

Henry, fork in hand, glanced up from the remains of his Caesar salad. He wore a roguish grin, an expression that took Joan back to her college years. "Why, Dr. Engel," he teased, "if I didn't know better, I'd say you were trying to pick me up."

"It was a simple compliment, Professor Conklin. That's all. Just a professional courtesy. I say it to all the visiting doctors."

"Ah . . . so that explains your current academic popularity." Henry stabbed a crouton, hiding a smile.

Joan feigned insult and snapped her napkin toward his hand.

"Ow." Henry rubbed his knuckles as if they stung. "Okay, okay . . . then I guess we'd best stick to business."

"Maybe we should," she said with a tired smile.

Thus far, their evening had been spent catching up on each other's pasts. Joan had nodded when Henry mentioned the death of his wife from cancer. Joan had heard the news from mutual friends. It was about the same time her own marriage had ended in a bitter divorce. Afterward, it seemed both had immersed themselves completely in their respective professions, becoming renowned in their fields. During this time, neither had sought out any intimate relationships, still shy from their wounded hearts. It seemed pain was pain, no matter what the circumstance.

"Have you learned anything new about the gold debris found inside the mummy's skull?" Henry asked more soberly.

Joan sat straighter, switching to her more professional demeanor. "Not much. Just that it's certainly not gold. It's more of a dense viscid liquid. At room temperatures, it's moldable, like warm clay. I suspect it's some type of heavy metal amalgam, perhaps mercury mixed with something else." She shrugged.

Henry's brows furrowed, and he shook his head slightly. "It doesn't make sense. The Incas' skill with metals was not considered advanced. Even smelting iron was beyond them. I find it strange they could create a new amalgam."

"Well, they must have learned something. They filled the mummy's skull full of the odd metal."

"Yes, I suppose . . ."

"But why do you think they did that?" she asked. "Fill his skull?"

"I can only theorize. The Incas revered the brain-case as a source of power. They even made drinking mugs from their slain enemies' skulls. My guess is that the Incas feared the friar's Christian god and performed this odd rite to avoid the wrath of this foreign deity."

Joan curled her nose. "So they drilled holes in the man's skull, removed the brain, and filled the space with the amalgam as an offering to the stranger's god?"

Henry shrugged and nodded. "It's a theory. The Incas seemed to have a fascination with trepanation. If you took all the skulls from around the world, they would not equal the number of Incan skulls found with such mutilations. So I wager there must be a religious significance to the act. But it's only a theory so far."

"And not a bad one, I suppose," she said with a smile. "But perhaps tomorrow I'll have more answers for you about the amalgam itself. I contacted Dr. Kirkpatrick at George Washington University, a metallurgy specialist. He owes me a favor. He's agreed to come by tomorrow and take a look at the substance."

Henry brightened with her words, his eyes glinting. "I'd like to be there when he examines the material."

"Sure . . ." Joan was momentarily flustered. She had been considering some way to arrange a meeting with Henry again before he left, and here he was dropping it in her lap. "Th . . . that would be wonderful . . . your company would be welcome anytime." Joan mentally struck her forehead with the heel of her hand. Why was she acting like a tongue-tied adolescent? She was forty-eight years old, for Christ's sake. When would these games between men and women ever grow more comfortable?

Joan found Henry smiling at her. "I'd enjoy working beside you again, too."

She blushed and wiped her hands on her napkin in her lap. She was saved from having to speak by the server's arrival with two platters of sizzling steaks. The two waited silently as dishes and silverware were exchanged. Once the waiter left, Joan spoke up. "So what about your end of the deal? Anything new on this Friar de Almagro?"

Henry's voice was subdued. "No . . . I'm still waiting to hear back from the archbishop's people."

She nodded. "When I was working on the metal, I got to thinking about the Dominican cross you found. I was wondering if it was really gold, or maybe another amalgam like the debris in the skull."

Henry glanced up quickly. "By God, I never considered that!"

She enjoyed his surprise and the look of admiration in his eyes. She continued, "Maybe it wasn't the Incas who created this metal. Perhaps it was their Spanish conquerors."

Henry nodded. "Now that's something I could more easily believe. The Spanish conquistadors! Maybe when this metallurgist reviews the material, we can at least put this part of the mystery to rest."

Joan grinned at his enthusiasm. There was nothing more attractive than a man who could share her passion for the mysteries of science—especially one as handsome as Henry.

"First thing when I get back to the Sheraton," Henry continued, "I'm gonna take a closer look at the cross again."

Joan tested her steak. It was a perfect medium rare. The chefs here never disappointed. "If you do, I'd like to know what you think as soon as possible."

"In that case . . . if you'd like, since you're dropping me off at the Sheraton, why don't you come up to the room and see for yourself? After working with the amalgam all day, you'd be the better one to judge it anyway."

Joan looked up from her steak to see if there was more of an invitation behind his words. She was not one to bed any man who happened to pique her interest, even an old friend . . . but she wouldn't mind extending their evening together.

Henry was working at his own steak with studied concentration. He glanced at her from above his glasses, his eyes questioning her hesitation.

Joan made her decision. "Why . . . yes, I'd love to take another peek at the cross."

Henry bobbed his head, returning to his steak. "Excellent."

Joan saw how his smile widened. She found her own grin growing brighter. They might as well be two teenagers out on a first date.

With the matter settled, both turned their attention to the table and the quality of the dinner. The remainder of the conversation consisted of the simple pleasantries of two diners: a review of the meal, shared stories of their different professions, even a discussion on the pending stormfront aiming at the coast from the Great

Lakes. By the time dessert was served—a delightfully rich vanilla crème brûlée shared with two spoons—both had grown out of their awkwardness and into a comfortable warmth.

"Whatever happened to us back at Rice?" Joan finally asked, feeling comfortable enough to broach an awkward topic. "Why didn't we work out?"

Henry fingered his cup of coffee. "I think there was too much life ahead of us. You wanted to pursue medicine. I wanted to get my master's at Texas A&M. I think at the time there was not much room for anything else, especially not a committed relationship."

"The woes of the career-driven," she mumbled. Joan's thoughts drifted to her own husband. It was his common complaint about their marriage. She was never home, never there for him.

Henry sipped his coffee. "Maybe. I suppose. But then eventually I met Elizabeth and you met Robert." Henry shrugged.

"Hmm . . ."

Henry sighed and set his cup down. "Maybe we should be going. It is getting near time for me to contact the team in Peru."

Joan glanced at her watch. It was almost ten o'clock. Where had the time gone? "And I've got an early day tomorrow myself. If we're to take a peek at that cross tonight, we ought to be going."

Henry insisted on paying the bill after a mild protest from Joan. "It's the least I can do after all you've done," he said, pulling out his wallet. "Besides, the tab will be coming out of my research grant anyway." He offered her a quirked grin.

Joan held up her palms, relinquishing any claims on the check. "If the government is paying, it's all yours."

Soon thereafter, following a short car ride, Joan found herself sharing an elevator with the professor. A degree of nervousness set in again as silence enveloped them. Henry fidgeted with the buttons on his suit. The doors chimed open on the seventh floor, and the two crossed down to Henry's hotel room.

"Excuse the mess," he said as he keyed open the door. "I wasn't expecting company." Henry held open the door for Joan to step through.

Joan stared at the ruins of the professor's hotel room. The bed had been overturned and the mattress shredded. Every drawer had been pulled and dumped; even the television lay on its side on the rug, its back panel unscrewed.

"My God!" Henry exclaimed, stunned.

"You said it was a mess, but I wasn't expecting this," Joan said in a halfhearted attempt at a joke.

Henry dashed into the room, giving it all a quick glance around. He sifted through some papers by the toppled desk and uncovered his laptop. He picked it up and tested it. A beep as it turned on revealed it had been undamaged. A sigh of relief escaped him. "All my research . . . thank God."

Joan cautiously entered the room. "You shouldn't touch too much. I'll call hotel security. Whoever burglarized the room might still be around."

Henry righted the desk and put the computer down. "Why didn't they take my laptop?"

Dialing the front desk, Joan spoke. "I suspect they were after bigger game. I'd wager that reporter's piece in the *Baltimore Herald* this morning caught the eyes of some petty thieves."

Henry seemed to jolt with her words. "The cross!" He strode across the room.

"Tell me you left it in the hotel safe," Joan said.

Shaking his head, Henry moved to one of the sconces on the wall. "After traveling through so many foreign countries, I've developed my own system of security."

As Joan related the burglary to the front desk, Henry used a Swiss army knife to unscrew the fixture from the wall and reached to the niche behind it. He retrieved a small velvet pouch, heavy with whatever was inside. He spilled out the large Dominican cross and silver ring into his palm.

Joan replaced the phone. "Security is on its way. You were lucky this time, Henry. Next time use the hotel's safe."

Henry looked around the room. "I think you're right. These thieves were damned thorough." Joan stayed silent as Henry examined the disheveled room. "Welcome back to America," he muttered sourly.

Joan's eyes strayed to a suit box from Barney's tossed in a corner. A register receipt was still taped to its cover. She eyed Henry's handsome suit. So it seemed the professor had done some last-minute shopping for their "date." She forced down a small smile and silently cursed the thieves who had ruined their evening.

Soon two large men in blue suits appeared at the open door. They flashed identification and entered. "We've called the police. They'll be here in a moment to take a statement. Another room is already being prepared for you."

Henry turned to Joan. "Why don't you head home. I can take care of matters here."

"I suppose I'd better. But tomorrow bring the crucifix with you to the lab. I'll have Dr. Kirkpatrick look it over. He'll know for sure if it's gold or not."

Henry looked about the room with a forlorn expression. "Thanks, I'll do that."

She moved to leave, but he stopped her with a touch on her arm. She turned to find him smiling at her. "As weird as this may sound considering the state of my room, I had a nice night."

She squeezed his hand and held it a fraction longer than professionally necessary. "I did, too." She returned his smile, if only a bit more shyly. "I'll see you tomorrow."

He nodded, and as she stepped from the room, he added softly, "I look forward to it."

Joan didn't turn, pretending not to have heard, when actually she feared her reddening face would reveal too plainly her heart. Only when she was safely in the elevator and the doors had closed did she let out a long sigh of relief. "Get ahold of yourself," she warned the empty elevator. "He's an old friend. That's all."

Still, as the elevator headed down, a small shiver of pleasure passed through her. Tomorrow could not come soon enough.

As another tumble of rocks echoed down from above, Sam glanced up from where he knelt. His eyes flicked to the others gathered around the three bands of hematite. Norman stared up toward the roof with a small flinch of his shoulders. Ralph only grumbled and continued swathing the yellow dye across his band with a small paintbrush. Denal sat to one side, running his hands slowly up and down the crowbar in his lap.

Only Maggie met his eyes. "The second level must be collapsed by now," she whispered.

Sam nodded with a deep sigh. None of them wanted to consider what that meant. He glanced to his watch. It was a little after ten in the evening. At this rate, there was little chance the pyramid would remain intact for another two days. To distract from the weight of rock slowly crumbling down upon them, they had attempted to keep busy. Sam's suggestion that they test his experimental dyes on the hematite bands had been grudgingly accepted.

"Now what?" Ralph asked. He stretched a kink from his back where he bent over his band.

Sam scooted closer. "Next you need to sponge the excess dye gently away with this lipophilic agent." He passed Ralph a dry sponge and a jar of clear solution.

"I'm ready, too," Maggie said, and reached for a second sponge.

With Sam directing, the other two students soon had the bands prepped for deciphering. Sam lifted the black Wood's lamp and switched it on. "Okay, extinguish the flashlight."

Once done, darkness suddenly collapsed tighter around them. A pool of purplish light was all that stood between them and absolute blackness. Bathed within the glow, the two bands fluoresced a soft green. The group clustered tighter.

"Amazing," Maggie exclaimed.

Under Sam's ultraviolet lamp, the ancient writing stood in stark relief, the green lettering glowing brightly, as crisp as the day it had been etched into the metal.

"Cool," Ralph said, patting Sam on the shoulder.

Holding back his own whoop of pride, Sam ran a finger along the lettering, carefully reading the writing on the first band. "*Nos Christi defenete. Malum ne fugat.*" Sam concentrated intently as he translated the scrawled Latin. " 'Christ protect us. May the evil never escape.' " A chill passed down Sam's spine.

"Not the words you want to hear trapped in a collapsed tomb," Ralph said.

"Especially when we're sitting right outside the cursed chamber," Norman added, eyeing Sam. "What was that you said about the pictograph in the next room? The gateway to Heaven, the gateway to Hell?"

Sam waved the photographer's fears away. "That's just a rough interpretation from a Judeo-Christian viewpoint. The ancient Peruvians didn't believe in a biblical heaven or hell, but in three distinct levels of existence: *janan pacha*, the upper world; *cay pacha*, our world; and *uca pacha*, the lower or interior world. They believed these three worlds were closely linked, and that certain sacred areas, named *pacariscas*, were where the three worlds came together." Sam glanced over his shoulder. "From the pictographs next door, I suspect that chamber was revered and protected as a *pacariscas*."

Norman stared toward the open doorway to the booby-trapped chamber. "A gateway to both the lower and upper worlds."

"Exactly."

Maggie elbowed Sam. "Enough already! Get on with the second band."

Sam cleared his throat and bent over the etched hematite, this time translating as he ran a finger along the Latin scribblings. " 'Lord above, keep us safe. We beseech you. We leave this tomb to Heaven. May it never be disturbed. Beware . . .' " Sam read the last two lines and his breath caught in his throat. He leaned away. "Oh, God!"

Maggie leaned nearer. "What?"

Sam glanced at the others. " 'Beyond lies the work-ings of Satan, the will of the Devil. I seal this passage against the Serpent of Eden, lest mankind be damned forever.' "

Five pairs of eyes turned to the open doorway.

"The Serpent of Eden?" Norman asked nervously.

Maggie explained, voice hushed. "Genesis. The cor-rupter of mankind, a tempter of forbidden knowledge."

"It's signed," Sam said, returning their attentions to the hematite bands. "Friar Francisco de Almagro, servant of our Lord, 1535."

Ralph glanced over Sam's shoulder. "Didn't your uncle say he thought the mummy was probably a Dominican friar?"

Sam nodded. "Yeah. This may be the fellow's last written testament. After sealing the tomb here, he must've been killed for some reason. But why?" Sam knelt back upon his heels. "What happened here? What was it about the next room that scared the man so much? It couldn't have just been the booby traps. Not with that reference to the Serpent of Eden."

Maggie nodded toward the open doorway. "What-ever the answer, it lies in there somewhere, maybe something the Moche discovered and the conquering Incas usurped. Something that spooked the bejesus out of our dead friar."

"I wish my uncle were here," Sam muttered. "We could use his expertise."

More boulders shifted overhead, grinding like old bones. "I don't think your uncle would share that wish," Norman said, eyeing the roof.

Maggie suddenly stood up and collected the flashlight. "I want to see that chamber again."

Sam noticed how her legs trembled for a second before she was able to take a step away. He suspected most of her stated curiosity was just a desire to move, to keep busy and distracted. He pushed to his feet. "I'll go with you."

Ralph stood up, too. "Norman and I'll go check the next level up."

Norman's eyes widened. "I will?"

Ralph glowered at the photographer. "Quit being such a pantywaist."

Norman scowled and rolled to his feet. "Oh, all right." He fished out the second flashlight. Denal had found the extra handlamp among the bag of tools abandoned by Gil's gang.

"Be quick," Sam warned. "It's not safe up there, and we need to conserve the batteries."

"Trust me," Norman said. "Between Ralph's company and falling slabs of granite, I'll be damned quick."

Denal also stood. He moved alongside Sam and Maggie, making his own decision on where to go.

With a wave, Norman and Ralph set off.

"C'mon," Maggie said behind him.

Sam and Denal followed her as she ducked through the doorway. Sam noticed Denal quickly touch his forehead and make the sign of the cross, a whispered prayer on his lips, before passing through the threshold.

In silence, the trio returned to the edge of the tiled floor. Gold and silver reflected their light brightly. The Incan king stood bright as a yellow star against the black granite stonework. The ticking of the machinery echoed in muffled time to Sam's own heartbeat. Tilting his Stetson, he studied the pictograph, tracing the flashlight's beam from the golden rectangle that represented the physical world, *cay pacha*, to the distant square that represented the upper world, *janan pacha*. A zigzag of gold tiles connected the two bases. "Well?" he asked. "What now?" Sam purposely kept the light away from the two bodies upon the floor.

Like a caged lioness, Maggie stalked back and forth before the puzzle. "There has to be a way across," she muttered. "Solve that and whatever prize lies here will most likely be revealed."

"The Serpent of Eden?" Sam asked.

Maggie turned to him, eyes bright in the reflected glow. "Don't you want to know what he meant?"

"Honestly, right now I'd just prefer to get our butts out of here."

"Well, until then . . ." Maggie swung back to the tiled pictograph. "I'm going to keep working." Without another word, Maggie stepped upon one of the gold tiles that made up the rectangle of gold at this edge.

"No, Miss Maggie!" Denal shouted.

Sam reached for her at the same time, but Maggie stepped onto a neighboring gold tile, out of his reach. "What are you doing?" he yelled.

She turned back—not to Sam, but the boy. "What's the safest path, Denal?"

Sam glanced to his side. The young Quechan stood trembling by the edge of the floor, eyes wild. "Maggie, what are you talking about?" Sam asked. "He doesn't know."

"He knows," she said. "He warned me from stepping on the floor the first time here." She stared intently at the boy. "I saw a look of recognition on your face, Denal."

The boy backed a step away.

Maggie continued. "I've solved part of the riddle. I stand on the section of the pictograph that represents our world." She pointed a hand toward the distant rectangle of gold on the far side of the room. "And I must reach *janan pacha*, the upper world. Isn't that so? But how do you move across the floor safely? The gold path is too obvious."

Denal just shook his head vehemently.

Sam lowered his flashlight. "Maggie, Denal can't know—"

Maggie's face hardened, and she swung away. She moved to step on one of the gold tiles that stair-stepped toward the distant rectangle.

"No!" Denal called out suddenly. Tears in his eyes. "I'll tell you."

Stunned, Sam stared at the teenager.

He seemed to sag under his gaze. "The old *amautas* of my people. They speak stories of a bad place like this. Very old stories. I no know for sure. But they say that life be balanced between *janan* and *cay*. To walk between them, you must balance the sun and the moon."

"The sun and moon?" Maggie said. She turned to the floor. "Ah sure! Of course." Maggie stepped onto a neighboring silver tile.

"Maggie! Don't!"

She ignored Sam and moved back to a gold square. "To follow the gold staircase of tiles, you have to alternate each step with a silver one. Balance the silver an' gold, the moon an' the sun."

Sam called out. "You can't know that for certain."

"I'm sure." Maggie continued across the room, stepping from silver to gold and back to silver again. She spoke hurriedly as she worked across the pattern. "Gold was considered by the Incas to be the sweat of the sun, while silver was the tears of the moon. Sun an' moon . . . gold an' silver . . ."

Sam stood at the edge of the floor, unable to breathe.

Denal mumbled in his native tongue, fear strong in his voice. "She goes . . . she no come back."

Sam barely heard him, his heart in his throat.

He tugged on Sam's arm. "Miss Maggie must stop," he beseeched. "The *amautas* say who travels to *janan pacha* can never return. She must stop!"

The boy's warning finally sank into Sam. He jerked as if he had touched flame. "Maggie!"

The surging panic in his voice drew her gaze.

"Denal says that if you cross the room, you can't come back!"

Maggie glanced toward the far wall, then back at Sam. She still stood on the same tile, but her voice shook. "Th . . . that makes no bloody sense. Why would the room be one-way?"

"I don't know. But now is not the time to test it."

Maggie sighed. "Maybe you're right . . ." She stepped back onto the silver tile she had just vacated.

"No!" Denal yelled.

The boy's scream saved Maggie's life. Flinching, she yanked back her leg just as the silver tile hinged open under her boot.

"Watch out!" Sam yelled. "Above you!" He had spotted the corresponding gold tile on the roof drop open. A thick rain of spears shot out, whistling, and disappeared into the pit opened under the silver tile.

Maggie had backed from the cascade of blades, legs trembling fiercely. She fell to her knees as the silver tile swung closed again. "Sam . . . ?"

Gesturing wildly, Denal explained, "She must no come back. If starts, Miss Maggie must finish."

The woman's eyes were wide with fear as she stared back at Sam across the six yards of floor. Sam could see a glaze of panic beginning to set in. What was he to do?

Suddenly the entire room shook violently. A thunderous roar accompanied it. Sam was thrown to the floor. Maggie ducked, covering her head with her arms. Two metal tiles dislodged from above and crashed with loud clangs.

Only Denal managed to keep his feet. The Quechan boy glanced toward the room's entrance. Dust and clouds of silt rolled toward them. "The temple! It falls!"

Sam rolled back to his feet as the floor settled. "Oh, God . . . Norman and Ralph . . ."

As if hearing his call, two figures suddenly burst through the cloudy silt. Coughing, Ralph skidded to a stop beside Sam. From head to foot, the large black man was grey with granite dust, as was Norman behind him. The photographer sneezed loudly.

Ralph was out of breath. "It's all coming apart!"

The groan of shifting stones seemed to come from all around them. Occasional loud crashes still erupted regularly, as close as the antechamber next door.

Norman wiped his nose on his sleeve. "There's nothing above us now."

Ralph pulled Sam to the neighboring wall of the short passage. "Feel."

Sam placed his hand on the wall of stacked granite stones. It trembled under his palm as the stresses from the tons of granite blocks and clay strained these last bulwarks. "All that's holding this place together is a lick and a promise," Sam realized aloud.

Norman suddenly drew their attention with an urgent call. He pointed toward the patterned floor. "Maggie!"

Sam swung around. Across the tiles, he spotted the Irish student sprawled on her side on the same gold tile. Her limbs twitched and spasmed. She was having another seizure.

"What the hell is she doing out there?" Ralph asked angrily.

"I don't have time to explain." Sam unslung his rifle and passed it to Ralph. "Stay here!" He darted onto the gold tiles.

Denal yelled a warning, but Sam ignored the boy. Sam danced from silver to gold as he climbed the staircase pattern toward *janan pacha*. Reaching Maggie's tile, he knelt beside her and cradled her head in his lap. His touch seemed to calm her slightly. Using this cue, he stroked her hair and called to her softly. Her trembling limbs quieted. "Maggie . . . if you can hear me, come to me. Follow my voice."

A small moan escaped from her lips.

"C'mon, Maggie . . . we need you . . . this is no time to be napping."

Her eyelids fluttered, and then she was staring at him. "Sam . . . ?"

He leaned down and hugged her tightly. The smell of her hair and sweat sharp in his nose. "Thank God!"

Maggie pushed from his embrace and quickly took in the scene. "You shouldn't have come out here," she scolded, but there was no heat in her voice, only relief. "The temple?"

"It's comin' down around our ears. This is the last level intact."

Maggie glanced up at Sam, an unspoken question in her eyes.

Sam answered, "An hour at most, I'd guess."

"What are we to do?"

Helping her to her feet, Sam stood. Maggie had to lean on his arm for support, her legs still weak. Her palms were hot on his bare skin. "You got me thinking earlier. Just why *did* the Moche or Incas build this room so it was one-way only?"

Maggie shook her head.

Sam glanced to the far wall. "It makes no sense . . . unless . . . unless there was another way out."

"A secret passage?"

"There must be more than just this booby-trapped room. Why the dire warning from the mummified friar? There's nothing here. Something must lie beyond this chamber."

"But if you're right, where's the entrance?"

Sam pointed to the large statue of the Incan king. It seemed to glower at them, gold against the dark stones. "If anybody would know, he would. A clue must lie with him." Sam met Maggie's eyes.

"So we'll have to cross over there," she said, swallowing hard. She offered Sam a wavery half smile. "One last puzzle."

The roof again rumbled ominously. "Right. We either solve it, or we kiss our asses good-bye."

Ralph called over to them. "What're you two doing? We're running out of time!"

Sam quickly related what they planned to do.

"That's insane! You're risking your lives on pretty thin guesses!"

Sam nodded toward the roof. "I'd rather take my chances than just wait for the sky to fall."

Ralph had no answer. He just shifted from foot to foot nervously. "Okay, boss, but be careful," he finally conceded.

Denal stepped onto the tile floor, his face ashen. "I come with."

"No!" Maggie and Sam called out in unison.

Denal just continued onward. "I know old stories. I help. I no die without a fight, too." He followed their path to join them. He glared up at Sam. "My mama, before she die, she teach me to be brave. I no shame her."

Sam stared for a moment, then clapped the boy on the shoulder. "Thanks, Denal."

He smiled weakly, but his eyes kept flicking between the Incan king and the patterned floor. With shaky fingers, he fished out a bent cigarette from a pocket and slipped it between his lips. He caught Sam eyeing the unlit cigarette and stared back defiantly. "Let's go."

Sam turned to leave. "You know those things will stunt your growth."

"Not if I don't light them," Denal said sourly.

"You find a way out of here," Sam said, "and you can smoke your lungs black."

Maggie trailed behind them. "Keep moving. This roof isn't goin' to last forever."

Sam continued in silence. Each step onto a new tile brought an ever-growing sense of dread. But nothing happened. Between Maggie and Denal, they seemed to have solved the riddle of the tiles, but what then?

Sam came to the midpoint of the floor and froze.

Maggie called from a couple rows back. "Why've you stopped?"

He stepped aside so she could see.

"Oh."

Sam was extra careful proceeding onto the next gold tile. The blood made the surface slick. He was mindful not to touch the torn and fouled body of Juan that shared the tile. The dead man's eyes seemed to track him as he passed. Sam glanced away, but the smell was strong this close, the metallic tang of blood mixed with the more earthy smell of decay. He continued on, sighing loudly once he stepped onto the next tile.

For a few rows, he sped faster, glad to escape the dead man. Neither of the other two spoke as they followed. Only the scuff of boots indicated they continued behind him. Farther across the room, he could hear Ralph and Norman mumbling nervously, but their words were too quiet to make out.

At last Sam stepped onto the four gold tiles that made up the pictograph of *janan pacha*. Bending in relief, Sam leaned his hands on his knees. He closed his eyes and thanked the heavens for his safe passage.

Maggie and Denal joined him.

"You both okay?" Sam asked, straightening.

Maggie could only nod. Her face shone with a sheen of sweat. Denal's cigarette trembled between his lips, but he bobbed his head, too.

Sam glanced to the wall. They were now grouped at the upper left of the pictograph. The last row of tiles was all silver. Only the statue itself, in the middle of the wall, stood upon a gold tile amid a small pile of gold and silver trinkets and offerings. "Now what? How do we reach the statue from here?"

Maggie turned in a slow circle. "Listen."

Sam frowned. "What—?" Then he realized what she meant.

Denal did, too. "It stopped."

Sam cocked his head. There was no trace of the ticking machinery that geared the booby trap.

"It ended as soon as we arrived here," Maggie said.

Sam nodded. "Our following the path correctly must have deactivated it."

"So it should be safe to follow the silver tiles to the statue?" Maggie asked, glancing toward Denal.

The Quechan boy shrugged. "I no know."

Sam took a girding breath and stepped off the gold tiles and onto the row of silver. He cringed for a heartbeat, but nothing happened. He glanced to Maggie.

"The gears are still silent," she said, meeting his eyes. "It must be okay."

Sam continued tile by tile to the golden statue. The others followed. Soon they stood before the Incan warrior. He seemed to be glaring down at them from under a headdress. The three studied their adversary.

The statue stood almost a full two yards taller than most men, posted with his back to a narrow silver archway in the granite wall. He bore a staff in one hand and a typical Incan bola in the other, three stones slung on llama tendon.

"Look at his *llautu* crown," Sam said, pointing to the figure's braided headdress topped by three parrot feathers and a fringe of tassels. "It definitely marks this one as a Sapa Inca. One of their kings."

"Yes, but the facial detail an' depiction of realistic musculature is unlike the Incas' usual stylization," Maggie whispered. "It's as perfect a work as Michelangelo's *David*."

Sam leaned closer to study the ancient king's face. "Strange. Whichever Sapa Inca is represented here was clearly worshiped as no other."

A step away, Denal cleared his throat. "The wall . . . it is not stone."

Sam turned away from the statue. The boy's gaze was not on the golden idol, but the black wall behind it. Sheer granite spread all around. "What do you mean?"

Maggie gasped. "Denal means it's not *stonework*. Look, there are no seams or joints. It's not stacked stone blocks like the temple."

Sam moved to the rock and ran a palm along it. "It's a wall of solid granite."

A voice called from across the room. "Did you find anything?" It was Norman.

Sam turned his head and yelled, "We found the mountain!" Sam arched his neck and examined the wall. "The pyramid must have been built at the base of this cliff face."

"But why?" Maggie asked.

Sam thought out loud. "The Incas revered mountains. But why build a *huaca*, or holy place, here? What was so special about this cliff?"

Maggie answered after a moment, "Wh . . . what if there was a cave?"

Sam slapped his hand against the granite wall. "Of course. Caverns were considered to be *pacariscas*, mystical places joining the three worlds of their religion. They were often used as places of ritual. It makes sense!"

"But where's the entrance?" Maggie asked.

"I don't know, but the statue must be a key. Did you notice the silver archway behind the statue? It's large enough to cover a narrow opening."

Maggie and Sam returned to the statue. Sam leaned his shoulder against it and tried to shove the idol aside.

"Be careful," Maggie warned.

Denal stood with one fist clenched at his throat.

But nothing happened. The statue could not be budged. "Damn it," Sam swore, taking off his Stetson and swiping his damp hair back. "The thing must weigh close to a ton."

Maggie frowned at him. "Brute force isn't the answer. With the complexity shown here, there has to be a mechanism to unlock the pathway." She elbowed Sam aside and approached the statue. Stretching on the tip of her toes, she examined it closely, her nose only inches from the golden surface. Slowly she worked her way down the statue's physique.

Sam grew impatient, especially when the floor began to tremble again. "This place isn't going to stand much longer," he mumbled.

"Aha!" Maggie exclaimed. She turned to Sam, her face at the Incan king's waist. "Here's the answer." She pointed to the statue's belly button.

"What are you talking about?"

Maggie reached and pushed her finger through the hole. Her entire finger was swallowed up. "The Incas considered the navel to be a place of power. They believed the umbilicus once joined the physical body of man to the gods of creation."

Sam crouched with Denal. "Another fusion of worlds."

Maggie slipped her finger out. "It's a keyhole. Now we just need to find the key."

Sam straightened, thinking aloud. "The navel links the gods of *janan pacha* to mankind in the physical world . . . to *cay pacha.* If this chamber is a point where all *three* worlds unite . . . then the key must be something from the lower world, from *uca pacha.*"

Maggie clutched his elbow in understanding. "By inserting the key into the navel lock, then all three worlds would be united."

"Yeah, but where do we find such a key?"

Denal nudged Sam. He pointed to the statue's feet, to where a small mound of gold and silver offerings were piled. "*Uca pacha* lies at bottom of feet."

"Och! We've been feckin' fools for sure." Maggie dropped to her knees and began sifting through the objects. "The lower world! Sometimes it's best to hide somethin' in plain sight."

Sam joined her. Working through the pile, he held up a golden figurine of a panther with ruby eyes, then cast it aside. "There's enough wealth here to finance a small nation."

"And it'll do us not a nit of good if we don't survive."

As if to remind them further, the temple rumbled and shook as another section gave way. The tiles overhead trembled and clanged. One of the booby traps sprang on its own, triggered by the roof's shaking: a huge granite block carved with a demon's face crashed to the floor and embedded itself in the silver tile below.

Maggie and Sam eyed each other grimly.

Ralph called from behind them, coughing slightly. "That's it! We're sealed in, folks! If there's another way out, I suggest you find it damn quick!"

Maggie whispered, "The structure of the floor and trap is coming apart. If Norman and Ralph are goin' to join us—"

"You're right. Keep searching." Sam stood up. "Ralph! Norman! Come on over! Now!" The two other students were obscured in a cloud of granite dust. But Ralph waved his flashlight in acknowledgment and started toward them.

Sam returned to Maggie. "They're coming. Any luck?"

She shook her head; her hand trembled as she picked through the pieces. "I can't think clearly. What if I miss a clue? We won't have a second chance." A small sob escaped her throat.

Sam knelt beside her. "We'll get out of here." He put an arm around her shoulders and held her tight.

She leaned into his embrace, silent for several heart-beats. Then a final shudder passed through her, and she seemed to relax again. Slipping from under his arm, she turned to Sam, her dusty face marred by trails of tears. She wiped at her cheeks and mumbled, "Thanks, Sam."

No words were needed. He nodded and returned to his own search alongside her. They worked as a team, sifting through the pile of objects. Sam almost tossed aside their salvation, but Maggie stopped him, grab-bing his wrist.

Sam held a foot-long golden dagger with a silver handle. "What?"

"Look at the carving on the hilt."

Sam raised it into the beam of the flashlight Denal was holding. It bore the figure of a man with prominent fangs. Sam recognized the figure from ancient ceramic pottery. "It's the fanged god Aiapaec."

Maggie nodded. "A god of the Moche tribes!"

Sam remembered his uncle's assessment of this buried pyramid. It was clearly Moche. Here was more proof. "This will make Uncle Hank happy . . . that is, if we get out of here to show it to him." He began to place the dagger aside.

Maggie stopped him again. "Wait, Sam. Some scholars say that the Incas may have incorporated the Moche god, Aiapaec, into their own pantheon of gods. But the Incas renamed him—Huamancantac!"

"The god of guano . . . bat dung?" Sam stared at her as if she were mad. What was her point? Then understanding dawned on him. "The god of bats . . . and *caverns*! A spirit from the lower world, *uca pacha*!"

Sam sprang to his feet, dagger in hand.

"It must be the key!" Maggie exclaimed.

Just then Ralph and Norman joined the trio by the statue. "I don't know what you're all excited about, but I'd suggest we get out of here." He pointed toward the rear of the chamber.

Sam turned. There *was* no rear of the chamber. With the dust settling from the last of the major rumbles, the back of the room was a tumbled pile of blocks. "Christ!" Overhead, a quarter of the heavy roof tiles hung crooked or tilted. And in the background, the continual groan of tons of granite sounded from above their heads.

Norman's voice was a squeak. "There's no place else to run."

"Maybe there is," Sam said. He turned and stabbed the dagger into the statue's belly. It sank to the level of the hilt.

Nothing happened.

Norman shifted his feet, staring at the impaled knife. "Okay, Brutus, you've stabbed Caesar. What now?"

Sam tried turning the knife like a key, but it refused to move. He pulled the dagger back out, his eyes on Maggie. "I was sure you were right." He held the gold dagger between them, clutching it tightly. "Th . . . this has to be the key!" he said between clenched teeth, frustration trembling his voice. "*It must be!*"

As he spoke the last word, the dagger shifted in his hands. The length of gold blade molded itself into a jagged lightning bolt. It shone brightly in the beam of the flashlights. Sam almost dropped the knife, but his left hand steadied his right, both palms now clutching the hilt. "Did anyone else see that? Or did my mind just snap?" Sam ran his fingers over the knife, searching for the catch that had triggered the transformation. He found nothing.

Another cascade of rock tumbled behind them. It was the chamber's roof collapsing, taking out half of the roof tiles. The clang of rock and metal echoed sharply. Death rolled toward them in a gnash of rock, but none of them moved.

Instead, Maggie raised her hands toward the dagger, then lowered them back again, clearly afraid of disturbing the miracle. "It's now the symbol of Pachacamac. The Incan god of creation." She met Sam's wide eyes. "Use it!"

Sam nodded and turned back to the statue. With the tip of the dagger trembling, Sam edged the knife into the belly of the Incan king. It took a bit of rocking back and forth to insert the jagged blade fully, but with one final push, the knife slid home.

A cracking grind of gears exploded, loud enough to vanquish the crash of boulders behind them.

As Sam held tight to the hilt of the dagger, the Incan statue split neatly in half, from crown to feet, a seam appearing from nowhere. The two halves pulled apart from the dagger's hilt, along with the silver archway behind it. Beyond the statue, a natural fissure in the rock was revealed.

Sam stood frozen before the split statue, the knife still in his grip, the blade now pointing toward the cavern entrance. "Holy shit!"

Stunned, Sam raised the dagger. It was once again just the straight blade he had first found. He let his arm drop and turned to the others. A blinding flash of Norman's camera caught him off guard. Sam rubbed at his eyes with the heel of his hand. "Warn a guy next time," he complained.

"And ruin that natural expression of awe?" Norman answered. "Not a chance."

The others all began talking at once—amazement, wonder, and relief ringing brightly. Ralph shone his flashlight down the throat of the fissure. It delved deep into the cliff face, beyond the reach of Ralph's light. "I hear what sounds like running water," he said. "The cavern must be plenty deep."

"Good," Sam said. He finally held up his dagger, getting the others' attention. "I have no idea what just happened here, but let's get our asses out of this temple before it crushes us flat as pancakes."

With more of the roof falling behind them, no one argued. They filed quickly past Sam and into the coolness of the natural cavern.

As Ralph slid by, he returned Sam's Winchester. "I have my own now," the large man said, lifting a snubby lever-action rifle.

Sam recognized it as Gil's weapon. "Where?"

Ralph jerked his thumb back at the tile floor. "I picked it up when Norm and I crossed. Gil must have run off in too big a hurry, abandoning it." Ralph hefted an ammo belt from his shoulder. "His loss . . . our gain."

"Hopefully we won't need either," Sam said.

Ralph shrugged and continued into the tunnel.

"You'd better try one last time to reach Philip," Maggie said, glancing back at the crumbling room.

"Let him know we're safe and not to give up on us. With water and shelter, we should be able to survive until help arrives."

"You're right. In the caves, I might not be able to reach him." Sam had forgotten all about Philip Sykes. He pulled the walkie-talkie free, stepped away from the threshold, and switched it on. Static immediately squealed when Sam hit the transmitter. "Sykes, can you read us? Over?"

The answer was immediate and choppy. ". . . alive? Thank God . . . the whole hill is gone . . . We're . . . as fast as we can! Over."

Sam smiled. He quickly summarized their discovery and the miracle of the dagger. "So we're gonna hole up in the caves here until you can free us. Did you get all that? Over."

The answer was scratchier as the walkie-talkie's battery weakened. ". . . caves? Don't wander too far. I'll try and . . ." Static drowned the rest.

Sam turned to stare at the pale faces of his friends. "Just hurry your ass, Philip!" he yelled into the walkie-talkie. "And get word to Uncle Hank as soon as possible!"

Static was his only response. The battery was too weak to send a signal through all the jumble of rock and clay overhead. Sam swore under his breath and turned off the walkie-talkie, conserving the little juice that was left. He prayed Philip had got all that.

Biting his lower lip, he joined the others. Beyond them lay a well of darkness. Though Sam was relieved at the escape from the crumbling pyramid, Friar de Almagro's warning still echoed in his head: *The Serpent of Eden . . . may it never be disturbed.*

Sam motioned them toward the black caverns. "Let's go."

The path through the rock was tight, so they proceeded single file. Ralph took the lead, and Sam brought up the rear. In the cramped space, Sam felt as if the rock were squeezing closed around him. At one point, they had to slide sideways, crushed between two walls of granite. Once through the jam, they could hear the echoing sound of rushing waters growing. The sound whetted Sam's thirst. His tongue felt like dry burlap in his mouth.

Ralph called back from the lead. "I think it opens up just ahead. C'mon."

Sam hurried forward, stepping almost on Maggie's heels. They had been climbing and scraping their way through the passage for close to an hour by then. At last, Sam felt a stirring of the air. He sensed a large space ahead. It coaxed them all to a faster clip.

The passage widened at last. The team could now proceed as a group. Ralph, a step ahead of the rest, held one of the flashlights. "There's something ahead," he mumbled.

Their pace slowed as the passage came to an end. Ralph raised his flashlight. "I don't believe it!" he gasped.

Sam agreed. The others stood silent beside him. Ahead lay an open chamber, a cavern with a river channel worn through the center of the floor. But that was not what triggered the stunned reactions from the others. Pillars linked roof to floor, their lengths carved with intricate images and fantastic creatures. In the stone, embedded silver reflected the flashlight, eyes from thousands of carved figures, sentinels from an ancient world.

Ralph lowered the light. "Look!" Across the floor of the dark cavern, a path of beaten gold wound from the passage's opening over to the rumbling river and followed the course deeper into the warren of caves. The bright path disappeared around a curve in the cavern wall.

"Amazing," Sam said.

Ralph spoke at his shoulder. "The other chamber must have been a decoy, a trap protecting what lies ahead."

Sam stepped forward, tentatively placing a boot on the gold path. "But what have we discovered?"

Maggie moved to his side as Norman snapped a few pictures. "We've found a place to rest. And that's enough for now."

The others mumbled their agreement, thirst and exhaustion overwhelming wonder and mystery.

Even Sam agreed. The mysteries could wait 'til morning. Still, as the others moved forward down the curving gold path toward the river, Sam could not help but notice how the shining track bore a distinct resemblance to a winding snake.

A golden serpent.

Henry sat by his computer and watched the on-screen phone connections whir through their internet nodes, the modem buzzing and chiming in sync. "C'mon, Sam, pick up the damn phone," he muttered to himself. It was at least the tenth time he had tried to reach the camp in Peru.

Various scenarios played in his head—from the mundane, such as a glitch in the site's satellite feed, to the more frightening scene of an armed attack on the camp by looters. "I should never have left."

Henry glanced to the clock in the upper right-hand corner of his laptop's screen. It was after eleven. He took a deep breath, calming his war of nerves. There might even be a simpler reason for the lack of response.

Because of the burglary and the ensuing paperwork with hotel security, Henry had been over twenty minutes late in making his call. The students probably gave up on him and were already sound asleep in their bunks.

Still, Henry waited one last time for the line to feed through to Peru. He watched the screen icon appear, indicating the satellite had been reached. The signal leaped for the metal transmitting dish at the Andean site. Henry held his breath. But again the signal died, no connection.

"Damn!" Henry slammed his fist on the desk as the modem switched off. Though there were a thousand other excuses for the lack of connection, Henry knew in his heart something was wrong. A creeping dread. Once before, he had experienced a similar fear, the day his brother Frank—Sam's dad—had died in the car crash. He recalled that phone call at four in the morning, the cold sensation of terror as he had reached for the receiver. He now felt a similar dread.

Something had happened down in Peru. He just knew it.

Henry reached for the computer once again, but before his hand touched a key, the phone beside the laptop rang loudly, startling him. His heart in his throat, he stared at the receiver, flashing back to that horrible morning years ago. He clenched his fist. "Get ahold of yourself, Henry," he said, forcing his fingers to relax. Closing his eyes and girding himself, he picked up the phone and raised it to his ear. "Hello?"

A woman's voice answered. "Henry? It's Joan."

Though relieved it was just his colleague, Henry recognized the stress in her voice. This wasn't a casual call. "Joan, what's wrong?"

His sudden worry must have caught her off guard. She stuttered for a moment, then spoke. "I . . . I just thought you should know. I dropped by my office after our date . . . um, evening together . . . and discovered someone had tried to break into the morgue where the mummy's remains are stored. The security guard startled them off, but he was unable to catch them."

"The mummy?"

"It's fine. The thieves never even got through the door."

"It seems that *Herald* reporter's story drew more flies than we suspected."

"Or maybe the same ones," Joan added. "Maybe after failing to find anything in your hotel room, they came here next. What did the police say?"

"Not much. They didn't seem particularly interested since nothing was stolen."

"Didn't they dust for prints or anything?"

Henry laughed. "You've been watching too many cop shows. The only thing they did was check the tapes from the security cameras in the hallway."

"And?"

"No help. The camera lenses had been spray-painted over."

Joan was silent for several breaths.

"Joan?"

"They did the same here. That's how the guard was alerted. He noticed the blacked-out monitor."

"So you think it was the same team of thieves?"

"I don't know."

"Well, hopefully the close call with the security guard will keep them from any further mischief." But Henry was not convinced.

Joan sighed loudly. "I hope you're right. I'm sorry I bothered you."

"It was no bother. I was up." Henry avoided telling her about his inability to reach Sam. Though it made no sense at all, Henry had a feeling that tonight's events were somehow intertwined: the burglary at the hotel, the attempted break-in at the morgue, his difficulty in reaching Sam. It was nonsense, of course, but the small hairs on the back of Henry's neck stood on end.

"I should let you go," Joan said. "I'll see you in the morning."

Henry frowned in confusion, then remembered his schedule to meet with Joan at the lab. After the night's hubbub and his nagging worry over his nephew, Henry had momentarily forgotten about the planned rendez-vous with Joan. "Yes, of course. I'll see you then. Good night." Just before he hung up the phone, he added a quick, "Thanks for calling," but the phone line was already dead.

Henry slowly hung up the receiver.

He stared at his computer screen, then clicked it off. There was no further reason to keep trying to reach the camp. He knew he would fail. Snapping shut the laptop, he made a whispered promise to himself. "If I can't reach the camp by tomorrow night, I'm on the first red-eye out of here." But even that decision did not calm his twanging nerves.

DAY THREE

Substance Z

Wednesday, August 22, 6:03 A.M.
Caverns
Andean Mountains, Peru

Sam studied the dagger's gold blade in the feeble light cast by the single flashlight. He had the last guard shift of the night. The others lay sprawled behind him, curled on the flat rock of the cavern floor, pillows made from rumpled shirts and packs. Ralph snored softly, but at least the big man was sleeping. Earlier, Sam had been unable to drowse, except for a brief catnap fraught with terrifying images of falling rocks and unseen monsters. He had been relieved when Norman had nudged him to take his shift.

Sam raised his eyes from the dagger and glanced about the cavern. All around him, silver eyes studied

Sam from the dozens of carved pillars, creatures that were half-human, half-animal. Incan gods and spirits. Nearby, the golden path reflected the meager light, a bright vein in the dark rock. Sam imagined the generations of Incan Indians that must have walked this trail. The footpath continued along the river's bank deeper into the series of caves, and Sam longed to follow it. But the consensus of the group was to make camp there, near a water source and the fissure opening, and await rescue. Exploration could come later.

Glancing at his watch, Sam suspected the sun was just now rising above the Andean mountains. Down there, however, the blackness seemed to grow deeper and more endless. Time lost all meaning; it stretched toward eternity.

Though Sam tried to ignore his hunger, his stomach growled loudly. How long had it been since any of them had anything to eat? Still, he shouldn't complain. At least, with the stream, they had water.

He just needed to keep himself distracted.

Sam fingered the blade of the dagger, pondering the mystery of its mechanism. How had yesterday's transformation occurred? He couldn't even fathom the trigger that unfolded the dagger into a jagged lightning bolt. It had done so with such smoothness and lack of mechanical friction, appearing to melt into the new form. The trick was too damned convincing. How intricate was the technology developed here? Friar de Almagro's warning of the Serpent of Eden suggested a source of forbidden knowledge, a font of wisdom that could corrupt mankind. Was this an example of it?

A cough drew his attention. Barefoot, Maggie sidled toward him. Even disheveled, she was striking. Covered only by a thin blouse, buttoned loosely, her breasts moved under the fabric. Sam's mouth grew dry. He dropped his eyes before he embarrassed himself, but his gaze only discovered the soft curves of waist and leg.

"You must quit fondling that thing, Sam," she said quietly. "People are goin' to start talking."

"What?" Sam asked, shocked, glancing up at her.

Maggie offered him a tired smile and nodded toward the dagger.

"Oh . . ." He tucked it away. "So . . . so you couldn't sleep?"

She shrugged, sitting beside him. "Rock doesn't make such a great mattress."

Sam nodded, allowing her this tiny falsehood. He suspected her restlessness was the same as his: bone-deep worries and the omnipresent press of the darkness around them. "We're going to get out of here," he said plainly.

212 • JAMES ROLLINS

"By trusting in good ol' Philip Sykes?" she said, rolling her eyes.

"He's an ass, but he'll pull us through."

She stared up at a neighboring pillar and was silent. After a time, she spoke. "Sam, I wanted to thank you again for coming out on the tiles when I had that last . . . that last seizure."

He began to protest that no such thanks were needed.

She stopped him with a touch to his hand. "But I need you to know something . . . I think I owe you that."

He turned to face her more fully. "What?"

"I am not truly epileptic," she said softly.

Sam scrunched his face. "What do you mean?"

"The psychologists diagnosed it as post-traumatic stress syndrome, a severe form of panic attack. When tension reaches a certain level"—Maggie waved a hand in the air—"my body rebels. It sends my mind spinning away."

"I don't understand. Isn't that a war-trauma thing?"

"Not always . . . besides there are many forms of war."

Sam didn't want to press her any further, but his heart would not let him stay silent. "What happened?"

She studied Sam for a long breath, her eyes judging him, weighing his sincerity. Finally, she glanced away, her voice dull. "When I was twelve years old, I saw a schoolyard friend, Patrick Dugan, shot by a stray bullet from an IRA sniper. He collapsed in my arms as I hid in a roadside ditch."

"God, how awful . . ."

"Bullets kept flying. Men and women were screamin', cryin'. I didn't know what to do. So I hid under Patrick's body." Maggie began to tremble as she continued the story. "His . . . his blood soaked over me. It was hot, like warm syrup. The smell of a slaughter-house . . ."

Sam slid closer to Maggie, pulling her to him. "You don't have to do this . . ."

She did not withdraw from him but neither did she respond to his touch. She gazed without blinking toward the darkness, lost in a familiar nightmare. "But Patrick was still alive. As I hid under him, he moaned, too low for others to hear. He begged me to help him. He cried for his mama. But I just hid there, using his body as a shield, his blood soaking through my clothes." She turned to Sam, her voice catching. "It was warm, safe. Nothin' could make me move from my hiding place. God forgive me, I forced my ears not to hear Patrick's moans for help." A sob escaped her throat.

"Maggie, you were only a child."

"I could have done something."

"And you could've been killed just as well. What good would that have done Patrick Dugan?"

"I'll never know," she said with the heat of self-loathing tears on her cheek. She struggled away from Sam's arm and turned angry, hurt eyes toward him. "Will I?"

Sam had no answer. "I'm sorry," he offered feebly.

She wiped brusquely at her face. "Ever since then, the goddamn attacks occur. Years of pills and therapy did nothing. So I stopped them all." She swallowed hard. "It's my problem, something I must live with . . . alone. It's my burden."

And your self-imposed punishment for Patrick's death, Sam thought, but he kept silent. Who was he to judge? Images of his parents' crumpled forms being yanked like sides of beef from the smashed car while he sat strapped in the backseat, watching it all, tumbled through his mind. Survivor's guilt. It was a feeling with which he was well acquainted. He still often woke with his bedsheets clinging to his damp skin, cold sweat soaking his body.

Maggie's next words drew him back to the black cavern. "In the future, Sam, don't risk yourself for me. Okay?"

"I . . . I can't promise that."

She stared angrily at him, tears brightening her eyes.

"Maggie—?"

They were interrupted by the appearance of Norman. "Sorry, folks, but I must talk to a man about a horse," the photographer grumbled, hair sticking up in all directions. He crossed over the gold path and headed for a nearby boulder, seemingly oblivious to the tension between the pair.

Sam turned to Maggie, but she would not meet his eyes. She pushed to her feet. "Just . . . just don't risk your life . . ." As she stepped away, Sam heard her mumble something else. The words had been meant only for herself but the cavern acoustics carried the words to him. "I don't want another death on my hands."

Leaning forward, ready to follow and console her, Sam paused, then relaxed back down to his seat. There was nothing he could say. He himself had heard all the platitudes before, after his parents had died. *Don't blame yourself. There was nothing you could do. Accidents happen.* No words had helped him then either. But at least Sam had had his Uncle Henry. Having just lost his own wife, Uncle Hank had seemed to sense that some things had to be faced alone, worked out in silence, rather than probed and prodded for an answer. It was this silence more than grief that had bound nephew to uncle, like two raw-edged wounds healing and scarring together.

Sam watched Maggie walk away, shoulders slumped. She had been right. It was her burden. Still, Sam could not suppress the urge to rush over to her, to take her in his arms and protect her.

Before he could act, a shriek drew him around. He flew to his feet, pulling out the dagger. He stepped to where his grandfather's Winchester leaned against a rock.

Norman came running around the boulder's edge, zipping up his fly, and glancing in panic behind him.

"What's wrong?" Sam asked as Norman stumbled to his side.

The photographer could not catch his breath for a moment. One arm kept gesturing back at the boulder as he gasped and choked. "B . . . Behind . . ."

Ralph drew beside them, bleary from his sudden awakening. He rubbed sleep from his eyes, Gil's lever-action rifle held in his other hand. "Goddammit, Norman. You scream like a girl."

Norman ignored Ralph's jibe, too panicked to care. "I . . . I thought they were just . . . just patches of lichen or spots of lighter rock. But something moved out there!"

"Who? What are you talking about?" Sam asked.

Norman shuddered, then finally seemed to collect himself. He waved them all back toward the boulder.

By then, Maggie and Denal hovered a few steps away. "I'm not sure." He led them back, but this time stayed well away from the rock and whatever lurked behind it.

Sam remained at the photographer's side. The dark stone on the far side of the rock lay in shadows. Streaks of quartz or white gypsum ran in streams up the nearby cavern wall. "I don't see anything."

Norman reached a hand back toward the others. "Gimme one of the lights."

Denal moved up and passed the second flashlight to the photographer. Norman clicked it on; light speared the inky gloom.

Sam twitched back in shock. It was not veins of quartz or gypsum that ran down the wall. These pale streaks flowed, streaming down the wall to pool at its foot. Even now, rivulets started spreading across the floor toward the gathered party. Sam shifted his own lantern. "Spiders . . ." Each was as pale as the belly of a slug and had to be a hand-spread wide. There had to be hundreds . . . no thousands of them.

Ralph stepped back. "Tarantulas."

"Albino tarantulas," Maggie moaned.

The army continued its scurried march. Scouts skittered to either side of the boulder. A few paused where the rock was damp and steamed slightly from Norman's morning relief, clearly drawn to the warmth.

"It's our body heat," Sam said. "The damned things must be blind and drawn by noise and warmth."

Behind him, Denal started gibbering in his native Quecha.

Sam swung around. The young Indian was gesturing in the opposite direction, toward the far side of the gold path. Norman turned his flashlight to where Denal pointed. As another flank of the army streamed down the other wall on pale, hairy legs, Sam suddenly had an awful sensation crawl up his back.

Sam arched his neck, raising his lantern high.

Overhead, the roof was draped by a mass of roiling bodies, crawling, mating, fighting. Thousands of pendulous egg sacs hung in ropy wombs of silk. The students had stumbled into the main nest of the tarantulas . . . and the army of predators was hunting for prey. They were already moving down the pillars, as if the carved figures were giving birth to them.

The group scattered from under the shadow of the monstrosity, fleeing back to their campsite.

As they retreated, Sam studied the huge spiders. Dependent upon the meager resources found in these caves, the tarantulas had clearly evolved a more aggressive posture. Instead of waiting for prey to fall into webs, these normally solitary spiders had adapted a more cooperative strategy. By massing together, they could comb the caves more successfully for any potential sources of a blood meal, taking down larger prey by their sheer numbers—and Sam had no intention of being their next course.

"Okay, folks, I think we've overstayed our welcome," he said. "Gather our gear and let's get the hell out of Dodge."

"Where to?" Maggie asked.

"There's a path through these caves, right? Those Indians who forged it must have done so for a reason. Maybe it's a way out. Anyone object to finding out?"

No one did. Five sets of eyes were still on the encroaching tarantulas.

Sam slipped the gold dagger into his vest and collected his grandfather's rifle. He gestured to the others to collect their few possessions. "One flashlight only," he said, as he led the way down the path. "Conserve the other. I don't want to run out of illumination down here." A shiver passed through Sam at the mere thought of being trapped, blind, with a pale army of poisonous predators encircling him. He tightened his grip on his rifle but knew it would do him little good if the lights went out.

Norman followed with the flashlight, glancing frequently behind him.

"As long as we keep moving, the spiders won't get you, Norman," Ralph said with a scowl.

The photographer still kept an eye on their back-trail. "Just remind me . . . no more bathroom breaks. Not until I see the light of day."

Sam ignored their nervous chatter. It was not what lay behind them that kept Sam's nerves taut as bow-strings, but the trail ahead. Just where in the hell would this path take them?

Unfortunately there was only one way to find out.

As they proceeded, Norman mumbled behind him. "Lions and tigers and bears, oh my . . ."

Sam glanced back, his brow furrowed in confusion.

Norman nodded to the gold path. "Sort of reminds me of the yellow brick road."

"Great," Ralph groused. "Now the fruit thinks he's Dorothy."

"I wish I was. Right now I wouldn't mind a pair of ruby slippers to whisk me home," Norman grumbled. "Or even back to a farm in Kansas."

Sam rolled his eyes and continued onward.

The remainder of the long morning stretched into an endless hike, mostly at a steady incline. Legs and backs protested as the cavern system led them higher inside the Andean mountain. If not for the lack of food and the growing exhaustion, Sam might have better appreciated the sights: towering stalagmites, cavern-ous chambers with limpid pools that glowed with a soft phosphorescence, cataracts that misted the gold trail at times with a welcome cooling spray, even a side cave so festooned with lacy crystals that it looked as if the chamber was full of cotton candy. It was a wonderland of natural beauty.

And everywhere they went, the carved pillars marked their way as grim sentinels, watching the group pass with unblinking silver eyes.

But as amazing as the sights were, the memory of what lay behind them never fully vanished. Breaks to drink from the stream were often accompanied by worried glances toward the rear. So far there had been no sign of pursuit by the tarantula army. It seemed they had left the spiders far behind.

Slowly, the morning wound to afternoon. The only highlight was a brief lunch to split a pair of Milky Way bars found stashed in Norman's camera case. Chocolate had never tasted so good. But even this small taste of heaven was short-lived, and only succeeded in amplifying everyone's hunger. Tempers began to grow short and attitudes sullen as they marched through the afternoon.

To make matters worse, a sharp pungency began to fill the cavern's normally crisp air. Noses wrinkled. "Ammonia. Smells like the ass end of a skunk," Sam commented.

"Maybe the air is going bad," Norman said with a worried expression on his haggard face.

"Don't be a fool," Ralph snapped. "The air would have been worse when we were deeper."

"Not necessarily," Maggie said. Her eyes had narrowed suspiciously, squinting at the darkness beyond the light. "Not if there was a source giving off the noxious fumes."

Ralph still scowled, clearly tired and irritated. "What do you mean?"

Instead of answering, Maggie turned to Sam. "All those tarantulas. From the look of them, they were well fed. What do the feckin' things eat down here?"

Sam shook his head. He had no answer.

"Oh God!" This came from Norman, who had taken the lead with the flashlight. The gold path led over a short rise into a neighboring cavern. From the echo of his exclamation, the chamber was large.

The others hurried to join him.

Maggie stared at the scene ahead, holding a hand over her mouth and nose. The sting burned their eyes and noses. "There's the answer. The source of the tarantulas' diet."

Sam groaned. "Bats."

Across the roof of the next cave, thousands of black and brown bats hung from latched toes, wings tight to bodies. The juveniles, squirming among the adults, were a paler shade, almost a coppery hue. Sharp squeaks and subsonic screeches spread the warning of intruders across the legion of winged vermin. Hundreds dropped from their perches to take flight, skirting through the air.

The source of the odor was immediately clear.

"Shit," Ralph swore.

"Exactly," Norman commented sullenly. "*Bat* shit."

The floor of the cavern was thick with it. Carved pillars, fouled with excrement, speared upward through the odorous mess. The reek from the aged droppings was thick enough to drive them all back with a stinging slap.

Norman tumbled away, choking and spitting. Bent at the waist, he leaned on his knees, gagging.

Ralph looked as if his dark skin had been bleached by the corrosive exposure. "We can't cross here," he said. "We'd be dead before we reached the other side."

"Not without gas masks," Maggie agreed.

Sam was not going to argue. He could barely see, his eyes were watering so fiercely. "Wh . . . what are we going to do then?"

Denal spoke up. He had hung back from the cavern's opening and so had borne the least of the exposure. Even now, he was not facing ahead, but behind. He had an arm pointed. "They come again."

Sam turned, blinking away the last of the burn. He took the flashlight from the incapacitated Norman. Several yards down the gold trail, three or four white bodies scurried across the rocky landscape. Scouts of the tarantula army.

"To hell with this," Ralph said, voicing all their concerns.

"What now?" Maggie asked.

Sam glanced forward and backward. Everyone began talking at once. Sam raised the light to get everyone's attention. "Stay calm! It won't do us any good to panic!"

At that moment, Sam's flashlight flickered and died. Darkness swallowed them up, a blackness so deep it seemed as if the world had completely vanished. Voices immediately dropped silent.

After a long held breath, Norman spoke from the darkness. "Okay, now can we panic?"

Joan ushered Henry into her lab. "Please make yourself at home," she offered, then glanced at her wristwatch. "Dr. Kirkpatrick should be here at noon."

Behind her, Henry had paused in the doorway to her suite of labs, his eyes wide. "It's like a big toy store in here. You've done well since our years at Rice."

She hid a smile of satisfaction.

Slowly, Henry wandered further into the laboratory, his gaze drifting over the plethora of equipment. Various diagnostic and research devices lined the back of the room: ultracentrifuge, hematology and chemistry analyzer, mass spectrograph, chromatograph, a gene sequencer. Along one wall was a safety hood for handling hazardous substances; along the other stood cabinets, incubators, and a huge refrigerated unit.

Henry walked along the row of machines and glanced into a neighboring room. "My God, you even have your own electron microscope." Henry rolled his eyes at her. "To book any time on our university's, it takes at least a week's notice."

"No need for that here. Today, my lab is at your full disposal."

Henry crossed to a central U-shaped worktable and set down his leather briefcase, his eyes still drifting appreciatively around the room. "I've had dreams like this . . ."

Chuckling to herself, Joan stepped to a locked stainless-steel cabinet, keyed it open and, with two hands, extracted a large beaker. "Here's all the material we collected from the walls and floor of the radiology lab."

She saw Henry's eyes widen as she placed the jar before him. He leaned over a bit, pushing his glasses higher on his nose. "I didn't realize there was so much," he said. The yellowish substance filled half of the liter-sized beaker. It shone brightly under the room's fluorescent lights.

Joan pulled up a stool. "From the amount, I judge it must have filled the skull's entire cranium."

Henry picked the beaker up. Joan noticed that he quickly grabbed it with his other hand. The stuff was heavier than it appeared. He tilted the jar, but the unknown substance refused to flow. Replacing the beaker on the table, he commented, "It looks solid."

Joan shook her head. "It's not." She grabbed a glass rod and thrust it into the material. It sank but not without some effort, like pushing through soft clay. Joan released the rod, and it remained standing straight in the jar. "Malleable, but not solid."

Henry tried to move the glass rod. "Hmm . . . definitely not gold. But the hue and brilliance are a perfect match. Maybe you were right before, a new amalgam or something. I've certainly never seen anything like it."

Joan glanced at him, eyebrows raised. "Or maybe you have. Let's compare it to the gold cross. You brought it with you, yes?"

He nodded. Twisting back to the table, Henry dialed the lock on his briefcase and snapped it open. "I figure it's safer with me than at the hotel." He removed the ornate Dominican cross and held it toward her.

The workmanship was incredible. The Christ figure lay stretched and stylized upon a scrolled cross; the pain of his agony sculpted in the strain of his limbs, yet his face was full of passionate grace. "Impressive," she said.

"And solid . . . . so I doubt it's made of the same amalgam." Henry placed the crucifix beside the beaker. The strange material and the cross glinted and shone equally.

"Are you sure?"

Henry met her eyes over the rim of his spectacles. He shrugged his brows. "I'll leave the final assessment to your expert."

She reached for the crucifix. "May I?"

"Of course, Joan."

Her hand hesitated for a heartbeat when Henry used her name. The intimacy and surroundings brought back sudden memories of when the two were lab partners during a semester in undergraduate biology. How strange and vivid that recollection was at the moment. More than just déjà vu.

Without meeting his eye, Joan took the cross from the table. The past was the past. She hefted the crucifix in her palm. It, too, weighed more than it appeared—but didn't gold always seem that way? She held the crucifix up to the light, tilting it one way, then the other, studying it.

Henry theorized aloud while she examined the relic. "It's definitely the work of a Spanish craftsman. Not Incan work. If the cross is confirmed to be composed of the same amalgam, then we'll know for sure the Spanish brought the substance to the New World, rather than the other way around . . ."

He continued talking, but something had caught Joan's attention. Her fingers felt small scratches on the crucifix's back surface. She reached to a pocket and slipped out her reading glasses. Putting them on, she turned the crucifix over and squinted. It was not the artist's signature or some piece of archaic scripture. Instead it seemed to be row after row of fine marks. They covered the entire surface of the crucifix's back side.

"What is this?" Joan asked, interrupting Henry.

He moved closer, shoulder to shoulder with her. Joan noticed the faint scent of him, a mix of aftershave and a richer muskiness. She tried to ignore it.

"What are you talking about?" he asked.

"Here." With a fingernail, she pointed to the marks.

"Ah, I noticed those. I think they're a result of the cross rubbing against the friar's robe, slowly abrading the soft gold over the years."

"Mmm, maybe . . . but they seem too symmetrical, and some of the marks are quite deep and irregular." She turned slightly to Henry, almost nose to nose. His breath was on her cheek, his eyes staring deep into hers.

"What are you suggesting?"

She shook her head, stepping away. "I don't know. I'd like to get a closer look."

"How?"

Joan led him around the corner of the table where sets of microscopes were positioned. She moved to a bulky binocular unit with a large glass tray under it. "A dissection microscope. Normally I use it to study gross tissues more closely."

She placed the cross facedown on the tray and switched on the light source. Illuminated from above, the gold glowed with an inner fire. Joan adjusted the light so it shone obliquely across the crucifix. Bending over the eyepiece, she made fine adjustments in the lenses. Under the low magnification, the surface of the cross filled the view. The marks on the crucifix were in stark relief, appearing as deep gouges in the metal, long valleys, clearly precise and uniform. The scratches composed a series of repeated tiny symbols: rough squares, crude circles, horizontal and vertical squiggles, hash marks, nested ovals.

"Take a look," Joan said, moving aside.

Henry bent over the scope. He stared a few moments in silence, then a low whistle escaped his lips. "You're right. These are not random scratches." His gaze flicked toward her. "I think there's even silver embedded in some of the grooves. Perhaps traces of the tool used to scratch these marks."

"For such painstaking work, there must be some reason to go through all that effort."

"But why?" Henry's lips tightened as he pondered this new mystery, his eyes slightly narrowed. Finally, he expelled a breath. "It may be a message. But who knows for sure? Maybe it's just an ordinary prayer. Some benediction."

"But in code? And why on the back of the cross? It must mean something more."

Henry shrugged. "If the friar notched it as a message while imprisoned, it may have been the only way he could keep it secure. The Incas revered gold items. If the cross was with him when he died on the altar, the Incas would have kept the crucifix with the body."

"If you're right, who was his message meant for?"

Henry shook his head slowly, his gaze thoughtful. "The answer may lie in this code."

Joan moved back to the scope. She slid a legal pad and a pen from a drawer, then sat down and positioned herself to copy the marks on her paper. "Let's check it out. I've always liked dabbling with cryptograms. If I don't have any luck, I can also run it by someone in the computer department, pass it through a decryption program. They may be able to crack it."

Henry stood behind her as she recorded the writing. "You've grown into a woman of many talents, Dr. Joan Engel."

Joan hid her blush as she concentrated on her task, copying the marks carefully. She worked quickly and efficiently, not needing to look up as she jotted what she saw. After years of making notes while studying a patient's sample under a microscope, she had grown skilled at writing blind.

In five minutes, a copy lay on the table beside her. Row after row of symbols lined the yellow paper. She straightened from her crouch, stretching a kink from her neck.

"Hold still," Henry said behind her. He slid a hand along her shoulder and gently lifted the cascade of hair from the back of her neck. His knuckles brushed her skin.

She suppressed a shiver. "Henry . . . ?"

"Don't move." His fingers reached to knead the muscles of her strained upper shoulders. At first, his skin was cool against her own, but as he worked, heat built under his strong fingers, warming her sore muscles.

"I see you've not lost your touch." She leaned into his fingers, remembering another time, another place. "So if I tell you to stop, ignore me," she said, feigning a nonchalance that the huskiness of her voice betrayed.

"It's the least I can do after all your help." His own words were heavier than usual.

A sharp rap on the laboratory door interrupted the moment.

Henry's hands froze, then pulled back.

Joan shifted from her chair, her shoulders and neck still warm from his touch. She glanced at her watch. "It must be Dr. Kirkpatrick. He's right on time."

Henry cursed the metallurgist's impeccable timing. He rubbed his palms together, trying to wipe away the memory of Joan's skin. *Get ahold of yourself, man. You're acting like a smitten teenager.*

He watched Joan walk away. One of her hands reached to touch her neck gently. Then she brushed her hair back into place, a midnight flow against her white smock. Mysteries or not, right now all he wished for was a few more moments alone with her.

Joan crossed to the door, opened it, and greeted the visitor. "Dale, thanks for coming over."

Dale Kirkpatrick, the metallurgy expert from George Washington University, stood a good head taller than Henry, but he was waspishly thin with an elongated face that seldom smiled. He tried to do so now with disastrous results, like a coroner greeting the bereaved. "Anything for a colleague."

Henry sensed the red-haired man had shared more with Joan than just a professional relationship. The pair's eyes met one another awkwardly, and the welcoming handshake was a touch longer than custom dictated. Henry instantly disliked him. The man wore an expensive silk suit and shoes polished to a glowing sheen. His heels tapped loudly as he was invited into the room. In his left hand, he carried a large equipment case.

Henry cleared his throat.

Joan swung around. "Dale, let me introduce you to Professor Henry Conklin."

Kirkpatrick held out his hand. "The archaeologist." It was a statement not a question, but Henry scented a trace of dismissal in his voice.

They shook hands, briefly and curtly.

"I appreciate your help in this matter," Henry said. "It's posed quite a mystery. We can't make heads or tails of this amalgam or whatever it is."

"Yes . . . well, let me just take a look." The man's attitude was again polite, but a touch haughty, as if his mere presence would bring light to darkness.

"It's over here," Joan said, guiding him to the worktable.

Once presented with the enigma, Kirkpatrick cocked his head, studying the strange substance in silence. Joan began to speak, but the specialist held up a finger, quieting her. Henry had an irrational urge to break that finger. "It's not gold," he finally declared.

"We sort of figured that out," Henry said sourly.

The man glanced back at him, one eyebrow held high. "Undoubtedly, or I wouldn't have been called in, now would I?" He turned back to the beaker and reached for the glass rod still embedded in the material. He fiddled with it. "Semisolid at room temperature," he mumbled. "Have you ascertained a true melting point for the substance?"

"Not yet."

"Well, that's easy enough to do." He told Joan what he would need. Soon they were gathered around a ceramic bowl warming over the low purple flame of a Bunsen burner. A sample of the metal filled the bottom half of the bowl with a thermometer embedded in it.

The metallurgist spoke as the material slowly heated under the hazards hood. "If it's an amalgam of different elements, the constituent metals should separate out for us as it melts."

"It's already melted," Henry said with a nod toward the bowl.

Dale swung his attention back, frowning. "That's impossible. It's only been warming for a few seconds. Even gold doesn't melt at such a low temp."

But Henry's observation proved true. Using tongs, Dale jostled the bowl. The substance now appeared as loose as cream, only golden in color. He looked up to Joan. "What's the temperature?"

Joan's face was bunched in consternation. "Ninety-eight degrees Fahrenheit."

Henry's eyes widened. "Body temperature."

Away from the heat source, the bowl quickly cooled and the metallic substance grew turgid as the trio pondered the result.

Henry spoke first. "I didn't see any breakdown into component metals like you said. Does that mean it's not an amalgam?"

"It's too soon to say." But Dale's voice had lost its edge.

"What next?"

"A few more tests. I'd like to check its conductivity and its response to magnetism."

In short order, they molded a sample of the soft metal into a cube and inserted two electrodes into it. Dale nodded, and Joan engaged the battery hookup.

As soon as the current flowed, the cube melted into a sludge that ran across the worktable.

"Switch it off!"

Joan flipped the toggle. The material instantly solidified again. Dale touched the metal. "It's cool."

"What just happened?" Henry asked.

Dale just shook his head. He had no answer. "Bring me the magnets from my case."

Henry and Joan positioned the two shielded magnets on either side of a second sample cube. Dale fastened a potentiometer on its side. "On my signal, raise the shields." He leaned closer to the meter. "Now."

Joan and Henry flicked open the lead dampers. Just as with the flow of electricity, the cube melted like ice in an oven, running across the table.

"Shield the magnets," Dale ordered.

Once done, the substance instantly stopped flowing across the tabletop, freezing in place. Dale again fingered the solidified metal. He now wore a worried expression.

"Well?" Henry asked.

"You said the substance exploded out of the mummy's skull when exposed to the CT scanner."

"Yes," Joan said. "It blew across the entire room."

"Then even the CT scanner's X rays affect the metal," Dale mumbled to himself, tapping a pen on the table's edge. "Interesting . . ."

Henry packed away the magnets. "What are you thinking?"

Dale's eyes cleared and focused. He turned to them. "The substance must be capable of using any radiant energy with perfect efficiency—electric current, magnetic radiation, X rays. It absorbs these various energies to change state." He nudged a trickle of the solidified metal. "I don't think there's even any heat given off as it changes form. It's an example of the perfect consumption of energy. Not even waste heat! I've . . . I've never seen anything like this. It's thermodynamically impossible."

Henry studied the contents of the beaker. "Are you suggesting the scanner's X rays triggered the mummy's explosion?"

He nodded. "Bombarded by that amount of concentrated radiation, some of the material might have changed state—this time from liquid to gas. The sudden expansion could have caused the violent explosion, expelling the liquefied metal. Once away from the radiation, it changed back to this semisolid state."

"But what is it?" Joan asked.

He held up that irritating finger again. "Let me try one more thing." Taking another sample cube of the soft metal, he squeezed it like a lump of clay. "Has it ever completely solidified?"

238 · JAMES ROLLINS

Joan shook her head. "No. I even tried freezing it, but it remained malleable."

Dale swung on his seat. "Professor Conklin, could you pass me one of the magnets' insulating sleeves?"

Henry had been wrapping the last of the heavy magnets in a copper-impregnated cloth. He undid his work and passed the wrap to Dale.

"The sleeve blocks the magnet's effects . . . so I don't accidentally damage some expensive electronics in passing. It shields almost all forms of radiation."

Henry began to get an inkling of the metal expert's plan.

Dale took the gold cube and wrapped it in the black cloth. Once it was totally shielded, he placed the shrouded cube back on the table. He then took a chisel and hammer from his case. Positioning the chisel's edge on the cube, he struck the tool a resounding blow with the mallet. A muffled clang was the only response. The cube resisted the chisel.

Quickly unwrapping the cube, Dale revealed the unblemished surface. He took the chisel again, and only using the force of his thumb, he drove it through the exposed cube. He explained these results. "All around us is low ambient radiation. It's always present—various local radio waves, electromagnetic pulses from the building's wiring, even solar radiation. This substance uses them all! That's why it remains semisolid. Even these trace energies weaken its solidity."

"But I don't understand," Joan said. "What type of metal or amalgam could do this?"

"Nothing that I've ever seen or heard about." Dale suddenly stood up, carefully lifting the soft cube in steel tongs. He nodded toward the neighboring room, to the electron-microscope suite. "But there's a way to investigate closer."

Henry soon found himself trailing the other two into the next room. He carried both the beaker of the strange metal, now sealed with a rubber stopper, and the mummy's Dominican crucifix. Already, Joan and Dale were bowed head-to-head as they prepared a shaving of the metal to use in the electron microscope.

Henry crossed to a small table off to the side, setting down the beaker and the cross. The large electron microscope occupied the rear of the room. Its towering optical column reached for the room's ceiling. A bank of three monitors was crowded before it.

Joan warmed up the unit, flipping switches and quickly checking baseline calibrations. Dale finished prepping the sample, locking it into place on the scanner's tray. He gave Joan a thumbs-up.

Henry, all but forgotten, scowled and sank to a stool by his table.

Across the small room, the optical column began to hum and click as its tungsten hairpin gun bombarded the sample with an electron beam. Dale hurried to Joan's side before the monitors. The pathologist jabbed at a keyboard, and the screens bloomed with a grey glow in the dim room. The words STAND BY could be seen even from where Henry sat.

"How long will this take?" Henry called over.

Joan glanced at him, her face a mixture of surprise and embarrassment. She must have finally realized how little she had acknowledged him. "Not long. The EM will need about ten minutes to compile and calculate an image." Joan offered Henry a weak, apologetic smile, then turned away.

Henry swung away himself, turning his attention back to the crucifix. He tapped its brilliant surface with a finger. After testing the unknown substance, the friar's cross was clearly composed of the real thing. "Mere gold," Henry muttered to himself. At least one mystery was solved, but that still left another enigma.

Grasping the crucifix, Henry flipped it over to study its back side and the rows of small scratches. What was Francisco de Almagro trying to say? Henry ran a finger along the marks. Was this some last message? If so, what was so important? As Henry fingered the cross, he felt a twinge of misgiving, similar to the one the previous night when his attempt to communicate with the camp failed. He pushed aside such irrational worries. He was being paranoid. But for the hundredth time that day, his thoughts drifted to Sam and the other students. How were they faring with the buried pyramid? Had they perhaps already discovered the answers to these puzzles?

Henry palmed the crucifix between his two hands, resting his forehead on his fingertips. So many oddities surrounded the dig. Henry sensed there was a connection, some way to bring all these strands together: mummified priests, mysterious metals, sealed crypts. But what was the connection? Henry felt the crucifix's outline pressed into his palms. A cross of gold and a coded message. Could this be the answer?

He imagined the young friar, crouched over his cross, etching it with some sharp tool. Painstaking work while his death neared. In Henry's hands were perhaps the last words of this man. But what did he want to say? "What was so important?" Henry whispered.

The image of the cross crystallized in Henry's mind, turning slowly before his inner eye.

Joan suddenly gasped behind him, pulling him out of his reverie. He twisted around. She faced his direction, but her eyes were not fixed on Henry. He followed the path of her gaze to his right elbow.

The beaker rested on the tabletop where Henry had placed it. His breath caught when he saw its contents.

"Henry . . . ?"

The beaker no longer contained a pool of the raw metal. Inside, leaning against the glass side, was a crude copy of the Dominican gold cross. Roughly cruciform in shape, the detail was blurred. The Christ figure was no more than a blunt suggestion upon its surface.

Joan and Dale moved closer.

"Did you do that?" Dale asked.

Henry glanced at the man as if he were mad. He pointed to its sealed stopper. "Are you kidding?"

As they all watched, the cross seemed to lose some of its detail. The edges became less sharp, and the figure slid from the cross to pool at the bottom of the beaker. Still, the cross itself persisted in its general shape.

Henry tried to explain, "I was just thinking about it when—"

A sharp chime rang from nearby, loud in the small room.

They all turned to see the monitors waver, then blink into greyscale images.

"Maybe we're one step closer to an answer," Dale announced tacitly. He stepped back toward the bank of monitors.

Henry and Joan followed. Their eyes met briefly. Henry could see the consternation and something that looked like fear in her eyes. Before he knew what he was doing, he reached out and gave her hand a quick reassuring squeeze. She acknowledged the gesture by moving a few inches closer to Henry's side.

With a final worried glance toward the cross in the jar, Henry joined the others at the monitors.

Dale stood bent over the keyboard, one finger tracing along the screen. Upon the monitor was an unearthly landscape, a rough terrain of oddly shaped peaks and valleys, as if someone had taken a black-and-white photo of the surface of Mars. "This is impossible," Dale said. He pointed to a section of screen that magnified a corner of the landscape. "Look. The metal is actually an aggregation of tiny particles. See how they're latched and interlinked."

On the screen, the cross-sectional view revealed tiny octagonal structures hooked to one another by six articulated legs. Each miniscule structure was joined to its surrounding neighbors in a dense tetrahedral pattern.

Joan reached to touch one of the grey particles displayed on the monitor. "They appear almost organic, like viral phages, or something."

The metallurgist grumbled, one hand indicating the general landscape across the rest of the screens. "No, definitely not viral. From the fracturing and internal matrix, the substance is distinctly inorganic. I'd almost say crystalline in structure."

"Then what the hell is it?" Henry finally asked, growing irritated with the man. "Metal, crystal, viral, vegetable, mineral?"

Kirkpatrick's gaze flicked toward the cross in the beaker, then he shook his head. "I don't know. But if I had to guess, I'd pick all of the above."

From the edge of the communication tent, Philip Sykes watched the sun begin to sink toward the mountains. This was the second day of his vigil by the collapsed ruins. What once had been a jungle-shrouded hill that hid the buried temple was now a cratered and broken ruin. Edges of toppled granite boulders and slabs from the temple jutted from the churned dark soil like exposed broken teeth.

If Philip had not gotten that call from Sam, informing him of the students' discovery of a natural cavern system, he would have thought them all dead. For the past half day, the mound no longer shifted or sagged. The noise from grinding rocks no longer groaned up from the earth. The dig site lay as silent as a grave. The temple had collapsed fully.

But Sam *had* called.

Philip clenched a fist. A part of him wished the arrogant Texan hadn't. It would have been easier to call them all dead; then Philip would be free to abandon the site, leave these cursed Indians to their black jungle. Every hour that Philip remained there he risked an attack from Guillermo Sala. Philip clutched his arms around himself as a chill breeze blew down from the mountaintop. Who would get there first—the rescue party called in by the pair of Indians or Gil's henchmen returning to finish their work?

The tension ground at Philip's nerves. "If only I could leave . . ." But he knew he couldn't, not before the rescue tunnel was completed. Philip stared toward the jungle's edge.

Nearby, the calls and low singing from the Quechan workers echoed up from the obscured work site on the far side of the mound. The looters' tunnel had been excavated a full fifteen yards that day. Though the Indians still shot him dark looks and muttered sharp words, Philip could not fault their hard work. The crew had split into three shifts and dug with pickax and shovel all night long and into the day.

It was even possible that Philip's estimation of two days to dig the others free might not turn out to be too far off the mark.

But would that be soon enough?

A sudden commotion rose from farther back in the jungle, where a few of the Indians were taking a break in the shade of the trees. Philip stood straighter, as if an extra inch of height would pierce the shadows of the forest. He held his breath.

An Indian, one of the workers, burst from the tree line. He waved an arm at Philip in the universal gesture to come. Philip refused to move; he even took a step back. As he hesitated, the Indians' voices grew more distinct as other workers gathered beyond the forest's edge. From the happy and relieved noises, Philip gathered that whatever new discovery had been made must not be a threat.

Philip girded himself with a firm breath, then stomped down from the height of the campsite toward the forest. Even the short exertion of crossing the clearing soon had Philip sucking for breath through his teeth. Tension and exhaustion had weakened his ability to handle the thin air. A seed of a headache bloomed behind his right temple by the time he neared the forest's edge.

Before he reached the eaves, a flow of excited Indians flocked into the clearing from the trees. They roiled around, grinning wide, teeth bright in the late afternoon sunshine. Soon the press of workers broke around Philip, like a rock in a stream. The way finally parted enough for Philip to see who the Indians were leading into camp.

Six figures, robed in mud brown attire and leather sandals, stepped from the trees, faces warm and open as they threw back the cowls from their heads. They too wore smiles upon their faces, but not the toothy grins of the crude Indians, only simple, kind countenances.

One of the robed men was clearly the leader. He stood a bit taller than the others and was the only one with a prominent silver pectoral cross.

"Monks . . ." Philip muttered in amazement.

Some of the Indians dropped to their knees at the feet of these religious men and bowed for a blessing. While the other monks placed palms atop heads and whispered prayers in Spanish, the head of this group approached Philip.

The man shrugged back his own cowl to reveal a strong, handsome face framed by black hair. "We have heard of your time of need, my son," he said simply. "My name is Friar Dominic Otera, and we've come to offer what aid we can."

Philip blinked. English! The man had spoken English! He suppressed an urge to step over and hug the friar. Instead, he tried to compose himself enough to speak. "How . . . how did you—?"

The monk held up a hand. "On our journey among the small nearby villages, we came upon the Indians you sent for help. I've sent them on to Villacuacha to alert the authorities, but in the meantime, we've come to offer prayers and consolation in the tragedy here."

Philip felt himself sag as his burden was finally eased. There were now others—others who spoke English—who could share his anxiety. Philip found himself blathering, unable to form a clear thought, blurting out a mixture of heartfelt thanks interspersed with his own worries. None of it made sense.

Friar Otera crossed to Philip and placed a cool palm upon his cheek. "Calm yourself, my son."

His touch centered Philip. "Yes . . . yes . . . where are my manners? You've all traveled far and must be thirsty and famished."

The monk lowered his face. "The Lord is all the sustenance we need, but as travelers we would be remiss in refusing your hospitality."

Philip bobbed his head like a fool; he could not help himself, so giddy with relief was he. "Then, please, come to my tent. I have juice, water, and can put together some quick sandwiches."

"That is most gracious. Then perhaps, out of the harsh sun, you can tell me what has befallen your group."

Philip led the monks toward the cluster of tents, though he noticed that three lagged behind, continuing their ministrations among the workers.

The friar noticed that Philip had paused. "They will join us later. The Lord's work must always come first."

Swinging back around, Philip nodded. "Of course." In short order, Philip and the friar were ensconced in his personal tent upon camp chairs. Resting between them was a platter of hard cheeses and sliced meats. The other two monks had shyly accepted glasses of fresh guava juice and had retired outside in the shadow of the tent, leaving Friar Otera and Philip in peace.

After sampling what Philip offered, the friar leaned back in the canvas chair with a sigh of gratitude. "Most delicious and kind." He placed both palms upon his knees, studying Philip. "Now tell me, my son, what has happened here? How can we help?"

Philip sipped his juice and collected himself. The simple duties as host had calmed his nerves, but he found himself unable to meet the friar's gaze. In the dim tent, the man's eyes were dark, penetrating shadows, wells that seemed to see into his soul. Philip had been raised Presbyterian but had never been particularly religious. Yet, he could sense power in this quiet figure who sat opposite him, and his initial relief had slowly changed to a mild trepidation in the presence of the man. He knew he could not lie to him; the monk would know his true heart.

Setting down his glass, Philip began his story of Gil's betrayal and subsequent sabotage. ". . . and after the explosion, the temple continued to collapse in on itself, driving those trapped deeper and deeper. There was nothing I could do to help them."

Friar Otera nodded his head, once, like a benediction. "Be at peace, Philip. You've done all you could."

Philip drew strength from these words. He *had* done all he could. He sat up straighter as he continued relating how the Indians were attempting to dig a rescue shaft, and how Sam and the others had discovered a secret tunnel behind a golden idol. He found himself going on and on. He even described Sam's discovery of the statue's key. "A gold knife that somehow transformed."

The friar's eyes grew wide at this last bit, slowing Philip's tale. The monk interrupted, "A gold knife and a hidden tunnel into the mountain?" The man's voice had grown strangely dark and deep.

"Yes," Philip said tentatively.

The friar was silent a moment, then returned to his normal even demeanor. "Thank the Lord for their salvation. At least your friends found a safe shelter. The Lord always opens a way for those of good heart."

"I hope to have the rescue shaft completed in two days or so. But if the Indians I sent can fetch more help—?"

Friar Otera suddenly stood. "Fear not. The Lord will watch over all those here. In his eyes, we are all his beloved sheep. No harm will come."

Philip quickly pushed from his own chair, meaning to accompany the friar.

The man waved him back down. "Rest, Philip, you've earned it. You've done the Lord's work here protecting your friends."

Sinking back into his chair, Philip sighed as Friar Otera bowed his way from the tent. "Thank you," he called as the monk departed.

Alone in his tent, Philip closed his eyes for a moment. He believed he could sleep. The burden was no longer his own, and the onus for his questionable actions had been absolved.

Philip stared at the closed flap of his tent. He remembered the smoldering power he had sensed in the man.

Friar Otera must be a *truly* religious man.

Well away from the tents, at the edge of the forest, Friar Otera met with one of his fellow monks. Otera forced his fingers to stop trembling. Could it be true? After so long?

The monk fished through his shoulder pack and passed Otera the radio. Stepping a few paces away under the forest's eaves, Otera dialed the proper channel and called to his superior.

He reverted to Spanish. "Contact has been made. Over."

A short burst of static, then a quick response. "And your assessment?"

"Favorable. The site appears golden. I repeat, golden." Friar Otera gave a terse summary of what he had learned from the pasty-faced student.

Even across the airwaves, Friar Otera heard the mutter of shock and the whispered words in Spanish, "*El Sangre del Diablo.*"

Friar Otera shuddered with the mere mention of that name. "And your orders?"

"Befriend the student. Earn his trust. Then light a flame under these workers. Dig a way to that tunnel." A long pause, then his final order. "Once contact is made, clean the site . . . thoroughly."

For the first time that day, Friar Otera smiled. He fingered the dagger in its wrist sheath. The haughty student here reminded him of those youths who had once spat upon Otera's poor upbringing, his mixed blood. It would be a pleasure to see this *americano* beg for his life. But more important, if what he suspected was true, there were even larger victories at stake. He had waited for so long, borne too many indignities from these Spanish missionaries who thought themselves his superior. No, if he was right, he would show them their mistake, their blindness. He would no longer be shunned and glanced over. Otera raised the radio to his hard lips, playing the good soldier. "Confirm contact and clean the site. I understand. Over and out."

Otera stepped back from the forest and returned the radio to the monk who stood guard. "And?" the fellow asked, packing away the radio.

Friar Otera straightened his pectoral crucifix. "We have a green light."

The other monk's eyes grew aghast. "Then it's true!" The man made the sign of the cross. "May the Lord protect us."

Friar Otera trudged back toward the camp. The words from the radio still echoed in his head.

El Sangre del Diablo.

Satan's Blood.

Maggie fumbled with the second flashlight, her fingers trembling. She thumbed the switch, and light flared out into the black caverns, blinding her for a second. The pale faces of her fellow students and the young Indian boy stared back along the trail. In that minute of darkness, more of the tarantula scouts had scurried onto the gold trail. To the side, more spiders approached, their albino limbs like pale-legged starfish against the black rock.

Sam glanced back toward the toxic bat cavern. "I . . . I don't know. The place will be swarming with tarantulas in a few minutes, but we can't trudge through waist-deep guano in the next cavern without dying from the fumes. There's got to be another way."

Maggie strode off the Incan footpath toward the nearby underground stream. It gurgled in its narrow channel, casting up a fine cool mist. "We swim," she said matter-of-factly, pointing her light at the rapidly flowing water.

"Swim?" Norman asked, his voice cracking. "Are you mad? That water's from snowmelt. We'll die of hypothermia."

Maggie swung around. "The current is swift but relatively smooth through this section of the caverns. We jump in and let the water shoot us through the bat cave and away from the spiders." She waved a hand across the river's fine mist. "This may even insulate us a bit from the worst of the toxic fumes."

Sam approached her side and glanced at her with appreciative eyes. "Maggie's right. It might work. But we need to stick together for this one. Once past the bats, we'll need to haul our asses out of this stream ASAP. If the current doesn't kill us, the cold may."

Denal sidled to the edge of the river's carved stone bank. The waters flowed about a meter below the lip. "I go first," he said, looking back. "Make sure it be safe."

"No, Denal," Maggie said and reached for him.

He stepped beyond her reach. "I be strong swimmer. If I make it to the far side, I yell." He glanced at the other faces. "Then you all come. If no call, then no come."

Sam moved toward the boy. "I'll do it, Denal," Sam said, patting the side pocket of his vest. "I have my Wood's lamp to light the way."

Denal pulled the lamp from his own pocket and flicked on the purplish light. "I no ask. I go." The boy then turned and jumped over the lip's edge.

"Denal!" Sam yelled, rushing to the river.

Maggie stopped Sam from leaping in after him. She followed the boy's path in the current. He bobbed in the water as it thrust him back and forth in the narrow channel, but he managed to keep the lamp thrust above the water, its purplish glow a beacon in the dark cave. Then the river carried him past a curve in the wall and down a tunnel.

"Damn kid picked my pocket," Sam muttered, a mixture of respect and worry in his voice.

"He'll make it," Maggie said.

The waiting quickly grew intolerable. None dared speak lest they miss Denal's call.

Only Ralph hung back at the footpath, keeping an eye on the spiders. "Here comes the main army," he warned.

Maggie swung around. It was as if a foaming white surf crested just at the edge of their light's reach. "C'mon, Denal, don't let us down."

As if the boy had heard her, a sharp distant cry echoed from farther in the caves. Denal had made it.

"Thank God," Sam sighed. "Let's get out of here."

Norman quickly finished packing his gear into a waterproof case while Ralph climbed over to join them, eyes still on the tarantulas.

Sam unslung the Winchester and nodded for Ralph to do the same with his rifle. "Try to keep your gun above water. The rifles could probably survive a short dip, but I'd rather keep them dry."

Ralph finally turned and eyed the water with a sick expression. "To hell with the rifle, I just hope I can keep my own head above water." He raised his face to the other three. "I can't swim."

"What?" Sam exclaimed. "Why didn't you tell us that before?"

Ralph shrugged. "Because Maggie was right. The river's the only way out of here."

Norman shoved up next to them. "I'll stick with Ralph. I did a stint in water rescue in the army."

Ralph frowned at him, disbelieving. "You were in the army?"

"Three years at Fort Ord, until I was discharged during a witch-hunt at my base." Norman's face took on a bitter cast. "So much for don't ask, don't tell."

Ralph shook his head. "I'll take my chances on my own."

The photographer's face grew fierce. He snapped at Ralph, "Like hell you will, you brain-addled jock. Quit this macho posturing and accept some help. It's not like I'm gonna try to cop a feel. You're not even my type!" Norman shoved his camera case at Ralph, his voice serious. "It's insulated with foam. It's meant to float after a raft capsizes. Keep the damn thing clutched to your chest, and I'll do the rest."

Ralph took the case reluctantly. "What about this?" He held up Gil's rifle.

Sam reached for it. "I'll manage both."

He reached for the gun, but Maggie snatched it first. "Two guns will weigh you down, Sam. The flashlight is waterproof and doesn't weigh nary a bit."

Sam hesitated, then nodded. "At the first sign of trouble, toss the rifle away. We need the light more than we need a second gun."

She nodded at his advice. "Let's go. The spiders aren't gonna like their meal escaping."

Sam waved for Norman and Ralph to go first, just in case of trouble. Sam and Maggie would follow.

Norman slid down to a small spit of rock just above the waterline, arms cartwheeling for balance. "Now," he called up to Ralph.

The large football player bit his lower lip, clutched the camera case to his chest, and jumped in before his fear of the water drove him away.

Maggie kept her light focused on them. Norman dived in smoothly, his lithe form coming up beside the floundering black man. "Lie on your back!" Norman yelled as the current dragged the two away. "Hug the case tight to your chest!"

Ralph fumbled around a bit more, coughing water and kicking frantically.

"Don't fight it!"

Ralph finally obeyed, rolling to his back.

Norman swam at his side, one hand snarled in the neck of Ralph's shirt, keeping the man's head above water. As the two drifted away, Norman admonished the big man with one final warning. "Keep tight to that case," he sputtered. "Lose my cameras, and I'll let you drown!"

"We're next," Sam said, shoving his Stetson into his pack. "You ready?"

Maggie took a deep breath and nodded.

"You gonna be okay?" he said, straightening and meeting her eyes.

Maggie knew he was referring to her panic attacks more than the threat from the water. "It was my idea, wasn't it? I'll be fine."

"You first then," he said.

She opened her mouth to argue when she felt a tickle on her leg. Glancing down, she saw a tarantula as large as a fist climbing up her khakis. Gasping in disgust, she knocked it away with her flashlight. Raising Gil's snub-nosed rifle above her head, she jumped gracelessly into the water.

Her back and bottom crashed into the water with a resounding splash. The brief sting of the impact was immediately replaced with lung-constricting cold. Her head burst above the water with a silent scream of shock. All her muscles cramped tight. She had to force her limbs to move. The cold burned through her clothes and froze the breath in her lungs.

Sam splashed just behind her.

Before she could turn or speak, the current grabbed her and started sweeping her down the channel. Maggie floated on her back, legs thrust before her so she could bounce off any unseen obstacles. She kept the flashlight above the water and used the stock of the rifle as a paddle to help her stay afloat.

Just at the edge of her light's reach, she saw Norman and Ralph disappearing down the throat of the river tunnel.

Sam called to her. "How you holding up?"

Maggie frowned. Now was not the time for a conversation. She spat out a mouthful of cold water after a sudden splash had caught her by surprise. The icy water froze even the fillings in her mouth. "Fine!" she sputtered.

Then the current dragged her into the black maw of the tunnel. The low roof flew by overhead, low enough that the tip of the rifle dragged along the rock above. Small sparks spat out where steel and rock rubbed. The scraping sound was eerily loud in the tight space.

Just as suddenly they were out of the tunnel and into the bat cave. Maggie's eyes instantly stung; her nose burned. Overhead, circling bats dove and glided through the edge of the flashlight's beam, still disturbed and wary of the two-legged intruders. A small sliver of sunlight lightened one corner of the arched roof. The bat's doorway. Too high and too small to do them any good.

But Maggie had little time for sight-seeing. The current had grown even swifter through this chamber, a mixed blessing. Though the swift waters churned a cloud of mist that washed away the worst of the guano fumes, the faster waters also frothed and tossed her body more vigorously.

Maggie's limbs grew leaden as the cold tried to freeze the marrow of her bones. Breathing became laborious. She gave up trying to keep the rifle above water and used it as a rudder to keep her from bouncing too hard against the jagged rocks on either side. She concentrated on just keeping the flashlight pointed forward.

Now nearly blind from the fumes and with her nose on fire, Maggie gasped and choked. Something suddenly scrabbled at her upraised arm, weighting it down, digging at her skin. Blinking, Maggie saw a huge bat perched on her arm, tiny claws scratching at her, leathered wings batting wildly. Sharp fangs glinted in the glow of the flashlight. She let out a strangled gasp. Wide eyes and huge ears swung toward the sound. Crying out, she shoved her arm underwater, taking her chances that the flashlight was insulated enough to take a short dunk. She was in luck; the flashlight shone brightly under the water, and the shock of the cold stream dislodged the bat.

It rolled through the water, bumping against her shoulder as it passed.

Maggie lifted the flashlight from the water, paddling fiercely.

Then the bat was on her again. Maggie felt a small tug on her hair trailing in the water. Like a hooked fish, the bat had snatched at this purchase. Now twisting and rolling, it climbed the tangled strands. Maggie felt tiny claws scratch at her scalp. The bat screeched wildly, almost in her ear.

The creature's distress call was answered from above. The cavern erupted with squeaks and supersonic piping, like fingernails dragged across a blackboard. Overhead, the roof seemed to drop lower as the entire massed colony took flight, diving toward the screeching bat tangled in Maggie's hair.

Oh, God! She beat at the winged creature with her flashlight, trying to club it away, but only succeeded in snarling it further. Claws ripped across her cold cheek, a line of fire.

Suddenly a hand appeared, pushing back her flashlight. "Hold still!"

It was Sam. He grabbed the squirming bat and ripped it from its nest in her hair, tearing out hundreds of roots along with the foul creature. He tossed it away. The bat hit the far bank with a wet smack.

"Here they come!" Sam yelled.

Maggie barely had time to see the dark cloud descend toward them, and even less time to take a breath, before Sam shoved her head underwater. Maggie would have panicked, but Sam held tight to her, his body close to hers, his touch the only warmth in the icy stream. She released control to him, letting him carry her as she held her trapped breath.

Soon the channel straightened, and the current grew swift and smooth. Maggie risked opening her eyes. The flashlight still glowed under the water, illuminating Sam's face. His blond hair, normally plastered under his Stetson, wove like fine kelp across his face. His eyes met hers. She drew strength from his solid gaze. He pulled her tighter to him. She didn't resist.

The current dragged them swiftly away, tumbling them to and fro. Maggie's lungs cried for air. Unable to hold out any longer, she wiggled slightly from Sam's grasp and pushed toward the surface. She would only risk a quick breath.

As her head popped from the water, she gulped air into her frozen lungs. She was ready to duck back down, when she noticed two things—the air had cleared of the burning sting and just ahead a small purplish glow lit the left bank.

Sam surfaced beside her with a whoosh of expelled air.

Maggie lifted her flashlight and pointed. "There!"

Sam twisted around. As they neared the site, Maggie spotted Norman helping Ralph from the water. The huge football player crawled on hands and knees. Atop the bank, Denal was limned in the eerie light of the Wood's lamp. His teeth shone a whitish purple as he waved the lamp overhead, signaling to them.

Together, Maggie and Sam kicked toward the shore, but they didn't have to struggle far. The channel curved with a deep natural eddy at the bend. The current tossed Maggie and Sam into the sluggish pocket. With limbs deadened by cold and clothes waterlogged, it was an effort to climb from the water. Like Ralph, Maggie found herself crawling onto the bank and collapsing on her back.

Sam threw himself across the rock beside her, tossing his Winchester up higher on the stony bank. "So much for keeping the guns dry."

Norman stepped beside Maggie. His teeth chattered as he spoke. "Y . . . you both need to keep moving. And . . . and get out of those wet clothes." He tugged off his own soaked shirt.

Maggie noticed Denal had already stripped to his skivvies, and Ralph was slowly kicking off his clinging pants.

"We're not out of danger yet," Norman continued. "That water was near freezing. We'll die unless we can get dry and warm."

Maggie found her limbs beginning to tremble. Sam glanced at her. "It's j . . . just the cold," she said, knowing what he was thinking.

"Up with the both of you," Norman said sternly.

Groaning, Sam pushed up as the photographer offered Maggie his arm. Too exhausted to object, she took Norman's hand and let him help her to her feet.

"Now strip," he said.

Maggie's fingers were numb and blue in the flashlight beam. She fumbled at her buttons and shrugged out of her shirt, too cold and exhausted to worry about exposing herself. *Hell*, she thought, yanking her zipper down, *a good blush would be welcome right now.*

Soon she stood in nothing but her wet bra and panties.

The others kept their eyes politely turned, except Denal, who stared widely at her. Once the boy realized he was caught gaping, he quickly looked away.

Maggie scowled to cover her grin. She slapped Sam on his damp boxers as she stepped past him. "Norman says to keep moving. We have to stay warm."

Maggie could feel Sam's eyes on her back as she moved away. The Texan mumbled behind her, "Oh, don't worry. Keep walking ahead of me dressed like that, and I'll be plenty warm."

This time she couldn't hide her smile.

"Th . . . this must lead somewhere," Sam said, trying to control his chattering teeth, as he pointed out the gold path that continued along the river.

No one answered, busy as they were shivering and rubbing frigid limbs. The icy water had lowered everyone's core body temperature and, with no way to start a fire, they were all at risk of hypothermia. They needed to find a dry, warm place . . . and soon.

Sam, who had moved ahead of them, suddenly called out. With his flashlight pointed over a rise in the trail, Sam's half-naked form was striking, limned in the back glow. Maggie had not realized just how fine a physique her fellow colleague had hidden under his baggy clothes. From broad shoulders down to his narrow waist and strong legs, Sam struck a handsome pose.

"Come see this!" Sam exclaimed, a broad grin on his face.

Maggie saw Norman grab for his camera case as she climbed to join the others.

Before her, spreading across a cavern as large as her university's soccer stadium, was a small dark city. Sam's light was the only source of illumination, but its dim glow was enough to light up the entire chamber. Houses of brick, some three stories high, dotted the floor, while up the walls climbed tier after tier of stacked granite homes, like a jumble of toy blocks. Empty windows stared back at them. Throughout the city, brighter splashes of gold and silver decorated many of the abodes. But what caught all their eyes was what stood in the town's center. Across the chamber, a massive gold statue stretched toward the ceiling, towering over the buildings. It was similar to the one that guarded the entrance to the cavern, but it was too distant and dark to make out any details.

"My God," Norman said, "it's a huge subterranean village."

As Maggie crossed to Sam's side, the mustiness of the chamber suddenly caught her attention, and she knew Norman's assessment was wrong. She recognized this smell—dusty decay mixed with the spiced scent of mummification herbs. "It's not a village," she corrected Norman, "but a *necropolis*. One of the Incas' underground cities of the dead."

Rubbing his arms and stamping his cold feet, Sam agreed. "A burial tomb . . . but I've never heard of one this extensive or elaborate."

Norman's flash exploded as the photographer snapped a series of rapid pictures. The added light froze the city in stark relief. "Maybe we can hole up in one of those houses and get warm. Pool our body heat like the Aleuts do in their igloos."

Maggie again noticed the deep ache from her cold limbs. "It's worth a try." She led the way toward the town's outskirts, following the gold path that ended at the city's edge.

Sam trailed behind. "I may have a better idea." But he did not elaborate when Maggie glanced over her shoulder. He just waved her ahead.

Maggie turned back, but not before noticing the purplish tinge to the Texan's lips. Behind Sam, the others fared no better. Ralph's limbs quaked and trembled as he followed. The big man seemed to fare the worst of all of them. He had swallowed a lot of icy water while traveling the stream and did not look well.

Hurrying, Maggie led the group quickly down the series of golden switchbacks to the cavern floor. She reached the town's edge, and the smell of earthy decay, like aged compost, filled her nostrils. She stared down the streets of this city of the dead. The tombs of the necropolis had been built like homes to keep the spirits of the deceased happy, reminding them of their prior lives, surrounding them with the familiar. Doorways bore sculpted lintels depicting various fanciful creatures, both mythological and zoomorphic—a mix of man and animal.

Just like the pillars that had marked the path.

Maggie touched one, a cross between a panther and a woman. "They depict the gods of *uca pacha*, protectors of the dead."

Across the avenue, Sam studied a brightly painted fresco on the side of a two-story building. He pointed. "And here are various *mallaqui* . . . spirits of the underworld."

Norman moved up to them. "I hate to interrupt your art history lecture, but Ralph is not looking so good."

Maggie glanced back. Ralph leaned against one of the doorways, head hanging. Even supported, his huge frame swayed slightly. "We need to find shelter. Get him warm."

Sam turned to Denal. "Are your matches still dry?"

The boy nodded. He pulled out a plastic-wrapped bundle from within his armful of damp clothes. It was the boy's extra box of cigarettes wrapped with a small box of matches. He passed the matches to Sam.

Maggie moved to Sam's side. "A fire? But what about kindling?"

As answer, Sam swung away and ducked into one of the neighboring abodes. From within, she heard shifting and sliding and realized in horror what Sam was planning. Sam backed out through the doorway, dragging something with him. With a grunt, he swung around, tossing his burden into the street. Bones cracked and clattered, and dust billowed up. It was a linen-wrapped mummy.

"They make good kindling," Sam said simply.

"Ugh!" Norman responded with disgust, and covered his mouth.

Having caught his breath, Sam crossed to the mummy and pulled free Denal's box of matches. Sam struck a match and soon had the linen wrap smoldering. Small flames grew as the old bones and leather inside fueled the fire. Orange flames spat higher and higher.

Maggie, while aghast at the source of kindling, still drew nearer the welcoming heat.

Sam, leaning on a wall now, jerked his arm at the surrounding necropolis. "If nothing else, we'll never have to worry about running out of wood."

Ralph sat as near to the flames as possible. After an hour, the heat had finally reached his cold bones. As he sat, he tried to ignore the source of the combustion. A mummified hand sprawled from the flames, quivering slightly from the heat. He glanced away.

Across the fire, Sam had taken apart both rifles and carefully cleaned and dry-fired them. Maggie half dozed in the warmth nearby, one arm around Denal. The Quechan boy stared into the flames, eyes wide and glazed. The day had taken its toll on all of them. Norman stood a few paces off. He had taken a couple of photographs, but Ralph could tell the photographer, as tired as he was, was itching to move deeper into the underground city. But not alone. The blackness, even with the fire, was like a physical presence, a dark stranger at their shoulders.

Norman seemed to catch Ralph studying him. He moved nearer. "How're you feeling?" Norman asked.

Ralph glanced away. "Better."

Norman settled on the stone floor beside him.

Before he could restrain himself, Ralph scooted an inch away.

Norman noticed the subtle shift. "Don't worry, big fella, I'm not making a move on you."

Ralph inwardly kicked himself. Old patterns were hard to erase. "Sorry . . ." he said softly. "I didn't mean anything."

"Yeah, right. Can't be caught sittin' next to the faggot."

"It's not that."

"Then what is it?"

Ralph hung his head. "Okay, maybe it was. I was raised strict Southern Baptist. My uncle Gerald was even a minister with the Church. We get that sort of thinkin' drilled into us."

"So what else is new? My parents were Mormon. They weren't too thrilled to learn I was gay either." Norman snorted. "Neither was the army, for that matter. I was kicked out of both families."

Ralph could not face Norman. While he had experienced prejudice during his life, Ralph at least had his family around him for support.

Norman stood up, camera in hand.

Ralph suddenly reached out and gripped Norman's hand. The thin photographer flinched. "Thanks. For back at the river."

Norman pulled his hand free, suddenly and uncharacteristically awkward. "No problem. Just don't try and kiss me. I'm not that type of girl."

"That's not what I heard," Ralph said.

Norman turned away. "Oh, man, Ralph, the comedian. I miss the bigoted jock already."

By the early evening, Henry felt even more out of place. He now trailed behind Joan and Dale as they marched through the deserted halls of Johns Hopkins. At this point in the evening, they were the last ones around. After the endless battery of tests in Joan's lab, they were retiring to her office to plan the next day's experiments.

As they walked, the two researchers were still deep in conversation about the mysterious material. "We'll need a complete crystallography assay of Substance Z," the gangly metallurgist said in an excited rush, using his new name for the strange element.

Henry sensed the man was already planning in which research journals to publish his findings.

"And I'd like to see how the material reacts in the presence of other radiation, especially gamma rays."

Joan nodded. "I'll check with the nuclear lab. I'm sure something can be arranged."

As Henry followed behind them, he lifted the beaker of the material and studied the crude replica of the Dominican cross. Substance Z. The other two scientists weren't seeing the forest through the trees. Here was the bigger mystery. The chemical and molecular attributes of the material, though intriguing, were nothing compared to the fact that the material had transformed on its own.

Neither of the other two seemed to place much weight on that fact. The metallurgist had attributed the transformation to the proximity of the material to the gold cross itself, theorizing some transfer of energy or electrons that made the material churn into its new form. "All metal gives off a unique energy signature," Dale had explained. "With the sample's acute sensitivity to various radiation, the material must have responded to the gold, changing its crystalline matrix to match the signature. It's amazing!"

Henry had disagreed, but had remained silent. He knew the answer lay elsewhere. He remembered how he had been pondering the code on the crucifix when the transformation had occurred. It was not the proximity to the cross that had changed Substance Z, but the proximity to *Henry*. Something had happened, but Henry was not ready to voice any wild speculations aloud—at least not yet. It was not his way, not until he had more information. One of the first lessons he taught his students—proceed with knowledge, not speculation. To Henry, the only thing certain about Substance Z was that it should not be dabbled with lightly. But the other two scientists were deaf to his rumblings of caution.

His right hand fingered the Dominican crucifix resting in the pocket of his sports jacket. Friar Francisco de Almagro knew something, something he had wanted to tell the outside world, his final testament. Henry suspected that the answers to the mysteries of Substance Z would not be found in nuclear labs or research facilities, but instead, in the crude scratches on the back of the friar's cross. Yet, before Henry dared to voice his own opinions or conduct his own experiments, he first planned to decipher this ancient code.

And Henry knew exactly where to start. Tomorrow he would again consult the archbishop. Perhaps some old records might mention a code among the Dominican friars.

"Here we are," Joan announced. She jingled her keys from a pocket and went to open the door. Grabbing the knob, the door gave way under her touch. "That's odd. It's unlocked. Maybe I forgot—"

She began to push the door open when Henry suddenly stopped her. "No!" He grabbed the pathologist by the elbow. Remembering that Joan had locked the door earlier, he yanked her away from the open doorway, tripping over a janitor's bucket behind him. He barely kept his balance.

"Henry!" she yelled in shock.

Dale scowled at him as if the archaeologist had gone mad. "What are you doing?"

Henry did not have time to explain. Danger signals reverberated up and down his spine. "Run!"

But it was too late.

Behind Dale's shoulder, a dark figure appeared in the doorway to Joan's office. "Don't move," the trespasser ordered coldly.

Startled, Dale swung around, his face draining of color. He backed up several quick steps in the opposite direction from Henry and Joan.

The man moved forward into the hall. He wore a charcoal suit over a black shirt and tie; his skin was coppery, with Spanish features, ebony hair, dark eyes. But what drew most of Henry's attention was the large pistol, outfitted with a thick silencer, in his right fist. He brandished it back and forth, covering both sides of the hallway. "Which of you has the gold crucifix? Relinquish it and you'll live."

Dale quickly pointed to Henry.

The assailant swung the barrel in his direction. "Professor Conklin, do not make me shoot you."

At that moment, the metallurgist's courage ran out. With the gunman's back turned, Dale made a run for it. His expensive shoes betrayed him, hard heels striking loudly on the waxed linoleum. The gunman did not even turn. He simply pointed his pistol back and fired; the shot was muffled by the silencer—but its effect was not. The force of the bullet knocked Dale off his feet. He went flying headfirst to the floor, skidding several feet before stopping, leaving a trail of blood across the white tiles. He tried to push up once, then collapsed back down, a dark pool spreading under him.

"Now, Professor Conklin," the burglar said, holding out his free hand. "The cross, please."

Before Henry could respond, a second dark-suited man stepped from Joan's office. He glanced at the fallen metallurgist, then back to the shooter. He spoke rapidly in Spanish, but Henry understood. "Carlos, I've destroyed all the paperwork and files."

The leader, Carlos, glanced to the other man. He lowered the pistol slightly. "And the computer?"

"The hard drive has been wiped and purged."

Carlos nodded.

Henry used the momentary distraction of the newcomer to slip the Dominican crucifix from his jacket pocket and flip it into the toppled janitor's bucket. Only Joan noticed. Her eyes were huge with fear.

Raising the pistol, Carlos turned to Henry. "I'm losing patience, Professor. The cross, please."

Henry stepped forward, placing himself between the shooter and Joan. He held out the beaker with the crude cross. He hoped the shape and the color would fool these thieves. He refused to lose the ancient relic.

The man's eyes narrowed suspiciously. He took the beaker and held it before him. Even distracted, the pistol never wavered from where it pointed, straight at Henry's heart.

The shooter's accomplice stood at the man's shoulders. "Is it . . . ?"

Carlos ignored the man, still staring at the mock-up of the original crucifix. Whispered words of a Spanish prayer flowed from his lips, a benediction. Then the cross in the beaker changed, melting before the man's gaze into a perfectly symmetrical pyramid.

Henry gasped.

The second man fell to his knees. "*Dios mio!*"

Carlos lowered the beaker, his hand shaking. "We've found it!" Exultant, he turned to his captives.

Henry backed into Joan. She clutched his hand fiercely. Henry sensed he had made a grave miscalculation. The thieves hadn't been after the Dominican crucifix because it was *gold*, but because they had suspected it was made of *Substance Z*. Henry had inadvertently handed them the very prize they had sought. Who were these people?

Carlos nodded toward Henry and Joan, but his brusque orders were for his companion. "Silence them."

The second man stood, pulling his own gun, much larger and more intimidating than the leader's weapon.

"Wait!" Henry begged.

Ignoring him, the man aimed his pistol at Henry and fired. Henry's chest exploded with fire. Joan screamed. Henry fell to his knees, his hand slipping from Joan's. He glanced up in time to see the man twist the gun toward Joan.

"No!" he moaned, raising one hand futilely.

Too late. A muffled shot.

Joan clutched her own chest and fell. She turned stunned eyes to Henry, then glanced down. Henry followed her gaze. Her fingers pulled out a feathered barb from between her breasts, then she fell backward.

Henry glanced to his own chest. There was no bleeding bullet hole, only a red-feathered spot of agony. Tranquilizing darts?

Words, in Spanish, floated around him as the drug took effect.

"Get the men up here now."

"What about the dead one?"

"Leave him in the office along with the janitor's body."

Carlos's face suddenly bloomed close to Henry's. His wavery dark eyes were huge. Henry felt lost in them. "We're going for a short ride, Professor. Pleasant dreams."

Henry slumped, but not before noticing the tiny silver cross dangling from a chain around the man's neck. He had seen it before. It was an exact match to the one found on the mummified friar.

A Dominican cross!

Before he could ponder this newest mystery, the black grip of the drug hauled him away.

DAY FOUR
Necropolis

Thursday, August 23, 7:45 A.M.
Caverns
Andean Mountains, Peru

Sam awoke on the stone floor of the cavern as someone nudged his side with a toe. Now what? Groaning a protest, he rolled away from the fire and found Norman standing nearby, staring out at the dark necropolis. The photographer had pulled the last guard shift. Even though the bat cave stood between them and the tarantula army, no one had been willing to take any chances.

"What is it?" Sam asked groggily, rubbing his eyes. After yesterday's labors and near deadly swim in the icy stream, he wished for nothing more than another half day beside the warmth of the crackling flames.

Even the smell was rather pleasant, considering the source of the fuel—almost a burnt cinnamon. From the heart of the bonfire, a charred skull glared through the flames at him. Stretching, Sam pushed up. "Why did you wake me?"

Norman kept staring at the shadowed tombs of the Incan dead. "It's getting lighter in here," he finally said.

Sam frowned. "What are you talking about? Did someone throw another log on the fire?" He glanced to the three bundled mummies stacked nearby like cords of wood, waiting to stoke the flames.

Norman swung around; he held a small device in his palm. It was his light meter. "No. While on guard, I checked a few readings. Since five o'clock this morning, the meter has been reading rising footcandles." Norman's glasses reflected the firelight. "You know what that must mean?"

Sam was too tired to think this early, not without at least a canteen of coffee. He pushed to a seated position. "Just spill it already."

"Dawn," Norman said, as if this made it all clear.

Sam just looked at him.

Norman sighed. "You really aren't a morning person, are you, Sam?"

By now the others were stirring slowly from their makeshift beds. "What's going on?" Maggie asked around a wide yawn.

"Riddles," Sam said.

Norman shot Sam a sour look and stepped closer to encompass the entire group as he spoke. "My light meter's been registering stronger and stronger signals since dawn."

Maggie sat up straighter. "Really?" She glanced beyond the firelight at the dark cave.

"I waited a couple hours to be sure. I didn't want to give anyone false hope."

Sam pushed to his feet. He wore only his pants. His vest still lay drying beside the fire. He had been using it as a pillow. "You're not suggesting—?"

Maggie interrupted, her words laced with excitement. "Maybe Norman's right. If the readings are stronger as the morning progresses, then sunlight must be getting down here from somewhere." She clapped Norman on the shoulder and shook him happily. "By Jesus, there must be a way out nearby!"

Her words sank into Sam's consciousness. *A way out!* Sam stepped to the pair. "You're sure the meter is not just registering flare-ups in the campfire?"

Norman frowned as Ralph and Denal edged around the fire to join the group. "No, Sam." He lifted his device. "It's definitely picking up sunlight."

Sam nodded, satisfied with the photographer's expertise. Norman was no fool. Sam squinted at the dark cavern. Firelight basked the walls and reflected off the monstrous gold statue in the center of the city. Sam prayed Norman was correct in his conclusions. "Then let's find out where that light's coming from. Can you use the meter to track the source?"

"Maybe . . ." Norman said. "If I keep it shielded from the torches and widen the f-stop . . ." He shrugged.

Ralph volunteered a suggestion. He seemed back to his old self since yesterday's trials, only perhaps slightly more subdued. "Maybe Norm and I could circle the camp and search out where the light reads the strongest. It should give us a direction to start."

Sam nudged the photographer when he did not immediately respond. "Norman?"

The thin man glanced at the wall of darkness at the edge of the fire's pool of light. He did not look like he cared for Ralph's idea, but he finally admitted reluctantly, "It might work."

"Good." Sam rubbed his hands and put a plan together. "While you reconnoiter, we'll finish breaking down the camp. Take the flashlight. You can click it on and off as you take your readings. But be careful, the batteries on this one are wearing down, too."

Ralph took the flashlight and tested it, thumbing the switch. "We'll be careful."

Norman glanced to the fire, then back to the darkness. "If we're gonna do this, we'd better hurry. There's no telling when we might lose the sunlight. Even passing clouds could block the footcandles stretching down to us." Contrary to his own words, Norman still hesitated, his face tight.

Sam noticed the photographer's tension. "What's wrong?"

Norman shook his head. "Nothing. I've just seen too many cheap horror movies."

"So?"

"Splitting up the group. In horror movies, that's when the killer starts knocking off the college co-eds."

Sam laughed, believing the photographer was cracking a joke—but Norman wasn't smiling. Sam's laughter died. "You don't seriously think—"

Suddenly something huge crashed into the bonfire. Flaming bits of wrap and bone exploded outward, stinging bare flesh and rattling across the stone floor. Smoke billowed, and darkness threatened to consume the group as the campfire was scattered. Luckily, a large flaming brand landed atop the stacked mummies nearby and set them on fire, returning the light. Shadows from the various pyres danced across the walls of the tombs.

Sam spun around, pulling Maggie behind him. Amid the ruins of their original fire rested a large square block, clearly a hewn-granite brick from one of the structures. He glanced up. There was no over-hanging cornice from where the huge block could have fallen.

Ralph voiced Sam's own thoughts. "That was no accident." The Alabama football player clicked on his flashlight and stabbed its beam into the darkness beyond the reach of the fires.

"Get the guns," Sam said. "Now."

Ralph nodded, tossing the light to Norman, then grabbed the rifle leaning against the stone wall. Sam bent and retrieved his own Winchester from beside his make-shift bed. Maggie kept close to his side, Denal at her hip.

Beyond the occasional crack and snap from the fire as dried bones burst from the heat, nothing could be heard. Yet all around them, Sam could sense move-ment. Shadows danced in the firelight, but some of the pools of darkness seemed to slink and slide. Something was out there, closing in on them.

"Ghosts come for us," Denal mumbled.

Maggie put her arm around the boy's shoulder. She comforted the lad, but no one argued against his words. The spread of the necropolis, limned in flame and thick with shifting shadows, made even their worst nightmares seem possible.

But what moved through the necropolis was much worse.

Norman's flashlight caught one of the slinking inter-lopers in his beam. It froze for a heartbeat like a deer in headlights—but this was no doe or buck. As pale as the albino tarantulas, it stood on two legs, naked, hunched, knuckling on one long, thickly muscled arm. Sam's first thought was ape, but the creature was hair-less, bald-pated.

It hissed at the light—at them—huge black eyes narrowed to angry slits, teeth pointed and sharp. Then it flew from the light, disappearing into the gloom, moving faster than Sam would have thought possible.

It had appeared and vanished so quickly that none of the group had time to comment. Sam had not even thought to raise his rifle; neither had Ralph. Norman's beam jittered as the photographer's arm trembled.

"What in bloody hell was that?" Maggie finally whispered.

Sam positioned his Winchester to his shoulder. In the distance, faint echoes could be heard all around them: the scrape of rock, strangled hisses, guttural coughs, even one piercing howl, clearly a challenge being trum-peted. It sounded as if scores of the creatures had them trapped, surrounded, but the cavern acoustics were de-ceptive. Ralph met Sam's gaze, fear glinting bright in the big man's eyes.

"What are they?" Maggie repeated.

"*Mallaqui*," Denal answered. Spirits of the underworld.

"And you wanted Ralph and me to go out there alone," Norman said, voice squeaking, flashlight trembling. "Let's take a lesson from horror flicks. We stick together from here on."

No one argued. In fact, no one said a word.

All eyes stared into the dark heart of the necropolis.

Henry woke and wished he hadn't. His head ached and throbbed as if someone had been using his temples for a drum solo. His mouth was full of sour acid and as sticky as Elmer's glue. He groaned because that was all he was capable of doing for the moment. Taking several breaths, he concentrated on making out his surroundings. The only light came from a slitted window high up the rear wall of the tiny room.

Memories of the attack in the halls of Johns Hopkins returned. One of his hands crawled across his chest to finger a tender spot in its center. The feathered barb was gone. Slowly he pushed up to find himself lying atop a frame bed, poorly cushioned by a worn mattress. He still wore his same clothes—Levi's and a grey shirt; only his Ralph Lauren sports coat was gone. Tossing aside a thin wool blanket, Henry pushed himself up.

The room was spartan. Besides the bed, the only other pieces of furniture were a wormwood desk huddled in the back corner and a prayer bench set before a plain wooden crucifix. Henry stared at the cross, its deep cherry stain stark against the whitewashed plaster. Before his mind's eye, he again pictured the silver Dominican cross hanging from around his attacker's neck. What the hell was going on?

He swung his feet to the floor, causing his ears to ring and his vision to dim for a fraction of a second. He took a deep breath, but not before noticing a strong, familiar smell from the tattered blanket on the bed. He fingered the coarse wool, which was slightly greasy. He raised it to his nose and sniffed. Llama. Wool from the llama was the poorest quality of the textiles produced in South American countries, used by the peasants only. It was seldom exported.

Understanding slowly dawned. South America?

Henry quickly stood, wobbling for a moment on his weak legs, then quickly regaining his strength. "No, it can't be!"

He stepped to the only door, short-framed but solid. He tested the latch. Locked, of course. Moving to the room's center, he stared up at the high window. Birds whistled in some nearby tree, and a warm breeze stirred the dust motes in the stream of sunlight. Too bright.

Henry sensed that this was not the same day when he had been shot by the tranquilizer dart. How long had he been out? The thin breeze smelled of frying oil, and in the distance rose the vague noises of a market, its strident voices hawking wares in Spanish.

Henry's heart sank as he realized the truth. He had been abducted, whisked out of the country. Another face appeared to him: straight fall of midnight hair, bright eyes, full lips. His breath caught in his throat as he remembered Joan pulling the feathered dart from between her breasts and slumping to the floor. Where was she?

More worried about Joan than himself, Henry stepped to the door and pounded his fist, shaking the planks in their frame. Before he could even call out, a small peekhole slid open near the top of the door. Dark eyes stared at him.

"I want to know what—!"

The peephole slammed shut. Muffled words, too low to hear distinctly, were exchanged a few paces down the hall. Someone left in a hurry. Henry pounded the door again. "Let me out of here!"

He had not truly expected a response; he had only been venting his frustration. So he was shocked when someone responded to his call. A voice called to him from down the hall. "Henry? Is that you?"

Relief flooded his chest, cooling his hot blood. "Joan!"

"Are you okay?" she yelled back.

"Fine. How 'bout you?"

"Sore, sick, and mad as hell."

Henry heard a lot of fear in her voice, too. He didn't know what to say. Apologize for getting her in this trouble? Offer false promises of rescue? He cleared his throat and called back. "Sorry . . . that wasn't much of a second date, was it?" he called out.

A long pause . . . then a soft chuckle. "I've had worse!"

Henry pressed both palms against the door. He longed to wrap his arms around her.

From outside the cell, the sound of someone approaching suddenly echoed down the hall. Joan must have heard, too; she grew quiet. Henry held his breath. Now what? A voice, firm and curt, spat just outside his door. Henry recognized the cadence of an order.

The grate of a sliding bolt sounded, then the door to his cell swung open. Henry did not know what he had expected, but he was shocked when he discovered two robed monks outside his cell. Their cowls were tossed back and prominent crucifixes hung from beaded chains around their necks.

Henry stepped away as his gaze fixed on the familiar face of the taller monk. It was the gunman from Johns

Hopkins, the one named Carlos. Once again, the man held a pistol in his grip, but this time there was no silencer. "Be cooperative, Professor Conklin, and all will go well."

"Wh . . . where am I? What do you want with us?"

Carlos ignored him, instead signaling his companion. The guard crossed to another door down the hall and freed the bolt. Swinging the door open, he barked in Spanish and pulled a gun from a slit at the waist of his robe. He waved its muzzle, signaling the occupant to vacate the room.

Joan stepped out cautiously, her eyes instantly finding Henry's. He saw the clear relief in her gaze. Tears glistened. She wiped brusquely at her face and needed no further prodding from the guard to join Henry and Carlos. Her eyes flicked a moment to the pistol in the taller monk's hand, then back to Henry. "Why are we here?" she whispered. "What do they want?"

Before Henry could answer, Carlos spoke. "Come. Your questions will be answered." Turning on his heel, the tall monk led them down the hall. The other monk, gun in fist, followed.

Joan slipped her hand into Henry's. He squeezed as much reassurance into her grip as possible. If these men had meant them dead, they wouldn't have drugged them and dragged them all the way here. But where was here? And what did they want? There was only one way to find out.

Henry followed Carlos. He studied the swish of the gunman's robe, sandals tapping quietly on the flagstone floor. And why these damnable disguises?

As they were led down a maze of halls and up two flights of stairs, Joan remained silent at his side. Her gait was stiff. They passed only one other monk in the hallway, a cowled figure, head bowed. He stepped aside to let the procession pass without raising his face. Henry heard a mumbled prayer upon the man's lips as he walked past. He never looked up.

Henry glanced back; the monk continued down the hall, either unaware or uncaring about the guns and prisoners.

"Strange," he mumbled.

At last, Carlos stopped before a set of large double doors, polished and waxed to a brilliant sheen. African mahogany, Henry guessed, and expensive. Carved in relief upon the doors was a mountain range with villages dotting the slopes. Henry knew the view. He had seen it many times while visiting Peru. It was a well-known region of the Andean mountains.

Henry frowned at the door as Carlos knocked.

A deep voice answered, "*Entrada!*"

Carlos swept open the doors on oiled hinges and revealed a room as handsome as the mahogany doors. An ornate prayer altar, adorned in silver and gold leaf, stood in the corner, while underfoot, an elaborate woven alpaca rug cushioned Henry's steps as he entered. To either side, shelves lined with dusty volumes filled the walls from floor to ceiling. In the center of the room, a massive desk rested, with an incongruous computer stationed at one end.

Behind the immense desk, a large man, elderly but still vigorous, pushed to his feet with a squeak of his chair. His size made even the desk seem small.

But Henry ignored the man and room, his eyes drawn to the wide windows beyond. Outside rose the steeple of a stately colonial church, towering above the surrounding town. Henry gaped at the view, shocked. He instantly recognized the landmark structure, knew with certainty where he was—Cuzco, Peru. Beyond the windows stood the Spanish Church of Santo Domingo, a Dominican church built atop the ruins of the Incas' Temple of the Sun.

Henry glanced back to the room at hand. Knowledge of where they had been imprisoned suddenly dawned. The monks, the view, even the figure now standing behind the wide desk, grinning a welcome . . .

Oh, God.

Henry stepped forward, eyes coming to rest on the large man, his captor. His features were distinctly Spanish, almost aristocratic. Henry recalled his conversation with the archbishop back in Baltimore. The bishop had promised to pass on the archaeologist's questions to a Dominican colleague in Peru. Henry remembered the name that the archbishop had mentioned. "Abbot Ruiz?" he said aloud.

The huge man bowed his head in greeting. "Professor Conklin, welcome to the Abbey of Santo Domingo." He seemed unperturbed by Henry's recognition. Abbot Ruiz's girth matched his height. His chest and belly swelled his cassock and black robe. His large size did not seem soft, more like a man who had once been solid with muscle, but whose shape had become bulky with age.

Henry faced his adversary. He had always considered himself a good judge of character, but the abbot confounded him. His manner was open and friendly. Silver-haired, he seemed a kindly grandfather. But Henry knew, considering the circumstances, that this judgment could not be further from the truth.

Joan shifted beside Henry. "You know this man?"

Henry shook his head. "Not exactly."

Abbot Ruiz waved them toward a pair of overstuffed chairs. "Professor Conklin and Dr. Engel, please make yourselves comfortable."

Henry stepped nearer the desk. "I'd prefer to stand until I get some answers."

"As you wish," he said, wearing a wounded expression. The abbot returned to his own seat, sinking into it with a sigh.

Joan joined Henry at the desk. "Just what do you want with us, goddammit?"

The abbot frowned, the false warmth melting from his face. "This is a holy place of our Lord. Refrain from blasphemies here."

"Blasphemies?" Henry said angrily. "Your man over there killed a colleague of ours, then drugged and kidnapped us. Just how many Commandments, let alone international laws, did he break?"

"We care not for secular laws. Friar Carlos is a warrior in the Lord's army and above any international rules. As for Friar Carlos's soul, do not fear. He has been absolved in Holy Confession, his sins forgiven."

Henry scowled. They were all mad.

Joan spoke up. "Fine . . . everyone's soul has been cleaned, pressed, and folded. Now why the *heck* have you kidnapped us?"

The abbot's face remained tight, angered—the kindly grandfather persona long gone. "Two reasons. First, we wish to learn more of what Professor Conklin has discovered at the ruins in the Andes. And second, what both of you have learned in the States from the mummy."

"We'll not cooperate," Henry said sternly.

Ruiz fingered a large seal ring on his right hand, twisting it around and around the digit. "That is yet to be seen," he said coldly. "Our order has grown skilled over the centuries at loosening tongues."

Henry's blood chilled at the man's words. "Who are you?"

Ruiz clucked his tongue. "I ask the questions here, Professor Conklin." The abbot reached to a desk drawer and pulled it open. He lifted a familiar object from within and placed it upon his desk. It was the laboratory beaker containing Substance Z. The golden material was still in the shape of the small pyramid. "Where exactly did you find this?"

Henry pictured the mummy's head exploding. He sensed he had better not lie, not until he figured out how much these others knew. Still, he refused to give away the complete truth. "We found it . . . in Friar de Almagro's possession."

Joan glanced sharply at him.

The abbot's eyes opened wider. "So our old colleague was successful in his mission. He *had* discovered the source of *el Sangre del Diablo*."

Henry's brows bunched as he translated the abbot's words. "The blood of the Devil?"

Ruiz studied Henry in silence for several moments, then steepled his fingers before him and spoke slowly. "I sense you know more than you're voicing, Professor Conklin. And though we've refined our tools over the centuries, I think simple honesty may gain your cooperation more easily and fully. You are, after all, a man of science and history . . . and curiosity may win out where threats fail. Would you hear me out?"

"As if I had any choice . . ."

Abbot Ruiz stood again. He collected the beaker and made it vanish within the folds of his vestments. "All men have free will, Professor Conklin. It is what damns us or saves us." The abbot stepped around his desk and waved for the monk named Carlos to lead the way. "The Sanctum," he ordered.

Henry noted the friar's shocked expression, then the quick nod and the turn of a heel. Carlos opened the office door and led them out.

Ever the good soldier of the Lord, Henry thought.

"Where are you taking us now?" Joan asked, sticking to Henry's side.

Ruiz marched beside them as they reentered the hallway. "To reveal the truth in the hopes that you will be equally open."

"The truth about *el Sangre del Diablo*?" Henry asked, prying for more information. "How do you know about it?"

The abbot sighed loudly, seeming to weigh whether or not to answer. Finally, he spoke. "The metal was first discovered by the Spanish conquistadors here in Cuzco." The abbot waved a hand. "It was found in the Incas' sacred Temple of the Sun."

"The ruins under the Church of Santo Domingo?" Henry asked. The temple had first been described by historian Pedro de Cieza de Leon as among the richest in gold and silver to be found anywhere in the world. Even the walls of the Incan temple had been plated with inch-thick slabs of gold—until the Spanish had ransacked and stripped it, tearing the structure down to the foundations to build their God's church atop it.

"Exactly," Ruiz said with a sigh. "The temple must have been a wondrous sight before it was pillaged. A shame really."

"And this Devil's blood?" Joan pressed. "Why that name?"

The group reached a long winding staircase leading deep into the heart of the Abbey. The abbot moved slowly down the steps, his great bulk hindering him. He wheezed slightly as he spoke. "The Incas had colorful names for silver and gold—the moon's tears, the sun's sweat. When the Spanish conquerors first learned of this other metal and witnessed its unearthly properties, they declared the material blasphemous, naming it just as colorfully *el Sangre del Diablo.* Satan's Blood."

Henry found himself being drawn into this story. This was his field of expertise, but he had heard no such stories. "Why are there no records of this discovery?"

The abbot shrugged. "Because the Church was summoned and agreed with the conquistadors. The metal was studied, its unusual properties noted, and was declared by Pope Paul III in 1542 to be an abomination in the eyes of our Lord. The work of Satan. The Dominicans who had accompanied the Spanish confiscated all such samples and returned them to Rome, for purification. All records of the metal's discovery were destroyed. To speak of it or write of it was deemed the same as communing with the Devil." The abbot glanced to the walls as they followed Friar Carlos. "Several historians were burned when they resisted the Pope's decree, here in this very building. It was our order's burden to preserve the secrecy."

"Your order . . . you keep saying that as if you're separate from the Catholic Church."

Ruiz frowned. "We are most definitely a part of the Holy Roman Church." The abbot glanced away, almost guiltily. "Unfortunately, most of Rome has forgotten us. Except for a handful of men in the Vatican, none still know this order's true mission."

"Which is?" Henry asked.

Ruiz shook his question away. "Come and you will see."

They had reached the bottom of the long staircase. Henry estimated they had to be at least fifty feet underground. A string of raw lightbulbs lit the way ahead. Henry glanced to the walls and was startled to see the characteristic work of the Incas—massive blocks of granite stacked and jigsawed together with immense skill.

The abbot must have noticed as Henry ran his palm along the wall. "We are now under the Abbey. Like the Church of Santo Domingo, the Abbey also rests on ancient Incan foundations. These passages actually merge and connect to the Temple of the Sun."

"Are we going there?" Joan asked. "To this temple?"

"No . . . we're going somewhere even more astounding."

With Carlos still leading, the group traveled the maze of passages. Henry noted the occasional wooden footbridge straddling open sections of the stone floor. At first, he attributed them to regions where the ancient Incan stonework had succumbed to earthquakes or simple wear. Then, as he crossed another of these bridges, he realized they were too regular and the pits too square. He suddenly suspected where the group traveled.

"This is the place of the pit!" Henry blurted out, staring back at the warren of hallways with their many twists and turns.

"So you've heard of this place?" Ruiz said with a smile.

"Place of the pit?" Joan asked.

"An underground labyrinth. A hellhole where Incan rulers tossed their most hated enemies. It was fraught with booby-trapped pitfalls lined by razored flint. They'd also throw in scorpions, spiders, snakes, even injured pumas, to torment the prisoners."

Joan studied the walls around them. "How awful . . ."

"It was one of the Incas' most infamous torture chambers. The Spanish conquistadors wrote extensively of it. It was supposed to be here in Cuzco, but it was believed long destroyed." Henry turned to the abbot. "Apparently it wasn't."

Carlos stopped at a bend in the corridor. He stood stiffly by a bare section of stone wall, almost at attention. From his narrowed angry eyes, the friar plainly did not agree with the abbot's decision to bring the captives here.

Abbot Ruiz stepped beside Carlos. "We've reached the center of the labyrinth. The Sanctum of our order."

Henry glanced up and down the corridor. All he saw were stacked granite blocks. There was no sign of a door.

The abbot approached the bare wall and pressed his large ruby ring against a small stainless-steel plate embedded in a shadowed cubbyhole. Then he stepped back as the grind of gears sounded from behind the bricks.

Henry tensed, not knowing what to expect.

Suddenly a section of the granite wall slowly dropped away, sinking into the floor. Bright light blazed from within, its effect almost blinding after the dimness of the dark hallways. With a groan, the section dropped fully away.

As the glare faded, Henry stared openmouthed.

Joan gasped beside him.

Ahead lay a large chamber, the size of a small warehouse. Starkly white and shining with stainless steel, it was an extensive state-of-the-art laboratory. Beyond the windows and vacuum-sealed glass doors, a legion of figures, dressed in sterile suits, labored at various stations. Muffled by the glass walls, the strains of Beethoven floated out from the laboratory.

Henry glanced back to the Incan stonework labyrinth, then back to the technologically advanced laboratory. "Okay, you've got my attention."

The expected attack never came. A full hour had passed by the time Sam stepped away from the large bonfire, rifle held tight to his shoulder. The dark necropolis rose to shadowed heights all around them. Firelight splashed across the nearest tombs, but most of the city of the dead was shrouded by an inky blackness. Only the towering gold statue at the center of town reflected the flames, a blazing pillar of brightness in the midnight cavern.

Nothing moved out there.

"Maybe they left," Norman whispered.

Sam disagreed. "They're still out there."

"It's the flames," Maggie finally said, her voice sharp but quiet, drawing the men's eyes momentarily from the tense vigil of the necropolis. "They tried to destroy the first campfire, hurling that big rock. But it was only chance that lit the stack of other mummies by accident. If the fire had failed us completely, we'd all be bloody dead."

"What do you mean?" Norman asked.

"They fear the flames," Sam said, realizing Maggie was right. He looked at her with renewed respect. "That's what's holding them back."

She nodded. "From the lack of pigment on the one we saw, it's clearly not a creature of sunlight. Most likely a cave dweller."

"But what *was* it?" Ralph asked.

"I don't know," Maggie snapped. The tension was making everyone edgy. She pulled Denal to her side. The boy's eyes were huge with fear, both real and superstitious. "But whatever it was, it was no spirit. No *mallaqui*. It was flesh an' blood. I don't know . . . maybe it's some type of bald gorilla or something."

Ralph shook his head, repositioning his own rifle slightly. Sam could guess the large man's arm was getting as tired as his own. "There are no large apes reported on the South American continent."

"But many parts of the Andes still remain unexplored," Maggie countered. "Like this place."

"But it looked almost human," Norman said.

Sam would not have used that term to describe the misshapen and bent-backed creature that had been caught in the flashlight's beam. He again pictured the beastly face armed with razored teeth. Definitely not human.

Maggie persisted. "All across the world, people report seeing strange hidden creatures in highland haunts—the Sasquatch of the Sierras, the Yeti of the Himalayas."

Ralph snorted. "Great. And we've discovered the abominable snowmen of the Andes."

The camp grew quiet again, the pressure of their situation discouraging any further talk. Total silence fell, except for the occasional pop or crackle from the fire. After a while, Sam began to hope Norman's first statement was true. Maybe the strange creatures had left.

Then, from deep in the cavern, a sharp bark erupted, followed by a guttural grunting from all around.

Everyone tensed. Sam fingered the trigger of his Winchester.

"The natives are growing restless," Norman whispered.

The coarse calls and gibbering escalated, echoing throughout the cavern. It sounded like hundreds of the creatures surrounded them.

Sam's eyes tried to pierce the darkness. "Fire or not, they may be gathering courage to attack."

"What should we do?" Norman asked.

"Two options," Sam answered. "One, we hole up in one of the tombs. Light a huge bonfire near the entrance and wait them out. Hold them off if they attack." Sam jiggled his pocket. "I've got maybe a dozen shells. And Ralph has around thirty."

Maggie glanced to the narrow entrance of one of the neighboring tombs. From her pinched expression, it was clear she did not care for that idea. "We'd be trapped in there. We could be swamped with no means of escape. And I'm afraid their fear of the firelight may wane."

"And what if the fire goes out?" Norman asked. "If we run out of mummies while holed up in there, who's going to go wandering out for more?"

Sam nodded at their concerns. "Exactly, not a great choice. So there is also option number two: We try to find that way out. We use Norman's light meter to guide us. We go armed and bearing torches. If flames scare them, then wielding burning brands may hold them off—at least long enough to get our asses out of here."

Ralph stood with his head cocked, listening to the growing howls. "Whatever we decide, we'd better hurry."

"Like I said before, they're growing more confident because we aren't doing anything," Maggie said. "But if we began moving, taking the fire with us, that ought to spook them again. Also, maybe this cavern is their home. If it's a territorial thing, by moving, showing them that we're leaving, they may not attack."

"That's a lot of maybes," Ralph countered.

Maggie shrugged. "I'd rather keep movin' than pin ourselves down. I don't think it's wise to stay in one spot too long. I vote for leaving."

"Me too," Denal quickly added, his voice small and scared.

Norman nodded. "We've overstayed our welcome here."

Sam eyed Ralph.

The large ex-football player shrugged. "Let's break camp."

"I'm for that." It heartened Sam to hear a unanimous decision, but he prayed it was the correct one. "Ralph and I need our arms free for the rifles. Everyone else grab a torch."

As the beasts shrieked and screeched, Ralph and Sam maintained a watch on the black necropolis. The others hurriedly worked at constructing torches. Another mummy was dragged from a nearby tomb, and its limbs were broken off, one each for Denal, Maggie, and Norman.

Norman stepped back, brandishing a thin mummified leg. "I've heard of pulling someone's leg, but this is ridiculous." His face shone with sweat from exertion and tension. The photographer crossed to the bonfire and lit the foot in the flames. "Something tells me I'm going to Hell for this." He glanced around the necropolis. "But then again, maybe I'm already there."

Ignoring his nervous chatter, Maggie and Denal followed his example. Soon each held aloft a flaming limb.

"I've got a spare torch just in case," Maggie said, pointing her thumb to the broken arm protruding from under the straps of her shoulder bag. "We can collect more on the way as we need them."

"If worse comes to worst," Norman said, "I also have a strobe flash on my camera as a last resort."

"Then let's head out," Sam said. "I'll take the lead. Norman's with me. We'll need his meter to guide us. Maggie, can you manage both your torch and the flashlight?"

She nodded.

"Then you follow us with Denal. Ralph will guard our rear. We'll cut through town first. We know there's no exit behind us . . . so our best bet is to move forward." Sam stared at the others. No one voiced any objections to his plan. "Let's go."

The team set off. The avenues between the necropolis's tombs were wide enough for them to cluster together. Norman walked to one side of Sam, reading his meter, shielding the unit from the torchlight with his body. Maggie marched on Sam's other side, her flashlight pointed forward. Denal kept to Maggie's hip. Only Ralph did as Sam had instructed earlier. He hung back and watched their rear.

As they tackled the maze of streets, heading toward the distant wall of the cavern, Maggie's earlier assessment proved only somewhat valid. The cacophony of howls did die down. The creatures were clearly shaken by the shifting firelight—but unfortunately not as completely as they had hoped. Cries and grunts still echoed around them, and even worse, the calls sounded closer.

Suddenly a huge blast of rifle fire exploded behind them. Sam spun around, heart in his throat, his Winchester ready at his shoulder. Ralph stood a couple yards back, the barrel of his rifle smoking.

"Damn!" Sam yelled, his ears still ringing from the blast. "Did you see something?"

Ralph shook his head and scowled at the shadowed necropolis. "Just a warning shot. If the fire didn't completely scare 'em, I thought the rifle might get their attention."

"Jesus, you nearly gave me a heart attack!" Maggie exclaimed. "Warn us before you do that again."

Ralph glanced back, his face growing sheepish. "Sorry. I just needed to do something. Those cries were crawling up my spine."

Norman picked himself up from the stony floor where he had ducked. "Do that again, and you're gonna owe me a new pair of undershorts."

Denal still stood by Maggie. "Listen," he said. "It quiet now."

With the ringing in his ears fading, Sam realized the boy was right. If nothing else, Ralph's rash act had subdued the howling. The cavern grew deathly still.

"Maybe that scared them away," Norman said hopefully, dusting off the seat of his pants.

"Don't count on it," Sam said. "Let's go."

The team continued into the maze of avenues and streets. Whoever had laid out the necropolis hadn't been much of a municipal planner, Sam decided. There was not a straight thoroughfare to be found, and many of the streets ended blindly. Their progress, as Sam judged by their proximity to the central golden statue, was slow, a snail's creep, requiring plenty of backtracking and stops to consult the light meter.

"We're gonna get ourselves lost in here," Norman complained at one point, hunched over the meter, cupping its aperture against the torchlight.

"There's got to be a way out," Sam argued.

The group grew more and more nervous—not because of any howling or signs of the creatures, but because the quiet had begun to chafe nerves. Without any clue to the beasts' whereabouts, every shifting shadow or scrape of rock made Sam twitch. Though no one said anything, they all knew the creatures were still out there, some primeval instinct that warned of hidden predators. The feeling of eyes staring at them, the sense of something breathing in the darkness.

As they continued, the silence pressed heavier. No one spoke anymore; even Norman's complaints died away. Sam glanced to the heights around them, wishing the howling would start again. Anything was better than this damnable quiet.

A growled scream sounded from overhead. Maggie stabbed her light to the roof of a neighboring tomb. Pale faces stared back at them. Huge black eyes reflected the light; lips pulled back in a keening cry, slashing teeth exposed.

"Back!" Sam screamed, shoving Denal and Maggie behind him.

Then the beasts leaped, heaving over the roof's edge toward them.

Ralph's rifle blasted. One of the misshapen creatures twisted in midair. Blood plumed out from its wounded neck. It spun and crashed to the stone floor, rolling and howling.

Sam herded the others back, retreating down the street. He sighted down the Winchester's long barrel. One of the creatures rose up from where it crouched on the street. Sam got his first good look at one of the beasts. It was as pale and hairless as the one spotted earlier, but this one was skinnier, emaciated. Each rib could be seen through the stretched skin. Even its limbs were just long bone and pale sinew, almost stretched like taffy. But it was its face that gave Sam pause. It was slightly muzzled like a bear, with teeth that seemed all fangs. Clearly a carnivore. But even more disconcerting were the huge black eyes. Sam sensed a rudimentary intelligence in its gaze: curiosity mixed with fury. A lethal combination.

But Sam recognized caution, too. The emaciated creature glanced back at its wounded companion, still writhing on the ground. When it turned around, its black eyes had narrowed into wary slits.

It hissed at Sam. Then in a flash of long pale limbs, it vanished down a side street, moving too fast for the eye to follow. Sam could not even shift his rifle sight in time. It was a blurred white ghost.

Damn, it moved fast.

Other of its brethren roiled from every opening, crawling from black windows, creeping from narrow doorways. As they moved, Sam noted subtle differences among them. Some were smaller, dwarfish models of the one he had just studied. Others were thicker-bodied. Some even bore what looked like vestigial wings sprouting from where the scapulas would be on a human. The only clear constants among them were the penetrating, hungry black eyes and the translucent skin.

"Sam . . . on your left!" Maggie called.

He spun. One creature, a squat brute bearing a huge brick above its head, raced toward them atop bowlegged limbs.

Sam had a heartbeat to aim. Instinct from years of pheasant and duck hunting served him well now. He sighted his target and squeezed the trigger. The bullet hit the beast square in the chest; the force of the collision stopped the creature's rush. It tripped to one knee, skidding slightly. Blood, black as oil against white skin, spilled down its bare chest. The stone brick toppled from its fingers, followed quickly by the bulk of the beast.

Another rifle shot drew his attention back to the right. By now, Ralph stood a few paces away. Sam saw another beast crumple to the floor. Ralph backed, waving an arm. "Keep going!"

A scream warned Sam again, but not from Maggie's throat this time. One of the bent-backed creatures, a female with pendulous breasts flat as pancakes, howled a ululating cry of attack. In her pale hands was a raised club.

He struggled to twist the rifle around.

"Sam!"

The club swung toward him, slicing faster than he had expected. He tripped back a step. But he was not fast enough. The club struck the Winchester's barrel with a resounding clang. The rifle tore from his grip and clattered onto the stone.

Sam's hand stung from the blow. The club circled back, toward his head this time. The female beast screamed her triumph. Off balance, Sam could not even duck.

Then his left ear suddenly flamed with pain. He yelped, both in distress and surprise.

"Sorry," Maggie gasped, shoving her flaming torch farther past his shoulder and into the attacker's face.

The beast's eyes widened in terror at the fire. Its triumphant scream changed in mid-peal to a cry of horror. The club fell from its trembling fingers as it shielded its face with an arm.

Maggie came around Sam's side and jabbed the torch.

The creature darted away, swinging around, and scrambled up the side of a tomb and away. Again moving with preternatural speed.

Maggie swung on Sam, frowning fiercely. "Grab your rifle!" She turned to Norman. "Use the torches." She jabbed an arm toward Ralph as another rifle blast echoed through the cavern. The black man was surrounded on all sides. "Go help him! I'll stick with Sam and Denal. We need to watch each other's backs as we retreat."

Norman started toward the embattled ex-football player, harrying away a pair of brutish forms with his flaming limb. "Retreat to where?" he called back.

"Anywhere but here!" Maggie answered.

Norman nodded, as if that were answer enough, and hurried forward, entering the fray around Ralph. More rifle fire and a swinging torch quickly cleared a space around the tall black man.

To the left, Sam heard Denal gasp. Swinging around with his rifle, Sam saw the small Quechan lad backing away from a trio of smaller creatures, miniature versions of the ones that had attacked Sam. They shuffled across the floor, knuckling on one forearm, remarkably reminiscent of small apes.

Using his free hand, Sam pulled Denal behind him, then raised his rifle. He aimed at the closest of the three, almost at point-blank range range, and blew away the back of the creature's skull. Splatter sprayed upon the other two, giving them reason to pause.

"Get back!" Sam yelled, drawing Maggie and Denal into a side street as the remaining pair approached. Another creature clawed at Maggie from a rooftop, but a swipe of her torch drove it away.

Then the pair of scuttling monsters on the street howled and leaped—but not at the humans. The pair tore into their fallen companion, ripping with teeth and claws, burrowing bloody muzzles into its flesh.

Sam, Maggie, and Denal continued their retreat.

"What the hell are those things?" Maggie mumbled, horrified.

Sam had no answer.

More and more creatures joined the meal, drawn by the scent of blood. Without the torches near, they boiled from every niche and shadowed alcove. They were all ravenous. Whatever tenuous neutrality had governed the creatures ended with the scent of fresh meat and blood.

A booming voice called out from around the corner. "Sam! Maggie!" It was Ralph. "We can't get to you now! There're too many!"

Sam watched the carnage. Driven by their wild bloodlust, Sam feared that fire would fail to cow these creatures now. "Don't try to reach us!" Sam yelled back. "We'll keep going this way! Head for the gold statue! Rendezvous there!"

More rifle fire exploded from around the corner.

Maggie shone her flashlight behind them. The way was momentarily clear. The feast in the other street had drawn the pack like moths to flame. "Hurry," Maggie urged. "Who knows how long the buggers will be satisfied with local fare?"

Sam needed no further encouragement. Herding Denal and Maggie before him, he urged them to speed down the avenues. Blindly, they took any turns that seemed to head toward the towering golden idol. All around, the screams of the monsters yowled and echoed, urging them forward. Sam reloaded his rifle on the fly, fingers fumbling shells into place. Once done, he shouldered the gun and closed the distance with Maggie.

"How're you holding up?" he wheezed between tight lips.

She glanced at him, her face pale and bright with sweat in the torchlight. "Okay," she said. "But ask me again when we stop running."

Sam reached and squeezed her elbow. He knew what she meant. While fighting and fleeing, the depth of their terror was held in check by adrenaline. True shock at their situation had yet to sink in fully.

Maggie patted Sam's hand. "I'll be okay."

Sam offered her a weak smile. "We'll get out of here."

She nodded—but he knew she didn't necessarily believe him. Neither of them was a fool. The creatures here were obviously scavengers and cannibals. From their pale skin and large eyes, they had been cave dwellers for generations. Maybe for millennia. Interbreeding, mutating . . . who knows what they once were? Maybe an unknown species of large ape, maybe even some prehistoric man. But if there was truly a way out of these caverns, why hadn't the beasts left?

Sam's mind ground on this puzzle, keeping his thoughts away from panic. Maybe Denal had been correct. Maybe these beasts were *mallaqui*, spirits of the underworld. If the Incas had come upon this trapped tribe of beasts, they could have believed they were beings of the *uca pacha*, the lower spirit level. Is that why they built such an extensive necropolis down here? Did they believe these monsters would protect their dead? Considering the attack upon Sam's group, the demonic beasts had proved themselves great guard dogs.

Sam shook his head, unsure of his own conclusions. A small part of him sensed that a vital piece of this puzzle was still missing—for the moment, there would be no further answers.

Sam, Maggie, and Denal ran on. In the distance, occasional blasts of rifle fire cut through the caterwauling screams, marking Ralph's and Norman's presence across the necropolis. But it was rare, startling Sam each time the blast echoed within the cavern.

"I hope they're doing all right," Maggie gasped after a volley of rapid rifle shots. She leaned against the sill of a window, catching her breath.

"They'll make it. With Ralph's strength and Norman's wit, how could they fail?"

Maggie nodded. She leaned forward to peer around the next corner. "By Jesus, there it is!" she said, stepping forward. She waved for Sam and Denal to follow.

Sam stepped around the corner and stared down the next street. It was long and straight, the first such thoroughfare in the cursed maze. Down the tomb-lined avenue, the base of the huge statue could be seen. This close, the statue was clearly an Incan king, a Sapa Inca, like the one that guarded the secret entrance to the caverns. The sculpture stood with its arms raised. Its palms touched the distant ceiling, as if supporting the roof over their heads.

Denal stared, mouth hanging open.

"It's the same king," Maggie said. She lifted her flashlight. It had to be at least twenty stories tall.

Sam followed where she pointed. Under a feathered and tasseled *llautu* crown, the king seemed to stare down at them, a slight scowl on his aristocratic face. It looked like the same king being honored here, too. "You're right. He must've been the Sapa Inca who had conquered the original Moche tribe, the ones who built the buried pyramid. I'd wager this was his way of placing his stamp upon this mountain citadel."

Maggie craned her neck. "Not a subtle guy."

"Well, let's go introduce ourselves." Sam led the way, still wary of attack from the denizens of the necropolis. Though he kept his rifle at the ready, this street seemed truly dead. No scrabbling sounds. The keening howls far away.

Sam, hurrying, meant to keep them that way.

The street proved much longer than it first appeared. The towering statue made the distance seem deceptively shorter. To either side, the tombs also grew in size and stature as they progressed toward the central plaza, further tricking the eye's assessment of distance.

The group's initial run eventually died down to a tripping walk on exhausted legs.

Maggie's flashlight played across the ornamentation of these elaborate mausoleums. Some stood four stories high, gilded with gold-and-silver designs, encrusted with rubies and emeralds. Fanciful creatures—dragons, winged leopards, human/animal hybrids—adorned the facades. She ran a finger along an elaborate mosaic depicting a ceremonial procession. "The tombs here must be of the *kapak*, the higher classes," she said, panting.

Sam nodded. "Clustered around the feet of their god, the Sapa Inca. Notice the position of his palms. Another symbol of how their king was a physical link between the upper world and this one."

Finally, the row of tombs ended, and the plaza beyond stretched to the gold feet of the statue. Sam glanced up. The statue climbed to the very roof of the chamber. "Wow . . ."

Maggie was not as impressed. She stood with her back to the sight, staring at the dark necropolis. Howls of the beasts echoed sporadically in the distance. "What the devil are those beasts?" she mumbled.

Sam crossed to her. "I don't know. But I think they bear some rudimentary intelligence. A few were using tools to attack. Rocks and clubs."

"I noticed, but they were only the thicker-limbed ones," Maggie said. "Did you notice that?"

Sam frowned and lifted his rifle. "I was sort of busy holding them off."

"Well, it's true. The others just fought with tooth and nail. It was almost like the pack was divided into four distinct classes. Each with its own function and abilities."

"Like bees? Workers, drones, and queen?"

"Exactly. First, there were those thin, lanky ones."

"Yeah, I saw one of those. They move as quick as cheetahs."

"But did you notice they never fought?"

"Yeah, now that you mention it. The skinny ones appeared first, then just sort of hung around at the fringes." Sam glanced to Maggie. "But what are they? A type of scout?"

Maggie shrugged. "Probably."

Sam pondered her theory in silence. He pictured the battle again in his mind. "What about those pitbull-looking things? The ones that weren't scared of the flames."

"Another class. Did you notice the lack of genitalia on them?"

"I really wasn't looking down there. But if they were sexless, I can guess what you're thinking—drones, just like the bees."

Maggie nodded. "Infertile workers of limited intelligence. Their fearlessness of the flames was probably more from stupidity than bravery. But who knows?"

"And the ones with the weapons?" Sam asked. "Those bigger ones with the muscles and weird vestigial wings. Let me guess. Soldiers."

Maggie shook her head. "Or maybe just laborers. I don't know. But did you see that gigantic fellow who hung back and seemed to bark orders? I'm sure he's some type of pack leader. I saw no one bigger than he."

"That's a lot of conclusions and suppositions on only a brief glimpse."

"It's what your uncle taught us to do. Extrapolate. Take the tiny shards of an ancient people and construct a civilization."

"Still, without more information, I'd be hard-pressed—"

Denal suddenly tugged on Sam's free arm.

He glanced down to the boy.

Denal stared into the dark necropolis. "Mister Sam, I hear no gunshots."

Sam turned, so did Maggie. She wore a deep frown. "Denal's right," she said. "We haven't heard any rifle fire for a while."

Sam studied the city, searching for any sign of Norman and Ralph. Echoing screams still rattled over the dark city. "Maybe they've outrun them."

Maggie swung in a slow circle, scanning the spread of tombs. From this point, the necropolis rose in a wide bowl around them. Seven avenues led out like spokes into the surrounding maze of tombs. "I don't see any sign of Norman's torch out there."

Sam stepped beside her. Silent. Where were they? Had they been caught? Fear for his friends knotted his stomach.

"They must be out there somewhere," he said quietly. "They must be."

Harried by a mob of beasts, Norman and Ralph backed through a tomb's doorway, ducking under its low lintel. The musty stench and odor of cinnamon filled the narrow space. It accentuated the cloying closeness of the cramped tomb. Beyond the doorway, pale creatures mewled and growled from hungry throats.

Swinging the flaming torch, now burnt down to the knobbed knee of the mummified leg, Norman drove back the scrabble of creatures from the doorway. So far the flames, feeble as they were, kept them at bay. "C'mon, Ralph," Norman begged. He risked a glance backward, his glasses sliding down his sweat-slick nose.

Deeper in the tomb, Ralph fought his rifle, struggling with the bolt. "Goddamn worthless piece of shit," he swore. "Still jammed."

"Well, unjam it!" Norman cried.

"What the hell do you think I'm trying to do?" Ralph attacked the rifle with more vigor, his muscles bunching in his thick arms, but with no better success. When Ralph raised his face, his expression was answer enough.

"Fuck." Norman poked his torch into a pale face that got too near. With a wail, the foul visage vanished. "What now? I'm running out of leg!"

"Hold on." A rustling and heaving sounded from behind. Norman dared not look back. The beasts were getting bolder and making grabs for his torch as the fear of the flames waned. Ralph appeared at his side, voice strained. "Move out of the way!"

328 · JAMES ROLLINS

Norman stepped aside as the large man dropped a bundle at the doorway. It was a desiccated mummy, wrapped in a fetal position. "Light it," Ralph ordered.

Norman brought his flaming brand to the dry wool bandages. Smoke billowed, filling the narrow space. The bright flames, like the light of salvation, bloomed upon the mummified corpse. More smoke choked the chamber. Norman's eyes stung; he coughed coarsely.

"Stand back," Ralph warned, then kicked the flaming bundle through the entryway. It skidded to a stop right outside the doorway and blazed brighter.

The creatures scattered, squealing like startled swine.

Norman backed up a step, sighing in relief. That should buy them a bit more time. "Can you get the rifle working?"

"I don't know. There's a shell jammed tighter than shit. I can't jimmy it free." Ralph shook his head as he stared at the flames. "Our only hope is that the others see the fire and come investigate."

"But they won't know the fire means we're in trouble. What if we tried screaming for help?"

Ralph glanced back, hopelessness in his expression. He shook his head. "Wouldn't do us any good. The acoustics in this place will only bounce the noise all around." Ralph glanced to Norman. "But I'm open to any other bright ideas."

Norman chewed his lower lip, turning in a slow circle, looking for some answer among the scattered pottery and tokens of the dead. "I think I do have a *bright* idea," he exclaimed, passing his torch to Ralph, then fishing through the camera bag slung across his back. He hefted out the flash unit and held it up. "A really *bright* idea!"

"What are you thinking?"

Norman waved away the question. "I need to get to that window slit." He pointed to a narrow gap in the brickwork near the ceiling. It was much too small for the beasts to get through, but it would suit his needs fine. "I need a boost. How strong are you?"

Ralph frowned. "I could lift four of your scrawny asses."

"One scrawny ass will do." Norman settled his camera bag on the floor. "Gimme a knee up."

Crouching, Ralph helped Norman climb from knee to shoulder.

"Now up," Norman said, kneeling atop Ralph's shoulders and balancing with one hand braced on Ralph's head.

With an explosive exhalation, Ralph heaved straight up, shoving Norman toward the high roof. Once his feet were steady, he hissed at Norman, "Hurry up with whatever you're doing."

Norman pulled up to the window's sill and peered outside. The view stretched all the way to the gold statue. Perfect.

"Hurry!" Ralph said from below.

Norman felt his balance shift under him. He grabbed the window's edge to keep from falling. "Steady there, big boy!"

"Get going! You're not as light as you look."

"Are you saying I'm fat?" Norman said with feigned offense.

"Enough wisecracks already. You're not funny!"

Norman grumbled, "Everyone's a critic." He freed his flash from his vest pocket. Holding the flash up, he triggered the bright light in quick bursts—three short, followed by three long flashes, ending again with three short. Then Norman waited a few seconds and repeated the signal.

The incandescent light was blinding as it reflected off the surrounding tomb walls. Norman squeezed out one more sequence of signals, then switched off the lamp, conserving the bulb. It would have to do.

With a final glance at the gold statue so tantalizingly close, Norman dropped back.

"What were you doing?" Ralph asked as Norman awkwardly hopped from his perch. Ralph rubbed his bruised shoulders.

"Making a 911 call." Norman pushed his flash unit back into his pack. "An old-fashioned S.O.S."

Ralph glanced up at the hole. "Smart," he mumbled.

"You're welcome," Norman answered, proud of his ingenuity. He straightened, slinging his camera bag over his shoulder. "Now if only someone spotted my signal."

Norman suddenly felt something squirm in his hair. He ducked and batted at it; his wrist hit something solid. Squeaking with shock, Norman rolled to the side and spun around.

One of the creatures continued to paw at him through the open window near the roof, its arm stretched toward him. Norman backed away. A leering face, wide with teeth, appeared upside down at the opening and growled at them. It seemed Norman's clever ploy had attracted someone—unfortunately not who he had hoped.

"Shit!" Norman whispered.

Overhead, scratching and scraping sounds began to echo from the rooftop. It sounded like a hundred crows scrabbling up there. In the back corner, one of the slab sections of the stone roof suddenly shifted an inch with a cracking grind of granite.

Both Norman and Ralph spun in horror to stare at the gap in the slabs. "They're forcing their way in!" Ralph groaned.

"How fucking strong are they?"

"With enough of 'em, they could probably tear this place apart."

The scrape of claws and the ominous grind of stone reverberated through the high, narrow chamber.

Norman stepped away, then glanced toward their only exit. Flames from the burning mummy blocked the doorway. They were trapped in a snare of their own making.

"Me and my bright ideas," he moaned.

Maggie was the first to spot the strobe of Norman's flash. "Over there!" she yelled, drawing the attention of Sam and Denal. "Sweet Jesus, they're alive." She had noticed a red glow a moment ago among the maze of tombs. At first, she wasn't sure it was them. Now she knew!

Sam sidled next to her. He had been circling the statue's base, searching, too. "Where?"

As answer, a second series of flashes exploded through the necropolis. It was not far, just past the end of one of the avenues that spoked away from the central plaza. "They must be in trouble," Sam said.

"What do you mean?" Maggie asked, her jubilation waning to worry.

"That's old Morse code. An S.O.S. signal."

Maggie stared toward the dark necropolis. "What are we going to do?"

Sam glanced at her. "I have to try and help them." The flare of flashing light blazed again, then died away. "They must be pinned down."

Denal spoke up, raising his torch a bit higher. "I go, too."

"And I sure as hell am not staying here alone," Maggie said. "Let's go." She started toward the avenue that led most directly toward the trapped students. A hand pulled her back.

"No," Sam said, "you and Denal stay here."

Maggie swung around, shaking out of his grip. "Like bloody hell! I'm not puttin' up with any of your chauvinistic bullshit, Sam."

"And I'm not asking you to. If I get the others free, we're gonna be running like scared rabbits with a pack of wolves on our heels. We're gonna need a hole to hide in." Sam stepped back to the statue. He raised his rifle and tapped its butt against the gold ankle. A dull clang reverberated up the leg.

"It's hollow," Maggie said, amazed.

"And a good place to hide," Sam said. "When I was circling around, I found a doorway on the far side. In the left heel of the idol." Sam reached to his waist and slipped out the gold dagger. He held its hilt out toward

Maggie. "I need you to pick that lock before I get back with the others."

Maggie accepted the dagger and the responsibility. "My da' was once a thief in his youth . . . here's hoping there's a genetic predisposition."

Sam smiled at her. "I always suspected there was something criminal about you."

She returned his smile. "I'll get the bloody door open. You just bring back the others." She held out her torch. "And be careful."

He stepped closer to accept the flaming brand. In the torchlight, she could see the intensity smoldering in his blue eyes. Grabbing the torch, he let his hand linger on hers. "You, too," he said, his voice a touch huskier. He hesitated another breath.

Maggie raised her face toward him. For a moment, she thought he was going to kiss her, but then he stepped away.

"I'd better get going."

She nodded. Somewhere deep inside her, in a place that seldom stirred, she felt disappointment and turned slightly to keep from betraying her feelings. "Don't you do anythin' stupid," she implored.

Denal spoke up from a pace away. "I see no more flashes. They stop."

Sam swung around . . . whatever tenuous moment they had shared faded away like scattered embers. He studied the spread of the necropolis. "That can't be a good sign," he said quietly.

"Hurry, Sam."

Nodding, the Texan raised his rifle toward the cavern roof. "Cover your ears."

She and Denal did so, but even with their palms clamped tight to the sides of their heads, the rifle blast was deafening.

After the ringing died away, Sam lowered the rifle. "Hopefully, that'll let them know the cavalry is coming."

Maggie frowned as Sam started down the avenue.

And will let the creatures know, too, she thought dourly.

"That had to be Sam!" Ralph said. "He must have seen your signal!"

Norman eyed the gap in the slabs overhead. After the single rifle blast, pale fingers had returned to tug and push on the granite, widening the space another inch. Black eyes stared in at the trapped pair. Norman jabbed his torch at the faces, but to little effect. The roof was too high. They simply backed away, then quickly returned.

"Sam won't make it here in time," Norman mumbled. "Not unless we find some way to chase these roof rats away."

Ralph turned from the doorway. "I may have an idea."

Norman watched as Ralph shrugged the ammo belt from his shoulder. "With the rifle jammed, we won't need this any longer." He held up the strap of leather with over twenty intact shells still on it, then stepped toward the entrance.

Norman began to get an inkling of Ralph's plan. "That might just work."

"And it might blast a way out of here for us, too." Ralph tossed the belt into the flames. In half a heartbeat, the shells began exploding like popcorn on a skillet, sputtering and cracking. Outside, ricochets pinged off the neighboring tomb walls. The mummy underneath the belt was riddled to shreds, and bits of it were scattered across the stone.

Overhead, beasts fled in a squealing rush from the noise and the cascade of flaming debris. Norman stepped nearer the gap to be sure they had actually fled. He raised his torch high toward the crevice in the roof. It was empty. No more peering faces or scrabbling fingers. He grinned. "It's working—"

"Get back!" Ralph hollered.

Fire suddenly tore into Norman's leg. Dropping his torch, he crumpled to the floor as bolts of agony shot all the way up into his belly. He cried out, mouth open for a moment in a silent scream, then a high-pitched whine escaped his lips: "Shhhiiittt!"

Ralph was instantly at his side, dragging him back toward the shadowed wall. "Goddammit, Norm, what did you think you were doing?"

Norman was not in the mood for a discussion of his shortcomings. With teeth clenched against the pain, he stared down at his right leg. A thick wetness soaked through the knee of his khakis. The room began to spin.

"You caught a ricochet," Ralph explained. He pulled off his shirt. "Why did you step from cover?"

Norman groaned and waved an arm toward the gap in the roof slabs. "I wanted to be sure—oh, the hell with it—I wasn't thinking." His face squeezed tight as Ralph gently examined the wound. "It's not like I tossed handfuls of bullets into campfires when I was a kid. But I guess with my army training I should've known better than to break cover."

"I don't think it hit any major arteries," Ralph said. "I don't see any spurting, but your knee is all shot to hell. I'm gonna have to wrap it tight to support it and to restrict any further seeping." Ralph took his own shirt, a thick flannel, and shredded it into strips. Taking a scrap, he touched Norman's leg. "This will hurt."

"Then let's *not* do it," Norman said sourly, grimacing.

Ralph frowned at him.

Norman sighed and waved him closer. "Oh, go ahead. Just do it."

Nodding, Ralph took his leg and bent it up. Norman's knee exploded with pain, like a stick of dynamite going off inside. But worse was the sick grate of bone on bone. Norman gasped, tears in his eyes. "Do you even know what you're doing?"

Ralph just continued to work, ignoring his agony. He wrapped his scraps of flannel shirt several times around Norman's knee from thigh to mid-shin. "Back at the University of Alabama, football players were always banging up their knees. If nothing else, I know how to place a quick support wrap." Ralph finished his handiwork with a final firm tug, cinching the wrap tight.

Norman's fists clenched; he writhed slightly. It felt like something with huge claws had clamped his knee. Then it was over.

His torturer scooted back. "That should keep you from dying."

Norman wiped the tears from his eyes. The pain subsided. "Great bedside manner, Doc."

Ralph eyed him a moment, worry creasing his brow as he studied the photographer. Finally, he glanced back toward the entryway. It was quiet. The bullets had long since stopped popping in the fire. "Now the bad news. We need to get out of here. My stunt's not going to keep those monsters away for long."

Norman glanced to the doorway. Pieces of the shredded and scattered mummy smoldered beyond the threshold, while distantly, spats of flames still dotted the stone floor. But at least the exit was open. He nodded and raised an arm. "Help me up."

Ralph stood, then used a muscled forearm to pull Norman from the floor.

Gasping from the movement, Norman was careful to keep his weight off his injured leg. Once up, he tentatively leaned on his heel, gauging the amount of pressure he could withstand. Pain throbbed, but the support wrap kept his knee immobilized. Norman hobbled a few steps, leaning heavily on Ralph's wide shoulder.

"Can you make it?"

Norman glanced up. Sweat beaded his forehead from this small exertion. He felt queasy from the continual throbbing in his leg. He offered Ralph a sick grin. "Do I have any choice?"

Overhead, something stirred. Claws again scrabbled on the rock. It sounded as if one of the beasts had hidden up there, but now with the streets quiet again, it was slinking off. The two men stood immobile, straining to listen, waiting to be sure the beast had moved away. Silence for ten full counts.

They dared not wait any longer. Where there was one, others might soon follow. "Let's get out of here," Norman said.

Ralph collected the torch from the floor. He fanned its embers into a brighter flame, then stepped beside Norman. "Grab my shoulder. Lean on me."

Norman didn't argue, but he held the man back for a moment. His voice was serious. "If we get in trouble . . . leave me."

Ralph did not answer.

He squeezed the larger man's shoulder harder. "Did you hear me?"

"I don't listen to fool's talk." Ralph raised a palm toward Norman's face.

"Oh, don't go Oprah on me, Ralph. I'm not talkin' to the hand." Norman pushed Ralph forward. They stumbled together toward the door. Norman kept speaking to distract himself from his pain. "I'm not saying you should throw me to the monsters as bait and hightail it away. I'm just saying . . . let's be practical. If we get in trouble, leave me in some cubbyhole and run. Put those ex-football player legs of yours to use."

"We'll cross that bridge when we come to it," Ralph muttered. He helped Norman ease through the low door.

Norman straightened, and the pair cautiously entered the street. The avenue was strewn with flaming bits of cloth. It looked like a war zone. "That was more of a show than I expected."

"But at least it helped chase those things off," Ralph said.

Norman glanced up and down the street. Ralph was right. There was no sign of the monsters. "Thank God." For the moment, they were safe.

"C'mon," Ralph said. "Let's get the hell away from here."

"Anything you say, boss."

Ralph set off with Norman in tow, their pace slow but steady. Soon they had left the smoldering remains of the mummy behind. Only a small pool of light cast by the stubby torch marked their progress. Norman had wriggled free his flash and held it ready, prepared to scare off any stragglers with the blinding light if necessary. At one-minute intervals, he also strobed a quick series of flashes to indicate their current location for Sam or any of the others to follow.

Of course, the flashes of light also gave away their position to the cave beasts, but it was a calculated risk. With Norman injured, they needed help, as in big guns, and that required a signal.

Norman lifted his flash and spat a series of blinding bursts toward the ceiling. "I feel like a goddamn firefly."

Ralph frowned, discouraging any conversation. They were already enough of a target.

Norman frowned at his companion's unspoken scolding but stayed silent, biting back a quip. He knew Ralph was growing more and more nervous. The large man had begun to pause, glancing quickly over his shoulder, as if he sensed something was tracking them.

Norman never heard anything, but his head now pounded continually. Still, he knew Ralph was mistaken about one thing. If they were being tracked, it wasn't a few whispered words that drew the creatures. Norman studied his leg. Blood seeped slowly from between the folds of the wrap. Considering the lack of light, he suspected the beasts' other senses were keen. *I'm a meal on the run*, Norman thought morosely.

Silently they continued onward, aiming for the gold statue. No attack came, but the cavern had grown strangely quiet. Only the occasional howl sounded from somewhere within the depths of the cavern. Ralph's shoulder became more and more hunched and tight under Norman's grip.

Finally, Norman slowed. By now, his skull felt two sizes too small, and his steps had become dizzied. "I need a rest break," he whispered.

"Already?" Ralph hissed, eyes wide on the surroundings.

Norman let go of Ralph's shoulder and hopped to a nearby tomb wall. "Just for a few moments."

Ralph scowled and swung the torch closer to Norman. The frustration in the large man's face waned to worry. "Shit, Norman, you look like crap."

"Good, because that's exactly how I feel." Norman slid down the cool stone wall and sat on his rump.

Ralph crouched beside Norman, his eyes back to surveying the length of the street. "It can't be much farther."

Norman bit his lower lip, then spoke the words he had been trying not to say for the past few minutes. "Ralph, you need to go on alone."

He shook his head—but not before hesitating a moment, Norman noticed. "I can't leave you here."

"Yes, you can." Norman forced as much false cheer into his voice as possible. "I'm gonna crawl into this tomb, cuddle up with the homey here, and wait for you to fetch that Texan with that big rifle of his."

Sighing, Ralph pondered his words. "Maybe . . ." He shoved to his feet. He even took a step away. Then he suddenly swung back. "Fuck that! You didn't leave me back at the river, and I'm not leaving you now!" Ralph held out his torch. "Take it!"

Norman grabbed the flaming brand. "What are you—?"

Ralph bent down and scooped up Norman under both arms, ignoring his squawk of protest. "I'll carry your ass out of here if I have to."

Norman squirmed a moment, then relented. "Let me down . . . if you're that determined, I can manage a little longer."

Lowering him back to his feet, Ralph hissed in his ear. "I don't want to hear anything else about abandoning you."

Norman grinned, inwardly relieved that Ralph had refused to leave. "And I didn't think you cared."

Ralph's brows bunched. "Just get your crippled ass moving."

Norman hopped a step forward, while Ralph's grip held him steady. "I hope you're right that it isn't far to the statue." Moving another painful step forward, Norman noticed Ralph hesitate. Ralph's hand remained clamped to Norman's upper arm, but he wasn't following.

Ralph's grip spasmed tighter for a moment, then relaxed.

Norman turned. "What's the holdup?"

His hand fell limply from Norman's shoulder. Ralph fingered weakly at his thick neck, disbelief on his face.

Blood poured over Ralph's fingers. The large black man reached for Norman with his other hand, pleading. "R . . . run!" Ralph gurgled.

Norman was unable to move. He stared transfixed by the spear of sharpened white bone protruding like a branch from the side of his friend's neck.

Ralph crashed to his knees. "G . . . Goddammit! Run!"

From behind Ralph, a tall, pale creature rose on spindly limbs. Their tracker had come out of hiding. Huge black eyes glared at Norman as the creature lifted a second spear of bone and leaped toward him, bounding high over Ralph's back.

Norman danced backward but was too slow on his injured leg. The beast plunged toward him, bone spear raised.

Ducking, Norman braced for the impact.

But Ralph suddenly bellowed with rage and lunged forward. He snatched the ankle of the creature as it flew past, a lineman grabbing a fumbled pass. He yanked the beast clear of Norman and swung the startled creature through the air, swatting it against the neighboring wall.

Its skull shattered like eggshells.

As its carcass collapsed in a tangle of limbs, so did Ralph. He struck the floor hard, too weak to break his own fall.

Norman rushed to his side, ignoring the pain as he fell to his hands. "Don't move! I'll get help! Sam can't be far." Norman gently turned his friend's face upward.

Glazed eyes stared back. Empty.

Norman's hand flinched back. Ralph was already gone. He crawled back, tears blurring his vision.

Around him, the cavern echoed again with the yammering howls and gibbering cries of the beasts. More trackers. They detected fresh blood and were drawn by their ravenous hunger.

Norman pressed his forehead against the cool rock and took several deep breaths. He was too tired to run, but he forced himself up. He would not let Ralph's sacrifice be for nothing. Glancing at Ralph's body, he stood unsteadily, torch in hand.

He turned on his good heel and swung around. Only three yards away crouched another of the foul creatures: squat, with thick arms and bent back. It growled at Norman.

Norman's eyes narrowed with rage. He shoved his torch high. "Fuck you!" he screamed, fists clenched and trembling. He put all his hate and sorrow into his cry, as tears rolled down his cheek.

Like those of a frightened deer, the beast's eyes flared wide, clearly startled by the unusual reaction of its injured prey. Disconcerted, it crept back, then scampered down a side street.

Norman's cry ended with a choking sob. He wiped at his face, then shoving his glasses higher on his nose, he limped forward. "You-all sure as hell better not get in my way! I'm not in the fuckin' mood!"

Maggie knelt by the door in the heel of the great statue. It was a long and narrow silver inset, about half a meter wide and two meters tall, flush almost with the surrounding gold walls. She was surprised Sam had even spotted it.

While Denal shone the flashlight, she once again worked the tip of the golden dagger into the narrow slot in the door's center. It had to be a keyhole, but so far no amount of manipulation of the gold dagger's tip would release the catch.

"Miss Maggie," Denal said quietly behind her, the flashlight's beam jittering. They rarely spoke, and only in whispers, afraid to attract the ears of the predators out there. "Mister Sam gone a long time."

She pictured Sam sneaking around the necropolis, alone, and pounded her fist against the unyielding surface in frustration. "I know that, Denal!" she hissed. Besides a flurry of rifle shots, sounding like an asthmatic machine gun, and one screamed shout, there had been no indication that anyone but the creatures still moved out there.

The boy mumbled a meek apology.

Sighing, Maggie leaned back, resting the dagger on her lap. "I didn't mean to snap at you, Denal. I'm the one who should be sorry. It's . . . it's just that I can't get this damn thing open, and they're counting on me." Maggie felt near tears.

He placed his hand on her shoulder.

Even that small bit of solace went a long way to calm her frayed nerves. She took a shuddering breath, forcing herself to calm down. Glancing at Denal, she patted his hand. "Thanks." She stared into the boy's scared eyes, then returned to study the door. "Denal, I'm sorry for getting you into this mess."

"No sorry. It were my choice to spy on Gil. I wanted to help you. My mama, before she die, she say I must help others. Be brave, Denal, she tell me."

"Your mother sounds like a wonderful woman."

Denal sniffed back tears. "She was."

Well, by Jesus, she thought silently, *I'm not going to let that wonderful woman's boy die down here.*

With renewed determination, she raised the gold dagger; the foot-long blade glittered in the flashlight beam. She remembered Sam's trick at transforming the dagger. She tilted the knife and examined its sculpted hilt, the fanged god Huamancantac. She ran her fingers along its contoured handle. She found no catch to trigger the change. "How did you do that, Sam?"

Maggie glanced to the door, then back up to the statue. She needed to think. Why a door in the back of the heel? The Greek myth of Achilles came to mind. The invincible warrior's only weak spot was his heel. But there was no such corresponding myth among the Incas or any of the Peruvian tribes.

Still, the coincidence kept nagging her. Could there be some connection? Many myths crossed cultures and continents. Just because she had never heard of such an Incan myth did not mean it did not exist. Without a written language, much of Incan heritage had been lost over the ages—perhaps tales of the Incan equivalent of Achilles had been lost, too.

Lifting the dagger, she recalled the Greek myth. The great Achilles was finally brought down by a blow to his heel. But it wasn't a knife that slew the magically protected warrior. It had been an arrow. She shook her head at this useless train of thought.

If only you were an arrow, she wished at the dagger.

In her hands, the hilt grew suddenly cool and the golden blade stretched and thinned, blossoming at its tip into a sharp arrowhead.

"Jesus!" Maggie blurted out, popping to her feet. She turned to Denal, holding out the transformed knife. "Look!"

Denal, though, was staring the other way, gaping out at the necropolis. He backed toward her, raising an arm. "Miss Maggie . . . ?"

With her gaze, she followed where he pointed. At the shadowed edge of the tombs, pale, monstrous shapes crouched. They had crept up on them so silently, even now not a growl or yowl escaped them. Maggie noticed several of the faces stared up at the gigantic statue— but not all of them. Several pairs of hungry eyes stared directly at them.

As if knowing they had been spotted, the creatures began to slink, crawl, and waddle out from the necropolis's edge. Silent, like twisted shadows. There had to be at least two dozen of them.

Maggie pulled Denal back with her into the small cubby between the two heels of the Incan king. Denal had a flashlight, and the remains of their one torch. It would not hold off the hordes. They needed help. She risked a step forward and yelled with all the wind in her lungs. There was no reason to hide in silence any longer. "Sam! Help!" Her call echoed throughout the large cavern.

A pair of the nearest beasts, angered by the noise, rushed toward her. They were of the soldier class of the pack, loping on muscular legs, eyes narrowed to black slits, fangs bared. They resembled hairless bears, muzzles stretched wide as they attacked.

Maggie brandished her only weapon, the dagger now shaped like an arrow. If she could kill one of them . . .

The nearest of the two raised up from its crouched run, ready to lash out at her, then its eyes flicked toward her only weapon. The beast howled as if struck and fell back, colliding with its partner. The two tangled together, claws raking each other as they fought to back away. Slitted eyes had widened in raw panic. Whining, they fled back to the others.

Maggie stepped farther from her hiding place. She lifted her weapon high. A squeal of fear ran through the massed beasts. Like a school of startled fish, they spun and darted away.

Lowering the transformed knife, she frowned at the gold arrow. What had just happened? She ran a finger down the shaft of the arrow. She glanced back at the locked door. More from the beasts' reaction than her own insight, Maggie suspected she truly held the key to the Incan statue. They had obviously feared it. But why? Did the beasts recall some frightening memory of the Incas who had once traveled here with this strange knife? If so, how? It had been so long ago, at least five centuries. Was it some type of collective memory, a genetic instinct among this diverse pack?

Stepping toward the silver door, she was determined to test her theory. Crouching, she slid the slender arrow through the slit. If this proved to be the key, then it also suggested the Incas had shared some common myths with the Greeks. This fact alone could be worth an entire doctoral thesis. Holding her breath, Maggie slid the arrow home.

A small *click* sounded—and the door swung open.

A dark chamber lay beyond.

Maggie hung back. She glanced to her hand. With the door open, the gold dagger had returned to its original shape. The long blade glinted in the light. Holding the weapon toward the doorway, she recalled the booby traps in the other chamber. Still, there was only one way to proceed. Without turning, she waved her free hand toward Denal.

"Bring me the flashlight."

Shining the light forward, she noticed that beyond the doorway lay a small, unadorned chamber, its floor of gold matching the statue. It was plenty large enough to house all of them. She leaned forward and cast the light up. There was no ceiling. The beam climbed into the hollow heart of the gold statue. It seemed to go on forever.

Pushing back out, she ran her light along the length of the Incan king. Overhead, his raised gold palms held up the roof of the cavern. For a hiding place, it was not exactly unobtrusive.

Maggie turned to face the dark necropolis. But where the hell were the others?

Sam froze when he heard Maggie's cry for help. He stared forward for a heartbeat into the maze of streets. For the past half hour, there had been no further sign of Ralph and Norman. The last he had heard was an explosive "fuck you," then nothing else. The streets lay silent.

Where the hell are you guys?

Sam had to accept the possibility that both were lost. He apologized silently if he was wrong and swung around. He headed back toward the statue at a dead run. No longer having to blindly track the two men, Sam could move faster. He knew the way back to the statue, knew which were the proper turns and which were dead ends.

Sam reached the last street, the straight avenue that aimed for the central plaza. From there, he even spotted the glow of Maggie's torchlight highlighting the statue's base. Tugging his Stetson snugly across his brow, he started down the street.

Before he had taken two steps, a cry of pain drew his attention to the right. Sam twisted around, rifle raised. Down a short side street, a figure slid along the left wall, hunched and feeble. The shape was too dark to be one of the cavern predators.

Sam raised his torch and, in turn, was blinded by a sudden explosion of light. Someone screamed at him: "Get away, you fuckin' shithead!"

Blinking back the glare, Sam lowered his rifle. "Norman?"

The figure had stopped a few yards back; a quieter, meeker voice answered. "Uh, Sam?" Norman lowered the flash he had used to blind the Texan.

Sam let out a whoop and hurried to Norman's side. His joy quickly deflated when he took in the photographer's injury. "Where's Ralph?"

Norman pocketed his flash and just shook his head. He would not meet Sam's eyes. Instead, he asked, "How about Maggie and Denal?"

"At the statue," Sam said, his voice subdued. The loss of Ralph was like a deadweight in his chest—but now was not the time to mourn. He straightened and reached to pull Norman under an arm. "We need to hurry. They may be in trouble."

Norman backed away, shoving at Sam's arm. Tears welled up. "I won't get anyone else killed."

"Bullshit, it's just your leg." Sam bullied up to Norman and scooped the photographer's shoulder under one arm. "How good were you at a three-legged race?"

Norman opened his mouth, clearly meaning to protest, but a fierce growling rose behind them from deeper down the street. They both glanced back; then Norman leaned more heavily on Sam. "Let's find out."

Sam nearly carried the injured photographer, but he was not going to leave the man behind. They returned to the main thoroughfare and headed out at a fast clip, limping and hopping. The yowling rose all around them now. It seemed to be paralleling their track.

"It's . . . it's my leg," Norman moaned at his ear. He started to lean away. "The blood is attracting them. If you leave me here, they might—"

"Sorry, no meals on this flight," Sam answered, pulling Norman closer, refusing to let the man sacrifice himself.

They hurried forward amid the escalating cries of the predators. The statue grew too slowly in front of them.

"We're not going to make it," Norman said, nodding toward a handful of pale forms leaping along the rooftops behind them, moving with incredible speed. One paused to howl at the cavern roof.

"Scouts," Sam said. "They've spotted us and are calling for reinforcements." Sam kept going, swinging his Winchester backward, and fired off one round. It was a blind shot. The bullet rebounded off the wall and bounced between the tomb walls to either side. Something yelped past the reach of their light.

Norman mumbled with grim satisfaction, "You've really got to watch those damn ricochets."

Shouldering the rifle, Sam hauled the photographer with him. The Winchester had only one shot in the chamber, then Sam would have to reload— which meant stopping. They would not survive the delay.

A voice called from down the street, drawn by his rifle blast. "Sam! Hurry! I have a way inside the statue!" It was Maggie. He spotted her small form at the end of the street, outlined in torchlight.

"Then get inside! Now!" Sam hollered back.

"Just move your asses! Don't worry 'bout me!"

Norman glanced at the mass of beasts upon their tail. "Personally I was worrying more about them," he said sourly.

Lungs on fire, legs burning, Sam forced them to a faster pace. He fought to close the distance with Maggie. He was now close enough to see her eyes widen at the sight of the company pursuing them.

"Holy shit," she said. "Hurry!" She ran toward them.

"Get back!" Sam gasped.

But she ignored him. She raced toward them with Denal at her heels. As Maggie drew near, she waved the gold dagger overhead and whistled a piercing note, a sheepherder calling his dogs.

What the hell did she think she was doing?

Sam glanced anxiously behind him. The forefront of the pale legion tumbled from the rooftops onto the street, almost at his heels. Sam shoved Norman forward and swung to face the coming onslaught with the single shell in his Winchester.

Maggie appeared at Sam's side. "Don't!" She shoved his rifle down and stepped forward. She brandished the long blade.

"Maggie!" But to Sam's shock, the squabble of creatures skidded to a stop, claws scraping rock. Black eyes were fixed on the knife. Even overhead, the scouts backed from the roof's edge, retreating. Those caught on the street crouched against the sight of the blade. They scrabbled slowly away.

Maggie indicated their party should do the same. "I don't know how long their fear will overwhelm the hunger for fresh meat." Maggie glanced at their group with concerned eyes. "Where's Ralph?"

"Dead," Norman said softly.

"Oh, God, no . . ." Maggie muttered, returning to guard the group with the dagger.

Sam kept at Maggie's shoulder. He glanced between the knife and the huddled pack. "Why do they fear it?"

"I don't know," Maggie answered tightly, voice strained with the news of Ralph. "Right now, all I care is that it works."

Sam agreed with her, but he could not keep his mind from working on the beasts' odd reaction. He remembered his earlier assessment that the creatures might be some inbred line of ape or prehistoric man, cave creatures the Incas had discovered down here and had revered as *mallaqui*, underworld spirits. But why would they fear this old Incan dagger?

Sam frowned, sensing he was still far from the true answer to the mysteries here. But as Maggie had said, the first thing a good researcher did when investigating something strange was to survive.

To either side, the line of tombs suddenly vanished. They had reached the central plaza.

"Around here," Maggie said, finally turning her back on the mass of creatures crouched down the street. She quickly led them to the door he had noticed earlier. Skirting around the heel, Sam saw the way now lay open.

"How did you manage to unlock it?" Sam asked.

Maggie passed him back the dagger. "It seems the weapon is also an all-purpose skeleton key. It changed to match this lock, too."

"You're kidding?" Sam flipped the dagger back and forth, examining it. "How did you get it to work?"

Maggie's brows furrowed. "That's the thing. I don't truly know."

Panting and wheezing, Norman pushed beside them, leaning on Denal now like a human crutch. "We've got company!" he gasped out, pointing back.

Sam turned. The pale beasts had begun to creep again from the shadowed streets and into the central plaza. Low growls began to flow. Sam herded everyone through the doorway in the golden heel. "It seems their hunger is winning out."

Maggie ducked in. "Hurry, Sam! Help me with the door!"

Without turning from the slathering pack, Sam backed to the narrow entry. As he struggled through, his rifle's strap caught on the door's hinge. Sam yanked on it, but only jammed the leather strap tighter. "Goddammit!"

Sensing his distress, one of the creatures bounded forward, growling and snarling, all teeth and claw. A soldier. As it neared, it hissed at Sam, drool foaming from its mouth, and swiped a razored claw at his throat.

Ducking back, Sam parried the attack with the gold dagger. The knife struck pale flesh, but it was a pinprick in a bull. The creature heaved up, screaming its rage. Blood splattered Sam from the injury, while he fought to unhook the rifle.

"Leave it!" Maggie yelled.

"It's our only weapon!" With one hand on his rifle, Sam kept the gold dagger between himself and his adversary. Other pale beasts squealed and cried behind the injured one. They had smelled the blood.

Sam met the eyes of the creature looming over him. In those black wells, Sam sensed a dark intelligence. It raised its injured arm, red blood drizzling down its pale flesh from the knife wound. A low growl of hate seeped from its throat. Sam tensed for the blow.

But instead the beast suddenly jerked away as if it were a marionette directed by some unseen hand. The raised arm blackened, starting from the clawed hand, then spreading down the arm like a flaming poison. Wisps of smoke trailed up from the limb. Howling in pain, the creature crashed backward into its brethren. Its arm, now charred, crumbled and fell away to ash, but still the burning spread. The beast rolled on the stone floor. In mere seconds, its pale torso and other limbs blackened to match the granite beneath it. Smoke swirled around the writhing figure; even spats of flame shone through cracks in its flesh.

Sam knew what he was witnessing. The rare phenomenon had been documented in the past, but never witnessed: *Spontaneous combustion.*

Stunned, Sam backed away, his rifle forgotten. Without him tugging any longer, the gun simply clattered to the floor. He left it where it fell, brandishing the dagger instead.

Beyond the doorway, the pale creatures retreated from their charred brother. The large beast lay unmoving, a sculpture of ash upon the stone floor.

Maggie crouched and grabbed the Winchester's stock and dragged it into the small chamber with them. "Help me with the door."

Sam nodded dully. He glanced at the gold dagger, then slipped it carefully into his belt. With his hands free, he joined Maggie in hauling the heavy door closed. Once shut, it snapped tight, the lock clicking in place.

Maggie leaned against the silver entry. "We should be safe now."

Suddenly the floor under them rumbled. Everyone tensed.

"Great, you had to say that," Norman whined, his eyes on the floor.

Under their feet, a deep-throated gurgling arose. It sounded like the rush and churn of a mighty river beneath the floor. The sound grew deafening, echoing up the hollow statue overhead.

"What the hell is that?" Maggie asked.

"Another trap!" Sam yelled.

"This way," Abbot Ruiz said, turning and walking down the long, sleek hallway.

Henry hung back as the abbot continued their tour of the research complex beneath the Abbey of Santo Domingo. Joan, her street clothes now masked in sterile white laboratory coveralls, walked alongside the large man, while Henry marched beside the stoic-faced Friar Carlos, who watched the group from under lowered lids, suspicious and vigilant. The foursome, now all dressed in matching white lab suits, seemed part of the research team that manned the suites of laboratories. Only the 9mm Glock carried in Carlos's tight fist suggested otherwise.

For the better part of the afternoon, Abbot Ruiz had passed from lab to lab, highlighting the advanced studies being done here: everything from botanical sciences to nuclear medicine, even a huge computer lab devoted to the human genome project. Henry did a mental calculation. Hidden within the heart of an

Incan labyrinth, the honeycomb of laboratories must encompass the entire heart of the abbey. Henry could not believe this complex had been kept secret for so long.

Joan spoke up as Abbot Ruiz continued down the hallway, asking the very question that had been nagging him, too. "Why show us all this?"

Ruiz nodded, clearly expecting the question. "As I said before, to gain your cooperation. But also to impress upon you the significance of the level of commitment here, so that what I show you next will be viewed within the proper context." The abbot turned a perspiring face toward Henry and Joan. "While I may operate from faith in my religion, I suspect you will need more concrete evidence. I suspect, like the Apostle Thomas, you will need to place your fingers in the wounds of Christ before you believe the miracle you are about to witness."

Henry edged closer to Joan, speaking for the first time in over an hour.

"Miracles? That's the first religious reference I've heard you utter while down here. Just what are you truly doing here?" Henry waved an arm to encompass the complex as they continued down the hall. "Discounting the murders and kidnappings, how is this all an undertaking of the Catholic Church?"

The abbot nodded knowingly. "Come. The answer lies just ahead."

Even with the 9mm Glock pointed at his kidneys, Henry was oddly intrigued. As a scientist and historian, whatever mystery lay hidden here, Henry needed no gun to keep him following. Just what had he stumbled onto?

Joan reached and took his hand as they approached the end of the hall. Though her eyes were also bright with curiosity, Henry could tell she was nervous. Her palm was hot in his. He gently drew her to his side.

Blocking the way ahead was an immense stainless-steel wall. In the center was a huge door, large enough for an elephant to pass through. Massive bolts secured the door tight. Off to one side was an electronic palm lock and keypad. It was obvious that before them stood the centermost chamber of the complex, the Inner Sanctum.

Without turning, Ruiz spoke. "None but the most devoted have ever stepped foot within this chamber. What lies ahead is mankind's hope for salvation and redemption."

Henry dared not speak, his curiosity too keen. He did not want to say anything that would dissuade the abbot from opening the vault. A man had been murdered to keep this secret, and Henry meant to find out what it was.

Joan did not have as much devotion to the mystery. "Why let us see?" she asked.

Ruiz still did not turn. His eyes were fixed on the doorway, his voice husky with reverence. "All answers lie within." He took his signet ring and pressed it into a niche. The palm pad lit up, and the abbot placed his left palm upon its surface; then with his other hand hidden by his bulk, he tapped a code to open the way.

Thick locks released with the roll of heavy bearings, and the bolts slid smoothly back, freeing the door. As Abbot Ruiz backed away, the massive door swung open toward them. It had to be at least two feet thick. From the opening, the perfumed scent of incense wafted out. After the sterility of the labs, the fragrance was cloying. A chill breeze carried the scent, as if the room beyond were refrigerated.

But neither the incense nor the chill seemed to bother Abbot Ruiz. The rotund man raised his arms in supplication as the door slowly opened.

Once the door was fully open, the abbot crossed himself solemnly and led the way forward. He spoke not a word, and Henry sensed that to speak would blaspheme the moment. He kept his lips clamped, but his eyes widened with anticipation.

As Abbot Ruiz stepped carefully through the entrance, sensors within the vault switched on a flood of halogen lights. The room burst with brightness, like a subterranean sunrise.

Joan gasped. From her vantage point, she had spotted what lay ahead. Henry had first to maneuver around the eclipsing form of the abbot to see what mystery the chamber contained. As he climbed over the threshold, his hand fell away from Joan's. He stumbled numbly into the room.

The chilly chamber was twenty yards square. At each corner, a small brazier smoked with a thin trail of incense. Upon each of the titanium walls hung monstrous silver crosses, each as tall as a man. An even larger crucifix hung from the ceiling three stories overhead.

But as stunning as all this was, it was nothing compared to what lay below the hanging cross. In the center of the room, upon an ornate silver altar, lay a life-size sculpture of a man. Henry moved nearer. The figure rested as if asleep, dressed in flowing robes, pillowed by his long hair, hands crossed upon his belly as if he lay at peace. The visage was relaxed in slumber. A profound peace emanated from the figure. Henry drifted to the side to view the face better.

Upon the figure's brow rested a crown of thorns.

Oh, God!

It was the figure of Christ—sculpted of solid gold!

No, not gold . . . Henry did not have to step any closer to recognize his mistake. The halogen spotlights blazed upon the figure of the sleeping Christ. The metal seemed almost to flow under the light. No, this was not gold! It was *el Sangre del Diablo*. The entire life-size sculpture had been molded from Satan's Blood.

Henry felt his knees grow weak. Words escaped him. The chill of the room crept into his bones. No wonder the room was refrigerated. At room temperature, the soft metal would likely lose its fine detail, like the cross had at Joan's lab back in Johns Hopkins.

Abbot Ruiz crossed to a plain wooden prayer bench that stood before the altar and knelt upon its hard surface, lips moving in silent worship. Once done, he climbed back to his feet, zippered open his sterile lab suit, and withdrew the beaker containing the golden sample from Joan's lab. The substance still retained the rough pyramidal shape. Abbot Ruiz kissed the tips of his fingers, then unstoppered the jar and reached within the beaker to remove its contents. Gently, the man's large hands dislodged the metal from the glass and lifted it free. Leaning forward, he reverently placed the pyramid atop the sculpture, near the folded hands of the Christ figure.

"Come," the abbot said solemnly, returning to his prayer bench. "It was your discovery, your gift, Professor Conklin. You should share in this."

Ruiz knelt again, bowing his head in prayer. Henry crossed to the abbot's shoulder with Joan at his side. Carlos still stood near the door, gun held steady, face hard.

Abbot Ruiz prayed, his words mumbled, face covered humbly with his hands.

Henry studied the figure, the room. He did not know what to expect. Still, what happened shocked him; Henry had to blink a few times to make sure it was not some optical illusion.

The pyramid composed of Substance Z melted and flowed across the sculpture. The folded hands parted enough to allow the molten metal to flow under them. As the golden fingers settled again, the flow of Substance Z formed a perfectly shaped lily, a redolent bloom and slender stem, grasped within the golden fingers of Christ.

The abbot sighed and lowered his hands, a beatific smile on his features. He pushed to his feet.

"What just happened?" Joan mumbled.

"Your sample has been added to ours . . . bringing us one step closer to our goal." The abbot backed from the altar, drawing the others with him.

"How did you do that?" Henry asked, nodding toward the statue.

"You have witnessed why the metal was thought demonic by the Vatican. It is the most unique property of *el Sangre del Diablo*." Ruiz turned to Joan. "We've read your notes and reports. Like you, we've learned over the years that the metal is responsive to any external source of energy: electricity, X rays, radiation, thermal. It uses any and all forms of energy with perfect efficiency, changing state from solid to liquid. But what you had yet to discover was the property the Incas demonstrated to the Dominican friars who first arrived."

"And what is that?" Henry asked.

Abbot Ruiz's gaze flicked toward Henry. "It also responds to human thought."

"What?" Joan gasped.

Henry, though stunned, remained silent. In his mind, he remembered how the sample had tried to form a replica of the Dominican cross when he had been holding and pondering the crucifix.

The abbot continued, "With focused concentration, it will respond to a brain's alpha waves just as it will to X rays or microwaves. It will melt and flow into whatever form is fixed in the supplicant's mind."

"Impossible . . ." Joan mumbled, but her voice held no force.

"No, not impossible. The brain can produce significant emanations. Quantifiable and measurable. Back in the early seventies, experiments in both Russian and

CIA think tanks demonstrated that certain unique individuals could manipulate objects or influence photographic film with nothing but the strength of their minds." Ruiz glanced back at the Christ figure. "But in this case it is not the individual that is unique, but the *substance*. It is attuned to the emanations of the human brain, the very thoughts of man."

Henry found his tongue, almost choking. "But this is an amazing discovery. Wh . . . why the secrecy?"

"To preserve mankind's hope for salvation," Abbot Ruiz stated solemnly. "Upon the Holy Edict of Pope Paul III in 1542, our Spanish sect of the Dominicans was given the mantle to pursue any end to keep the demonic metal from corrupting mankind. To keep its existence secret and to sanctify it."

Henry's eyes narrowed. "You keep saying that— *your sect*. What do you mean by that? Who exactly are you?"

The abbot stared at Henry as if judging whether or not he was worthy of a response. When he spoke it was low and with an undercurrent of threat. "Who are we? Our order is one of the Dominican's oldest, founded in the thirteenth century. We were once called the Keepers of the Question. It was our order that first accompanied the conquistadors into the New World, into the land of heathens. As discoverers of *el Sangre*, we were granted the task of confiscating every ounce of the demonic metal and putting everyone associated with its discovery to the Question, until knowledge of *el Sangre* vanished into the folds of the Church."

Understanding slowly dawned in Henry. He remembered the symbol of the crossed swords on Friar de Almagro's ring. "Oh, God," he mouthed.

Abbot Ruiz straightened, unashamed. "We are the last of the Inquisitors."

Henry shook his head, disbelieving. "But you were disbanded. Rome disavowed the Spanish Inquisition in the late nineteenth century."

"In name only . . . the Holy Edict of Pope Paul III was never revoked."

"So you fled here?" Henry asked.

"Yes, far from prying eyes and closer to the source of *el Sangre del Diablo.* Our order considered our mission too vital to abandon."

"Mission to do what?" Joan asked. "Surely with all your research here, you don't still believe the metal to be tainted by the devil?"

Her words drew a patronizing smile from the abbot. "No. On the contrary, we now believe *el Sangre* to be blessed." A smile grew at their consternation. "For the metal to be able to divine the mind of man and turn his thoughts into physical reality, the hand of God must be involved. Within our labs, our sect has worked for centuries to refine the material and to expand the metal's receptivity to pure thought."

Henry frowned. "But to what end?"

The abbot spoke matter-of-factly. "So we can eventually reach the mind of God."

Henry could not hide his shock. Joan moved closer to him, reaching for his hand.

Ruiz continued, "We believe that with enough technologically refined ore, we can build a vessel sensitive enough to receive the mind or spirit of our Holy Lord."

"You must be joking," Joan gasped.

The abbot's expression was somberly stoic.

"And what then?" Henry asked, sensing something was being left unsaid.

The abbot cocked his head. "Professor Conklin, that's our most guarded secret. But if we are to win your cooperation, I suppose I must show you everything. The final revelation." Ruiz stepped toward the altar. "Come. You must understand."

Henry sensed that the abbot, though he might whisper of guarded secrets, actually enjoyed this little dog-and-pony show for his guests. In some ways, it worried Henry. To reveal these secrets so openly suggested that the sect had no real concern that Joan or Henry would ever be sharing such knowledge with the world. The abbot's confidence and willingness to talk, more than anything, made Henry edgy.

Once at the altar, Abbot Ruiz waved an arm over the golden figure. "Here is our ultimate goal."

"I don't understand," Joan said. Henry shared her confusion.

The abbot touched the sculpture with a single trembling finger. "Here is an empty vessel, responsive only to our thoughts. But with enough raw material, we hope to reach the spirit of God Himself. To bring his will into physical form."

Henry stared at the sleeping figure of Christ. "You're not suggesting—"

"We believe it was by providence that *el Sangre* was delivered into the hands of the Church when first discovered in the New World. It was a challenge to our faith. A test of God. If we bring together enough of this divine substance, God's mind will reach out and enter our vessel here, bring it to life." Abbot Ruiz turned to Henry, his eyes bright with zeal. "Our goal is to bring a living God back to this earth."

"You're talking about initiating the Second Coming!" Joan exclaimed.

Abbot Ruiz nodded, turning to stare across the golden figure. "Christ born again here on Earth."

Henry shook his head. This was insane. "So why us? Why do you need us?"

Ruiz smiled and drew them away. "Because you discovered the remains of Friar Francisco de Almagro, one of our predecessors. In the sixteenth century, he was sent to search for a rumored deposit of *el Sangre*, a strike so large that it was said by the Incas to 'flow from the mountaintops like water.' He never returned and was assumed killed. But when I received word from Archbishop Kearney in Baltimore, our hope was renewed. Maybe our ancestor had discovered the mother lode, only to die before he could bring back the knowledge." He glanced at the slumbering Christ figure. "We pray, Professor Conklin, that you've stumbled upon our means to reach God."

"You truly think this mythical mother lode is at my dig?"

The abbot raised his eyebrows. "Word has reached us from our agent on-site there. Signs look promising. But after that accident at the underground temple, it'll take us a while to—"

Henry tensed. "What accident? What are you talking about?"

Ruiz's face grew grim. "Oh, yes, that's right. You would have no way of knowing about the collapse." The abbot quickly related what had happened at the ruins.

The blood drained from Henry's face.

"But fear not, though the students are trapped, their last transmission suggested that they'd found a natural cavern in which to take shelter."

"I need to get up there! Now!" Henry blurted out, pulling from Joan's grasp. All interest in anything here died to cold ash. Oh, God . . . he had forgotten all about Sam. He had not even considered that his nephew might be in danger, too.

"There is nothing you can do. I'm in contact with my men up there. Any change, one way or the other, and I'll tell you immediately."

Henry's blood, which had drained from his face, rushed back. "You'll get no cooperation from me! Not until I know my nephew is safe!"

"Calm yourself, Professor Conklin. I've already sent a team of mining experts to assist in the rescue."

Henry wrung his hands together. Joan stepped nearer, drawing an arm around his shoulders. He stood stiffly in her embrace. After the death of his wife and brother, Sam was his only family. Henry had no room for anyone else. If he had not been so enamored of his old college flame, Henry might have been thinking more clearly and avoided this whole mess. Stepping out of Joan's embrace, Henry spoke to the abbot through clenched teeth. "If any harm comes to Sam from this, I will kill you."

Abbot Ruiz backed up a step, while Friar Carlos moved in with his Glock, warning Henry off. The abbot's voice trembled slightly. "I'm sure your nephew is safe."

Another booby trap!

As the gold floor trembled underfoot, Sam pulled Maggie to his side. She had been attempting to unlock the statue's door, but it had locked tight behind them. "Brace yourselves!" Sam yelled above the growing roar of rushing water below. "Be ready to act!" Through his bootheels, the reverberations thrummed up his legs and tingled his ribs and spine.

A step away, Denal supported Norman; the young Quechan's eyes were huge saucers.

The rumble below grew deafening in the small space, and the floor bucked under Sam's boots. "Hang on!"

Suddenly the roar filled the space around them; the floor trembled as if holding back an immense pressure. Then the loud knock of catches releasing echoed all around them. The platform shot upward under them. Norman fell to his hands and knees, crying out in pain as his injured limb struck the metal floor. No one else spoke, hushed with fear, frozen in tense postures.

The platform rocked and jolted, but continued on its upward course—slowly at first, then faster, spinning slightly as it ascended the shaft. Underfoot, the floor continued to tremble with whatever force propelled it.

"Hydraulics!" Norman cried out over the roar. He was helped to his feet by Denal.

"What?" Sam asked.

Maggie pushed free of Sam's embrace and studied the floor. "They must've tapped into an underground river, perhaps a tributary of the one we swam in yesterday. It's a bloody hydraulic lift!"

Sam stared up into the throat of the passage above. "But where is it taking us?"

Maggie frowned. "If they wanted to kill intruders, this is an overly elaborate way to do it," Maggie said, eyeing the flow of smooth walls. "I think it's taking us all the way up."

"To the roof?" Sam said, remembering the stance of the Incan king, arms raised up, palms on the ceiling as if supporting the roof of the cavern. He pictured the statue's form. It was a straight shot up.

"Hopefully not just to crush us up there," Norman said sourly. "That would ruin an otherwise perfectly good day."

"I don't think so," Maggie answered, her voice unsure.

Denal suddenly cried out. He pointed overhead. "Look!"

Maggie swung her flashlight up, but there was no need. Far above them the end of the passage came into sight, a dome of gold, the interior crown of the statue's skull. Light streamed from regularly spaced cracks in the roof's surface. Then like the petals of a flower, six sections of the roof peeled fully open. Bright sunlight flowed down toward them.

"It's a way out!" Sam exclaimed. He whipped off his Stetson and let out a whoop of joy. "We've made it!"

Norman added more quietly, "Some of us, that is."

Sam's smile faded. He replaced his hat, picturing Ralph's face. Norman was right. It was inappropriate to cheer their own salvation when one of their friends was not beside them.

Maggie moved nearer to Sam. Her eyes were bright with both relief and sadness. She craned her neck to study the opening dome.

Sam put his arm around her. "I'm sure Ralph would be glad we escaped."

"Maybe . . ." she mumbled softly.

He hugged her tighter. "The dead do not begrudge the living, Maggie—not Ralph, not even your friend Patrick Dugan back in Ireland . . ." And to this list, Sam silently added his own parents.

Maggie leaned into him, her voice tired. "I know, Sam. I've heard it all before."

Holding her, he gave up on words. He knew that sometimes forgiving yourself for living was harder than facing death itself. It was something you had to do on your own.

Slowly now, the elevator climbed toward freedom, and the platform pushed up into the opened dome. Finally, it settled to a stop. The six sections of the dome had retracted fully. Underfoot, the click of latches bumped the floor, locking the platform in place once again. Below them, the whoosh of water receded, flushing down the shaft.

"We're home," Norman said.

After the dimness of the cavern, the late-afternoon sunlight was blinding, even when filtered through the heavy mists that seemed to cloak the skies overhead.

"But where the hell are we?" Sam asked, stepping forward. He craned his neck all around.

They appeared to be in some deep wooded valley. Towering steep walls of reddish black rock surrounded them on all sides, impossible to scale without mountaineering equipment and considerable skill. Overhead, mists roiled and obscured the sunlight to a bright haze.

"What's that smell?" Norman asked.

The air, thin and warm, was tainted by the odor of rotten eggs. "Sulfur," Maggie said. She turned in a slow circle, then pointed an arm. "Look!"

Near the north wall of the valley, a plume of steam shot skyward from a crack in the rock near its base. "A volcanic vent," Sam said. This region of the Peruvian Andes was still geologically active, riddled with volcanic cones, some cold and silent, others still steaming. Earthquakes rattled through the mountains almost daily.

Maggie waved an arm. "This is no rift valley. We're in some type of volcanic caldera."

Norman limped closer, eyes on the rock walls. He frowned. "Great. Why is the phrase 'out of the frying pan, into the fire' coming to mind right now?"

Ignoring the photographer's dour words, Sam studied the heights around them. "If you're right, Maggie, we must be among that cluster of volcanic peaks east of our camp." He nodded his head to a dark shadow to the south. Another cone, its rocky silhouette masked in steam, seemed to climb from the south wall itself, towering over their volcanic valley. "Look how many there are."

Maggie nodded. "You're probably right. This region's never been explored. Too steep and dangerous to trek through."

Denal spoke up, sticking close to Norman's side. He wiped his brow with a shirtsleeve. "Warm in here," he muttered.

Sam agreed, taking off his Stetson and swiping back his damp hair. At this altitude, wearing only his vest, he should be chilled as twilight approached, but instead the breeze was warm, almost balmy.

"It's the steam vents," Maggie explained. "They're keeping this place heated and humid."

"Like some tropical greenhouse," Norman said, his eyes on the jungle surrounding the gold dome. "Look at all this growth." He struggled to free his camera.

Around them spread a dense forest. Draped with vines, the tangle of trees spread in all directions. From their vantage point higher in the valley, they could spot a few open meadows, breaks in the jungle canopy, mostly near the ubiquitous volcanic vents. Otherwise, within the walls of the volcanic cone, the forest appeared undisturbed. Under its insulating canopy, a profusion of wild growth flourished. Giant ferns, with fronds longer than a man was tall, obscured the forest floor, while hundreds of orchids with fist-sized yellow blooms hung from the crooks of trees. Even some form of jungle rose climbed on thorny creepers along limbs and vines.

Norman snapped a few photographs, while the others wandered along the forest's edge.

Within this verdant and flowered splendor, birds whistled and piped in alarm, disturbed by their presence. A small flock of blue-winged parrots darted across the misty skies. Closer, the barking calls of monkeys warned them away, echoing off the rock walls. Their tiny bodies darted and flew among the trees and vines, flashes of fiery fur and whipping tails.

Beyond this wall of greenery, the babble of water over rock promised the presence of some spring-fed creek nearby.

"It's like some lost Eden," Norman said.

Sam nodded, though a seed of worry took root. He remembered the Latin warning etched on the hematite bands by Francisco de Almagro: *Beware the Serpent of Eden*.

A similar thought must have passed through Maggie's mind. Her lips were pinched sternly, and her eyes narrowed in suspicion. "We've got company," she suddenly whispered.

Sam tensed, eyes instantly on the alert. "What?"

Maggie stood immobile, only her eyes moved, indicating a direction in which to look.

Behind them, a sudden grind of metal sounded. The dome was closing back up, their only means of retreat from the volcanic caldera vanishing.

Sam searched the section of jungle Maggie had indicated. Finally, he spotted a small face in the shadows, staring back at him. The figure must have known he had been spotted and rose from his crouch. He stepped from the dense thicket at the jungle's edge. From other spots, seven more men slipped into the clearing around the gold dome.

Mocha-skinned and dark-eyed, the men were clearly of Quechan heritage. They stood only to about Sam's shoulder, but bore spears a good head taller than the Texan. They wore traditional Indian garb: unadorned *haura* trousers and shirts fancifully decorated with parrot and condor feathers.

The leader, wearing a crimson headband, stepped forward and spoke sternly in his native tongue.

Denal translated, face scrunched. "He wants us to follow him."

The small hunter turned and stepped back to the forest's edge. He pushed aside the giant frond of a tree fern to reveal a hidden path. The man ducked under the leafy growth and started down the trail. The other hunters hung back to ensure Sam's group followed.

Without any reason yet to fear them, Sam waved. "Let's go . . . maybe they know a way back to the dig." Still, as he eyed their long weapons, Sam cinched his Winchester more snugly over his shoulder. If trouble should arise, he wanted to be ready.

Denal touched Sam's elbow. The boy's eyes were narrowed in suspicion, too. He seemed about to say something, then shook his head and fished out a bent cigarette from a pocket. He mumbled something in his native tongue as he slipped the filter to his lips.

"What is it, Denal?"

"Something no right," he grumbled but said nothing more. Ahead, the boy helped Norman under the frond and onto the path.

Sam followed last with Maggie beside him. As the jungle swallowed them up, they proceeded in silence for several minutes.

"What do you make of them?" Maggie finally whispered.

"They're obviously a Quechan tribe. Hundreds like them live as hunter-gatherers out in the wilds."

Maggie pointed a thumb back toward the clearing. "And they just ignore a dome made of beaten gold?"

Sam pondered her words. She was right. The hunters had seemed more shocked to see them than the wealth at their backs. Denal's consternation also nagged at him. What was wrong here?

He studied the Indians as they marched onward. They moved silently, spears carried comfortably, pushing vines from their way. Soon the path crossed a small stream forded by a series of large stone blocks set in the flow. Who were these hunters?

The answer to his question appeared around a bend in the path.

The thick jungle opened, and a village appeared as if by magic. The cluster of stone homes surrounded a central plaza and spread in terraced steps up into the jungle itself; almost all of the homes were half-buried in the growth, shadowed by the high canopy. Jungle flowers festooned stone rooftops and grew in planted yards. The fragrant blooms negated the sulfurous smell of the volcanic vents.

Sam stared, his mouth gaping open. Llamas and small pigs moved around the narrow streets, while men and women came to doorways and windows to gawk equally at the four strangers. There had to be over a hundred inhabitants here, dressed in poncholike *cushmas,* or sleeved shirts with small capes, or long Indian *anacu* tunics.

The homes were as equally decorated as their inhabitants: lintels and window edges were sculpted elaborately, while silver and gold adornments glinted in the setting sun's haze.

Norman limped ahead, leaning on Denal's shoulder. From a doorway, one of the younger women, dressed in a wool *llikla* shawl, nervously approached Norman. She held out a loose wreath of blue flowers woven with yellow parrot feathers. The thin photographer smiled and bowed down. Taking the opportunity, the woman darted forward and slipped the handwoven adornment over the photographer's head. Norman straightened as she giggled, a hand over her lips, and danced away.

Norman turned to Denal, fingering the gift with an embarrassed grin. "Does this clash with my shirt?" he asked, and limped onward. The photographer seemed oblivious to what they had stumbled upon.

Sam and Maggie, though, stood frozen at the village's edge. In his mind, Sam stripped away the jungle growth from the homes and erased the people and animals from the streets. He recognized the layout of this town. The central plaza, the spoked avenues, the terraced homes . . . it was the same spread as the necropolis below!

Maggie grabbed his elbow. "Do you know what this place is?" she whispered, staring up at Sam with huge eyes. "This is not some Quechan tribe, eking out a fist-to-mouth existence."

Sam nodded. "These are Denal's ancestors," he said, coming to the same conclusion as Maggie, his voice numb with shock.

They had stumbled upon a *living* Incan village!

As the sun set, Philip heard a noise he had not thought to hear: the rasp of static from the camp's radio. He jolted to his feet, knocking over the camp stool on which he had been sitting. Friar Otera and the other Dominicans were all down at the excavation site. A pair of experienced miners had arrived just past noon today and were helping direct the Quechan laborers.

Philip tore open the communication tent's flap and dived into its shadowed interior. He snatched up the receiver. "Hello!" he yelled into the handpiece. "Can anyone hear me?"

Static . . . then a jittery response. ". . . ilip? It's Sam! The walkie-talkie's battery . . . We made it out of the caves . . ." Garbled static flared up.

Philip adjusted the radio's antennae. "Sam! Come back! Where are you?"

Words fought through the static. "We're in one of the volcanoes . . . east, I think."

Philip's heart sang. If the others were safe, there was no further reason to continue to excavate the shaft. It was all over! He'd be able to leave soon! He pictured his own apartment back at Harvard, where his books, computer, and papers were all neatly organized and cataloged. He glanced down at his torn shirt and filthy pants. After this expedition, he was done with field-work forever!

His glee made him miss some of Sam's last words, but it no longer mattered. ". . . helicopters or some other aerial surveillance. We'll set up a signal fire on the ridge. Search for us!" Sam asked one final question. "Have you got word to Uncle Hank yet?"

Philip frowned and hit the transmitter. "No, but I'm sure word's reached Cuzco by now. Help's arriving here already. It shouldn't be long."

A squelch of static erupted when Philip released the button.

Sam's voice was more faded. "You won't believe what we've found up here, Philip!"

He rolled his eyes. Like he really gave a damn. But Sam's next words drove away even his profound apathy: "We've found a lost Incan tribe!"

Philip hit the transmit button. "What?"

". . . too long a story . . . battery weak . . . call same time tomorrow."

"Sam, wait!"

"Search for our signal fire!" Then the static ground away all further communication.

Philip tried for another few minutes to raise Sam again, but to no avail. Either the battery had grown too weak, or the bastard had switched off his walkie-talkie. Philip slammed the receiver in place. "Fucker!"

Suddenly the slap of canvas drew his attention around. The slender figure of Friar Otera slid within the tent. The tall monk straightened by the doorway, outlined by the setting sun behind him, his face masked in shadows. "Who were you talking to?" the man asked—harshly.

Philip guessed the monk was fatigued by the day's efforts at digging. Standing, Philip welcomed him further inside. "It was Sam!" he said excitedly. "He and the others made it out of the caverns!"

Philip was pleased to see the man's shocked expression. "How? Where are they?"

After quickly retelling Sam's story, Philip concluded, "We'll need some way to spot his signal fire . . . a helicopter or something."

The friar nodded, eyes hooded. "That's good," he mumbled.

"But that's not even the biggest news," Philip said smugly, as if the discovery had been his own. "Sam thinks he's found an actual group of Incas up there, some lost tribe."

Friar Otera's eyes flicked toward the student.

Philip gasped at what he glimpsed in those hard eyes, something feral and dangerous. He stumbled back a step, tripping over a discarded mug. By the time he caught himself, Friar Otera was already at his side, gripping his elbow tightly.

"Are you all right?" the man asked.

Cringing, Philip glanced up. Whatever he had seen in the friar's eyes had vanished. Only warmth and concern shone in the monk's face. It must have been a trick of the light before. Philip cleared his throat. "I . . . I'm fine."

Friar Otera released his elbow. "Good. We wouldn't want anything to happen to you." He turned away. "I must share your good news with the others," he said, then bowed out of the tent.

Philip let out a long sigh of relief. He didn't know what it was about Friar Otera that made him so edgy. The guy was only a dirt-water monk after all. Still, Philip had to rub the goose bumps from his arms. Something about that man . . .

Sitting with Maggie on the stairs at the edge of the plaza, Sam stared at the firelit celebrations below. Torches and fires dotted the open space in the center of the Incan village. Musicians bore instruments of every size and shape: drums made of llama skin, tambourines ringing with tiny silver cymbals, trumpets made of gourds and wood, flutes constructed of reeds or various lengths of cane, even several pipes fashioned from the large pinions of the mountain condor. All across the town, voices sang in celebration at the arrival of the newcomers.

Earlier, before the sun had set, the village shaman, or *socyoc*, had tossed his mystical *chumpirun*, a set of small colored pebbles, upon the ground to tell their fortune. The grim-faced, tattooed man had studied the stones, then risen up, arms high, and declared Sam's group to be emissaries of *Illapa*, the god of thunder. He had ordered this night's celebration in their honor.

Against their objections, the small group had been bustled off and treated like visiting royalty. Washed, groomed, and dressed in clean native wear, the team had regathered for the night's feast and celebration. The dinner had been endless, course after course of local fare: roasted guinea pig, bean stew with bits of parrot meat, a salad made of spinachlike amaranth leaves chopped with a type of native carrot called *arracacha*, and herbed pies made from *oca*, a relative of the sweet potato. After not eating for so long, the group had stuffed themselves, refusing nothing offered lest it offend their hosts.

Only Norman had eaten sparingly. He had started to run a fever from his injuries and retired early to the stone-and-mud hut assigned them. Denal had gone shortly thereafter, not sick, just sleepy-eyed and exhausted, leaving Sam and Maggie to oversee the remainder of the night's celebration alone.

Yawning, Sam ran a hand over the knee-length beige tunic he now wore and readjusted the short, knotted *yacolla* cape that he had slung over one shoulder. Unwilling to part with his Stetson, he tugged the hat lower over his brow.

Once comfortable, he leaned back on his hands. "How could these folks have remained hidden here for so long?" he mumbled.

Maggie stirred beside him. "Because they wanted it that way." She was decked out in a long sienna tunic that reached to her ankles. It was secured by an ivory white sash and matching shawl. She fingered the gold dragon pin holding the shawl in place. "Did you notice that most of the village is purposefully hidden in the jungle? Almost camouflaged. I doubt even satellite scans could pick out this hidden town, especially with all the geothermal activity around here. It would confound any thermal scans."

Sam stared at the misted night skies. Few stars could be seen. "Hmm. You may be right."

Maggie changed the tack of the conversation. "So, Sam, how does it feel to be a messenger of the thunder god?"

He smiled lazily. "Prophetic pebbles or not, I think that shaman must have heard echoes of our rifle blasts. I think that's why he associated us with *Illapa*."

Maggie glanced quickly at him. "I never even considered that. It's a great theory."

Sam enjoyed the praise, grinning slightly.

"But what about the necropolis down below? How does that fit in? It's almost a mirror image of this place."

Sam frowned. "I don't know. But considering its location, it may have something to do with the Incas' three levels of existence. If this village was considered to be part of the middle or living world—of *cay pacha*—then the village below this one would certainly be thought of as *uca pacha*, the lower world."

"The world of the dead."

"Exactly . . . a necropolis."

Maggie's brows drew together in thought. "Hmm . . . maybe. But if your theory is sound, where's the third village?"

"What do you mean?"

"The Incas were very structured. If they built matching cities in the lower and middle worlds, where's the village of the upper world, of *janan pacha*?"

Sam shook his head, growing tired. "I don't know. But we'll get more answers tomorrow. For now, let's just enjoy the celebration in our honor." He raised his mug of *chicha*, a fermented corn drink, and took a long sip. He grimaced at the bitter taste.

Maggie settled back. "Not to your liking," she teased.

"It'll never replace a cold bottle of Bud. But, sheesh, this brew packs quite a kick." Sam found himself becoming a little light-headed. By then, the celebration had run long into the night. Even the moon had set.

Maggie smiled and leaned into him a bit. He took a chance and put his arm around her. She did not pull away or make a joke of it. Sam took another swig of the corn beer. He hoped the moment's warmth was not all from the fermented brew.

Before them, a new group began an elaborate dance around the central fire pit. The celebrants, both men and women, wore gold or silver face paint and danced in precise rhythm to a tune played on the skull of some jungle deer, the horns of which acted as a flute.

"It's beautiful," Maggie said. "Like a dream. Stories we've read come to life."

Sam pulled her closer to him. "I only wish Uncle Hank were here to see it."

"And Ralph, too," Maggie said softly.

Sam glanced at the woman in his arms. She was staring into the firelight, her eyes ablaze, the warm glow bathing her face.

She must have sensed his scrutiny. She turned to him, their faces close, too close. "But you were right,

Sam," she said softly. "Before . . . when you said the dead don't begrudge the living. You were right. We're alive . . . we're here. And we mustn't waste this gift with guilt an' sorrow. That would be the true tragedy."

He nodded. "It's wrong to live a life as if you were dead." His voice was just an exhaled whisper. Sam remembered the years following the loss of his parents. He and his uncle had shared their sorrow together, leaning on each other. But in truth, the two of them were not unlike Maggie. In part, they, too, had barred outsiders, using their shared tragedy as a barrier against getting close to others. He didn't want to do that any longer.

Sam dared to inch a little nearer to Maggie.

She stared up into his eyes, her lips slightly parted.

He leaned nearer, his heart thundering in time with the drums—then suddenly the music ended. A heavy silence descended over the plaza.

Maggie glanced away at the interruption, ending the intimate moment. "It seems the party's over."

Sam's heart squeezed tight in his chest. He could not trust his voice. He swallowed hard, freeing his tongue. "I . . . I guess it is," he choked out.

A figure crossed toward them. It was the shaman, whose name they had learned was Kamapak. On his tattooed face, he wore a wide smile as he approached, climbing the stairs. Sam and Maggie rose to greet him. He babbled in his native tongue, arms lifted in both thanks and farewell, clearly wishing them a good night's rest. Already the fires around them were being extinguished.

Standing, Sam's head spun slightly with the effects of the *chicha* beer. Steadying himself for a breath, he stared at the fading flames, a mirror of his own inner hopes and passions. He turned away. It hurt too much to look.

Chaperoned by the shaman, Sam and Maggie drifted back toward the rooms assigned them. The Inca still talked excitedly as he led them.

Sam wished Denal were still there to translate for them, but he was able to discern a few familiar words. Something about one of their mythic gods, Inkarri. Not understanding, Sam just smiled and nodded in the universal manner of the nonfluent.

When they reached the row of homes bordering the square, Kamapak finally grew quiet and patted Sam on the shoulder. The shaman bowed his head, then whisked away to oversee the end of the celebration.

Maggie paused, watching him leave. Her room was separate from the men's. Sam stood awkwardly, wondering if that moment ago could be rekindled, but Maggie's next words doused cold water on those embers. "What was all that about Inkarri?"

Sam shrugged, recalling the Inca's epic story. Supposedly, Inkarri was the living son of Inti, the Sun, and the last god-king of his people. It was said he was captured by the Spanish conquerors and beheaded, but his decapitated head did not die. It was stolen away and hidden in a sacred cave—where, to this day, it had supposedly been growing a new body. When the body was complete, Inkarri would rise again and restore the Incas to their former splendor.

But this was, of course, just plain myth. The last leader of the Incas had been Atahaulpa. He had been garroted to death by the Spanish army led by Pizarro in 1533, and his body cremated. Sam shook his head. "Who knows what the shaman was suggesting? Maybe in the morning we could have Denal talk to him."

Maggie frowned. "It's still strange. I'd always thought that myth originated when tales of the Spanish conquest were mixed with Biblical stories brought by missionaries, stories of Christ's resurrection. It's odd to hear the *socyoc* of this isolated tribe recounting the same tale here."

"Well, whatever the source, he sure as hell seemed excited."

Nodding, Maggie continued to stare out at the terraced village as the campfires were extinguished and the torches ground into the sand. Darkness spread across the stone homes, swallowing them away. Finally, she sighed and turned away. "I guess I'd better turn in. We have a long day tomorrow. Good night, Sam."

He waved her off, then turned to the reed mat that hung over his own door. As he pushed aside the barrier, stories of Incan gods faded into the background, replaced by the memory of Maggie staring up at him, eyes bright with the promise of passion. Sam's chest still ached at the untimely interruption.

Maybe he had read too much into that fiery moment. Still, he knew the memory of her lips would haunt his dreams this coming night.

Sighing, he ducked into his room.

DAY FIVE

Inkarri

Friday, August 24, 6:30 A.M.
Cuzco, Peru

Joan had not slept all night. She sat at the small desk in her cell, a tiny oil lamp illuminating her work. The crinkled sheet of yellow legal paper was spread upon the wormwood desk. The sliver of a pencil in her hand was now worn dull, the eraser rubbed down to its metal clasp. Still, she worked at deciphering the row after row of symbols. It was her handwritten copy of the coded message found on the back of Friar Francisco de Almagro's crucifix. Nobody had thought to confiscate the paper from her, but why would they? No one but she and Henry knew the significance of the scrawled symbols.

Joan tapped the pencil against her lips. "What were you trying to warn us about?" she mumbled for the thousandth time since returning to her cell after dinner last night. She had been unable to sleep, her mind fraught both with worry over her imprisonment and curiosity about the revelations in the Abbey's laboratory.

And her fellow prisoner down the hall had offered her no solace.

After learning of his nephew's danger, Henry had grown distant from her, his eyes hard and angry, his manner closed. He had not spoken a single word over dinner. As a matter of fact, he had hardly touched his lamb chops. Any attempt of hers to allay his fears was met with a polite rebuff.

So Joan had returned to her cell, tense and anxious. At about midnight, she had begun working on the code after her failed attempt at slumber.

Joan stared at her night's work. Large sections of the message had been translated, but many gaps still existed. Her success so far was mostly due to the one large clue provided by Abbot Ruiz himself: the name *el Sangre del Diablo*. From the wide variety of runelike symbols, Joan had already estimated each mark corresponded to a letter of the alphabet, a simple replacement code. So it was just a matter of finding a matching sequence of symbols that would correspond to the same sequence of letters in *el Sangre del Diablo*. She had prayed that somewhere in the cryptogram the friar would mention the name.

And he had!

With that handful of symbols now assigned specific letters, it was just a matter of trial and error to decipher the rest of the cryptogram. But it was still difficult. She was far from fluent in Spanish. She wished Henry had been there to help her—especially since it was so disconcerting to realize that the tidbits she had deciphered so far were glimpses into a man's last words, his final warning to the world.

She held the paper up. A chill passed through her as she read: *Here is my last willed words. May God forgive me . . . the Serpent of Eden . . . pestilence. . . . Satan's Blood corrupts God's good work . . . Prometheus holds our salvation . . . pray . . . may the Serpent never be loosed.*

Sighing, Joan laid down her pencil and paper, then rubbed her tired eyes. This was the best she could accomplish. Friar de Almagro had been either insane or scared witless, but after what she had witnessed in the vault below, Joan could not be sure his ravings didn't hold some kernel of truth. Whatever he had found, it had terrified him.

The sound of approaching footsteps echoed down the hall, interrupting her reverie.

Quickly, she folded the yellow paper and pocketed it again. If she had a private moment with Henry, she would get his feedback . . . that is, if he would listen to her. She remembered how stubborn Henry had been as a youth, full of deep moods that she could never touch back then. But she wouldn't let that stop her now. Even if she had to twist his arm, she would make him hear her out. Francisco de Almagro had feared something up in the mountains, something associated with the mysterious metal. If Henry's nephew was in the thick of things up there, Henry had best listen to her.

A sharp knock on her door was followed by a voice. "The abbot wishes to see you both." The curt voice was Carlos's. Joan swung around as a jangle of keys unlocked her door.

Now what?

Henry sat once again in the abbot's study. Rows of books lined the walls, and the wide windows were cracked open upon a view of the Church of Santo Domingo, its cross bright in the morning sunlight. Behind him, another monk stood guard, pistol in hand.

But Henry saw none of it as he sat huddled in on himself. In his mind's eye, he pictured Sam buried under piles of rubble and tons of granite blocks. His fists clenched. It was his fault. What had he been thinking when he left the excavation site to a handful of inexperienced students? He knew the answer. He had been blinded by the possibility of proving his theory. Nothing else had mattered. Not even Sam's safety.

The creak of heavy doors announced the arrival of someone else. Henry glanced back over his shoulder to see Joan escorted in by the dark-eyed Carlos. Her eyelids were puffy, and from the wrinkled state of her blouse and pants, it looked like any attempts at sleep had failed her, too.

Joan offered Henry no smile when she entered the room. But why should she? She was yet another person whose life had been threatened by Henry's folly. He had reentered her life only to endanger it.

"Sit down," Carlos ordered the woman roughly. "Abbot Ruiz will be joining you shortly." The friar then mumbled something in Spanish to the other guard, his words too rushed and quiet for Henry to make out. Then Carlos left.

Joan sank into the other cushioned chair before the wide mahogany desk. "How are you holding up?" she asked.

Henry did not feel like talking, but she deserved at least the courtesy of a response. "Okay. How about you?"

"The same. It was a long night." Joan glanced toward the guard and leaned a little closer. She touched Henry's knee, feigning intimacy, just two lovers consoling one another. Her words were no more than soft breaths. "I think I've deciphered most of the code on your mummy's crucifix."

Despite his despair, Henry was jolted. "What?"

His startled reaction drew the eye of the guard. The monk glared at him, lifting his pistol higher.

Henry lowered his voice, then reached and touched Joan's cheek. It did not require much acting to play the lover of this woman. "What do you mean?" he whispered. "I tossed the cross away back at the lab."

Joan reached to a pocket in her blouse and pulled out the corner of a yellow sheet of paper. "My copy."

Henry's eyes grew wide. Here he had been wallowing all night in his own guilt and anger, and Joan had spent the hours laboring at the crucifix's cryptogram. Shame flushed his cheeks. But why should her action surprise him? She had always been so resourceful.

Joan continued in hushed tones. "It warns that this mysterious metal is dangerous. His last words seemed to be a garbled warning about some disease or pestilence associated with Substance Z. Something I think his order knew nothing about . . . and still doesn't."

Henry found himself drawn into the mystery. He could not help Sam directly from here, but knowledge could be a powerful weapon. "What was he afraid of?"

Joan shrugged her face. "I couldn't decipher it all. There are gaps missing and strange references: the Serpent of Eden, the Greek myth of Prometheus." She stared intently at Henry. "I need your help in figuring it out."

Henry's gaze flicked toward the guard. He wanted to get a peek at her translation, but there was no way with the guard looking on. "The Serpent of Eden is surely a reference to the tempter of forbidden knowledge in the Bible, a metaphoric reference to something that both tantalizes and corrupts."

"Like Substance Z, perhaps."

Henry's brows lowered. "Maybe . . ."

"But what about the Prometheus reference?"

Henry shook his head. "I don't see that connection at all. He was one of the mythic Titans who stole fire from the gods and brought it to mankind. He was punished by being chained to a rock and having his liver eaten out by a huge vulture each day."

Joan frowned. "Strange . . . why mention that?"

Henry leaned back into his chair and silently pondered the mystery. It was better than uselessly worrying over Sam. He took off his glasses and rubbed at his eyes. "There must be a reason."

"That is assuming the man was still sane when he etched the cross."

"I don't know. Let me think about this. According to Abbot Ruiz, Francisco was pursuing the mother lode, the true source of *el Sangre*. He already knew of its transformational property, so I think your earlier assumption was correct. He discovered something up in the mountains, something that changed his mind about the metal."

"And something that scared the hell out of him."

Henry nodded. "But he was also eventually executed and mummified, suggesting he had been captured by the Incas after making this discovery. If he wanted to get a warning out to his order, a message on the cross was a smart move on his part, a calculated chance. He must have known that the Incan shamans would have left unmolested any personal items, especially gold, on the body of the deceased. It was his one chance of getting his message out, even if he did not. He must have hoped his body would be returned to the Spaniards, rather than mummified and buried like it was."

"So what does all this suggest?"

Henry turned to Joan, worry in his eyes. He had no answer.

Any response from Joan was cut off as the door opened again. Abbot Ruiz marched into the room, his face red from either exertion or excitement. Carlos followed in his wake and took up a station beside the other guard. Ruiz continued to his desk, sighing as he eased his large bulk into his seat. He eyed Henry and Joan for a few silent moments. "I have good news, Professor Conklin. Word from the mountains reached us early this morning."

Henry sat up straighter. "Sam and the others?"

"You'll be pleased to hear they've made it out of the buried temple. They're safe."

Henry swallowed back a sob of relief. Joan reached a hand out to him, and he clutched it gratefully. "Thank God."

"Indeed you should," Ruiz said. "But that is not all."

Henry raised his eyes. Joan still held his hand.

"It seems you've trained your nephew well." Ruiz wore a broad smile.

"What do you mean?" Henry asked, his voice hard.

"He and his fellow students have made an astounding discovery up in the mountains."

Henry's eyes narrowed.

The abbot leaned back in his chair, clearly enjoying the suspense. "He's found a lost Incan tribe, a village nestled high in a volcanic cone."

"What?" Shocked, Henry clutched Joan's hand harder. He did not know what to make of this pronouncement. Was it some trick of the abbot's? But Henry could think of no motive. "Are . . . are you sure?" he asked, dismayed.

"That is what we are going to verify," Ruiz said. "I've spent all morning making arrangements and getting everything in order for our journey."

"*Our* journey?"

"Yes, both you and I. We'll need your expertise up there, Professor Conklin. We'll also need your presence to convince your nephew to cooperate fully with us." Abbot Ruiz quickly told of Sam's radioed message and of the students' escape through caves to the hidden site of the village. "So you see, Professor Conklin, we don't know exactly where this volcano is. There are hundreds in the area. Your nephew has proposed signaling us by a set of bonfires, and with you alongside us, I'm sure he'll do so posthaste."

Henry sat stunned by the news. It was too much to assimilate at once. Sam was safe—but if Henry got involved, if he went along with Ruiz's plan, then he could put Sam into more danger. On the other hand, out in the field, perhaps he'd have a chance to warn his nephew, stop whatever Ruiz schemed. Imprisoned here, he had little chance of doing anything to help his nephew.

Joan squeezed his hand, clearly sensing his distress. He found comfort in her grip.

Abbot Ruiz stood up. "We're set to leave by helicopter in ten minutes," he said. "Time is critical."

"Why?" Henry asked, taking strength from Joan.

Ruiz stared Henry down. "Because we have come to believe your nephew has uncovered more than just an Incan tribe. He may have unearthed the site of *el Sangre del Diablo*'s mother lode. Why else would a small clan of Incas still be hiding up there? Unless they were guarding something."

Joan and Henry exchanged concerned glances.

"We must hurry." The abbot waved to Carlos, who shuffled forward in his robe, his 9mm Glock again in his hand.

"Move," the guard said harshly, jabbing his gun into Henry's throat.

The abbot seemed oblivious to his aide's rough manner. As if washing his hands of the matter, he circled around the desk and headed to the door.

At gunpoint, Henry and Joan stood.

"Not you," Carlos said, indicating Joan. "You're staying here."

Joan's brows crinkled with fear.

Still holding her hand, Henry pulled her closer. "She comes with me, or I don't leave."

By the door, the abbot paused at the commotion. "Fear not, Professor. Dr. Engel simply remains here to ensure your cooperation. As long as you obey our orders, no harm will come to her."

"Fuck that! I'm not going!" Henry said fiercely.

A nod from the abbot and Carlos struck faster than Henry could react. The large man swung his arm and slapped Joan a resounding blow across her face. She fell to the floor, a surprised cry on her lips.

Henry was instantly at her side, kneeling beside her.

She lifted her hands from her pale face. Her fingers were bloody, her lip split.

Henry turned to take in both Ruiz and Carlos. "You goddamned bastards! There was no need for that!"

"And there is no need for profanity either," Ruiz said calmly from the doorway. "The lesson could've been much worse. So I'll invite you again, Professor Conklin, please come with me. Do not disobey again, or Carlos will not be so lenient next time."

Joan nudged Henry away. "Go," she said around her tears, her voice shaky. "D . . . Do as they say."

He leaned closer to her. He knew he had to leave. Still . . . "I can't abandon you here."

She pushed to her knees and swiped at the blood trailing down her chin. "You have to," she said tremulously, near to sobbing. Joan then reached out and hugged him, falling into his arms. She whispered in his ears, her voice instantly dropping from its frightened demeanor to a firmer tone. "Go, Henry. Help Sam."

Henry was stunned by the transformation, suddenly realizing the "shrinking violet" act was for the benefit of their captors.

Joan continued, "If the bastards are right about the mother lode being up there, you're the only one who knows of Francisco's warning. So go. I'll manage what I can from here."

Henry could find no words to match this woman's strength. "But—?"

She hugged him tighter, faking a sob, then hissed into his ear, "Oh, quit this chauvinistic crap. I thought you were better than that." She leaned her cheek against his own. Her voice grew louder again for the benefit of Carlos and Ruiz. "*Oh, please, do . . . do whatever they ask of you. For my sake. Just come back to me!*"

Even considering the circumstances, Henry could not hold back a tight grin. He buried his expression in the folds of her thick raven hair. "Okay, now you're laying it on a bit too thick."

She kissed him gently by the earlobe, her breath hot on his neck, her voice a whisper again. "I meant every word. You had better come back for me, Henry. I won't have you disappearing from my life like you did after college."

They held each other for a few silent seconds. Then she shoved him brusquely away. *"Go!"*

Henry rose to his feet, his neck still warm from her kiss. He saw new tears in Joan's eyes that he suspected were not faked. "I'll be back," he said softly to her.

Carlos grabbed his elbow. "Come on," he spat sourly, and yanked him away.

Henry did not resist this time. He turned to the door, but not before catching Joan as she mouthed one final warning, her bloody fingers touching her breast pocket.

As Henry was led away, Joan's last message echoed through his thoughts—both a mystery and a warning.

Beware the Serpent.

Two things struck Sam when he awoke the next morning and crawled out of his bed of straw. First, amazement that he could have slept at all. Around him, scattered throughout the stone room were countless examples of Incan handiwork: pottery with enameled designs, woven tapestries hung upon the walls depicting gods in battle, simple wooden utensils and stone tools. He really was in a living Incan village! He could not believe the dream from last night was still real.

Second, he realized that the Incas' *chicha* beer had created the most brain-splintering hangover he'd ever had. His head pounded like one of the drums from last night, and his tongue felt as furry as a monkey's tail. "God, I didn't even drink that much," he groaned. He stretched, adjusted the loincloth he'd donned the day before, and rolled to his feet. "It must be the altitude," he decided aloud.

Searching for his tunic, he found it in a corner and slipped into it. Rounding up his Stetson, he headed toward the door. He noticed Denal and Norman were already up and about. Their beds were empty.

Shoving aside the reed mat that hung across the doorway, Sam blinked against the painful glare of late-morning sunlight. Too bright for his bleary eyes. Nearby, birds sang from the treetops, and a scent of lavender almost overpowered the ever-present reek of sulfur from the volcanic vents. Sam groaned at the morning.

"About time," Maggie said from nearby. Norman and Denal were at her side. "You'll be happy to know the Incas also developed a form of coffee."

Sam raised both hands and ambled toward the sound of her voice. "Give me!"

His eyes slowly adjusted to the light, and he found his three companions, dressed in matching tunics, gathered around two women who were working at a small brick stove with an open baking hearth beneath it. The trio smiled at his sorry state.

He hobbled over to them. Thick earthenware pots rested on small openings atop the stone oven, bubbling warmly with morning porridges and stews. The smell of baking bread arose from the oven, along with another odor he could not place.

Sam bent and took a deep whiff from the oven, clearing his head of the cobwebs.

"Llama dung," Maggie said.

Sam straightened. "What?"

"They use llama dung to fuel their ovens."

Taking a step back, Sam frowned. "Delightful."

The pair of young Incan women who were cooking chattered amongst themselves, skirting quick glances toward the strangers. One of them was pregnant, her belly swelling hugely. Sam knew the work ethic of the Incas was severe. Everyone worked. They had a saying: *Ama sua, ama lulla, ama quella.* Do not steal, do not lie, do not be lazy. The only nod toward pampering the pregnant women was the presence of a low wooden stool, or *duho*, providing them with the opportunity to settle their weight while they worked. It was one of the few pieces of furniture the Incas built.

Sam accepted a mug of a thick, syrupy brew from Maggie and looked at it doubtfully.

"It helps," Maggie said with a wan smile. It seemed she had not completely escaped the aftereffects of the wicked brew either.

Sam sipped at the Incan coffee. It tasted nutty with a hint of cinnamon. Satisfied that it tasted better than it looked, he settled in with his drink. He sipped quietly for a few precious moments. Maggie was right. The Incan coffee helped clear his head, but his thoughts remained fuzzy at the edges. He swore off *chicha* forever. Finally, he lifted his face from the steam of his mug. "So what's the morning's plan?"

Norman answered. "Morning? It's almost noon, Sam. I'm ready for a short siesta." His words were jaunty, but his pale face gave him away. Sam hadn't noticed at first, but the photographer's skin had a sickly sheen to it. Sam saw how he had to lean heavily on Denal as he limped away from the wall.

"How's the leg?" Sam asked.

Norman hiked up the edge of his tunic. His knee was bandaged, but it was obviously swollen.

One of the women leaned closer, studying Norman's leg. She babbled something in Inca. Three pairs of eyes turned to Denal.

He translated. It was lucky his Quechan language was so similar to the native Inca from which it was derived. Otherwise, the group would be hard-pressed to communicate there. "She says Norman needs to go to the temple."

"Temple?" Sam said.

"I'm not gonna have some witch doctor work on me," Norman said, dropping the edge of his tunic. "I'll tough it out until help arrives. Speaking of which, have you tried to reach Philip at the camp?"

Sam shook his head, worry for the photographer crinkling his eyes. "I'll do it now. If we can't get a helicopter up here tonight, maybe you'd better consult the witch doctor. The Incas were known for their proficiency at natural medicines. Even surgery."

Norman rolled his eyes. "I don't think my HMO will cover the costs."

Sam waved him back to the shelter. "Then at least go lie down. I'm going to call Sykes right now."

Denal helped Norman back to the room. Sam followed to get his walkie-talkie from the pack. He cast a concerned look at Norman when the man gave out a soft cry as he settled atop the straw bed. "Make sure he drinks plenty today," Sam said to Denal. "Once you've got him settled, join me. I'll need your help in some translation with the natives."

Sam then slipped through the reed covering and stepped a few paces away, clicking on the walkie-talkie. The battery indicator was in the red range. It would not last much longer without a recharge. "Sam to base. Sam to base. Over."

Maggie came over to listen in.

The response was almost immediate. "About time, Conklin!" Philip whined at him. Static frosted his words.

"Any luck arranging a rescue up here? Norman's injured bad, and we need a quick evac."

The excitement in his fellow student's voice could not be completely masked by white noise. "Your uncle's coming! The professor! He's just leaving Cuzco! He should be here with a helicopter and supplies by dawn tomorrow."

Maggie clutched Sam's elbow excitedly.

Philip continued, "I didn't get to speak to him. Radio's still out. But word passed from Cuzco, to the nearby town of Villacuacha, then to our base by a makeshift walkie-talkie network some monks set up this morning. Word just reached us this past hour!"

Sam's emotions were mixed. Uncle Hank was coming! But still a frown marred his lips. He had hoped for rescue *today*, but such a hope was not realistic. They were hundreds of miles away from anyplace with even a crude form of airport. He clicked the transmit button. "Great news, Philip! But get that helicopter up here as soon as possible. Light a fire under Uncle Hank if you can. We'll keep a fire burning here all night long, just in case he's able to arrive any earlier." The red light on his battery indicator began blinking ominously. "I gotta go, Philip! I'll call you at sunset for an update."

Static ate most of Philip's response. The scratchy white noise began tweaking Sam's residual headache. He cursed and clicked the walkie-talkie off. He hoped his last message reached Philip.

"Dawn tomorrow," Maggie said, relief clear in her voice. She turned to stare at the village. "It'll be great to have Professor Conklin here."

Sam stepped next to her. "I'm still worried about Norman. I really think we should talk to Kamapak, the shaman. See if the Incas here at least have the equivalent of aspirin or a pain reliever."

Off to the side, Denal bowed through the reed mat. He crossed toward them. "Norman sleeps," the boy said as he joined them, but his lips were tight with concern.

"Maybe we'd better find that shaman," Maggie said. "Can you help us, Denal?"

The youth nodded, and turned toward the village. "I ask." He hesitated before going, squinting at the homes. "But something no right here."

"What do you mean?"

"There no children," Denal said, glancing up at them.

Maggie and Sam frowned at each other, then stared out at the spread of stone homes. "Sure there are . . ." Sam started to say, but his voice died away. They had not noticed any youngsters when they had arrived yesterday, but the sun had been close to setting. The celebration had run late into the evening, so the lack of children had not struck Sam as odd enough to notice.

"He's right," Maggie said. "I've been up for at least an hour, and I've seen no wee ones either."

Sam pointed toward where the two women still worked at the ovens. "But she's pregnant. The children must be somewhere. Maybe they're hiding them from us as a precaution."

Maggie scrunched up her nose, unconvinced. "They seemed to accept us so readily. No guards or anything."

"Let's go ask," Sam said, nodding toward the pregnant Incan woman.

He led the others back to the oven. Sam nudged Denal. "Ask her where the children are kept."

Denal stepped closer and spoke to the woman. She seemed uncomfortable so near the boy. She guarded her belly with a hand. Her answer was clearly agitated, involving much arm movement and pointing.

Sam glanced to where she indicated. She was pointing toward the neighboring volcanic cone that overlooked this caldera.

Denal finally gave up and turned back to Sam. "There no children. She say they go to *janan pacha*. Heaven." Denal nodded to the towering volcano.

"Sacrifices, do you think?" Maggie said, stunned. Infanticide and blood rites with children were not unknown in Incan culture.

"But *all* their children?"

Maggie crossed to the woman. She cradled her arms and rocked them in the universal sign of baby. "*Wawas . . . wawas . . . ?*" she asked, using the Quechan word for baby. Maggie then pointed to the woman's large gravid belly.

The woman's eyes widened with shock, then narrowed with anger. She held a hand pressed to her belly. "*Huaca*," she said firmly, and spoke rapidly in Quecha.

"*Huaca*. Holy place," Denal translated. "She say her belly be home now only to gods, no longer children. No children here for many, many years. They all go to temple."

The woman turned her back on them, dismissing them. Clearly offended by their line of questioning.

"What do you suppose she's talking about, Sam?" Maggie asked.

"I don't know. But I think we have another reason now to seek out that shaman." Sam waved Denal and Maggie to follow him. "Let's go find Kamapak."

Their search ended up being harder than Sam had thought. Most of the men had gone to work the fields or hunt, including the shaman. Denal managed to glean some directions from a few of the villagers who had duties within the town's limits. Sam's group soon found themselves trekking down a jungle path. They passed groves of fruit and avocado trees being harvested and pruned. And a wide plowed meadow where fields of grainlike quinoa alternated with rows of corn, chili pepper plants, beans, and squash. Both men and women worked the fields. In an unplanted area, men were using *tacllas,* or foot plows, to turn the soil, while women helped, using a simple hoe called a *lampa.* Maggie and Sam paused to watch them labor, amazed to see these ancient Incan tools at work.

"I can't believe this," Sam said for the hundredth time that day.

Denal nudged Sam. "This way," he said, urging them on.

Sam and Maggie followed, still looking over their shoulders. They reentered the jungle and within a short time came upon a clearing. The shaman stood with a handful of other men. Cords of hewn wood were stacked on sleds. The gathered Incas could have been brothers, all strong, muscular men. Only the shaman's tattoos distinguished him from the others. Kamapak, at first, was startled by their appearance, then smiled broadly and waved them all forward. He spoke rapidly.

Denal translated. "He welcomes us. Says we come in time to help."

"Help with what?"

"Hauling wood back to town. Last night, at the feast, the many campfires burned their stores."

Sam groaned, his head still pounding slightly from his hangover. "Emissaries of the gods, or not, I guess we're expected to earn our keep." Sam took up a position beside Kamapak, taking up one of the many shoulder straps used to haul the sled. Denal was beside him.

Maggie walked ahead, helping to clear chunks of volcanic stone and make a path.

With six men acting as oxen, dragging the sled proved easier than Sam expected. Still, one of the men passed Sam a few leaves of a coca plant. When chewed, the cocaine in the leaves helped offset the altitude effects . . . and his hangover. Sam found his head less achy. He wondered if the leaves might help Norman's fever and pain.

Feeling better now, Sam conversed with the shaman as he hauled on the sled. Denal translated.

Sam's inquiry about children was met with the same consternation. "The temple receives our children from our women's bellies. This close to *janan pacha*"—again a nod to the towering volcanic cone to the south—"the god, Con, has blessed our people. Our children are his children now. They live in *janan pacha*. Gifts to Con."

Maggie had been listening and glanced back. Sam shrugged at her. Con was one of the gods of the northern tribes. In stories, he had epic battles with Pachacamac, creator of the world. But it was said that it was the god, Con, who created man upon this earth.

"This temple," Sam asked, speaking around his wad of bittersweet leaves. "May we see it."

The shaman's eyes narrowed. He shook his head vehemently. "It is forbidden."

From the man's strong rebuff, Sam did not pursue the matter. *So much for being emissaries of the god of thunder,* he thought. It seemed Illapa was not high on this village's totem pole.

Maggie slipped back to Sam's side. She whispered, "I was thinking about Denal's observation about the missing children and got to thinking about the village's makeup. There is another element of this society that is missing, too."

"Who?"

"Elders. Old people. Everyone we've seen has been roughly the same age . . . give or take twenty years."

Sam's feet stumbled as he realized Maggie was right. Even the shaman could not be much older than Sam. "Maybe their life expectancy is poor."

Maggie scowled. "Life is pretty insulated here. No major predators, unless you count those things down in the deep caves."

Sam turned to Kamapak and, with Denal's help, questioned him about the missing old folk.

His answer was just as cryptic. "The temple nurtures us. The gods protect us." From the singsong way the words were spoken, it was clearly an ancient response. And apparently an answer to most questions. When Maggie made her own inquiries—into health care and illness among the members—she received the same answer.

She turned to Sam. "It seems the old, the young, the frail, and the sick end up there."

"Do you think they're being sacrificed?"

Maggie shrugged.

Sam pondered her words, then turned to Denal, trying a different tack on this conversation. "Try describing those creatures we saw in the caves."

The boy frowned, tiring of his role as translator, but he did as Sam asked. The shaman's brows grew dark with the telling. He called a halt to the sled. His words were low with a hint of threat as Denal translated. "Do not speak of those who walk through *uca pacha*, the underworld. They are *mallaqui*, spirits, and it is ill to whisper of them." With those words, the shaman waved the sled on.

Sam glanced at the volcanic mountain to the south. "Heaven up there, and hell below us. All the spiritual realms of the Inca joined in this one valley. A *pacariscas*, a magical nexus."

"What do you think it means?" Maggie said.

"I don't know. But I'll be glad when Uncle Hank arrives."

Soon the team of haulers and their load of wood reached the village's edge. By now it was well past noon, and the workers tossed off their harnesses and began meandering into the village proper. The spread of homes once again was full of chattering and happy people. It seemed even the workers in the field had returned for a midday rest.

Sam, Maggie, and Denal wandered back to their own shelters. Ahead, Sam noticed that the women who had been cooking at the stove were now spooning out roasted corn and stew into stone bowls. He smiled, suddenly realizing how hungry he was.

"We should wake Norman," Maggie said. "He should try an' eat."

Denal ran ahead. "I get him," the boy called back.

Maggie and Sam took their places in line before the stove. Other ovens around the village also steamed into the air, like mini volcanic vents. Like most Incan townships, this village was broken into distinct *ayllu*, extended family units or groupings. Each *ayllu* had its own open-air kitchen. Among the Incas, meals were always eaten outdoors, weather permitting.

Reaching the head of the line, Sam was handed a bowl of steaming stew topped by a ladle of mashed roasted corn. Poked into it was a small chunk of dried meat, *charqui*, jerked llama steak.

Sam was sniffing at it when Denal burst from the nearby doorway and hurried toward them, his boyish face drawn and serious.

"What is it?" Maggie asked.

"He gone," Denal glanced around the area. "I find his blanket and straw all messed up."

"Messed up?" Sam asked.

Denal swallowed hard, clearly worried and scared. "Like he fighting someone."

Maggie glanced to Sam. "Before we panic," he said, "let's simply ask." Sam waved Denal back to the pregnant women dishing stew. The boy interrupted her serving.

Denal spoke rapidly. The woman nodded, a smile growing on her face. When Denal turned to Sam, he was not sharing her smile.

"They take Norman to the temple."

By late afternoon, Joan found herself ensconced with a young monk in one of the many laboratory cubicles deep in the heart of the Abbey. Faithful to his word, the abbot had left orders that Joan be treated as a guest. So her request to observe the Abbey's researchers at work was grudgingly allowed—though her personal guard dog was never far away. Even now, Joan could see Carlos through the observation window. He rested one palm on his holstered pistol.

A young monk named Anthony drew back her attention. "Of course, we all have our own personal theories," he said matter-of-factly, his English fluent. "It is not as if we let our faith cloud our experimentation. The abbot always says our faith should withstand the vigors of science."

Joan nodded and leaned a bit closer to the man. They now stood before a bank of computers and monitors. Several technicians worked a few cubicles down, dressed the same as they were, in sterile white lab suits, but otherwise they were alone.

Anthony logged onto the computer. Near his elbow was a tray of minute samples of the Incan metal, row after row of miniscule gold teardrops embedded in plastic wells. Fresh from the freezer, a slight fog of dry ice still clung to the tray. She had learned the lab was trying to learn the nature of the metal in an attempt to accelerate their desired goal of bringing Christ back to earth. They had already developed methods to rid the metal of contaminating impurities, heightening the miraculous abilities of the substance.

Joan studied the teardrop samples. To test her own theory, she needed one of those pearls of gold. But how? The samples were so close, but with so many eyes watching, the tray might as well have been locked behind iron bars. Joan tightened her fists, determined not to fail in her mission. She needed just a moment's distraction. Taking a deep breath, she readied herself.

"I'm almost set," the young monk said, working at the keyboard.

And so was she.

Joan leaned her left breast more firmly against his shoulder as she peered at the tray. She had picked Anthony as her guide because of the youth's age; clean-shaven and dark-haired, he could not be much older than twenty. But besides his impressionable age, she had selected him from all the others for another reason. When she had first entered the labs, guarded by Carlos, Joan had noticed how the young man's eyes had widened in appreciation. She saw how his gaze had settled upon her breasts, then darted away. Back at Johns Hopkins, she had taught enough undergraduates to recognize when one seemed interested in more than just a scholarly education. Usually, she gently rebuffed any advances, but now she would exploit these feelings. Cloistered here among the monks, Joan suspected this youth could be easily unnerved by the attentions of a woman—and from the youth's reaction now, she had been proven right.

Anthony swallowed hard, his cheeks reddening. He pulled away slightly from her touch.

Joan took the advantage. She slid onto the neighboring stool, one hand crossing to rest on the youth's knee. "I'd be most interested in hearing your own theories, Anthony. You've been here a while. What do you think of *el Sangre del Diablo*?" She squeezed his knee ever so slightly.

Anthony glanced back to the glass partition, toward Carlos. Her hand was hidden from view by their bodies. The young monk did not pull away this time, but his face was almost a shade of purple. He sat frozen, stiff as a statue. If Joan's hand had wandered any higher up his leg, she expected she would have discovered exactly how stiff the young man was.

She had spent the entire afternoon brushing against him, touching him, whispering close to his ear. With gentle cajoling and urging, she had finally guided him to this last lab, where actual samples of the mysterious metal were being analyzed. Now the truly tricky part began.

Joan tilted her head, attentive to the young monk. "So tell me, what do you think the metal is, Anthony?"

He almost choked on his words, "Maybe nan . . . nanobots."

Now it was Joan's turn to startle, her hand slipping away from his knee. "Excuse me?"

Anthony nodded rapidly, relaxing slightly, now able to discourse on familiar territory. "Several of us . . . the younger researchers among us . . . think maybe the metal is actually some dense accumulation of nanobots."

"As in nanotechnology?" Joan said. She had read a few theoretical articles that had discussed the pos-

sibility of building subcellular machines—nanobots—
that could manipulate matter at the molecular or even
atomic level. A recent article published in *Scientific
American* described a crude first attempt to construct
such microscopic robots by scientists at UCLA. In her
mind, she remembered her own electron microscope
scan of the metal: the tiny particulate matrix linked together by hooklike appendages. But nanobots? Impossible. The youth here had obviously been reading too
much science fiction.

"Come see," Anthony said, suddenly excited to be
able to show off for his audience. He reached to the
tray and lifted one of the pellets of metal with a pair
of stainless-steel tweezers. He fed it into the machine
before him. "Electron crystallography," he explained.
"It's our own design here. It can isolate one unit of the
metal's crystalline structure and construct a three-
dimensional picture. Just watch." He tapped a monitor
screen with the tweezers.

Joan leaned closer, fishing out her eyeglasses, forgetting for the moment her seduction of the young monk.
When she had asked Anthony to show her the metal,
she hadn't meant such a *close* look. But now the scientist in Joan was intrigued.

An image appeared on the screen, in crisp detail, rotating slowly to show all surfaces. Joan recognized it.

A single microscopic particle of the metal. It was octagonal in shape with six threadlike appendages: one on top, one on bottom, and four radiating out from midsection. At the end of each were four tiny clawed hooks, like sparrow's talons.

Anthony pointed to the screen with the tip of a pen. "In overall shape and architecture, it bears a clear resemblance to a hypothesized nanobot proposed by Eric Drexler in his book *Engines of Creation*. He theorized a molecular machine in two sections: *computer* and *constructor*. The nanobot's brain and brawn, so to speak." He tapped at the central octagonal core. "Here's the central processor, its programmed brain, surrounded by six nodes, or constructors, that manipulate the arms." The young monk moved his pointer along to the thin talonlike hooks. "Here is what Drexler called its molecular positioners."

Joan frowned. "And you think this thing can actually manipulate matter at the molecular level?"

"Why not?" Anthony said. "We have enzymes in our bodies right now that act as natural *organic* nanobots. Or take the mitochondria inside our cells . . . those organelles are no more than microscopic power stations, manipulating matter at the atomic level to produce ATP, or energy, for our cells. Even the thousands of viruses in nature are forms of molecular machines." He glanced to her. "So you see, Mother Nature has already succeeded. Nanobots already exist."

Joan slowly nodded, turning back to the screen. "This thing looks almost viral," she mumbled. Joan had seen blowups of attacking viral phages. Under the electron microscope, they had appeared like lunar modules landing on cell membranes, more machine than living organism. This image reminded her of those viral assays.

"What was that?" Anthony asked.

Joan tightened her lips. "Just thinking out loud. But you're right. Even the prions that cause mad cow disease could be considered nanobots. They all manipulate DNA at the molecular level."

"Yes, exactly! *Organic* nanobots," he said, his face flushed with excitement. He pointed back at the screen. "Some of us think this may be the first *inorganic* nanobot discovered."

Joan frowned. Maybe it was possible. *But to what end?* she wondered. *What is its purpose?* She remembered Friar de Almagro's warning etched on the crucifix. He had been frightened of some pestilence associated with the metal. If the monk was correct, was this a clue? Many of the natural "organic" nanobots she had mentioned to Anthony—viruses, prions— were disease vectors. She sensed that with more time she could unravel the mystery. Especially with the use of this facility, she thought, glancing around the huge laboratory.

But first, she had one experiment to perform. Before handling disease vectors, it was always best to have a way of sterilizing them. And the dead friar had hinted at a way in his cryptogram: *Prometheus holds our salvation.*

Prometheus, the bearer of fire.

Was that the answer? Fire had always been the great sterilizer. Joan remembered the assessment made by Dale Kirkpatrick, the metallurgist. He had noted that Substance Z used energy with perfect efficiency. But what if the metal received too much heat, like from a flame? Maybe as sensitive as it was, it couldn't handle such an extreme.

Joan had come down here to test her theory, to steal a sample of metal on which to experiment. She risked a quick glance back at Friar Carlos. Her guard dog was clearly bored, too confident in the defenses of the Abbey to be worried about a mere woman.

Casually, Joan removed her glasses, then leaned more tightly into Anthony as he reached for a pen. The young man flinched at the sudden contact and jerked his arm back. His elbow knocked Joan's glasses from her hands. She made sure her eyewear landed atop the tray of precious samples. Small gold droplets danced and rolled across the desktop, like spilled marbles.

Anthony jumped up. "I'm sorry. I should have watched what I was doing."

"That's okay. No harm done." Joan scooted off her stool. She quickly palmed two of the rolling teardrops. Others tumbled to the floor. Technicians scurried forward to help Anthony gather the stray samples. Joan backed away.

Carlos appeared suddenly at her side, gun at the ready. "What happened?"

Joan pointed with one hand, while quickly pocketing her pilfered samples with the other. She nodded toward the flurry of activity. "It seems not even this blessed lab can escape Murphy's Third Law."

"And what's that?"

Joan turned an innocent face toward Carlos. "Shit happens."

Carlos scowled and grabbed her by the elbow. "You've been down here long enough. Let's go!"

She did not resist. She had what she had come for— and more.

From where he knelt on the laboratory floor, Anthony raised an arm in farewell. She graced him with a smile and a wave. The young man deserved at least that.

Carlos quickly led her back through the under-ground labyrinth. She thought it fitting that the dregs of the Spanish Inquisition should end up holing them-selves in the equivalent of an Incan torture chamber. She wondered if the choice of location was purposeful. One torturer taking up residence after another.

Soon Joan found herself before the door to her own cell.

Carlos nodded for her to enter.

But Joan hesitated, turning to him. "I don't suppose you have a cigarette on you." She didn't smoke, but he didn't know that. She scrunched up her face in feigned discomfort. "It's been two days, and I can't stand it any longer."

"The abbot forbids smoking in the abbey."

Joan frowned. "But he's not here, is he?"

An actual smile shadowed his lips. He glanced up the hall, as a packet of cigarettes appeared in his hands. Nothing like the communal secrecy of a closet smoker. He shook out two. "Here."

She pocketed one and slipped the other to her lips. "Do you mind?" she mumbled around the filter, lean-ing toward him for a light.

The perpetual scowl returned, but he reached to his robe and removed a lighter. He flamed the tip of her cigarette.

"Thanks," she said.

He just nodded toward the door of her cell.

She backed up, pulled the latch, and entered her cell.

"Those things will kill you," Carlos mumbled behind her, closing and locking the door.

Joan heard his footsteps retreat, then leaned against the door with a long sigh, smoke trailing from her lips. She held back a wracking cough. She had done it. After allowing herself a few moments to savor her victory, she pushed off the door and set to work. The missing samples might be discovered.

She crossed to the small desk and sat down. Removing the cigarette from her lips, she carefully rested it on the edge of the table. Suddenly fearing hidden cameras, Joan hunched over her desk and slipped out the few abstracts and articles on nanotechnology that the young monk had sent her. She planned on reading more about the young monk's theory. As she scooted the papers aside, a highlighted sentence from a personal paper caught her eye: *We have come to believe that each particulate structure of the metal may actually be a type of microscopic manufacturing device. But this raises two questions. To what purpose was it designed? And who programmed it?*

Joan straightened slightly, pondering these last two questions. *Nanotechnology?* She again pictured the nanobot's crystalline shape and hooked appendage arms. If the young researcher was correct, what the hell was the purpose of this strange metal? Had Friar de Almagro long ago discovered the answer? Was this what terrified him?

Leaning over the desk to cover her subterfuge, Joan slipped out one of the two gold droplets. Regardless of the answer, she knew one thing for sure. The metal had terrified the mummified friar, and he had possibly hinted at a way to destroy it.

Joan rolled the gold tear across the oak tabletop. Now warmed, the metal was like a piece of soft putty. She had to handle it carefully. Using her pen, she scooped a tiny bit onto the pen's tip and wiped it on the desktop. She had to be frugal. The test sample was about the size of a small ant.

Once done, she retrieved her cigarette, knocked off the ash, and lowered its glowing tip toward the metal. "Okay, Friar de Almagro. Let's see if Prometheus is our salvation."

Licking her lips, she touched the gold.

The reaction was not loud, no more than a firm cough, but the result was fierce. Joan's arm was thrown back. The cigarette flew from her fingers. Woodsmoke curled into the air. Her own gasp of surprise was louder than the explosion. She waved a hand through the smoke. A hole had been blown clear through the oak desktop.

"My God," she said, thanking her stars that she hadn't used the entire teardrop of metal. It would have taken out the entire desk and probably the wall behind it.

She glanced to the door, listening for footsteps. No one had heard.

Grimly, she stood and stepped to the door. She touched the lock, a plan coming to mind. She fingered the remaining golden samples, weighing them, calculating. She must get word out—especially to Henry.

But did she have enough of the volatile metal to blast her way to freedom? Probably not . . . She stepped away from the door. She would bide her time until the right moment.

She must wait, be as patient as Friar de Almagro. It had taken him five hundred years to get his message out. Joan stared at the smoldering hole in the desk— but someone had finally heard him.

As the sun set, Henry waited while the large helicopter refueled at the jungle-fringed landing strip. The abbot's crew of six men worked to load the final supplies into the cargo bay. Henry stood off to the side, at the edge of the dilapidated runway. Rotorwash scattered empty oil cans and trash across the hard-packed dirt strip. Nearby, in the shadow of a wooden shack, Abbot Ruiz, who had discarded his robes and stood dressed in a khaki safari outfit, argued with the pinched-face Chilean mechanic. It seemed the price of petrol was a heated debate.

Henry turned his back on them. Off to his left, two of the abbot's armed acolytes stood guard over him, ensuring that he, a sixty-year-old professor, did not make a break for the jungle. But the guards were unnecessary. Even if he could disarm the guards and bolt, Henry knew he would not survive ten steps into that jungle.

Beyond the edge of the forest, Henry had caught flashes of sunlight on metal, guerrillas hidden from sight, protecting their investment. This weed-choked strip was clearly a base for drug and gun smugglers. Henry also noted the crates of Russian vodka stacked by the side of the shack. *Black-market central*, he judged.

He resigned himself to his fate. They had traveled all afternoon from Cuzco to this unmarked landing strip. From there, he estimated it would be a four-hour hop to another secret refueling stop near Machu Picchu, then another three to four hours to reach the ruins. They should arrive just as the sun rose tomorrow.

He had until then to devise a way to thwart the abbot's group.

Henry recalled his brief contact with Philip Sykes. The student had clearly sounded relieved, but fear also traced his voice. Henry cursed himself for getting not only his own nephew into this jam, but all the other students, too. He had to find some way to protect them. But how?

A voice called out from near the helicopter. The tanks were topped and ready for the next leg of the journey.

"Finish loading!" Ruiz yelled back over the growl of the rotors. The abbot passed a fistful of bills to the tight-lipped Chilean. It seemed a price had been set.

Beside the helicopter, the last crates of excavation and demolition equipment still waited to be loaded. Among the gear, Henry noted four boxes with Cyrillic lettering burned into the wooden side planks. Clearly Russian contraband: grenades, AK-47 assault rifles, plastique. *Lots of armament for an archaeological team,* Henry thought sourly.

The abbot waved for Henry's guards to herd him back toward the pair of helicopters. Henry was under no delusions. He was just one more piece of equipment, another tool to be used, then discarded. Once the abbot had what he wanted, Henry suspected he would end up like Dr. Kirkpatrick back at Johns Hopkins, lying facedown, a bullet in the back—as would Joan, Sam, and the other students.

Henry was led back to the helicopter. He knew better than to resist. As long as Joan was captive, he had to wait, alert for any opportunity that might arise. As Henry crossed the hard dirt runway, he thought back to their last moment together. He remembered the scent of her hair, the brush of her skin as she whispered in his ear, the heat of her breath on his neck. His hands grew clammy thinking about the danger she faced. No harm must come to her. Not now, not later. He would find a way to free her.

Abbot Ruiz was all smiles when Henry reached the waiting helicopter. "We're off, Professor Conklin," he hollered, and climbed into the cabin. "Up to your ruins."

Frowning at the man's jovial manner, Henry was nudged by a guard to follow. Once inside, Henry strapped himself into the seat beside the abbot.

Leaning his large bulk forward, Ruiz talked to the pilot, their heads together so they could hear each other. The pilot pointed to his radio headpiece. When Ruiz turned back to Henry, his smile had faded away. "There seems to be more trouble up there," he said.

Henry's heart beat harder in his chest. "What are you talking about?"

"Your nephew had brief contact with the student at the ruins. It seems that the *National Geographic* photographer has got himself into a bit of a bind."

Henry remembered Philip's description of Norman's injury. He had not been allowed to talk long enough to get any details, other than that the photographer was hurt and needed medical attention. "What's the matter?"

The abbot was climbing back out of the helicopter. "Change in plans," he said with a deep frown. "I need to haggle for more fuel, enough to take us directly to the ruins. No more stops."

Henry grabbed Ruiz's arm. "What's happening?"

One of his guards knocked Henry's hand away, freeing the abbot. But Ruiz answered, "Your nephew seems to think the Incas are going to sacrifice the photographer."

Henry looked startled.

Abbot Ruiz patted Henry's knee. "Don't worry, Professor Conklin. We might not be able to rescue the photographer. But we'll get up there before the others are killed." Then the large man ducked under the idling rotors, holding his safari hat atop his head.

Henry leaned back into his seat, clenching his fists. Blood rites. He had not even imagined that possibility but, considering the Incan religious ceremonies, he should have! Sam and the others were now trapped between two bloodthirsty enemies—the disciples of the Spanish Inquisition and a lost tribe of Incan warriors.

From outside the window, Henry saw the abbot give the pilot a thumbs-up as lackeys of the guerrillas rolled two spare fuel tanks toward the waiting helicopter.

Narrowing his eyes, Henry suspected it was not altruism on the abbot's part that motivated this change in plans. It was not to save the other students' lives, but to protect Ruiz's stake in what might lie up there. If Sam and the others were killed, the site of the *Sangre* mother lode might be lost, possibly for centuries again. Abbot Ruiz was not taking any chances. Another two fistfuls of bills passed to the now-smiling Chilean.

Under the carriage of the helicopter, Henry felt the bump and scrape as the spare fuel tanks were loaded in place. The abbot crossed back toward the helicopter, hurrying.

Henry leaned his head back, a soft groan escaping his throat.

Time was running out—for all of them.

Maggie watched Sam stalk back and forth across the stone room, like a prodded bull awaiting the ring. He held his Stetson in a white-knuckled grip, slapping it repeatedly against his thigh. With their own clothes clean and dry, he had changed back into his Wrangler jeans and vest. Maggie suspected his change in dress was a reflection of Sam's anger and frustration with the Incas.

Though she understood Sam's attitude, she and Denal still wore the loose Incan wear, not wanting to offend their hosts.

Sam had tried all afternoon to get the shaman to allow them access to the temple or to bring Norman back. Kamapak's answer was always the same; Sam could translate it himself by now: "It is forbidden." And with no way of knowing where this sacred temple was hidden, they could not plot any rescue. The forested valley easily covered a thousand acres. They were at the mercy of the Incas.

"I contacted Philip and let him know the situation," Sam said, speaking rapidly, breathless, "but he's no help!"

Maggie stepped forward and stopped Sam's pacing with a touch to his arm. "Calm down, Sam."

Sam's eyes were glazed with guilt and frustration. "It's my fault. I should've never left him alone. What was I thinking?"

"They'd welcomed us as part of their tribe, accepted us warmly. There was no way you could've anticipated this."

Sam shook his head. "Still, I should have taken precautions. First, Ralph . . . now Norman. If only I had . . . if I had just—"

"What?" Maggie asked, now grabbing Sam's arm in an iron grip. She was going to make him listen. His ranting and breast-beating was doing them no good. "What would you have done, Sam? If you had been there when the Incas came to take Norman, what do you think you could have done to stop them? Any resistance would probably have gotten us all killed."

Sam shuddered under her grip, the glaze clearing from his eyes. "So what do we do? Wait while they pick us off one at a time?"

"We use our heads, that's what we do. We need to think clearly." Maggie let Sam go, trusting him to listen now. "First, I don't think they're going to pick us off. Norman was injured, so he was taken to the temple. We aren't hurt."

"Maybe . . ." Sam glanced at Denal, who stood by the reed mat that covered their doorway, peeking out. Sam lowered his voice. "But what about him? They take children there, too."

"Denal is past puberty. To the Incas, he's an adult. I doubt he's at risk."

"But did you see how they stare at him when he passes? It's like they're curious and a little confused."

Maggie nodded. *And fearful, too*, she added silently. But she did not want to set Sam off again.

Denal spoke up from the doorway. "People come."

Maggie heard them, too. Those who approached were not being secretive. The chattering of many excited voices sounded from beyond their shelter. Some were raised in song.

Sam crossed to join Denal. "What's going on?"

Denal shrugged, but Maggie saw his hands tremble a bit as they held the reed mat open. Sam placed a protective hand on the boy's shoulder and took up his Winchester in the other. Armed now, Sam pulled back the covering. The Texan stepped out, his back straight, confrontational.

Maggie hurried to join them. She didn't want Sam doing anything rash.

Outside, the sun had fully set. Night had cloaked the terraced village while they had discussed Norman's plight. Throughout the spread of homes, a scatter of torches bloomed, bright as stars in the darkness, while the full moon overhead served as the only other illumination.

As they watched, the neighboring plaza filled with a growing number of Incas. Some bore torches, while others held aloft pieces of flint, striking them together and casting sparks like fireflies into the night. Across the plaza, a rhythmic drumbeat stirred a handful of Incan women to dance, their tunics flaring around their legs. In the center of the square, a fire suddenly flared.

"Another celebration," Maggie said.

One of the men with the flints neared, smiling white teeth at them. He sparked his stones, matching the drums' rhythm. Flutes and pipes joined the chorus.

"It's like the fuckin' Fourth of July," Sam muttered.

"Definitely a party of some sort," Maggie agreed. "But what are they celebrating?" From Sam's stricken expression, Maggie suddenly wished she had remained silent. She stepped closer to him, knowing what he was thinking. Maggie had studied the Incan culture, too. A village would always celebrate after a blood ritual. A sacrifice was a joyous occasion. "We don't know this has anything to do with Norman," Maggie reasoned.

"But we don't know it doesn't," Sam grumbled.

Denal, who had been keeping close to the doorway, suddenly pushed forward. "Look!" he said, pointing.

Across the plaza, the mass of bodies entering the square parted. A lone figure wandered through them, dressed in an umber-colored robe and black *yacolla* cape knotted at one shoulder. He seemed dazed and walked with a slight drunken sway to his step.

Sam's voice matched the man's confusion. "Norman?"

Maggie grabbed Sam's elbow. "Sweet Mary, it's him!"

The two glanced at each other before rushing toward Norman. Around them, the celebrants were in full swing. The music grew louder, the chanting and singing along with it. Before they could reach Norman's side, Kamapak appeared from the crowd, blocking their path. In the firelight, the shaman's tattoos were spidery traces on his cheeks and neck: abstract symbols of power and strange feathered dragons.

Sam started to raise his rifle, but Maggie pushed the barrel down. "Hear him out."

The shaman spoke grandly. Denal translated. "Your friend has been accepted as worthy by the gods of *janan pacha*. He is now *ayllu*, family, with the Sapa Inca."

"The Sapa Inca?" Maggie asked, still holding the barrel of Sam's rifle. "Who?"

But the shaman was already turning away, inviting them forward to Norman's side. The photographer finally seemed to spot them. He waved a weak arm and stumbled in their direction. His face was still pale— not the ashen complexion of fever or illness, but more of shock. Sam hurried to his side. Maggie and Denal stayed beside the shaman.

Kamapak witnessed the reunion with clear pleasure. Maggie repeated her question with Denal's help.

"I don't understand. Sapa Inca?" Maggie had never thought this small village had any distinct leader, let alone one of the revered god-kings of the Incas. "Who is your Sapa Inca?"

The shaman frowned when Denal translated her words, then spoke slowly. Denal turned to her. "He say he gave you the name of the Sapa Inca before. It be Inkarri. He live at the Temple of the Sun."

"Inkarri . . . ?" Maggie remembered the mention last night of the beheaded warrior king. Her brows bunched together.

Any further inquiry was interrupted by Sam's reappearance with Norman. "You are not going to believe this," Sam said as introduction. He nodded to Norman. "Show her."

Norman reached to his robe and parted it enough to reveal his bare knee. For a single heartbeat, Maggie frowned, leaning a bit forward but saw nothing out of the ordinary. "I don't see—" Then it struck her like a dive into a cold lake on a hot day. "Jesus, Mary, and Joseph!"

Norman's knee was healed. No, not healed. There was absolutely no sign of the bullet damage. No puckered entry wound, no scar. It was as if Norman had never been injured.

"But that's not the most amazing thing," Norman said, drawing both Maggie's and Sam's attention.

"What?" the Texan asked.

Norman raised his palms to his face. "My eyes."

"What about them?" She noticed the photographer's thick eyeglasses were missing.

The photographer glanced around the plaza, his voice awed. "I can see. My vision is a perfect twenty-twenty."

Before either student could react, Kamapak raised his arms and voice. His words, booming off the stone walls and stretching across the square, were meant not just for them, but for the entire gathered Incan tribe.

"What's he saying?" Sam asked Denal as he shouldered his rifle.

Before the boy could answer, Norman spoke dully. "He says this night, when the moon rises to its zenith, the Sapa Inca will come. After many centuries, he will descend from his gold throne and walk among his people."

Kamapak pointed to the group of students.

Norman finished, wearing a surprised look on his face, " 'Here stands the future of our tribe. They will take Inkarri back to *cay pacha*, the middle world. The reign of the Incas will begin again.' "

A roaring cheer rose from the gathered Incas.

Only their group remained silent. Sam stared with his mouth hanging open. Maggie found no words either, so awed was she. *How could Norman have known what the shaman had said?* Denal moved closer to Maggie, his eyes fearfully locked on Norman.

Shrugging, Norman said, "Hey, don't look at me for an explanation, guys. I failed first-year Spanish."

As the celebration continued, Sam sat with Norman on the steps of the plaza. He wanted answers. "So tell us what happened. What is this Temple of the Sun?"

Norman shook his head. He ran a finger over his knee. "I don't know."

"What do you mean?" Maggie asked. She sat on Norman's far side, while Denal rested on a lower step, his eyes on the continuing celebration. The boy was smoking one of the last of his precious cigarettes. Its tip flared like a torch with each long inhalation. After the terrors of the day, Sam could not begrudge Denal this one vice. "What did the temple look like?" Maggie persisted.

Norman turned to her, his eyes both worried and angry. "That's just it . . . . *I don't know.*"

"Then what *do* you know?" Sam asked.

Norman turned away, his face aglow in the reflected firelight. "I remember being snatched from my bed in our room. I tried to struggle, but I was too weak to offer more than a couple of good kicks at my kidnappers. Soon I was being carried, none too gently, I might add, between two warriors along a path heading south. After about three-quarters of an hour, we hit the south wall of the cone, with that other big black volcano hanging over us. There was a steep climb, and then I saw a sudden dark cut in the rock. A tunnel opening, right through the side of the volcano."

"Where did it go?" Sam asked, drawing Norman's gaze.

"I don't know. But I saw daylight at the end of the tunnel. I'm sure of it."

"Maybe it connects to the other volcano," Maggie said. "A path to the Incas' *janan pacha*."

"What else?" Sam asked the photographer.

Norman slowly shook his head. "I remember being carried a good way down the shaft until a side cavern appeared ahead. Torchlight was coming from it. As we neared, someone stepped out, greeting my kidnappers with a raised staff." The photographer glanced away and frowned.

"And?"

"And after that, my mind's a blank. The next thing I recall is being led back out of the tunnel, the last rays of the setting sun blinding me." Norman picked at the robe he wore. "And I was wearing this."

Maggie leaned back on her stone seat, digesting Norman's story. "And you could understand the Incan language . . ." She shook her head. "Maybe some hypnotic learning process. It could explain the memory lapse. But the level of healing—your knee, your eyes—this is far beyond anythin' even Western medicine could do. It's . . . it's almost miraculous."

Sam frowned. "I don't believe in miracles. There's an answer here. And it lies in that temple." He met Norman's gaze. "Could you find your way back there?"

Norman pinched his lips for a moment, then spoke. "I believe so. The trail was clear, and there were these stone trailside markers every hundred yards or so. The warriors would stop and quickly spout a few mumbled words and go on."

"Prayer totems," Sam mumbled. At least he was relatively certain he could find this Temple of the Sun if necessary. He would have to be satisfied with that for now. Tomorrow Uncle Hank would arrive, and Sam could leave these strange mysteries to his uncle's expertise. As worrisome and frightening as the day had been, Sam was just relieved Norman had been healed, no matter how or why.

Across the plaza, the raucous drums died away, and the dancers slowed and stopped. A single Incan woman climbed atop a stone pedestal and began to sing softly, her voice lonely in the fiery night. Soon, the gathered throng solemnly joined in her song, their hundred voices rising like steam toward the midnight sky. Nearby, Denal began softly singing along. Though the words were not translated, Sam sensed joy mixed with reverence, almost like a Christian hymn.

Maggie's words played through his mind. *Miracles.* Had the Incas stumbled upon some wondrous font of healing? The equivalent of Ponce de Leon's mythic fountain of youth? Sam's mouth grew dry at the thought of discovering such a find.

Listening to the crowd quietly sing, Sam looked over the square; he again was stunned that there were no children, no babes in arms or toddlers clinging to their mothers' hems. Nor were any elders mixed with these younger men and women. All the faces singing up at the full moon overhead were too uniform, all near the same age.

Who were these people? What had they discovered? A sudden shiver, which had nothing to do with the cooling valley, passed through Sam.

Finally, a hush spread like a wave over the square. Sam's eyes were drawn to the plaza's south side as the celebrants all fell to their knees. The small woman who had led the singing climbed off her pedestal and knelt, too. Soon only a solitary figure remained. He stood on the far side, unmoving, tall for an Inca, at least six feet. He bore a staff with a sunburst symbol at its top.

Maggie urged them all to kneel, too. "It must be the Sapa Inca," she whispered.

Sam settled to his knees, not wanting to offend this leader. Any cooperation would depend on this fellow's good graces.

The man slowly moved through the crowd. Men and women bowed their foreheads to the stones as he passed. No one spoke. Though not borne atop the usual golden litter of the Sapa Incas, the man wore the raiments of kings: from the *llautu* crown of woven braids with parrot feathers and red vicuna wool tassels, down to a long robe of expensive *cumbi* cloth decorated with appliqués of gold and silver. Even his sandals were made of alpaca leather and decorated with rubies. In his right hand, he bore a long staff, as tall as the man himself, topped by a palm-sized gold sunburst.

Norman mumbled, "The staff. I remember it. From the tunnel shaft."

Sam glanced at the photographer and saw the man's nervous fear. He touched Norman's shoulder in a gesture of support.

As the king neared, Sam studied his features. Typical Incan: mocha-colored skin, wide cheeks, full strong lips, dark eyes that pierced. In each earlobe was a disc of gold stamped with a sunburst icon that matched his staff's headpiece.

The Sapa Inca stepped to within three yards of the kneeling trio. Sam nodded in a show of respect. It was not fitting to stare directly at Incan rulers. They were the sun's children, and as with the sun itself, one's eyes must be diverted from the brightness. Still, Sam refused to touch his head to the stones of the plaza.

The Incan king did not seem to take offense. His gaze was intense but not hostile. With a look of burning curiosity, he took one more step toward them. His shadowed face was now aglow in the fiery light from a nearby torch, forging its ruddy planes into a coppery gold.

Maggie gasped.

Sam's brow crinkled at her reaction, and he dared stare more openly at the man—then it struck him, too. "My God . . ." he mumbled, stunned. This close, there could be no mistaking the resemblance, especially with the torch bathing the king's countenance in a golden light. They had all seen this man before. He matched the figure sculpted in gold back in the caverns, both the life-size idol guarding the booby-trapped room and the towering statue in the center of the necropolis.

The Sapa Inca took one step closer. With the torchlight gone from his face, he became just a man again. He studied them all for several silent moments. The plaza was as quiet as a tomb. Finally, he lifted his staff and greeted them. "I am Inca Inkarri," he said in English, his voice coarse and guttural. "Welcome. May Inti keep you safe in his light."

Sam remained kneeling, too stunned to move.

The king tapped his staff twice on the stone, then raised it high. On this signal, warbling cheers rose from a hundred throats. Men and women leaped to their feet, the drums thundered, flutes and tambourines added their brightness.

The Sapa Inca ignored the commotion and lowered his staff.

Kamapak appeared like a ghost from the dancing crowd. The shaman's face beamed with radiant awe, his tattoos almost glowing against his flushed skin. "*Qoylluppaj Inkan, Inti Yayanchis,*" he intoned, bowing slightly at the waist, and continued to speak. Even without any translation, Kamapak was obviously begging some boon from this king.

Once the shaman was finished, the Sapa Inca grunted a terse answer and waved Kamapak away. The shaman's smile broadened, clearly having obtained a favorable answer, and stepped back. The king nodded soberly at Sam's group, his eyes lingering a moment on Denal; then he swung back around and followed the shaman through the clusters of celebrants.

"I guess we passed muster," Sam said, breathing again.

"And were summarily dismissed," Maggie added.

Sam turned to Norman. "What were they saying?"

The photographer leaned back on his heels, his eyes narrowed. "Kamapak wanted to talk in private with the king"—Norman faced Sam—"about us."

Sam frowned. "What about us?"

"About our future here."

Sam did not like the sound of that. He watched the shaman and the king cross the plaza toward a large two-story home to the left of the square. "What do you make of this Sapa Inca fellow?" he asked Maggie.

"He's obviously had some exposure to the outside world. Learned a little English. Did you notice his face? He must be a direct descendant of that ancient king of the statues."

Sam nodded. "I'm not surprised at the similarity. This is a closed gene pool. No outsiders to dilute the Incan blood."

"Until we arrived, that is," Norman said.

Sam ignored the photographer's words. "But what about him claiming to be the mythic Inkarri?"

Maggie shook her head.

"Who's this Inkarri?" Norman asked.

Maggie quickly explained the story of the beheaded king who was prophesied to rise again to lead the Incas back to glory.

"The Second Coming, so to speak," Norman said.

"Right," Maggie said, frowning slightly. "Again clear evidence of Christian influence. Further proof of some Western intrusion here."

Sam was less convinced. "But if they've been out of the valley, why do they continue to hide?"

Maggie waved a hand toward Norman. "They obviously discovered something here. Something that heals. A volcanic spring or something. Maybe they've been protecting it."

Sam glanced at Norman, then back to the Incan king who disappeared into the home along with Kamapak. All the mysteries here seemed to start and end at the temple. If only Norman could remember what had happened . . .

"I'd love to be a fly on the wall during their conversation," Maggie muttered, staring across the plaza.

Norman nodded.

Sam sat up straighter. "Why don't we?"

"What?" Maggie asked, turning back to him.

"Why not eavesdrop? They have no glass on their windows. Norman can understand their language. What's to stop us?"

"I don't know," Norman said sourly. "Maybe a bunch of men with spears."

Maggie agreed. "We shouldn't do anything to make 'em mistrust us."

Sam, though, continued to warm to his idea. After a day spent wringing his hands over Norman's fate, he was tired of operating in the dark. He cinched his Winchester to his shoulder and stood. "If the shaman and king are discussing our fate, I want to know what they decide."

Maggie stood, reaching for his elbow. "We need to talk about this."

Sam stepped away from her grip. "What do you say, Norman? Or would you rather be dragged to the altar in the morning? And I don't mean to be married."

Norman fingered his thin neck and stood. "Well, when you put it that way . . ."

Maggie was now red-faced. "This isn't the way we should be handling this. This is stupid and a risk to all our lives."

Sam's cheeks flushed. "It's better than hiding in a hole," he said angrily, "and praying you're not killed."

Maggie stepped away from him, blinking in shock, a wounded look on her face. "You bastard . . ."

Sam realized Maggie thought he had been referring to her incident in Ireland, using her own trauma to knock aside her arguments. "I . . . I didn't mean it that way," he tried to explain.

Maggie pulled Denal to her side and turned her back on Sam. Her words were for Norman, dismissive. "Don't get yourself killed." She stalked off toward the row of homes.

Norman stared at her back. "Sam, you've really got to watch that mouth of yours. It's no wonder you and your uncle are bachelors."

"I didn't mean—"

"Yeah, I know . . . but still . . . next time think before you speak." Norman led the way around the edge of the plaza. "Come on, James Bond, let's get this over with."

Sam watched as Maggie ducked into her room; then he turned to follow Norman. His heart, on fire a moment ago, was now a burned cinder in his chest. "I'm such a jackass."

Norman heard him. "No argument here."

Sam scowled and tugged at the brim of his Stetson. He passed Norman with his angry stride. "Let's go."

As the celebration raged around them, they reached the squat two-story home. It was clearly the abode of a *kapak*, the nobleman of the Incas. The windows and door were framed in hammered silver. Firelight blazed from the uncovered windows, and muffled voices could be heard from inside.

Sam searched around to ensure no one was watching, then he pulled Norman into the narrow alley beside the home. It was cramped, allowing only enough room for them to move single file. Sam crept along first. Ahead, flickering light could be seen coming from a courtyard that was closed off by a shoulder-high wall. As they neared, Sam spotted small decorative holes piercing the walls: star-shaped and crescent moons. A perfect place from which to spy.

Waving Norman onward, Sam slunk up to one of the holes and peeked through. Beyond was a central garden courtyard, rich with orchids and climbing flowering vines. Sleeping parrots rested on perches, heads tucked under wings. Amid the riotous growth, a fire pit blazed in the center of the courtyard.

Two figures stood limned against the flames: Kamapak and Inkarri.

The shaman touched one of his tattoos with a fingertip, mumbling a prayer, then opened his *chuspa* pouch and cast a pinch of powder upon the fire. A spat of blue flames chased embers higher into the sky. Kamapak spoke to the king as he stepped in a circle around the fire, tossing more powder into the flames.

Norman, positioned at a neighboring spy hole, translated. His lips were near Sam's ear, his words breathless.

The shaman spoke. "As I told you, though they are pale-skinned and came from below, they are not *mallaqui*, spirits of *uca pacha*. They are true people."

The king nodded, pensively staring into the flames. "Yes, and the temple has healed the one. Inti accepts them." Inkarri stared back at Kamapak. "Still, they are not Inca."

Kamapak finished whatever ritual he had been performing and crossed to one of the reed floor coverings and folded himself smoothly to the floor, legs crossed under him. "No, but they do not come with murder in their hearts either . . . like the others long ago."

The king sat on a woven mat beside the shaman. His voice was tired. "How long has it been, Kamapak?"

The shaman reached to a pouch and pulled out a long string of knotted rope. He spread it on the stones of the courtyard. Sam recognized it as a *quipu*, an Incan counting tool. Kamapak pointed to one knot. "Here is when we discovered the Mochico in this valley, when your armies first came here, five hundred and thirty years ago." He moved his fingers down several ropes. "And here is when you died."

Sam pulled back and stared quizzically at Norman. *Died?* The photographer shrugged. "That's what he said," Norman mouthed.

Frowning, Sam started to return to his eavesdropping when a shouted bark startled him. Torches flared at either end of the alley. Sam and Norman froze, caught red-handed. Harsh orders were yelled at them.

"Th . . . they want us to come out," Norman said.

Sam touched the rifle's stock, then thought better of it. He'd wait first to see how this all played out. "C'mon."

He pushed past Norman and slid down the alley toward the waiting guards. Angry faces met them at the plaza. A circle of men, some bearing torches, all bearing spears, surrounded them. The music had stopped. Hundreds of sweating bodies stared in their direction.

From the doorway, the shaman and the king appeared. A spatter of words were exchanged between the guards and the shaman. The king stood stoically at the doorway.

Finally, the Sapa Inca lifted his staff, and all grew silent. Turning to Sam, he spoke in strained English, "At the temple, Inti whispered your tongue in my ear so I could speak to you. Come then. Learn what you seek in dark corners." He turned and reentered the stately abode.

Kamapak frowned, clearly disappointed with them, and waved them both inside the same courtyard upon which they had eavesdropped.

The Sapa Inca gestured to woven rugs on the floor.

Sam and Norman sat.

The king strode to the fire, speaking to the flames. "What be it that you seek?" he asked.

Sam sat straighter. "Answers. Like who you really are."

The Sapa Inca sighed and slowly nodded. "Some now call me Inkarri. But I will speak my true name to you, my first name, my oldest name, so you will know me. My birth name be Pachacutec. Inca Pachacutec."

Sam furrowed his brows. Pachacutec was a name he knew. He was the ancient founder of the Incan empire, the leader who expanded the Incas from their sole city of Cuzco to a dominion encompassing all the lands between the mountains and the coast. "You are a descendant of the Earth Shaker?" Sam asked, using the Incan nickname for their founder.

The king glowered. "No, I *am* the Earth Shaker. I *am* Pachacutec."

Sam frowned at this answer. Impossible. Clearly this man had the delusions of all kings—that they were the embodiment of their ancestors, the dead reincarnated in the living.

Kamapak spoke up in his native tongue. The shaman's hands were very animated. He picked up the length of knotted rope, the *quipu*, from where it had been left. He shook it at them.

Norman translated, "Kamapak claims everyone here in the valley is over four hundred years old. Even their king."

"So this Sapa Inca believes he's the *original* Pachacutec."

Norman nodded. "The real McCoy."

Sam shook his head, dismissing all this Incan mysticism. But in a small corner of his mind, he pondered Norman's cure and new abilities. Something miraculous was definitely going on, but could this tribe have lived for that long? He remembered his own thoughts about a fountain of youth. Was it possible?

Sam asked the question that had been nagging him since arriving here. "Tell us about this Temple of the Sun."

Pachacutec glanced to the sunburst symbol on the staff in his hand, then to the bonfire. His face suddenly took on a tired look, his eyes so old that for a moment Sam could almost believe this man had lived five hundred years. "To understand, I must tell stories I hear from other mouths," he whispered. "From the Mochico who first came to this sacred place."

Sam's heart clenched. So the Moche had been here first! Uncle Hank had been right.

The Sapa Inca nodded to the shaman. "Tell them, Kamapak, of the Night of Flaming Skies."

The shaman bowed his head in acknowledgment and crossed to the fire's edge. His voice took on a somber tone. Norman translated. "Sixty years before Inca Pachacutec's armies conquered this valley, there came a night when the skies were ablaze with a hundred fiery trails, bits of flaming sun chasing each other across the black skies. They fell from *janan pacha* and crashed into these sacred mountains. The Mochico king ordered his hunters to gather these bits of the sun, finding them in smoking nests throughout the mountains."

Sam found himself nodding. Clearly this was a description of a meteor shower.

Kámapak continued, "This gathered treasure was brought back to the Mochico king. He named the pieces, the Sun's Gold, and ensconced his treasure in a cave here in this secret valley."

Pachacutec interrupted. "But then I come with my armies. I kill their king and make the Mochico my slaves. I force them to take me to this treasure. I must kill many before the way be opened. Here I find a cave full of sunlight you can touch and hold. I fall to my knees. I know it be Inti himself. The god of the sun!" The king's eyes were full of past glory and wonder. It seemed to revitalize him.

The shaman continued the story, as Norman translated. "To honor Inti and to punish the Mochico for imprisoning our god, Pachacutec sacrificed every Mochico in this valley and the village below. Once done, Pachacutec prayed for seven days and seven nights for a sign from Inti. And he was heard!"

The shaman opened his bag and, with a mumbled prayer, tossed a bit of purplish dust on the fire; blue flames flared for a heartbeat. Then he continued. "As reward for his loyalty, a wondrous temple grew in the cave, a *huaca* constructed from this hoard of Mochico sun gold. In this sacred temple, Inti healed the sick and kept death from those who honored the sun god."

Sam had to force himself to breathe. Had these ancient Indians truly discovered some otherworldly fountain of youth? Sam only had to stare at Norman, healed and translating, to begin to believe.

"Pachacutec gave up his crown to his son and retired to this valley, leaving the governing of the Incan empire to his descendants. He and his chosen followers remained here, worshiping Inti, never dying. Soon, even the children born in the valley were made into gods by the temple's power and given as gifts to *janan pacha*."

With these words, the king's eyes flicked toward the south, where the tall neighboring volcano loomed. A certain brooding look grew in his eyes.

Sam had to admit a perverse internal logic to the story. If these valley dwellers never died, then sacrificing children was good population management. The resources of this volcanic valley were not unlimited and continued births would soon overwhelm the resources. The tale also succeeded in explaining the lack of elderly residents. No one aged here.

Pachacutec interrupted again, his tone bitter. "But the time of peace ended. A hundred seasons passed, and men in tall ships came, men with strange beasts and stranger tongues."

"The Spanish," Sam mumbled to himself.

"They kill my people, drive them from their homes. Like the jaguar, there be no escaping their teeth. They come even here. I speak to them. Tell them of Inti. I show them the temple and how it protects us. Their eyes grow hungry. They kill me, meaning to steal Inti from us."

"They killed you?" Sam blurted out before he could stop it.

Pachacutec rubbed the back of his neck, as if kneading out some stubborn pain. He waved his other hand at Kamapak, motioning him to continue.

The shaman's words grew dour as Norman translated. "The Spanish came with lust in their hearts. And as Pachacutec had slain the Mochico king, the foreigners slew our king. Pachacutec was taken to the center of the village." The shaman waved toward the plaza beyond. "And his head was cut from his body."

Sam's excitement about discovering the fountain of youth dried in his chest. This last story was clearly preposterous. And if this was false, then all of the others probably were, too. Just fireside fables. Whatever cured Norman had nothing to do with these stories. Still, Sam was compelled to listen 'til the end. "But you live now. How is that?"

The shaman answered, glancing almost guiltily down. "The night the Sapa Inca was slain I heard the Spanish speak of burning his body. Such a cruelty is worse than death to our people. So I sneaked out and stole my king's head from where he lay dead. With the Spanish in pursuit, I took my king to the temple and prayed to Inti. Again the god heard and proved his love." The shaman threw another pinch of dust on the fire, a clear obeisance to his god.

Pachacutec continued the last of the tale. "The temple carried me back from death. I opened my eyes as my head lay on the altar. From my bloody mouth, I warned the strangers of Inti's anger. This show of Inti's strength made warriors into women. They screamed, wailed, tore at their hair, and ran away. The dogs sealed the lower entrance, but word of my death be already flying. The killers were captured, and their shaman sacrificed."

Sam frowned. He knew one way to test the veracity of these stories. "What was the name of this Spanish shaman?"

Kamapak answered, voice tight with old hatred, hands balled into fists: "Francisco de Almagro."

Pachacutec scowled at the name and spat into the fire. "We had this shaman dog captured for his blasphemies. But he fled like a coward and fouled a sacred site with his own blood. After his death, we made holes in his skull and drove out his god with ours."

Sam sat shocked. He remembered his uncle's story of the golden substance that exploded from the mummy's skull. The ancient and modern stories seemed to match. But what these two were describing—immortality—how could it be true?

As Sam's mind roiled, the shaman finished the story as Norman continued to translate the ancient Inca language. "After the foreigners fled, the temple slowly grew Pachacutec another body. Inti warned our king that these strange men from across the sea were too strong and too many, and Inti must be protected. So the path here was left sealed. We allowed ourselves to be forgotten. But Inti had promised Pachacutec that there would come a day when the path would reopen, a time when the Incan dynasty would begin again. When that day came, for our loyalty, our people had been promised not only their own lands back, but also the rest of the world."

Pachacutec's eyes blazed with fire and glory. "We will rule all!"

Sam nodded. "Inkarri reborn from his secret cave."

Pachacutec turned his back on the fire and them. "So my people have named me after my rebirth. Inkarri, child of the sun."

"When does this path to the world below reopen?"

"When the gods of *janan pacha* are ready to leave," Pachacutec answered, waving an arm toward the south. "Until then, we must live as the temple tells us. All who threaten Inti must be sacrificed."

The shaman turned his back, too. Norman quietly translated, color draining from his face. "You have shown your deceit this night, hiding your shame in the cloak of night." His last words came out pained. "At dawn, when the sun rises and Inti can see our loyalty, you will be sacrificed to our god. Your blood will stain the plaza."

The shaman signaled with his right hand.

Sam shot to his feet, but he was too late. Incan warriors swarmed from adjacent rooms and swept over them. Sam fought, but with no success. His rifle was knocked to the stones. Disturbed parrots screamed in the trees.

"No!" Sam yelled, but neither the shaman nor the king would face them as they were dragged away.

Dressed in her own khakis and shirt, Maggie huddled in the shadow of the courtyard wall. Holding her breath, afraid to move, she watched Sam and Norman being dragged away. *Sweet Jesus, what was she going to do?* She silently cursed the mule-headed Texan. He had to go charging blindly into danger. She turned and leaned her back on the stone wall. Hiding as still as a mouse, she had heard most of Pachacutec's and Inkarri's stories and knew there was no way to talk them out of this jam.

At least, she had hid Denal before coming here.

Earlier, she had heard the music in the plaza stop abruptly. She had peeked out and watched as Sam and Norman were seized. While instinct had told her to run with Denal as far and fast as possible, she had fought against it. The other two were her friends, and she could not abandon them without trying to help. So she had whisked Denal into the jungle's edge and told him to stay out of sight. Then she had sneaked back here to discover the fate of her friends.

Now she knew. Maggie peeked through a crescent-shaped hole in the courtyard wall. It was empty. Even the king and the shaman were gone. Maggie stared at the sole reason she still tarried here. Sam's Winchester rifle lay on the granite cobblestones of the courtyard. If a rescue was going to succeed, she would need that weapon.

Listening for voices, she studied the surrounding rooms for any sign of motion. It seemed clear. Her hands trembled with fear at what she was about to attempt. She bit her lip, refusing to let panic into her heart. Sam and Norman were depending on her. Taking a final deep breath, she grabbed the top of the wall, pulled herself up, and hooked a leg over the edge. She struggled for a few moments, then managed to boost herself over.

With her heart thundering in her throat, Maggie dropped into the courtyard. A blue-and-gold macaw ruffled its feathers, watching her, still tense from the excitement a few moments ago. Maggie willed the bird to remain quiet and crept to the foliage's edge. The rifle lay only ten meters away. She just needed to dash across the open space, grab the rifle, then flee back over the wall.

It sounded easy until Maggie's legs began to tremble under her. She knew she would have to act now or lose herself to panic. Clenching her fists, she pushed from the shadows of the trees and ran across the cobbles. Her hands settled upon the stock of the rifle just as voices sounded behind her. Someone was returning! She froze like a deer in headlights, fear paralyzing her. She could not move, could not think.

Suddenly, a log in the fire popped, loud as the blast from a starter's gun.

It was what she needed. A gasp of fear escaped her throat, releasing her. She snatched the rifle and ran, not caring who might hear her. Terror gave her legs. She flew through the foliage and over the wall in a heartbeat.

She sank gratefully into the shadows, rifle clutched to her chest.

The voices behind her grew louder. Gulping air as silently as she could, she turned and peeked into the courtyard. It was Kamapak and Pachacutec returning. She watched the tattooed shaman cross to the yard's center and throw a handful of powder into the fire. Azure flame danced to the rooftops, then died back down.

The two men spoke in their native tongue. The only word decipherable was the name *Inkarri*. The king seemed reluctant to do what the shaman wanted, but finally his shoulders sagged, and he nodded.

Straightening and stepping near the fire, Pachacutec reached to his shoulder and pulled the gold *tupu* pin that held his robe. The fine cloth fell like a flow of water from his body to pool around his ankles. The

Sapa Inca stepped free of his robe, naked of all except his *llautu* headpiece and his staff.

A hand flew to Maggie's lips, clamping away her cry of shock. But something must have been heard. The king glanced to the courtyard wall, staring for a long breath, then turned away.

Maggie's stomach churned with acid. But she knew better than to move. She could not risk the scuff of stone alerting them further to her presence. She stared.

From the neck up, the king's skin was the familiar mocha brown of the Andean Indians, but from the neck down, his skin was as pale as something found under a rock. It reminded Maggie of the beastly predators that haunted the caverns below. But Pachacutec's skin was even paler, almost translucent. Vessels could be seen moving blackish blood under his skin; bones appeared as buried shadows. The man's belly and chest were flat, hairless. Not even nipples or a navel marred the smooth surface. He was also sexless, completely lacking external genitalia.

Sexless and unnaturally smooth. Maggie found one word coming to mind as she stared at this strange apparition. *Unformed.* It was as if the king's body were a blank slate waiting to be molded, like pale clay.

Oh, God. The realization dawned on her.

The story of Inkarri was true!

DAY SIX

The Serpent of Eden

Saturday, August 25, 4:48 A.M.
Andean Mountains, Peru

Henry stared out the window as the helicopter banked over the jungle-stripped ruins. He had not slept all night. Worries and fears had kept him awake as their bird flew over the midnight jungles. He had yet to come up with any plan to thwart his captors. And without the additional stop to refuel, their flight from the guerrilla airstrip had been shortened. Time was running out.

Below, the campsite was still dark. The sun had yet to rise. Only a set of work lights near the base of the buried pyramid illuminated the dig. Apparently, even after the news of the students' escape, work continued to open the temple. The abbot's people sought every scrap of their precious *Sangre del Diablo*.

The abbot, wearing a radio headpiece, yelled over the roar of the rotors. "We're here, Professor Conklin! I assume that I do not need to remind you what will happen if you fail to cooperate fully!"

Henry shook his head. *Joan.* She was still being held hostage at the Abbey. Any punishment for failings on his part would be exacted against her. Henry cleared his throat and pointed to the abbot's radio headpiece. "Before we land, I want to speak to Dr. Engel. To make sure she's unharmed."

The abbot frowned, not in anger but in disappointment. "I am faithful to my word, Professor Conklin. If I say she will remain safe, she will."

Only until you have what you want, Henry thought dourly. His eyes narrowed. "Excuse me if I doubt your hospitality. But I would still like to speak to her."

Abbot Ruiz sighed and shrugged his large bulk. He slipped his headset off and passed it to Henry. "Be quick. We're landing." The abbot nodded toward a cleared square not far from the students' tents.

The helicopter righted its banking turn and began to settle toward the flat stone plateau. Below, Henry spotted men with flashlights positioned at the periphery of their landing site, guiding the chopper down.

Henry did not fail to notice the mud brown robes the flashlight-bearers wore. More of the abbot's monks.

Henry pulled the headpiece in place and positioned the microphone.

The abbot leaned forward and was talking to the pilot, pointing to the radio. After a minute of static, a scratchy voice filled his earphones. "Henry?"

It was Joan! He held the microphone steady. "It's me, Joan. Are you okay?"

Static blazed, then words trailed through. ". . . fine. Have you reached the camp?"

"Just landing now. Are they treating you well?"

"Just like the Hyatt here. Only the room service is a little slow."

Despite her light words, Henry could hear the suppressed tension in her voice. He pictured those tiny crinkled lines that etched her eyes when she was worried. He had to swallow hard to speak. He would not let anything happen to her. "Slow room service? I'll see what I can do from here," Henry said. "See if I can light a fire under hotel management."

"Speaking of fire, Henry, remember back at college we shared that classical mythology class together? I was in the Abbey's library today. They have the professor's book here. Can you believe that? Even that chapter I helped him write about Prometheus."

Henry's brows drew together. "Small world, isn't it?" he answered blandly, going along with her ploy. Back at Rice University, the two had *never* shared such a class. Clearly Joan was trying to get a message to him. Something about the myth of Prometheus, a definite reference to Friar de Almagro's etched warning.

He heard the heightened tension in her voice. "Remember the difficulty we had in translating the line *Prometheus holds our salvation*?"

Henry chuckled with false mirth. "How could I forget it?" He clenched his hands in his lap. What was Joan hinting at? Something about *fire*. But what? What does fire have to do with salvation? And time was running short. The helicopter was about to land.

Joan must have sensed his confusion. She spoke rapidly, practically just blurting it out. "Well, I also reread the section where Prometheus slays the great Serpent. Do you remember that? Where fire was the final solution?"

Henry suddenly tensed as he realized what she was saying. *The Great Serpent. The Serpent of Eden.* Understanding dawned in him. She was offering him a way of destroying *el Sangre del Diablo*. "Sure. But I thought that event was said to be done by Hercules. Are you sure your interpretation is accurate?"

"Definitely. Prometheus packed a vicious punch. You should have seen the picture in the book. Think plastic explosive."

"I . . . I understand."

A shudder suddenly shook through the helicopter's frame. Henry jumped in his seat, startled. Outside, the helicopter's skids bumped on the granite stones, then settled to a stop.

The abbot's face appeared before Henry's, yelling to be heard above the slowing rotors. "You've talked long enough. We've landed!" He turned to the pilot and made a slashing motion across his neck.

Henry was about to be cut off. "Joan!"

"Yes, Henry!"

He clutched his microphone tightly, struggling with words he thought he'd never speak to another woman. "I just wanted to tell you that . . . that I—" Static blasted in his ears as the radio contact suddenly ended.

Wincing, Henry stared at the radio. What had he wanted to say to Joan? That he was falling in love with her? How could he presume she shared any deeper feelings than mere friendship?

The radio was taken from his numb fingers.

Either way, the chance was gone.

As two Incas stood guard, Sam struggled with the woven grass ropes that bound his hands behind his back, but he only succeeded in tightening them.

Beside him, Norman sat on the stones of the plaza, shivering slightly. The photographer had long given up trying to free himself, resolved as he was to the inevitability of their deaths.

Already the skies paled to the east, heralding the approach of dawn, but the village still lay cast in grays and blacks. Once the sun fully rose and the streets were bathed in golden light, the two would be sacrificed to the sun god, Inti.

But at least, it was just the *two* of them.

Maggie and Denal had managed to escape. All night long, men had been searching the terraced village and surrounding jungle, but with no luck. Maggie must have heard the commotion from Sam's capture and run off with the boy, disappearing into the dark jungle. But how long could the two remain hidden once the sun was fully up? Sam prayed Denal and Maggie could avoid capture until his uncle arrived with help. But when would that be? He had no way of knowing. His walkie-talkie was still inside his vest, but with his arms bound behind him, there was nothing he could do.

He yanked on his bonds. If he could only free a hand . . .

A rifle blast suddenly pierced the quiet dawn. The crack echoed over the valley, but it clearly came from the east. *Maggie!* She must have been discovered.

Both guards turned in the direction of the rifle shot. They spoke hurriedly as more men poured into the square, led by Kamapak. With much chattering, the group of barefooted hunters took off toward the forest's edge. The tattooed shaman waved even the two guards away to aid in the search.

Bound tight, Sam and Norman were not a threat.

Once the square was empty, Kamapak crossed to them. He wore a worried expression.

Sam suspected the shaman feared his god's wrath if *all* these foreigners were not slain at dawn.

In his hands, Kamapak bore small bowls of paint. He knelt beside Norman and spoke to the photographer as he placed down his dyes, then slid a long narrow flint knife from his sashed belt.

As the man spoke, Sam stared hungrily at the shard of sharpened stone. How he longed to grab that weapon.

Norman groaned after the shaman finished his explanation.

"What is it?" Sam asked.

"It seems the shaman has come to prepare us for the sacrifice," Norman said, meeting Sam's eye. He nodded to the dyes. "Marks of power are to be written on our bodies."

The shaman dipped a finger in the red dye, intoning a prayer loudly, then picked up the splinter of flint.

Norman's gaze followed the blade, his face paling. He glanced sidelong at Sam, but he kept one eye on Kamapak.

"What else?" Sam asked, sensing something unspoken.

"Before the sun rises, he also plans to cut out our tongues . . . so our screams don't offend Inti."

"Great . . ." Sam said sourly.

Kamapak raised his knife toward the growing dawn. As he continued his chanted prayer, the bright edge of the sun rose above the eastern lip of the volcanic cone. Like an awakening eye, Sam thought. For a moment, he understood the Incas' worship of the sun. It was like some immense god peeking down on their lowly world. Kamapak sliced his thumb with his knife, greeting the sun with his own blood.

Even though Sam's own life was threatened, a small part of him watched the ritual with clear fascination. Here was an actual Incan sacrificial rite, a dead tradition coming to life. He studied the tiny pots of natural dyes: red from rose madder, blue from indigo, purple from crushed mollusks.

As Kamapak continued his prayers, Norman suddenly stiffened beside the Texan. Sam glanced up from his study of the dyes to see a figure break from the cover of a nearby doorway. He almost gasped as he recognized the figure: *It was Maggie.*

Behind Kamapak's back, she dashed across the stones, barefooted like the hunters—but, also like the warriors, she was *armed*. In her right hand was a long wooden cudgel.

Kamapak must have sensed the danger. He began to turn, but Maggie was already there. She swung the length of hardened wood and struck a fierce blow to the side of the shaman's head. The blow sounded like a softball struck by a Louisville Slugger. Kamapak was knocked to his hands, then fell to his face, unmoving. Blood welled through the man's dark hair.

Sam stared, too shocked to react for a few seconds. He turned to face Maggie. She seemed equally stunned by her act. The cudgel fell from her limp fingers to clatter on the granite cobbles.

"The knife," Sam said, drawing her gaze from the limp form of the shaman. He nodded toward the sliver of flint and twisted around to indicate his roped wrists.

"I've got my own," Maggie said, alertness returning in a rush. She glanced around the plaza and drew forth the gold dagger from her belt. She hurriedly sliced Sam's bindings.

Sam jumped to his feet, rubbing his wrists. He stepped over to check on Kamapak. The shaman lay unmoving, but his chest did rise and fall. Sam let out a relieved breath. The man was just unconscious.

Maggie passed Sam the gold dagger after freeing Norman, then helped pull the photographer to his feet. "Can you both run?"

Norman nodded weakly. "If I have to . . ."

Voices sounded from nearby. Somewhere a woman's voice was raised in alarm. "It looks like you'll have to," Maggie said.

In unison, they all turned to run, but they were already too late.

Around the square, armed men and women entered from streets and alleys. Sam and the others were herded to the center of the plaza and surrounded.

Sam noticed Norman had the shaman's shard of flint gripped in one fist. The photographer lifted it. "If they mean to take my tongue, they're gonna have to fight me for it."

"Where's Denal?" Sam whispered.

"I left him with the rifle," Maggie answered. "He was supposed to lead the others away so I could try and free you. We were to rendezvous in the jungle."

"I don't think that plan's gonna work," Norman said. He pointed his flint knife. "Look."

Across the square, one of the hunters held Sam's Winchester in his grip. He handled the weapon as if it were a poisonous snake. The man sniffed slightly at the barrel's end, crinkling his nose.

"Denal . . ." Maggie mumbled.

There was no sign of the boy.

A gruff voice sounded behind them. They turned.

Pachacutec pushed through the crowd. He was in full raiment, from feathered crown to fanciful robe. He lifted his staff. The golden sunburst caught the first rays of the rising sun and glinted brightly.

The king spoke slowly in Inca, while Norman translated. "We have captured the strangers in our midst. Inti rises for his sacrifice. Revive Kamapak so the gods can be honored."

Off to the side, a trio of women worked on Kamapak. They bathed his face in cold water and rubbed his limbs while chanting. Slowly Kamapak's arms began to move. Then his eyes flickered open. He seemed blind for a moment until the memory of his assault returned. Anger shone in his gaze. Weakly pushing away the women, he shoved to his feet. He wobbled a bit, but one of the hunters helped steady him.

Kamapak ambled shakily toward his king.

Pachacutec spoke again, this time in English, drawing the eyes of the students. "It be an honor to give blood to Inti. You disgrace our god with your fighting."

By now, the sun had risen enough that the center of the square was bathed in sunlight. Sam brandished his dagger, bright in the morning light. Disgrace or not, he wasn't going to give his blood without drawing the same from his attackers. He raised the knife higher, wishing he had a more intimidating weapon, something to strike terror.

With this thought, the handle of the dagger grew warm and the length of gold blade shimmered and twisted, spreading and curving, until the form of a striking snake sprouted from the hilt. Sam froze, afraid to move, unsure what had just happened.

He stared at the transformed dagger. Gold fangs were open to the sun, threatening the gathered throng.

Pachacutec had taken a step back when the transformation had started. He now took a step nearer, eyes wide with awe.

Sam did not know how the transformation had occurred, but the miracle of the dagger was clearly something the Incas had never seen. Sam raised the golden asp high.

Pachacutec lifted his staff, mimicking Sam's pose. His eyelids lowered slightly, as if in prayer. Suddenly the golden sunburst symbol atop his staff flowed and transformed to match the serpent. Two snakes stared each other down.

Now it was Sam's turn to back away. Pachacutec met the Texan's gaze. Sam no longer saw anger in the man's eyes, but tears.

To the king's side, Kamapak fell to his knees, bowing his head toward Sam. The gathered throng followed suit. Foreheads pressed to the stones.

Pachacutec lowered his staff. He stepped toward them. Arms wide. "Inti has blessed you. The sun god of the Mochico listens to your dreams. You be one of the chosen of Inti!" The king crossed to stand before Sam. He offered his hand. "You be safe in our house. All of you!"

Sam was too confused to react. The sudden change in the Incas was unnerving. But he could not quite trust the transformation, any more than he could understand what had happened to the dagger.

Maggie pushed beside Sam. "What about Denal?"

Pachacutec heard her. "The boy. He be not fourteen years. Too young for *huarachicoy*." He smiled as if this explained it all.

Sam frowned. *Huarachicoy* was the ceremonial feast where a boy was accepted as a man into a tribe, when he was given his first *huara*, the loincloth of an adult tribesman. "What do you mean 'too young'?"

Kamapak raised his face and spoke. Norman translated. "It was decided that the boy, like all the tribe's children, was to be taken to the temple. He was to be gifted directly to the gods."

Maggie turned to Sam. "Sacrifice," she said with fear.

"When?" Sam asked. "When was this to be done?"

Pachacutec glanced to the rising sun. The bright disk was fully above the volcanic edge. "It be done already. The boy be with the gods."

Sam stumbled backward. "No . . ."

The Texan's reaction confused the king. The Sapa Inca's bright smile faltered. "Be this not Inti's wish?"

"No!" Sam said more forcefully.

Maggie grabbed Sam's elbow. "We need to go to that temple. Maybe he's still alive. We don't know for sure that he's dead."

Sam nodded at her words. There was a chance. He faced Kamapak and Pachacutec. "Take us to the temple."

The king bowed his head, offering no argument to one of the chosen. Instead, he waved, and the shaman stood. "Kamapak will guide you."

"I'm coming with you," Maggie said.

"Me too," Norman added, swaying a bit on his feet. Clearly the transformation and the long, stressful night had taken its toll on him.

Sam shook his head. "Norman, you need to stay here. You can speak the local lingo. Get the Incas to light a signal fire on the highest ridge so the evac helicopter can find us." Sam reached to his vest pocket and pulled out the walkie-talkie. "Here. Contact Sykes and get a status report. But more importantly . . . get Uncle Hank up here ASAP!"

Norman looked worried with the burden of his assignment, but he accepted the walkie-talkie with a slow nod. "I'll do what I can."

Sam clapped the photographer on the shoulder, then he and Maggie hurried away, stopping only to collect Sam's Winchester.

"Be careful!" Norman called to them. "There's something strange up there!"

Sam didn't need to be told that. All he had to do was look at the golden viper mounted on the dagger's hilt in his hand.

Bright sunlight glinted off its sharp fangs.

He shivered. Old words of warning rang in his head: *Beware the Serpent of Eden.*

Henry trudged toward the collapsed subterranean temple. Even from here, he saw how the crown of the hill had fallen in on itself. Sodium lamps highlighted the excavation on the lee side of the slope, where workers still struggled to dig a rescue shaft into the buried ruins.

As Henry walked, Philip's litany of the events of the past few days droned on: ". . . and then the temple started to implode. There was nothing I could do to stop it . . ." Philip Sykes had come running up to Henry as soon as the professor had cleared the helicopter's rotors, wearing a smile that was half panicked relief and half shame, like a dog with his tail tucked between his legs. Henry ignored his student's ceaseless explanation. The theme was clear from the start: *I'm not to blame!*

Henry finally touched Philip's shoulder. "You've done a great job, Mr. Sykes. Considering the circumstances and confusion here, you've managed admirably."

Philip bobbed his head. "I did, didn't I?" He ate up the praise with a big spoon . . . and then thankfully grew quiet, content at being absolved for any of the tragedy. Henry, though, knew the student was hiding more than he was telling. Henry had heard the disparaging comments whispered from some of the Quechan workers as they passed. He knew enough of the local Indian dialect to tell that the laborers resented Philip. Henry suspected that if he questioned the workers, a different view of the events of the past few days would come to light . . . and that Philip would not come out looking so squeaky clean.

But right now, Henry had more important concerns.

He eyed the two guards who flanked them. They no longer brandished their guns, but they kept their hands on holstered pistols. Abbot Ruiz marched ahead of them, wheezing through nose and mouth. The altitude and exertion in climbing through the ruins were clearly taxing the heavy man.

As they finally reached the site where a black tunnel opened into the side of the buried temple, a man dressed in the brown robes of a friar stepped toward them. He was darkly handsome with cold eyes that seemed to take in everything with a sharp glance.

Abbot Ruiz stared hungrily at the tunnel opening. "Friar Otera, how do things fare here?"

The monk remained bowed. "We should reach the temple ruins by noon, Your Eminence."

"Good. Very good. You have done brilliantly." He stepped past the bowing man without a glance, dismissing him.

Henry, though, caught the glint of white-hot anger in the monk's eyes as he straightened, the man's face settling back to passive disinterest. But Henry knew better. A few words of faint praise were not going to satisfy this man as they had Philip. Closer to him now, Henry noted some Indian features mixed with his Spanish heritage: a deeper complexion, a slightly wider nose, and eyes so deep a brown they seemed almost black. Friar Otera was clearly a *mestizo*, a half-breed, a mixture of Spanish and Indian blood. Such men had hard lives here in South America, their mixed blood often a mark of humiliation and ridicule.

Henry followed the abbot, but remained attuned to the friar's movements. He knew he had better keep a close watch. There were dangerous layers to this man that had nothing to do with the abbot's schemes. Henry noticed how even Philip gave the man a wide berth as the student clambered up the loose soil toward the tunnel opening.

Friar Otera took up a pace behind Henry.

As they reached the excavated tunnel, the sun climbed fully into the sky. The clear blue skies promised a hot day to come.

Suddenly a crackle of static drew their eyes toward Philip. The student reached inside his jacket and pulled free a walkie-talkie. "It must be Sam," Philip said. "He's early."

Henry stepped nearer. His nephew had said he would contact base around ten o'clock. The call was a few hours ahead of schedule.

"Base here," Philip said, lips pressed to the receiver. "Go ahead, Sam."

Static and interference whined for a few seconds, then . . . "Philip? It's not Sam. It's *Norman*."

Philip glanced over the radio to the others, brows raised. Henry understood the Harvard student's shock. From Sam's last radio message, Norman had been at risk of being sacrificed last night. Thank God, he was still alive!

Norman continued, speaking rapidly. "When do you expect the helicopters? We need them up here now!" Panic etched his voice.

"They're right here!" Philip yelled back. "As a matter of fact, Professor Conklin's with me." Philip held out the walkie-talkie.

Henry took it, but not before noticing the narrowing of Abbot Ruiz's eyes. A warning against any slip of the tongue. Henry raised the radio. "Norman, it's Henry. What's going on up there?"

"Denal's in danger! Sam and Maggie have gone to rescue him. But we need help up here ASAP. Within the hour, several signal fires should be blazing near the cone's western ridge. They should be visible through the mists. Hurry!"

Henry eyed the Abbot. He was already waving some of his men back toward the helicopter. They had thought to have a few hours until Sam called, but clearly Abbot Ruiz was more than happy to accelerate the schedule, especially with Norman's next words.

"There's something strange up here . . . borders on the miraculous, Professor. Must see to . . ." The static was growing worse, eating away words.

The abbot met Henry's gaze, his eyes bright with religious hope. Ruiz nodded for Henry to question the photographer.

"Does it have anything to do with a strange type of gold?" Henry asked.

Norman seemed not to have heard, cutting in and out, ". . . a temple. I don't know how . . . heals . . . no children though."

The choppy transmission was clouding any clear meaning. Henry gripped the walkie-talkie firmly and pressed it closer to his lips. If he had any hope of warning Sam and the others, it would have to be now. "Norman, sit tight! We're coming! But tell Sam not to do anything rash. He knows I don't *trust* him to act on his own."

Beside him, Philip startled at his words. Henry prayed Norman would be as equally shocked by such a statement. The entire team knew Henry held his nephew in the highest esteem and would never disparage Sam or any of them in this manner, but Abbot Ruiz didn't know that. Henry pressed the receiver again. "I mean it. Do nothing. I *don't trust* Sam's judgment."

"Professor?" Norman's voice was full of confusion. Static raged from the unit. Any further words dissolved away.

Henry fiddled with the radio but only got more static. He thumbed it off. "Batteries must have died," Henry said morosely. He prayed Norman had understood his veiled warning, but if not, at least no harm had been done. Abbot Ruiz seemed oblivious of Henry's attempt at a secret message. He handed the radio back to Philip.

Philip returned the walkie-talkie to a pocket, then opened his mouth. "What do you mean you don't trust Sam, Professor. Since when?"

Henry took a step forward, trying to signal the Harvard grad to shut up.

But Abbot Ruiz had already heard. He swung back to Henry and Philip. "What's all this about?" he asked, his face narrowed with suspicion.

"Nothing," Henry answered quickly. "Mr. Sykes here and my nephew have an ongoing rivalry. He's always thought I favored Sam over him."

"I never thought that, Professor!" Philip said loudly. "You trusted all of us!"

"Did you now?" Ruiz asked, stalking up to them. "Trust seems to be something that all of us are losing at this moment."

The abbot waved a hand, and Friar Otera appeared behind Philip with a bared blade.

"No!" Henry yelled.

The thin man grabbed a handful of the student's hair and yanked Philip's head back, exposing his throat.

Philip squawked but grew silent when he saw the blade. He stiffened when the knife touched his throat.

"Is another lesson in order so soon?" the abbot asked.

"Leave the boy be," Henry begged. "He doesn't know what he's saying."

The abbot stepped beside Philip, but his words were for Henry. "Were you trying to pass a warning up there? A secret signal perhaps?"

Henry stared Ruiz full in the face. "No. Philip just misspoke."

Ruiz turned to the terrified student. "Is that so?"

Philip just moaned, closing his eyes.

The abbot leaned and spoke in Philip's ear. "If you wish to live, I expect the truth."

The student's voice cracked. "I . . . I don't know what you're asking."

"A simple question. Does Professor Conklin trust his nephew?"

Philip's eyes flicked toward Henry, then away again. "I . . . I guess."

The abbot's face grew grim, clearly dissatisfied by the vague answer. "Philip," he intoned menacingly.

The student cringed. "Yes!" he gasped out. "Professor Conklin trusts Sam more than any of us. He always has!"

The abbot nodded, and the knife left the student's throat. "Thank you for your candor." Ruiz turned to

Henry. "It seems a further lesson is needed to convince you of the value of cooperation."

Henry felt ice enter his veins.

"For your deception against the path of God, a severe punishment is in order. But who should it be exacted upon?" The abbot seemed to ponder the question for a moment, then spoke. "I think I shall leave this up to you, Professor Conklin."

"What do you mean?"

"You get a choice on who will bear the burden of your sins: Philip or Dr. Engel?"

"If you're going to punish anyone," Henry said, "then punish me."

"We can't do that, Professor Conklin. We need you alive. And making this choice is punishment enough, I imagine."

Henry blanched, his knees weakening.

"We have no need for two hostages. Whoever you choose—Philip or Dr. Engel—will be killed. It is your choice."

Henry found Philip's eyes upon him, begging him for his life. What was he to do?

"Make your decision in the next ten seconds or *both* will die."

Henry closed his eyes. He pictured Joan's face, laughing and smiling over their dinner in Baltimore, candlelight glowing on her cheeks. He loved her. He could no longer deny it, but he could also not dismiss his responsibility here. Though Philip was often a thoughtless ass, he was still one of his students, his responsibility. Henry bit his lips, tears welling. He remembered Joan's lips at his ear, her breath on his neck, the scent of her hair.

"Professor?"

Henry opened his eyes and stared angrily at the abbot. "You bastard . . ."

"Choose. Or I will order both of them slain." The abbot raised a hand, ready to signal the friar. "Who will die for your sins?"

Henry choked on the words, "D . . . Dr. Engel." He sagged after he spoke Joan's death sentence. But what other choice did he have? Though many years had passed since their time together at Rice, Joan had not changed. Henry still knew her heart. She would never forgive Henry if he preserved her life at the cost of Philip's. Still, his decision cut him like a huge jagged dagger in his chest. He could hardly breathe.

"So be it," Abbot Ruiz stated mildly, turning away. "Let it be done."

Sam followed Kamapak as the shaman trotted out of the jungle's fringes and into the brightness of the morning sun. Even with the cloak of mist overhead, the sun's brilliance was painful after the dim light of the shadowed jungle.

Shading his eyes, Sam stumbled to a stop. Maggie pulled up beside him. Both were winded from the high-altitude jog. A headache rang in Sam's skull as he surveyed the land beyond the jungle's edge.

A hundred yards away rose an almost vertical wall of bare volcanic stone, a cliff of crenellated rock, knife-sharp, and as coppery red as fresh blood. Above it loomed the black cone of the neighboring volcanic mountain, imposing in its heights.

Ahead, a thin trail zigzagged up the wall to the opening of a tunnel seventy yards above the valley floor. It looked like a hard climb. Two men could be seen working their way down the slope from the opening. Sunlight flashed off the spears they carried. Denal was not with them.

"C'mon!" Sam said, pointing his transformed dagger toward the men.

Maggie nodded, too winded to speak. Adjusting Sam's rifle over her shoulder, she cinched it higher and followed.

Kamapak led the way through a small field of wild quinoa, a type of highland wheat, along the forest's edge. Beyond the green fields, at the base of the cliff,

508 · JAMES ROLLINS

lay a wide apron of scraggled scrub and tumbled volcanic rock. A handful of vents steamed nearby, collared
with yellow stains of sulfur. The air was humid and
warm, a foul-smelling sauna.

They met the other two Incas at the trailhead that
led up to the tunnel above. As Kamapak spoke to the
guards, Sam studied the spears the two men brandished. Their blades were gold like his dagger. But
more importantly, the weapons appeared unbloodied.
Sam tried to listen to the conversation, but he could
understand none of it. Finally, the shaman waved the
men back toward the village and began the steep climb,
leading them upward.

Sam stopped Kamapak with a touch to his shoulder.
"Denal?" he asked.

The shaman just shook his head, pointed up, and
continued the journey.

"What do you think?" Maggie asked.

"I don't know. But apparently the answer lies up
there."

Maggie glanced worriedly toward the opening far
above. "At the temple?"

Sam nodded grimly, and the two followed Kamapak
up the series of switchbacks that climbed the wall. Any
further talk was cut off by the need to breathe. Sam's
grip on his knife grew slick. He heard Maggie panting

behind him. The muscles of his legs began to protest from the exertion.

Only Kamapak seemed unaffected. Acclimated to the altitude and moist heat, the shaman seemed unfazed by the climb. He reached the opening before they did and waited for them. He spoke as they approached. The only word recognizable to Sam was *Inti*, the god of the sun.

Sam glanced behind him and surveyed the spread of valley. Below, the village, half-covered in jungle, was barely discernible. Then suddenly a series of small fires climbed the rocky ridge off to the left, reaching to the lip of the volcanic cone. The signal fires. "Good going, Norman," he wheezed quietly.

Maggie joined him. "Let's hope your uncle gets here soon," she said, eyeing the fires. Then she nudged Sam toward the tunnel. "Let's get going."

Kamapak struck a torch to flame and led the way inside. The tunnel was wide enough for four men to walk abreast and seemed to stretch straight ahead. No curves or turns. The walls around them were smooth volcanic stone.

"A lava tube," Maggie said, touching the stone.

Sam nodded and pointed ahead. The darkness of the tunnel had seemed at first impenetrable. But as Sam grew accustomed to the gloom, he noticed a vague light coming from far ahead. Sunlight. "Norman was right," he said. "The tunnel must connect either to another valley or a cavern open to the sky."

Before Maggie could respond, Kamapak stopped ahead. The shaman lit two torches embedded in the right wall. They framed a small cave that neither Sam nor Maggie had noticed in the darkness. Kamapak knelt before the entrance.

As flames blew forth, a glow from the side chamber reflected back the torchlight into the main tunnel. Drawn like moths, Sam and Maggie moved forward.

Sam reached the entrance first. He stumbled to a stop as he saw what lay in the side chamber. Maggie reached his side. She tensed, then grabbed the Texan's upper arm. Her fingers dug in tightly.

"The temple," she whispered.

In the neighboring cave stood a sight to humble any man. The space was as large as a two-car garage, but every surface was coated with gold—floor, ceiling, walls. It was a virtual golden cavern! And whether it was a trick of the light or some other property, the golden surfaces seemed to flow, whorling and eddying, sliding along the exposed surfaces but never exposing the underlying volcanic rock. In the center of the room's floor was a solid slab of gold, clearly an altar or bed. Its top surface was contoured slightly, molded to match the human physique. Above the altar, hanging like a golden chandelier, was a fanciful sphere of fili-greed gold, strands and filaments twined and twisted into a dense mesh. It reminded Sam of a spider's egg sac, more organic than metal. Even here the illusion of flowing gold persisted. The entwined mass of strands seemed to wind and churn slowly in the flickering torchlight.

"Where's Denal?" Maggie asked.

Sam shook his head, still too shocked to speak. He pointed his serpent-shaped knife at the central altar. "No blood."

"Thank God. Let's—" Maggie jumped back a step.

A small spiral of gold filament snaked out from the mass above the altar and stretched toward Sam. "Don't move," Sam mumbled, freezing in place himself.

The thread of gold spun through the air, trailing like a questing tentacle. It seemed drawn toward Sam's extended dagger. Finally it stretched long enough to brush against the gold serpent, touching a fang. In-stantly, the golden sculpture melted, features dissolving away, surfaces flowing like warm wax. The hilt grew cold in Sam's grip as heat was absorbed from it. Then the gold reshaped itself, stretching and sharpening, into the original dagger.

The questing filament retreated, pulled back into the main mass like a reeled-in fishing line.

Sam held the dagger before his eyes. "What the hell just happened?"

Maggie found her tongue, crossing into Sam's shadow, keeping his wide shoulders between her and the gold cave, the temple. "It's not gold. It can't be. Whatever your blade is made of, it's the same as the temple. What the Mochico called *sun gold*. Some metal culled from meteors."

"But it almost seems alive," Sam said, backing away with her.

Kamapak rose to his feet, eyes full of awe for Sam. He mumbled something at Sam, then bowed his head.

"I don't think we should tinker with it, Sam. Let's find out what happened to Denal, and leave this until more experienced scientists arrive."

Sam nodded dully. "This is what Friar de Almagro saw. It's what must have scared the man into sealing off this caldera. The Serpent of Eden."

"That an' the decapitated head of Pachacutec," Maggie mumbled.

Sam turned to her. On the way to the temple, Maggie had told him how she had eavesdropped on Norman and Sam's fireside conversation, knew the fabricated story of Inkarri. "You don't buy into that nonsense of the beheaded king, do you?"

Maggie glanced down. "There's something I didn't tell you, Sam."

"What?"

"I wanted more time to think about what I saw before speaking." She glanced up at him. "I sneaked into the courtyard after you an' Norman were dragged away. I saw Pachacutec without his robe. His body was . . . was wrong."

"What do you mean?"

"It was like—"

A scream suddenly echoed down the passage, cutting off the conversation. Sam and Maggie froze.

"Denal!" Maggie gasped out as the cry echoed away. "He's alive!"

Sam stepped farther down the tunnel, toward the point where the vague glow of sunlight could be seen coming from ahead. "But for how much longer? Let's go."

Kamapak raised an arm to block them. He shook his head fiercely, babbling clear words of warning. The only understandable syllables were *janan pacha*. Incan Heaven. Sam recalled how the children of the villagers were said to be given as gifts to the gods at *janan pacha*. It was where they must have taken Denal! Kamapak stared defiantly at Sam, forbidding them passage.

"Fuck this!" Sam mumbled angrily. He brandished his dagger before Kamapak. "We're going, buddy. So either move or I'll carve a door in you."

The tone of his voice must have breached the language barrier. Kamapak backed away, fear in his eyes at the dagger. Sam did not wait for the shaman to change his mind. He led the way at a fast clip. Kamapak, though, trailed behind them, muttering prayers under his breath.

Soon they were at the exit of the tunnel. It emptied onto the floor of another volcanic caldera. But the mists there were thicker, the sunlight filtered to a twilight glow. Even drapes of heavy fog obscured the forested jungle ahead. The reek of sulfur was strong enough to burn the eyes, and the heat was stifling. A clear path led into the jungle.

"We must be in the neighboring caldera," Maggie whispered.

Sam nodded and continued into the valley. Maggie followed, and after a moment's hesitation, so did Kamapak. The shaman's posture was slightly hunched, his eyes on the strange skies, like he feared something would reach out and grab him. Clearly, the shaman had never been there. Some strong taboo.

"Not exactly my idea of heaven, that's for sure," Sam said as he led the way into the jungle, wiping the sweat from his brow. Under the canopy, twilight became night.

Around them, the jungle was quiet. No bird calls or the rustle of animals. In the gloom, Sam did spot a few monkeys hidden in the canopy overhead, but they were motionless, quiet. Only their eyes tracked the strangers in their midst.

Maggie already had the rifle unslung, and Sam hoped she was the experienced marksman she claimed to be. Especially since their only other weapon was Sam's dagger.

No one dared even whisper as they followed the path to where the jungle opened ahead. As they reached the brighter light, Sam crouched and held up a hand, halting them. They needed a plan. He glanced to Maggie. Her eyes were wide with fear and worry. Kamapak huddled behind her, wary.

Then another scream erupted, piercing the jungle like an arrow. It came from just ahead. "Help me!" The terror was clear in the boy's voice.

"To hell with caution," Sam blurted, and stood. "C'mon!" He raced down the last of the path, Maggie at his heels.

They burst from the jungle cover into the outskirts of another Incan village. There, too, terraced stone homes climbed the gentle slopes and lay half-hidden in the fringes of the jungle. But that was the only similarity. The jungle had encroached on the village, claiming it. Everywhere weeds and bits of forest grew from between the slabs of granite, sprouting as if from the stone itself. Nearby, a tree grew from one of the cracked rooftops, spreading its limbs to envelop the house.

But as unkempt as the village was, the smell was even worse.

The streets were full of refuse and offal. Old animal bones lay scattered like broken glass in an alley, many with pieces of hide or fur still clinging to them. Underfoot, shattered shards of pottery crumbled.

"Jesus," Maggie said, covering her mouth. "It's the third city."

"What?" Sam whispered.

"Remember from the celebration the first night. You guessed the necropolis was built as a city of *uca pacha*, the lower world, while the other village was of *cay pacha*, the middle world. Well, here's the *third* village. A city of the upper world, of *janan pacha*."

Sam glanced at the fouled and ruined streets in disgust. This was no heavenly city. But he dared not stop to ponder the mystery. Waving them on, Sam led them down the avenue.

As they ran, Kamapak stared at the ruined village with horror, eyes wide with disbelief.

Obviously this is not his idea of Heaven either, Sam thought.

Ahead noises began to be heard: grunting and soft angry squeals. But through the noise, one sound drew them on. Sobbing. It had to be Denal.

Sam slowed as the street emptied onto the village's main square. He peeked around the corner, then fell back. "Damn . . ."

"What?" Maggie whispered. She crept to the corner and looked.

Sam saw her shoulders tense. He joined her at the corner, forcing back his initial shock. Stripped naked as a newborn, Denal stood in the center of the square, dazed and terrified.

And with clear reason.

Around him, the square was crammed with pale creatures. Some as large as bulls, others no bigger than muscled calves. Sam recognized the sickly forms. These were the same beasts that had haunted the necropolis below. They circled the boy, sniffing, snuffling at his heels. Occasional fights broke out, sudden hissed screams and slashes of razored claws. They had yet to decide what to make of the boy.

But one thing was clear. They were hungry. Saliva drooled from almost all their lips. They looked near starved. All knobbed bones and skin.

One of the nearest creatures suddenly spun in their direction. It was one of the spindly-legged beasts. One of the pack's scouts. Sam and Maggie barely slid back into hiding before being spotted.

Sam nudged Maggie back.

The tattooed shaman looked just as confused and horrified. Clearly he had never suspected what his *janan pacha* had truly hidden. Before Sam could stop him, Kamapak stepped around the corner, arms raised. With tears in his eyes, the shaman lifted his voice in song, bright with religious fervor. Kamapak strode toward the pack of creatures.

The beasts on the square grew quiet.

Sam pulled Maggie farther back. He whispered in her ear. "We need to circle around. Take advantage of the shaman's distraction. See if we can free Denal."

She nodded, and the pair took off at a run, diving down a cross street that paralleled the plaza. They heard Kamapak's song droning on. Sam tried to race as quietly as possible, avoiding bones and pottery.

"This way!" Maggie hissed and darted into an alley between two homes.

Sam followed and soon found himself crouched again before the square, but this time, Denal lay directly ahead of them. The boy had not noticed them;

he had fallen to his knees, his eyes fixed on where the shaman stood.

The beasts had also been attracted by the singing. The monstrous throng had drifted away from the terrified boy and toward the new oddity. A path lay open.

If they were to rescue Denal, it was now or never.

Sam took a deep breath, then crept out, keeping low to the ground. Maggie followed, rifle at her shoulder.

Across the plaza, Sam spotted the shaman, now surrounded by the beasts. A few of the dwarfish members of the pack, the sexless drones, picked at the robe Kamapak wore. Others, the taller, more muscled hunters, kept back warily, heads cocked, studying the newcomer, listening to the singing. But how long would his song keep the monsters cowed? Sam immediately had his answer. One of the hunters raced forward and clubbed the shaman to the stones of the plaza. Sam took a step toward Kamapak, but Maggie restrained him with a grip on his elbow.

Kamapak slowly pushed up and touched his bloody forehead. The pack stared as the shaman raised his red fingers. Then the beasts caught the scent of his blood and all else was forgotten. The pale forms surged and leaped forward, scrambling and swamping the shaman. Kamapak screamed in terror and pain. Screeches and howls accompanied the attack. Even from where he stood, Sam could hear bones snap and flesh rip.

Denal turned away from the horrible sight and finally spotted Sam. He struggled to his feet and ran toward the pair on wobbly legs. The boy's eyes were puffy from tears, his face pale with terror. He opened his mouth to speak, but Sam raised a finger to his own lips. Denal clamped his mouth closed but could not stop a small whimper from escaping.

Sam and Maggie were soon at his side. As Sam pulled the boy to him, the growls and hisses began to die down across the plaza. Kamapak's own screams had already been silenced.

"We need to get clear of here!" Maggie whispered.

Across the square, handfuls of the beasts had settled to the stones with their meals. Bits of torn robe were everywhere. Blood lay in a trampled pool on the stones. But Kamapak himself was gone, shredded apart and torn by the claws and teeth of the creatures. All that remained were bloody gobbets being gnawed and fought over.

But, unfortunately, there was not enough of the thin shaman to go around. Several of the beasts now searched, sniffing, for another source of food. Their feral eyes fell back upon the boy. Their group was spotted.

"Damn it," Sam muttered.

Screeches rose again from the remaining creatures. Even those with fresh meat raised bloody muzzles to see what else might be claimed.

"Denal, how'd you get down here?" Sam asked, retreating across the square, no longer needing to be quiet. "Is there another way out?"

The boy shook his head. "The guards took me to the temple. Made me lie down on the altar. Then I wake up . . . I here, dizzy, no clothes." Denal's voice cracked. "Th . . . then these things come!"

"What the hell are they?"

Denal stuttered. "Th . . . their gods."

One of the nearest beasts lunged at them. Maggie eyed it through the rifle's sight and fired. The creature flew back, half its skull blown away. "Well, these feckin' gods bleed."

The dead beast was set upon by some of its brethren. More meat for the feast. But it did not slow the others down; bloodlust and hunger had driven them into a near frenzy.

Sam, Denal, and Maggie continued to retreat until new growls arose behind them. Sam swung around. More of the creatures shambled and crept into the back of the square, latecomers to the party, drawn by the fresh blood and screams. From the rooftops all around, other pale beasts clambered and howled their hunger.

"I think the dinner bell's just been rung," Sam said dourly.

Joan worked in her cell. She had spent the morning poring over various journal articles, abstracts, and typed notes on the theory of nanotechnology supplied to her by the earnest young monk. She was especially intrigued by the paper on the theory of biomimetic systems, the idea of constructing microscopic machines by imitating already existing biological models, such as mitochondria and viruses. The article by a Dr. Eric Drexler proposed using proteins and nucleic acids as the building components of a micromachine, or nanobot. The article expounded on how present-day biology could inspire the generation of "synthetic, nonbiological structures."

Joan leaned back, picturing the microscopic octagonal units that composed Substance Z. Their shape had struck her as familiar, almost an imitation of viral phages. Were these units actual examples of biomimetic constructs?

Reaching to the tabletop, Joan rifled through her papers until she came across a printout from the scanning probe microscopy analysis. It broke down the component parts of the strange unit.

Assay 134B12

SPM analysis: utilizing phase imaging, force modulation, pulsed forced microscopy (results cross referenced with mass spectrograph analysis #134B8)

Initial findings:

Shell architecture: macromolecules of Si (silicon) and H(hydrogen), specifically cubosiloxane ($H_8S_{18}O_{12}$) plus tectosilicates

Articulated arms: Si (silicon) nanotubes interfaced with Au(gold)

Core: Unable to analyze

Joan tapped at the sheet of paper. So the arms of the nanoparticle contained gold, hence the hue of Substance Z. But what intrigued her more was the shell composition. It was mostly silicon. In nature, almost all biologic building blocks were based on hydrocarbons—molecules of hydrogen, oxygen, and *carbon*. But here was a construct that replaced carbon with *silicon*.

"Hydrosilicons," she mumbled, naming this new class of molecule. Though hydrocarbons made up most of biology, in *geology*, it was silicon that made up the dominant element in the earth's crust. Could this structure be some link between biology and geology? Or as the young monk had proposed, was this the first *inorganic* nanobot to be discovered?

Lastly, her eyes rested on the last line of the report. The composition of the core. *Unable to analyze.* Here was the crux of the mystery. The exterior was known and quantifiable, but the inner workings were still an enigma. This brought her back to the ultimate question raised by the young monk in his own personal papers: *What is the purpose of this microscopic machine? And who had programmed it?*

Before Joan could ponder the mysteries any deeper, she heard the scrape of heel on stone from down the hall. She glanced to her watch and furrowed her brow. It was much too early for anyone to be fetching her lunch. She bit her lower lip. Whoever approached probably had nothing to do with her, but she could not take that risk.

Joan hurriedly straightened up the contents of her desktop. She shifted the research papers into a neat pile, then folded the worn sheet of legal paper with Friar de Almagro's code and stuffed it in a pocket. Next she slid the single book allowed in her room, a King James Bible, over the ragged hole she had blown through the oak desktop, hiding the result of her experimentation last night.

Finally, she rolled the cigarette she had bummed from Friar Carlos off the desk and tucked it into her breast pocket. She surveyed her handiwork, satisfied that no sign of her secret experiment with Substance Z had been discovered.

And luckily she did. The footsteps stopped right outside her door. Joan tensed. A key was fitted into the lock and turned.

She swung around as the door was pulled open. It was Friar Carlos with his 9mm Glock. She stood, brows raised in question. "What is it?"

"Out," he said brusquely, waving his pistol. "Come with me."

Joan hesitated; fear that she had been caught iced her blood.

"Now!" Carlos barked.

Nodding, Joan stepped forward and through the door. One hand fingered the collar of her blouse. On the underside of the removable plastic stay of her collar were the two teardrop-sized pearls of Substance Z. She could not risk leaving the samples in her cell. The room might be searched, or she might be reassigned to a new cell. So she had devised this way to keep the golden drops hidden and in her possession.

Carlos nodded her forward. She followed his directions. She expected him to lead her down to the labs, but instead he herded her to a new section of the Abbey. She frowned at the unfamiliar surroundings. "Where are we going?"

"You'll see when you get there."

The friar, never a warm fellow, was even more tight-lipped today. His tense attitude heightened her nervousness. What was going on? This wing of the Abbey was spartan. Plain stone floors with a string of bare bulbs illuminated the way. There were no lines of small doors opening into tiny domiciles. Joan glanced up and down the long hall. They had not passed a single of the Abbey's denizens since entering this wing.

"Is th ... there something wrong?" she asked, unable to keep the tremble from her voice.

Friar Carlos did not answer. He simply guided her to a small staircase at the end of the hall. It was only six steps and led to a thick oak door banded in iron. A small crucifix etched in silver marked the door. Above the crucifix was a pair of crossed swords.

Joan remembered Henry remarking on such a symbol found on Friar de Almagro's heraldic ring. She remembered its meaning. It was the mark of the Inquisition.

Nervousness became a clammy fear as Carlos backed her to the side at gunpoint and knocked on the door.

His rap was clearly a code. A latch was slid open from inside, the grate of iron on wood loud in the empty, bare hall.

Carlos stepped back as the door was swung open. Joan felt the heat of the next room flow out like the breath of a dragon. She was not allowed to back away. The 9mm Glock was pressed firmly into her side.

A heavy figure, his bared chest gleaming with sweat, stood in the doorway. He had shrugged his monk's robe from his shoulders and let it hang from his sashed belt. He ran a hand over his bald pate, which was also gleaming, and spoke in clipped Spanish. Carlos answered. The big monk nodded his head and waved them inside.

"Go," Carlos ordered.

With no other choice, Joan followed. The next room was something from old horror movies. To the left was a row of barred cells, straw-floored, with no beds. To the right was a wall upon which were hung neatly coiled chains. A row of leather whips hung from pegs. In the center of the room was a brazier, red hot with flickers of flames. Amid the glowing coals, three long iron poles were embedded.

Branding irons.

Joan glanced around the room. She was in a mock-up of a medieval dungeon. *No,* she corrected herself. She could smell a familiar scent. Something from her days at the emergency room. *Blood and fear.* This was no mock-up, no wax museum set. It was real.

"Why . . . why am I here?" Joan asked aloud, but in her heart she already knew the answer. Henry had made some mistake. As frightening as her surroundings were, Joan felt a twinge of worry for Henry. What had happened to him? She faced Carlos. "Am I to be punished?"

"No," the friar said, his words as casual as if speaking of the weather. "You are to be killed."

Joan felt her knees weaken. The heat of the room suddenly sickened her. She could hardly breathe. "I . . . I don't understand."

"And you don't need to," Carlos answered. He nodded to the large monk.

Using a pair of leather gloves, the thick man judged his irons. He pulled them from the coals and eyed their glowing tips. He pursed his lips, content, then spoke in Spanish.

Carlos raised his pistol. "Move to the far wall."

Joan did not trust her legs. She glanced around the room, then back to Carlos. "Why all this? Why this way?" She weakly pointed at his gun. "You could have killed me in the room."

Carlos's lips grew grimmer. He studied the tools of interrogation, the tools of the Inquisition, and answered, "We need the practice."

Maggie stared down her rifle and squeezed the trigger. The pale face flew back, the mouth a bloody ruin. Pivoting on her toe, Maggie swung the barrel at her next target. The blasts of the Winchester had deafened her by now to the screeches and howls. She operated on instinct. She fired again, blowing back one of the pale scouts that had wandered too near. Its high-pitched squeal as it was set upon by its brethren managed finally to slice through her numb ears.

She lowered her rifle, wheezing between clenched teeth. The five beasts she had slain so far were at least keeping the throng momentarily occupied.

Something touched her shoulder. She butted the rifle's stock at it.

"Whoa!" Sam yelled in her ear. "Hold on! It's me!" He gripped her shoulder more firmly.

Maggie licked her dry lips, shaking slightly. "What are we going to do?" she moaned. The beasts still had them boxed in the center of the plaza and were not backing down. She had made no headway in blasting a path to freedom. For every creature she shot down, more would leap and scramble to fill the gap.

Sam released his grip. "I've been counting. You have only one more round left."

Maggie glanced at the rifle. "Jesus!" She raised the weapon. Her last shot had better be good. She forced her hands not to tremble.

Sam pushed her gun down. "Let me try."

"With what?" she hissed at him.

He raised his gold knife. "Remember the creatures at the necropolis?"

"Sam, you're gonna have to let them come damn close," she argued, pulling the rifle free of his grip.

"Maybe not." Sam stepped in front of her. Taking off his Stetson, he lifted the gold dagger high and waved his hat with his other hand. He screamed a raw bellow of challenge.

Hundreds of eyes lifted from their meals and growled back at Sam.

The Texan replaced his hat, leaving only the dagger held in an upthrust fist. The growls from the massed throats died down as gazes flicked to the gold knife. A trickle of whimpering sounded to one side. Sam seemed to have heard it, too. He swung toward the noise, the weak spot in the throng. He waved his dagger with long sweeping motions, repeating his bellow of anger.

The wall of pale forms began to pull back from him, breaking apart.

"Stick to my back," Sam whispered at Maggie and Denal.

Maggie waved the naked boy ahead, then covered their rear with the Winchester. *One bullet,* she kept reminding herself.

Sam began a slow approach toward the throng, brandishing his dagger, jabbing, swiping, growling.

With bleating cries, several of the beasts galloped out of his path. The standoff broke down. More and more of the beasts fled, dragging off the bloody chunks they had managed to scavenge.

"I think it's working," Sam said.

Suddenly, something lunged at Sam. Vestigial wings beat on its back, identifying it as one of the hunters. Sam stumbled back, tripping over Denal.

Maggie danced away, keeping her feet and swinging her rifle.

But she was too slow.

Sam fell atop the boy as the creature leaped atop them. Denal screamed in terror. Sam shoved his only weapon up. *The dagger.* The screeching beast impaled itself on the blade. It seemed a small weapon compared to the hooked claws and shredding fangs of the attacker—but the effect was anything but small.

The tiny wings of the beast seemed suddenly to work. The creature appeared to fly straight up off Sam's blade, squealing a noise that made even Maggie cringe. It rolled to the stones of the plaza and lay belly up. Small flames could be seen lancing from between the clawed fingers that clutched its wounded abdomen.

Around them, the pale throng froze and became silent, eyes wide, unblinking.

The flames spread from the beast's belly. Like a wildfire in dry grass, the blaze blew through the creature. It arched and writhed; jaws stretched wide in a silent scream of agony. Flames shot out of its throat, flickering like some fiery tongue, and then its head was consumed. The creature's bulk collapsed to the stone, dead. Flames still danced along its blackened form, a sick pyre.

Sam and Denal were already on their feet. "Let's go," Sam said.

The Texan threatened again with his dagger, but this time, there was no challenge. The remaining beasts in his path cleared out. Huddled in a tight group, they crossed toward the exit. All three held their breath.

Maggie stared at the smoldering form of the attacker. *Spontaneous combustion.* She tried to add this piece to the growing puzzle. She shook her head. Now was not the time.

She turned her attention forward.

Sam continued to threaten the few beasts who still hovered at the edges of their path. An especially large monster, all muscle and bone, still glared from one side. Its eyes were narrowed with wary hatred. Of all the creatures there, this one appeared well fed. It hunched on one knuckled fist, like some silverback gorilla, but naked and pale. Maggie recognized it as one of the rare "leaders" of the pack. She noticed it lacked any external genitalia. *Like Pachacutec's body*, she realized.

One of Maggie's eyes twitched as a horrible realization began to dawn. She was so shocked that she failed to notice what the hulking beast held in its other clawed fist. "Sam!"

The creature swung his arm and threw a boulder the size of a ripe pumpkin at the Texan. Sam glanced over but could not move in time. The chunk of granite struck Sam's fist. The dagger flew from his grip. It landed in the middle of a clutch of the beasts.

The giant stone-thrower roared in triumph, raising on its legs and striking its barreled chest with one of its gnarled fists. Its triumphant bellow was echoed by others all across the plaza. Without the dagger, they had no defense now.

Maggie raised her rifle toward the howling gorilla. "Shut up, asshole!" She pulled the trigger, and the monster fell backward, crashing to the stones. Its legs tremored in death throes for a breath, then grew still.

As the echoes of her rifle blast died down, silence returned to the plaza. No one moved. With the death of the leader, the pack was momentarily cowed.

Finally, Maggie hissed, "Sam, that was my last shell."

"Then I'd say we've overstayed our welcome here."

As if hearing him, the creatures began to creep slowly toward them again.

The Texan turned to Denal. "How fast can you run?"

"Just watch me!" Denal flew down the empty street ahead.

Sam and Maggie took off after the boy, racing together through the fouled village.

Angry screeches and hungry howls erupted behind them. The chase was on. With the prey on the run, the pack abandoned their wariness. Bloodlust overcame fear. Scouts ran along neighboring streets, white blurs between homes, tracking them. Behind them, hunters gave chase, howling their challenge.

Maggie struggled to keep up with Sam, fighting to get the Winchester over her shoulder.

"Leave it," Sam yelled back.

"But—?"

Sam slowed and grabbed the rifle from her. He whipped it over his head and threw it behind them.

The prized Winchester clattered and skittered across the rock. "I'd rather save you than a damned rusted rifle."

Unburdened and strangely energized by Sam's words, Maggie increased her pace. They ran side by side, matching stride. Soon they were out of the village and onto the jungle path. Trees and whipping branches strove to slow them down, but they pushed onward, scratched and bloodied.

Denal was a few meters ahead of them, leaping and running naked through the woods.

"Make for the tunnel!" Sam called ahead.

"What tunnel?" Denal called back, almost tripping.

Maggie realized Denal had no memory of getting here. She yelled. "Just stick to the trail, Denal. It leads right to it!"

The boy increased his stride. Sam and Maggie struggled to follow. Behind them, they could hear the snap of branches and the yipping barks of the hunters.

Gasping, neither tried to speak any longer. Maggie's vision narrowed to a pinpoint and, as she ran, her legs spasmed and cramped. She began to slow.

Sam's arm was suddenly under her, pulling her along.

"No . . . Sam . . . go on." But she was too weak even to fight him.

"Like hell I will." He hauled her with him. The chase seemed endless. Maggie did not remember the trail being this long.

Then finally sunlight returned. The jungle fell behind them. Ahead, the black eye of the tunnel lay only a handful of meters ahead. Denal was already there, hovering at the entrance.

Sam half carried her up the short slope to the entrance. "Get inside!" he called to the boy.

Maggie glanced over her shoulder. Pale forms burst through the jungle foliage, ripping away clinging vines. Some loped on two legs, some ran on all fours.

"Get inside! Now, Denal!"

"I . . . I can't!" the boy whined.

Maggie swung forward. Denal still crouched by the entrance. He would take a step toward the shadowed interior, then back away.

Sam and Maggie joined him. The Texan pushed her toward the tunnel. "Go!"

Maggie stumbled into the entrance, her vision so dimmed that the gloom of the tunnel was blinding. She twisted around to see Sam pull Denal into his arms.

The boy screeched like a butchered pig as Sam leaped into the tunnel beside her. Denal writhed and contorted in the man's arms.

"What's wrong with him?" Maggie asked, as she and Sam limped deeper down the throat of the tunnel.

Denal's back arched in a tremored convulsion. "I think he's having a seizure," Sam said, holding the boy tight.

Behind them, the screeches of the beasts echoed up the passage. Maggie glanced over her shoulder. The beasts piled up at the entrance, twisted forms limned in the sunlight. But none entered. None dared pursue their escaping prey into the tunnel. "They won't come in here," Maggie muttered. She frowned as she swung around. *Like Denal,* she added silently.

Sam finally fell to his knees, exhausted, legs trembling. He laid Denal down. The boy's eyes were rolled white, and a frothing saliva clung to his lips. He gurgled and choked.

"I don't understand what's the matter with him," Sam said.

Maggie glanced back to the writhing mass of beasts at the tunnel's opening. She slowly shook her head.

Finally, Denal coughed loudly. His body relaxed. Maggie reached toward the boy, thinking he was expiring. But when she touched him, Denal's eyes rolled back. He stared at her, then sat up quickly, like coming out of a bad dream. "*Qué pasó?*" he asked in Spanish.

"I had to drag you inside," Sam said. "What was wrong?"

Denal's brows pinched together as he struggled back to English. "It would not let me come inside."

"What wouldn't?"

Denal pressed a finger against his forehead, eyes squeezed shut. "I don't know."

Maggie suspected the answer. "It was the temple."

Sam glanced over the boy's head at her. "What?"

Maggie stood. "Let's get out of here."

Sam helped the boy up. They followed her as she slowly trudged back toward the distant exit. Ahead, the two torches that framed the golden alcove, the Incan's Temple of the Sun, could be seen flickering from their notches in the wall.

As Maggie drew abreast of the cave, she slowed and stopped, studying the golden altar and the webbed mass of golden filaments above it.

Sam drew up to her, but his eyes were still cautiously watching their backtrail for any renewed sign of pursuit. He mumbled as he joined her. "If that was Incan Heaven back there, I hate to see their idea of Hell."

Maggie nodded toward the golden temple. "I think it's right here."

Denal hung back, keeping as far from the shining room as possible.

Sam stepped beside her. "I know. It's hard to believe the Incas would feed their children to those monsters."

"No, Sam. You don't understand. Those monsters *are* their children." Maggie turned toward Sam. She ignored his incredulous look. She needed to voice her theory aloud. "They told us the temple takes their children, turns them into gods, and sends them to *janan pacha*." Maggie pointed back toward where the last of the beasts still cavorted and whined at the entrance. "Those are the missing children."

"How . . . why . . . ?"

Maggie touched Sam's shoulder. "As I tried to tell you before, I saw Pachacutec without his king's robes. His body was hairless, pale, with no genitalia. His body looked just like one of those beasts. Like that big creature I shot. One of the pack's leaders."

Sam's brows bunched; his eyes shone with disbelief. He glanced to the temple. "You're saying that thing actually grew him a new body?"

"As well as it was able. As Sapa Inca or king, it gave him the body of a pack leader."

"But that's impossible."

Maggie frowned. "As impossible as Norman's healed knee?" she asked. "Or his repaired eyesight? Or his ability to suddenly communicate with the Incas? Think about it, Sam!" She nodded to the temple. "This thing is some biological regenerator. It's kept the Incas alive for hundreds of years . . . it grew their leader a new body. But why? Why does it do that?"

Sam shook his head.

Maggie pointed once again toward the beastly caldera. "That's the price for eternal life here. The children! It takes their offspring and . . . and I don't know . . . maybe experiments with them. Who knows? But whatever the purpose, the temple is using the Incas' children as biologic fodder. The villagers are no more than cattle in a reproductive experiment."

"But what about Denal?" Sam asked.

She glanced to the boy. He was unchanged . . . mostly. She remembered his reluctance to enter the tunnel. "I think the temple needs more malleable material, earlier genetic cells, like from newborns. Denal was too old. So it did to him like it does to all its experiments. Once finished, it instilled some mental imperative to cross to the next caldera and implanted phobic blocks on returning. You saw Denal's inability to enter here, just like the creatures'. I suspect those beasts we found at the necropolis two days ago had migrated from the caldera through other tunnels, perhaps looking for another way out, and became trapped down there. I think the beasts are allowed to go anywhere *except* into the villagers' valley. That is forbidden."

"But why?"

"Because the temple is protecting its investment from its own biologic waste products. It can't risk some harm coming to its future source of raw genetic material. So it protects the villagers."

"But if these creatures are a risk, why doesn't it just destroy the experiments once it's done with them? Why let them live?"

Maggie shrugged. "I'm not sure. Maybe the neighboring caldera is a part of the experiment, some natural testing ground for its creations. It monitors how they adapt and function in a real environment."

"And what about the way they burn up when I stabbed them?"

"Spontaneous combustion. A fail-safe mechanism. Did you notice how Denal's guards had spears made of the same gold? A blow from one of these weapons, even a scratch, must set off some energy cascade. It's just another level of protection for the villagers."

Sam stared at the temple, horror growing in his eyes. "It still sounds crazy. But considering what happened to Norman, I can't deny that you might be right." He turned to Maggie. "But, if so, why is the temple doing all this? What is its ultimate goal? Who built it?"

Maggie frowned. She had no answer. She began to shake her head when a new noise intruded into the tunnel.

. . . *whump, whump, whump* . . .

Sam and Maggie both turned toward the tunnel's other end. It was coming from the valley beyond.

"C'mon," Sam said excitedly. He led them at a fast clip toward the bright sunlight.

As they reached the end, squinting at the late morning's glare, Sam pointed. "Look! It's the cavalry!" Circling through the mists overhead was a dark shadow. As it descended farther, the green-black body of a military transport helicopter came into sight. "It's Uncle Hank! Thank God!"

Maggie also sighed with relief. "I'll be glad to get the professor's take on all this."

Sam put his arm around her. She didn't resist.

Then deeper down in the valley, a new sound challenged the beat of the rotors. A more rapid thumping: *drums*! It seemed the Incas had also spotted the strange bird entering their valley. The sharp clangs of beaten gongs began to ring through the valley, strident and angry.

Maggie glanced at Sam. "War drums."

Sam's arm dropped from her shoulder; his grin faded. "I don't understand. Norman should've warned the Incas not to fear the professor or the others."

"Something must've gone wrong."

Sam now wore a deep frown. "I've got to reach my uncle and warn him." He began to lead the way down the steep switchbacks.

Below in the valley, the helicopter descended toward the flat field of quinoa planted at the jungle's edge. The shafts of the plants were beaten flat by the rotor's wash.

Maggie followed. "But what about Norman?" she yelled over the roar of the helicopter.

Sam did not answer, but his pace increased.

Norman hid in the fringes of the jungle as the helicopter landed in the green meadow beyond. He kept tucked behind the leaves of a thorny bush; tiny green ants marched down a frond before his eyes, too busy to be bothered by the thumping beat of the helicopter as its skids settled into the field.

Norman, though, felt every thudding *whump* deep in his chest. Cringing, he prayed he was wrong and hoped he had misinterpreted Professor Conklin's words. "After all that's occurred this last week," he mumbled to himself, "maybe I'm just being paranoid." Still, Norman remained hidden as the passenger compartment of the chopper slid open. A part of him knew that he was *not* wrong. Professor Conklin had been trying to warn Norman about something. But what?

The answer was soon apparent. A mix of men, some dressed in fatigues and jungle camouflage, others dressed in the brown robes of monks, clambered from the helicopter. The men, even the monks, moved too efficiently to be just a rescue team. Crated gear was offloaded from a hatch and cracked open. Norman saw assault rifles passed from hand to hand. Several of the men knelt and attached grenade launchers to their weapons.

Norman hunkered down even lower. Oh, God! He hadn't been paranoid enough.

From deeper in the jungle, the drums and clanging gongs that had sounded from the Incan village fell silent. Norman held his breath. He was glad he had warned Pachacutec to prepare the village. If there had been no danger, the plan was for Norman to accompany the professor back to the village, halting any bloodshed and making introductions.

Norman considered returning to the village now. The Incas were prepared for hostilities, but not for this. He should warn them to flee. But Norman knew Pachacutec never would. The two had shared a long talk this morning, and it was clear the Incan king would brook no challenge to the tribe's autonomy. Pachacutec would not run.

So Norman remained hidden, peering through the fronded branches of his lookout post. The leader of the men, a rotund fellow outfitted in a safari suit and matching hat, barked orders and aligned his men for a march to the village. The men were quick to obey. In only ten minutes from the time the skids hit the ground, the assault team was under way. They operated with military precision.

A pair of men took the point. Crouching, they ran from under the blades of the helicopter and raced to the trailhead that led to the village. From their reconnaissance in the air, Norman was sure the twisted trails to the village had been mapped. The other four men followed more slowly, cautiously, guns at the ready. The large leader, red-faced and covered in a sheen of sweat, moved behind them, armed with a pistol and flanked by a single guard for protection.

Norman waited until the entire troupe had vanished into the jungle to finally breathe. He sat hunched, unsure what to do. He had to get word to Sam. Trying to peer toward the cliff face that contained the temple's tunnel, he could determine nothing about their fate. The jungle blocked his view.

If he could maybe work his way through the jungle . . .

He started to shift when new voices froze him in place. He trembled, half-crouched. From the far side of the helicopter, two other men climbed out. Norman instantly recognized the professor. He was unshaven, and his clothes looked like they had been slept in for a few days, but there was no mistaking his proud demeanor.

Henry stumbled a step forward, shoved at gunpoint by a tall dark man dressed in a monk's robe. The gunman had dark black hair and an even darker scowl. A silver cross glinted on his chest.

Norman did not understand all this religious garb. Clearly it was some ruse.

Voices reached him as the pair stepped farther away from the helicopter. "You will cooperate with us fully," the dark man said, "or the student at the dig will suffer the same fate as the woman friend of yours."

Norman saw Henry's shoulders slump slightly, defeated. He nodded.

From his hiding place, Norman clenched his fists in helpless frustration. The gunman had to have been referring to Philip. The Harvard student must be held hostage back at the camp.

"The collected prisoners will be questioned," the man continued. "You will help in the interrogation."

"I understand," Henry snapped back. "But if my nephew or any of the others are harmed, you can all go fuck yourselves."

The man's countenance grew even darker, but he just stepped back. He used his free hand to slip out a cigarette.

Norman shifted his crouched position, his right hand landing upon a chunk of volcanic rock. He clutched the rock and stared back at the sole man holding the professor captive. Norman worked the red rock free. If he sneaked along that ridge of basalt, it would put the helicopter between him and the guard. Norman already began to move, sidling along the jungle's edge. He knew even the chopper's pilot had left with the assault team, leaving only the single guard. It was a risk, but one that could save them all. If he could free the professor, they could flee together and join Sam's group.

Norman reached the folded ridge of volcanic basalt, took a deep breath, then broke from cover and dashed across the open few yards to reach the cover of the ridge. He dived back into the welcome shadows, waiting for bullets to pepper the slope behind him, sure he had been seen. Nothing happened. He leaned a moment on the rough rock. He raised the chunk of volcanic stone, suddenly questioning how smart this was. Before fear could immobilize him, he pushed onward, scuttling like a crab in the shadow of the basalt ridge.

Once he was sure he had gone far enough, he risked a quick peek over the ridge. He was right. The bulk of the helicopter stood between him and the gunman. Norman climbed over the ridge as quietly as possible. The soft scrape of rock sounded explosively loud, but Norman knew it was all in his head. Besides, he was committed. Out in the open.

He ran with the rock clutched to his chest, his heart pounding so loudly that even the Incas at the village could probably hear it. But he made it to the shadow of the helicopter. He knelt and spotted the feet of the two men on the far side. They seemed unaware of his presence.

Crawling under the helicopter, Norman moved around the extra fuel tanks. Strands of quinoa tickled his arms as he sneaked to the far side of the chopper. Ahead, both the professor and the gunman stood, their backs to him. The pair stared toward the jungle. The robed guard exhaled a long trail of smoke.

Holding his breath and biting his lip, Norman slipped free. He could either creep slowly, thus avoiding any obstacles . . . or simply make a mad dash toward his quarry. But Norman didn't trust his shaky legs with speed. So he stepped cautiously, placing one foot after the other, edging toward the gunman.

He was only an arm's length away when all hell broke loose.

Explosions suddenly rocked the valley. The center of the jungle ripped far into the sky, flaming shards raining down.

Norman gasped at the sight, unable to stop his surprised response.

Hearing him, the gunman twisted on a heel and dropped to a crouch.

Norman found himself staring at the business end of a pistol. "Drop it!" the man ordered.

There was no need for words. The rock in Norman's hand was already falling from his numb fingers.

From the jungles, screams and yells echoed forth. Gunfire rattled like a cupful of teeth.

Over the man's head, Norman spotted Henry. He wore a look of hopelessness and defeat.

Norman slumped, matching the expression. "I'm sorry, Professor."

Sam stumbled to a stop when the first explosion tore through the valley. He crouched slightly at the rain of flaming debris. "What the hell—?"

Denal crouched down, too.

Maggie was at Sam's shoulder, her eyes wide. "They're attacking the village!"

Sam stayed low. "Uncle Hank would never do that."

"What if it's not the professor?" Maggie said. "Maybe someone else saw the signal fires. Thieves. *Huaqueros.* Maybe even the same bastards who tried to tunnel into our dig last week. Maybe they intercepted our radio messages an' beat Uncle Hank here."

Sam sank to the slope. "What are we going to do?"

Maggie's eyes were fierce. "Stop them." She nodded toward where the helicopter rested in the field, half-obscured by a peninsula of jungle. "Take that out, and these thieves aren't going anywhere. Then call the professor and warn him to come with the police or army." She turned to Sam. "We can't let them murder and steal what we found here."

Sam was nodding with her words. "You're right. We have to at least try." He stood up. "I'll go and reconnoiter the site. See what's up."

"No," Maggie argued. "We remain together."

Sam frowned, but Maggie's expression did not budge.

Even Denal nodded his head. "I go, too." Sam caught the way the boy glanced up at the tunnel entrance. Denal was not being heroic; he just didn't want to be left alone . . . especially naked and weaponless.

Sam stood and surveyed the valley.

Automatic gunfire echoed up from the jungle. Other explosions would occasionally erupt, tossing trees and rocks into the sky. Amidst the weapons fire, whispers of Incan war cries mixed with the screams of the dying. Smoke billowed up and through the jungle.

"Okay," Sam said. "We all go. But stick together and keep quiet. We'll sneak to the jungle's edge and creep as close to the chopper as possible. Find out if there are any guards."

Maggie nodded and waved him forward.

Sam hurried down the last of the switchbacks and led them through the escarpment of volcanic boulders and scrub bushes. Soon the shadows of the jungle swallowed up the trio. Sam raised a finger to his lips and guided them with hand signals. Within the embrace of the forest, the sounds of warfare grew muffled.

Crouching, Sam picked a path through the foliage. They had to get to the helicopter before the thieves finished subduing the village. Sam prayed that there were some backup weapons in the helicopter. If they were to hold the valley until Uncle Hank got there, they would need their own firepower.

The shadowy jungle grew brighter ahead. It was the forest's edge. Sam slowed his approach. Now was not the time to be caught. He signaled the others to hang back. Sam alone crept the last of the way. Just as he was fingering away a splayed leaf of a jungle fern, a familiar voice reached him.

"Leave the boy alone, Otera! There's no reason to hurt him."

Uncle Hank!

Sam pulled back the leaf to view the open meadow beyond. The large military helicopter squatted like some monstrous locust upon the field of quinoa. But closer still was a sight that froze Sam's blood. His uncle stood before a man dressed in a monk's habit, but the man was no disciple of God. He bore in his right fist a large pistol. Sam, familiar with guns, recognized it as a .357 Spanish Astra. It was a weapon capable of stopping a charging bull—and it was pointed at his uncle's chest.

Over his uncle's shoulder, Sam spotted a third member of this party. It was Norman! The photographer's face was pale with fear.

The man named Otera glared at Sam's uncle. "Since when are you the one giving orders here?" He suddenly swung his gun and viciously struck Norman across the face. The photographer fell to his knees, blood welling from a cut on his brow.

"Leave him alone!" Uncle Hank said, stepping around to shield Norman.

Otera, his back now slightly turned to Sam, raised his pistol. "I think you've outlived your usefulness, old man. From the messages, these students know where the gold is hidden. So with this fellow here, I see no need to keep you around." Sam distinctly heard the gun cock.

Oh, God! Frantic, Sam slid from his hiding place and ran across the wet field.

The motion drew his uncle's attention. Henry's eyes widened in surprise. Sam saw his uncle struggle to stifle any further reaction—but even this small response was noticed.

Otera pivoted around just as Sam reached him, gun at chest level. Sam yelled and leaped at him, then an explosion of gunfire stung his ears. Sam was flung backward, away from his uncle's captor. He landed in the meadow on his back.

"No!" he heard his uncle yell.

Sam tried to push to his elbows, but he found he could not move. Not even breathe. It felt as if some huge weight sat on his chest. Pain lanced out in all directions. From the corner of his eye, he saw his uncle leap on the back of the robed gunman, tackling and crushing him to the ground.

Sam smiled at the old man's fierceness. *Good for you, Uncle Hank.*

Then all went black.

From a couple meters away, Maggie had spotted Sam suddenly burst from his hiding place and out into the open. What was the damned fool doing? She hurried forward with Denal beside her. As she reached Sam's hiding place, the crack of a single gunshot sounded from beyond the leafy fern.

Panicked, Maggie ripped away the fronds. She saw Sam collapsed in the flattened meadow, his arms twitching spastically. Even from her hiding place, she could see a gout of blood welling from a huge chest wound. Blind to all else, she ran from cover. She would no longer hide in a ditch while a friend died. "Sam!"

As she ran, she finally noticed the struggle beyond the Texan's body. It made no sense. The professor sat on the back of a struggling monk. The gun, still smoking in the wet grass, was just beyond the man's reach. Suddenly, as if in a dream, Norman appeared out of nowhere. He bore a huge red rock over his head. He brought it down with a resounding blow atop the pinned man's head. The man went limp, and Professor Conklin climbed off him.

It was then a race to see who could reach Sam first.

Sam's uncle won. He fell to his knees beside his nephew. "Oh, no . . . oh, God!"

Norman and Maggie reached him at the same time.

Falling to his hands and knees, Norman reached and checked for a pulse. Maggie sank more slowly. She saw the glassy way Sam stared up at the skies. She knew no one was there; his eyes were empty.

Norman just confirmed it. "He's dead."

At gunpoint, Joan crossed toward the wall of chains. She knew if she allowed herself to be bound to that dungeon wall that she was a dead woman; any hope of escape would be gone. Her mind spun on various plans and scenarios. Only one idea came to mind.

As she was prodded by Friar Carlos's pistol, her fingers clutched her collar. She slipped out the plastic stay that held her collar stiff and scraped one of the soft teardrop samples of Substance Z into her palm. She had to time this right.

On the way toward the wall, she sidled near the large, bare-chested monk who still stoked the flaming brazier. He leaned over his handiwork, stirring the glowing coals with one of the iron brands. Joan noted the slight bubble of drool at the corner of his lips. The thick-limbed brute clearly lusted to test his irons on her flesh. He caught her staring and grinned, a flash of desire.

Joan suddenly felt no guilt for what she was about to do.

Nudging past him, she flicked the pebble of metal into the brazier, then turned her back and ducked— and lucky that she did. The explosion was more force-ful than she had expected. She was thrown forward, crashing to the stone floor, and skidded on hands and knees. Her back burned. The smell of singed silk struck her nose. She rolled around, twisting her sore back to the cool stone.

Behind her, the brazier was a twisted ruin. The iron brands were scattered; one was even impaled through a wooden support pillar. The echo of the explosion slowly died in her ears, the ringing replaced with a pained howling. Her gaze shifted to the large monk. He lay on his back several meters away. His bare chest was charred and blistered. A hand rose and knocked a coal from his belly with a groan. The man sat up, one side of his face blackened. At first, Joan thought it was just soot; then the man cried out, and his burned skin split open, raw and red. Blood ran down his neck.

Oh, God. She turned her face away.

Carlos, unharmed, was already on his feet. He crossed to a telephone on the wall and barked in Spanish. A call for help. Once done, he slammed the receiver down and stepped over the wounded man. The monk clutched at Carlos's pant leg, but the friar shook him loose and crossed to Joan.

He pointed his gun. "Get up."

Joan pulled to her feet, gasping as her singed shirt peeled from her back. Carlos frowned and forced Joan around so he could view her injuries. "You'll live," he said.

"But for how long?" Joan asked with a sour look. "Until the next time you decide to kill me?" Joan waved a hand around the room. "What just happened?"

Carlos scowled at the man still moaning on the floor. "An apprentice. It seems he has much to learn still."

Joan bowed her head, hiding her grim satisfaction. Carlos blamed the monk for the explosion. Good. Now for the next step in her plan. At her collar, she scraped a second dollop of gold under a fingernail, then reached to her pocket. She fingered out the cigarette Carlos had given her yesterday. With trembling fingers, she brought it to her lips. "Do you mind?" she asked, raising her face.

He frowned harshly at the moaning monk. "Go ahead. We've got a few minutes until someone comes for him." He reached out, and a lighter appeared in his fingers.

Bending, she lit the cigarette, then nodded her thanks. She took a long drag, sighing appreciatively and loudly. "That's better," she said heavily, exhaling in Carlos's direction.

Joan saw him eye the glowing tip of her cigarette. His pupils dilated at the scent of nicotine.

She took a second drag, then passed him the cigarette, sighing out the smoke languidly. "Here. Thanks. But that's enough for me."

He accepted her offering with a tight smile. "Afraid for your health?"

She shrugged, too tense to trust her voice. She spotted the glint of gold on the underside of the cigarette, a quarter inch from its glowing tip. "Enjoy," she finally said.

Carlos held up the cigarette in a salute of thanks. Then he grinned and drew it to his lips. Joan took a small step away, turning her shoulders slightly.

She watched the friar take a long drag on the cigarette. Its end grew red hot as it burned toward the filter. Joan swung away as the white paper flamed toward the smear of gold.

The explosion this time was not as severe.

Still, it threw her to her knees.

Joan twisted around, her head ringing with the blast. Carlos still stood, but his face was a cratered, smoking ruin. He fell backward, landing atop the burned monk, who now screamed in horror.

Joan rolled to her feet and recovered the friar's Glock from the floor. She crossed to the wailing monk. Crouching, she roughly checked his burns. Third degree over sixty percent of his body. He thrashed from her touch, crying out. She stood. He was a dead man, but didn't know it yet. He would not survive these burns. "Not so fun playing with fire, is it?" she mumbled.

She raised her pistol and aimed between his eyes. The monk stared at her in terror, then fainted away. Sighing, she lowered the Glock. She couldn't do it, not even to give him a quick end. She moved away.

Time was crucial. She had a gun and a remaining sliver of gold. Nothing must stop her from escaping.

She hefted the pistol and stepped clear of the two prone bodies. She eyed the friar's corpse for a moment.

"You were right, Carlos," she said, turning to the door. "Smoking kills."

Maggie touched Henry's shoulder as he knelt over his nephew's body. His shoulders were wracked with painful sobs. Maggie knew no words could ease his pain. Her years in Belfast had taught her that much. On both sides of the fighting, Irish and English, Catholic and Protestant, there were just grieving mothers and fathers. It was all so stupid. So insane.

Behind her, gunfire continued to bark throughout the jungle, though by now it had died to sporadic fits. The most intense fighting had already ended. The Incas had no prayer against such armament.

She stared at Sam, unable to look at the ragged wound, the blood. She found her gaze resting on his face. His Stetson had been knocked off when he fell. He seemed almost naked without it. His tousled sandy hair was mussed and unkempt, like he was just sleeping. She reached and touched a lanky lock, tucking it behind an ear. Tears she had been holding back finally began to flow. Her vision blurred.

Henry reached to her hand, sensing her pain, needing support himself. His cold fingers wrapped around hers. Where words failed, simple human contact soothed. She leaned into the professor's side. "Oh, Sam . . ." her voice cracked.

Norman knelt across from Sam's body. Behind him, Denal stood quietly. The naked boy was now covered in Norman's poncho, leaving the photographer only a pair of knee-length breeches. Norman cleared his throat. "Maggie, what about the temple?" he said softly. "Maybe . . . maybe it could . . ." He shrugged.

Maggie raised her teary eyes. "What?"

Norman nodded to Sam's body. "Remember Pachacutec's story."

Horror replaced sorrow. Her eyes widened. She pictured the Sapa Inca's pale body and remembered what lay in the neighboring valley. She slowly shook her head. The temple held no salvation. She could not imagine giving Sam's body over to it.

Henry spoke, his voice coarse with tears. "Wh . . . what temple?"

Norman pointed toward the volcanic wall. "Up there! Something the Incas found. A structure that heals." Norman stood and exposed his knee. He told of the injury he sustained.

The professor's face grew incredulous. He turned to Maggie for confirmation.

She slowly nodded her head.

"But Sam's d . . . dead," Henry said.

"And the king was beheaded," Norman countered. He looked to Maggie for support. "We owe it to Sam at least to try."

Henry stood as another grenade exploded, and gunfire grew heated again. The weapons fire sounded much closer. "We can't risk it," he said sternly. "I need to get you all into hiding. It's our only hope of surviving."

Maggie had stopped listening after the word *hiding*. A part of her wanted to agree with the professor. *Yes, run, hide, don't let them catch you.* But something new in her heart would not let her. She stared at Sam's still face. A single tear sat on his cheek. She reached with a finger and brushed it off. Patrick Dugan, Ralph, her parents . . . and now Sam. She was done hiding from death.

"No," Maggie said softly. She reached and took Sam's Stetson from where it had fallen in the damp grass, then swung to face the others. "No," she said more forcefully. "We take Sam to the temple. I won't let them win."

"But—"

Maggie shoved to her feet. "No, Professor, this is our choice. If there is even a chance of saving Sam, we attempt it!"

Norman was nodding. "I saw a stretcher in the helicopter when I got the rope to tie up the monk."

Maggie glanced to where the man who had shot Sam still lay unconscious in the grass. His breath was ragged, his pallor extreme. He would probably die from the blow to the skull, but as an extra precaution, they had lashed his legs and arms. They stopped at gagging him, mostly because of his labored breathing. Her chest tightened with anger at the sight of him. She glanced away, to the helicopter. "Get the stretcher!"

Norman and Denal hurried to the chopper's open door.

Henry stepped to her side. "Maggie, Sam's dead. Not only is this wrong, it's likely to get everyone killed."

Maggie stood up to the professor. "I'm done hiding in ditches," she said. She remembered Sam's scathing words last night when she resisted eavesdropping on the shaman and the king. She had tried to justify her reluctance, but Sam had been closer to the truth. Even then, *fear* had ruled her—but no longer. She faced Henry. "We're doing this," she said firmly.

Norman and Denal arrived with a khaki-colored army stretcher, ending further discussion. Henry frowned but helped lift Sam onto the stretcher. Soon they were under way. Henry stopped only to grab the monk's pistol from the weeds and stuff it into his waistband.

With the four of them, Sam's weight was manage-able. Still, the climb up the switchback seemed endless. Maggie's nagging fear and the need for speed stretched time interminably. Once they reached the tunnel, she checked her watch. Only twenty minutes had passed. But even that was too long. The jungle gunfire had grown ominously silent.

"Hurry," Maggie said. "We need to be out of sight!"

With straining arms and legs, they trundled into the gloom of the passage.

"It's just a bit farther," she encouraged. "C'mon."

Ahead, the torches still glowed at the entrance to the gold chamber, though now they just sputtered. As they pulled even with the temple, Maggie heard the professor gasp behind her. She turned, helping to lower Sam.

Henry gaped at the chamber, his face a little sick. "It's *el Sangre del Diablo*," he mumbled, setting Sam down.

Maggie knew enough Spanish to frown at his words. "The blood of the Devil?"

"It's what the abbot's men have come searching for. The mother lode—"

Norman interrupted, "We need to get Sam in there. I'm sure there's a time factor involved in this resurrection business."

Henry nodded. "But what do we do? How do we get it to work?"

They all looked at each other. No one had an answer.

The photographer pointed into the chamber. "I don't have an operator's manual. But there's an altar. I'd say first thing is to get Sam on it."

Henry nodded. "Let's do it."

They hauled Sam up, each person grasping a limb, and eased him onto the gold altar. Maggie's skin crawled as she stepped into the chamber. It was like a thousand eyes were staring at her. Her fingers brushed against the altar's surface as she placed Sam down. She yanked her hand away. The surface had felt warm, like something living.

With a shudder, she retreated from the room, along with the others. Standing in the passage, they all stared, transfixed, waiting for something to happen, some miracle to occur. It never did. Sam's body just lay on the altar. His blood dripped slowly from his chest wound and down the side of the altar.

"Maybe we waited too long," Maggie finally said, breaking the room's spell.

"No," Norman said. "I don't think so. Kamapak took half a day to get Pachacutec's decapitated head here, and the temple still grew him a new body."

"Sort of," Maggie countered. She turned to Norman. "What did Kamapak do after bringing the head here? Was there any clue?"

Norman answered sullenly, "All he said was that he prayed to Inti, and the god answered."

Maggie frowned.

Henry suddenly stiffened beside her. "Of course!"

She turned to the professor.

"It's prayers! Concentrated human thought!" Henry stared at them as if this was answer enough. "This . . . this gold, Devil's blood, whatever the hell it is . . . it responds to human thought. It will mold and change to one's will."

Now it was Maggie's turn to lift her brows in shock, but she remembered the transformation of Sam's dagger. It had changed as their needs dictated. She remembered how it had transformed in her own hands, when she had been so desperate for a key to the necropolis's gold statue. "Prayers?"

Henry nodded. "All we have to do is concentrate. Ask it . . . beg it to heal Sam!"

Norman dropped to his knees, drawing his palms together. "I'm not above begging."

Henry and Maggie followed suit. Maggie closed her eyes, but her thoughts were jumbled. She remembered the pale beasts in the next chamber. What if something like that happened to Sam? She clenched her fists. She would not let that happen. If prayers worked, then she'd let the others pray for healing. She would concentrate on keeping the temple from making any additional "improvements" in the man.

Bearing down, she willed it to heal Sam's injuries, but *only* his injuries. *Nothing else!* She strained, knuckles whitening. *Nothing else, damn you! Do you hear me?*

Denal suddenly gasped behind her shoulder. "Look!"

Maggie cracked open her eyes.

Sam still lay upon the altar, unmoving, but the ball of webbed strands above the bed began to unwind, to spread open. Thousands of golden stands snaked and threaded from the nest to weave and twine in the air. Tips of the strands split into even tinier filaments, then these split again. Soon the threads were so fine, the room seemed filled with a golden fog. Then, like a heavy mist settling, the golden cloud descended over Sam's body. In a few seconds, his form was coated from crown to toes with the metal, making him a sculpture in gold. And still the gold seemed to flow. Like some shining umbilical cord, a thick twined rope connected the golden statue of Sam to the node above the altar. The cord writhed and pumped like a living structure.

Maggie felt slightly sickened at the sight. She stood up; Henry and Norman soon followed.

"What do you make of it?" Henry asked. "Will it work?"

No one answered.

"How long it will take is the better question," Norman said. "I don't think the army down there is going to give us all day to hang around."

Henry nodded. "We need to think about setting up a defense. Is there another way out?" The professor glanced down the tunnel toward the other caldera.

"Not that way," Maggie said.

Henry turned back around and rubbed at his tired eyes. "Then we'll need weapons," he mumbled. "I spotted an extra case of grenades in the helicopter, but . . ." The professor shook his head sourly.

Norman spoke up. "Grenades sound good to me, Doc. Preferably lots of them."

"No," Henry said dismissively. "It's too risky to go back down there."

"And it's too risky *not* to," Norman argued. "If I'm quick and careful . . ."

Denal added, "I go, too. I help carry. Box heavy."

Norman nodded. "Together, it'll be a cinch." He was already stepping away with the boy.

"Be careful," Maggie warned.

"Oh, you can count on that!" Norman said. "The *National Geographic* doesn't offer combat pay." Then he and the boy were off, hurrying down the corridor.

Henry returned to staring at the temple. He mumbled, "The structure must be using geothermal heat as its energy source. This is amazing."

"More like horrible. I can see why Friar de Almagro called this thing the Serpent of Eden. It's seductive, but beneath its charms lies something foul."

"The Serpent of Eden?" Henry furrowed his brows. "Where did you come by that expression?"

"It's a long story."

The professor nodded toward the temple. "We have the time."

Maggie nodded. She tried to summarize their journey, but some parts were especially painful to recount, like Ralph's death. Henry's face grew grim and sober with the telling. At the end, Maggie spoke of the beasts and creatures that haunted the neighboring valley. She explained her theory, finishing with her final assessment. "I don't trust the temple. It perverts as much as it heals."

Henry stared down the long corridor toward the distant sunlight. "So the friar was right. He tried to warn us of what lay here." Now it was Henry's turn to relate his own story, of his time with the monks of the Abbey of Santo Domingo. His voice cracked with the mention of the forensic pathologist, Joan Engel. Another death in the centuries-long struggle to possess this strange gold. But Maggie read the additional pain behind the professor's words, a part of the story left unspoken. She didn't press.

Once done, Henry wiped his nose and turned to the temple. "So the Incas built here what the abbot dreamed. A structure large enough to reach some otherworldly force."

"But is it the coin of God?" she asked, nodding toward Sam. "Or the blood of the Devil?" She glanced to the next caldera. "What is its ultimate goal? What is the purpose of those creatures?"

Henry shook his head. "An experiment? Maybe to evolve us? Maybe to destroy us?" He shrugged. "Who knows what intelligence guides the temple's actions. We may never know."

Muffled voices and the scrape of heel on rock drew their attention around. It was too soon for Norman and Denal to be returning. Flashlights suddenly blinded them from the tunnel's entrance. An order was shouted at them: "Don't move!"

Maggie and Henry stood still. What else could they do? There was no escape behind them. But in truth, neither was willing to abandon Sam. They waited for their captors to approach. "Do whatever they say," Henry warned.

Like hell I will! But she remained silent.

A huge man, who from the professor's story could only be Abbot Ruiz, crossed to the professor. Maggie was given only the most cursory glance. "Professor Conklin, you've proven yourself as resourceful as ever. You beat us here." He frowned at Maggie. "Of course, the tongues you needed to free were a little easier than ours, I imagine. These Incas proved themselves quite stubborn. Ah, but the end result is the same. Here we are!"

The abbot stepped past them to view the chamber. He stood, staring for a moment at the sight. Then his large form shuddered, trembling all over. Finally, he fell to his knees. "A miracle," he exclaimed in Spanish, making a hurried sign of the cross. "The sculpture on the table appears to be Christ himself. Like in our vault at the Abbey. It is a sign!"

Maggie and Henry glanced at each other. Neither corrected the abbot's misconception.

"See how it trickles down from the roof. The old Incan tales spoke of the mother lode. How it flowed like water from the mountaintops! Here it is!"

Maggie edged closer. She knew, sooner or later, the abbot would discover his mistake. She could not let these men interfere with Sam's healing. She cleared her throat. "This chamber is just a trinket," she said softly.

The abbot, still kneeling, turned to her. His eyes still shone with the gold. "What do you mean?"

"This is just the temple, the entrance," she said. "The true source lies in the next valley. The Incas call it *janan pacha*."

"Their heaven?" the abbot said.

Maggie nodded, glad the man had some knowledge of the Incan culture. She glanced to Henry. He wore a deep frown, clearly guessing her plot. He didn't approve, but he remained silent. Maggie returned her attention to the abbot. "This temple is just a roadside prayer totem. A gateway to the true wonders beyond."

The abbot shoved to his feet. "Show me."

Maggie backed a step. "Only for a guarantee of our safety."

Abbot Ruiz glanced down the corridor. One eye narrowed suspiciously.

"Heaven awaits," Maggie said, "but without my help, you'll never find it."

The abbot scowled. "Fine. I guarantee your safety."

"Swear it."

Frowning, Abbot Ruiz touched the small gold cross hanging from his neck. "I swear it on the blood of Jesus Christ, Our Savior." He dropped his hand. "Satisfied?"

Maggie hesitated, feigning indecision, then finally nodded. "It's this way." She headed down the corridor.

"Wait." The abbot hung back a moment. He waved to one of his six men. "Stay here with the good professor." He crossed toward Maggie. "Just to keep things honest."

Maggie felt a sick tightness in her belly. She continued down the passage, forcing her legs to stop trembling. She would not give in to her fear. "Th . . . this way," she said. "It's not too far."

Abbot Ruiz stuck close to her shoulder, all but breathing down her neck. He wheezed, his face as red as a beet. Prayers mumbled from his lips.

"It's just through there," she said, as they neared the exit to the tunnel.

The abbot pushed her aside, marching forward, determined to be the first through. But when he reached the exit, he hesitated. His nose curled at the stronger stench of sulfur here. "I don't see anything."

Maggie joined him and pointed to the trail in the jungle ahead. "Just follow the path."

The abbot stared. Maggie feared he would balk. She was sure he could hear her heart pounding in her throat. But she maintained a calm demeanor. "*Janan pacha* lies just inside the jungle. About a hundred meters. It is a sight no one could put into mere words."

"Heaven . . ." Abbot Ruiz took a step into the caldera, then another—still he was cautious. He waved his five men ahead of him. "Check it out. Watch for any hostiles."

His men, rifles at shoulders now, scurried ahead. The abbot followed, keeping a safe distance back. Maggie was forced to leave the tunnel to maintain the ruse. She held her breath as she reentered the foul nest of the creatures. Where the hell were the monsters?

She took a third step away from the entryway when she heard a rasp of rock behind her. She swung around. Perched over the rough entrance to the tunnel was one of the pale beasts. One of the scouts. It clung by claws, upside down. It knew it had been spotted. A hissing scream burst from its throat as it leaped at her.

Maggie froze. Answering cries exploded from the forest's edge. It was a trap, and here was the sentinel. Maggie ducked. But the scout was too quick, lightning fast. The beast hit her. She fell backward and used the attacker's momentum to fling it down the short slope behind her. She did not wait to see what happened. She scrambled to her feet and dived for the tunnel.

Behind her, spats of gunfire exploded; screams of terror and pain accompanied the weapons fire. But over it all, the wail and shriek of the beasts.

In the safety of the tunnel, Maggie swung around, facing the opening. She saw the abbot level his pistol and fire pointblank into the skull of the beast that had attacked her. It flopped and convulsed on the ground. The abbot glanced to the forest's edge, where his men still fought for their lives. He turned his back on them and ran toward the passageway, toward Maggie. He spotted her; hatred and anger filled his eyes. No one thwarted the Spanish Inquisition.

Maggie backed down the tunnel as the abbot pulled up to the entrance. Heaving heavily, the obese man struggled to breathe. He gasped out, "You bitch!" Then he leveled his pistol and stepped inside.

Jesus! There was nowhere to run.

"You will suffer. That I guarant—" Suddenly the abbot was yanked backward with a squawk of surprise. His gun went off, the shot wild. The bullet ricocheted past Maggie's ear.

A scream of horror erupted from the man as he was dragged from the tunnel and flung around. A hulking pale monster, another pack leader, had his expensive safari jacket snagged in a clawed fist. The other hand grabbed the abbot by the throat. More beasts soon appeared, more razored fists snatching at the choice meal. His gun was knocked from his grip. The abbot's scream became strangled as he was dragged away from the tunnel's entrance. A pale face, mouth bloodied, appeared at the tunnel opening. It hissed at her, then dived to the side, joining in the feeding frenzy.

She swung away and turned her back on the slaughter.

Behind her, a sharp screech of pain died into a wet gurgle. She hurried farther down the passage, toward the torchlight, away from the howling.

At the temple's entrance, she saw the lone guard. He stepped toward her, gun pointed. "*Qué hiscistes?*" he barked in Spanish, asking her what she had done. She saw the terror in his eyes.

Suddenly, Henry stepped behind him and pressed the barrel of a pistol to the back of the guard's head. It was the weapon the professor had taken from the monk by the helicopter. "She was taking out the garbage." He pressed the barrel more firmly. "Any problem with that?"

The man dropped his rifle and sank to his knees. "No."

"That's better." Henry crossed in front of the man and kicked the rifle toward Maggie. "You know how to use that?"

"I'm from Belfast," she said, retrieving the gun. She cocked it, checked the magazine, and lifted it to her shoulder.

Henry turned to his prisoner. "And you? Do you know how to fly the helicopter?"

The man nodded.

"Then you get to live."

Suddenly a groan sounded from the next room. Henry and Maggie swung around. They watched the golden umbilicus spasm and the gold coating begin to slide from Sam's body. Like a large siphon, it drew the metal from his skin, then coiled up on itself, churning and slowly twisting overhead.

Another groan flowed from Sam.

The guard stared into the temple, mouth gaped open in surprise. He crossed himself hurriedly.

"He's breathing," Henry said. He stepped toward the entrance.

Maggie grabbed his elbow. "Be careful. I don't know if we should interfere yet." Her words were strained, speaking while holding her breath. Dare she hope . . . ?

Sam pushed to one elbow. His eyes were unfocused. His other arm rose to swipe at his face, as if brushing away cobwebs. He moaned slightly, wincing.

Henry reached a hand out. "Sam?"

He seemed to focus on the voice, coughing to clear his lungs. "Un . . . Uncle Hank?" Sam shoved up, weaving slightly. His eyes finally seemed to focus. "God . . . my head."

"Move slowly, Sam," Maggie urged. "Take it easy."

Sam swung his feet to the floor with another groan. "I could use a bucketful of aspirin." He finally seemed to realize where he was. He craned his neck and stared up at the twined ball of golden strands. "What am I doing here?"

"You don't remember?" Maggie asked, concerned. He sounded lucid, but was there some sustained damage?

Sam frowned at his chest. The fingers of his right hand trailed to his bullet-torn vest. He stuck a finger through the hole, then pulled open his vest. There was no wound. "I was shot." His statement had the edge of a question.

Maggie nodded. "You died, but the temple cured you."

"Died?"

Both Maggie and Henry nodded.

Sam pushed to his feet, stumbled a step, then caught himself. "Whoa." He moved more slowly, deliberately, concentrating. "For a dead man, I guess I shouldn't complain about a few aches and pains." He crossed toward them.

Henry met Sam at the entrance and pulled his nephew to him. Their embrace was awkward due to the pistol in the professor's right hand. "Oh, God, Sam, I thought I lost you," he said, his eyes welling with tears.

Sam hugged his uncle fiercely, deeply.

Maggie smiled. She wiped at her own cheeks, then knelt by the stretcher and retrieved Sam's Stetson.

Henry pulled away, rubbing at his eyes. "I couldn't face losing you, too."

"And you don't have to," Sam said, swiping a hand through his hair.

Maggie held out his hat. "Here. You dropped something."

He took it, wearing a crooked smile, awkward, half-embarrassed. He slipped it to his head. "Thanks."

"Just don't die again," she warned, reaching and straightening the brim.

"I'll try not to." He leaned toward her as she adjusted his hat, staring into her eyes.

She didn't pull away from him, but she didn't move closer either. She was too conscious of the professor's presence and the weight of the rifle over her left shoulder. They stared for too long, and the moment began slipping away. Maggie gritted her teeth. To hell with her fears! She reached toward him—but Sam suddenly turned away.

A new voice suddenly barked from the darkness behind them, "Drop your weapons!" A figure stepped into the edge of the torchlight. He held Denal in his arms. The boy's mouth was clamped tightly shut, a long military dagger at his throat. The stainless-steel blade reflected the glow of the torches. The boy's eyes were wide with terror.

"Otera!" Henry hissed.

Norman fled through the jungle, crashing through the underbrush. His vision was blurred by tears. He attempted halfheartedly to keep his flight quiet, but branches snapped and dried leaves crunched underfoot. Still, he stumbled on—in truth, he did not care who heard him any longer.

Again he pictured the friar leaping to his feet from the grassy meadow. The bastard had been playing possum, lying in wait for Norman and Denal as the pair had crossed toward the helicopter. The friar had grabbed the boy before Norman could react, twin blades flashing out from wrist sheaths. Norman's response was pure animal instinct. He had leaped away from his attacker, diving into the jungle and racing away.

Only after his panicked heart had slowed a few beats did Norman recognize the cowardice of his act. He had abandoned Denal. And then he'd not even attempted to free the boy.

Logically, in his mind, Norman could justify his action. He had no weapons. Any attempt at rescue would surely have gotten them both killed. But in his heart, Norman knew better. His flight had been pure cowardice. He recalled the terror in Denal's wide eyes. What had he done?

Fresh tears flowed, almost blinding him.

Suddenly the jungle fell away around him. The gloom of the forest broke into brightness. Norman stumbled to a stop, brushing at his eyes. When his vision cleared, he gasped in horror at the sight.

A small clearing had been blasted into the jungle by grenade and gunfire. Bodies lay strewn all around, torn and broken. Both men and women. All Inca. The smell gagged him as he stumbled back: blood and excrement and fear.

"Oh, God . . ." Norman moaned.

Flies already lay thick among the corpses, buzzing and flitting around the clearing.

Then suddenly on his left, a huge shape rose up, looming over him, the dead coming to claim him. Norman spun to face the new threat. He would no longer flee. He *could* no longer flee. Exhausted and hopeless, he fell to his knees.

He raised his face as a huge spear was lifted in threat, its golden blade shining in the brightness overhead.

Norman didn't flinch.

I'm sorry, Denal.

Henry stepped toward Otera, gun raised. "Let him go!"

The trapped boy's limbs trembled as the knife was pressed harder to his tender throat. A trickle of blood ran down his neck. "Don't try it, Professor. Get back! Or I cut this boy open from neck to belly."

Fighting back a curse, Henry retreated a step.

The friar's eyes were wild and fierce. "Do as I say, and everyone lives! I don't care about you or the boy. All I care about is the gold. I take it with me, and you all stay here. A fair bargain, yes?"

They hesitated. Henry glanced to Maggie, then to Sam. "Maybe we should do as he says," he whispered.

Maggie's eyes narrowed. She stepped to the side and spoke to the friar, her voice fierce. "Swear on it! Swear on your cross that you'll let us go."

Scowling, Otera touched his silver crucifix. "I swear."

Maggie studied the man for a long breath, then carefully placed down her weapon. Henry did the same. The group then backed a few steps away.

Otera crossed to their abandoned weapons, then shoved Denal toward them.

The boy gasped and flew to Maggie's side.

The friar returned his long dagger to a hidden wrist sheath. Henry now understood how the man had managed to escape his ropes. He mentally kicked himself. None of them had thought to search the unconscious man.

Grinning, Otera crouched and retrieved his pistol. He passed the rifle to the guard who still knelt to the side of the passage. But the man refused to take it. He just stared numbly into the temple, lips moving in silent prayer.

Otera stood and finally swung to face the room himself. He froze, then stumbled back, overwhelmed. His face glowed in the golden light. A wide smile stretched his lips. "*Dios mio* . . . !" When he turned back to them, his eyes were huge.

"Impressive, isn't it?" Sam said.

The friar squinted against the torches' glare. He finally seemed to recognize the Texan. "I . . . I thought I killed you," he said with a frown.

Sam shrugged. "It didn't take."

Otera glanced to the cave of gold, then back to them. He leveled his gun. "I don't know how you survived. But this time, I'll make sure you die. All of you!"

Maggie stepped between the gunman and Sam. "You swore an oath! On your cross!"

Otera reached with his free hand and ripped off the silver crucifix. He tossed it behind him. "The abbot was a fool," he snarled at them. "Like you all. All this talk of touching the mind of God . . . pious shit! He never understood the gold's true potential."

"Which is what?" Henry asked, stepping beside Maggie.

"To make me rich! For years, I have endured the abbot's superior airs as he promoted others of pure Spanish blood above me. With this gold, I will no longer be half-Indian, half-Spanish. I will no longer have to bow my head and play the role of the lowly *mestizo*. I will be reborn a new man." Otera's eyes shone brightly with his dream.

Henry moved nearer. "And who do you think you'll become?"

Otera leveled his pistol at Henry. "Someone everyone respects—a rich man!" He laughed harshly and pulled the trigger.

Henry cringed, gasping and falling back.

But the shot went suddenly awry, striking the roof and casting blue sparks.

As the gun's blast died away, a new noise was heard. "Aack . . ." Otera choked and reached for his chest. A bloody spearhead sprouted from between his ribs. The friar was lifted off his feet. Gouts of blood poured from his mouth as he moaned, mouth opening and closing like a suffocating fish. His pistol fell with a clatter from his fingers.

Then his head slumped, lolling atop his neck, dead.

His limp body was tossed aside by the spear-bearer.

From behind him, a large figure stepped into view. He wore singed and torn robes.

"Pachacutec!" Sam cried.

The man suddenly stumbled forward, falling to his knees before the Incan temple. Tears streaked his soot-stained face. "My people . . ." he mumbled in English. "Gone."

A second figure appeared out of the darkness behind the man.

"Norman!" Maggie ran up to the photographer. "What happened?"

Norman shook his head, staring at the impaled form of the friar. "I ran into Pachacutec on the trail, amid the slaughter. He was coming to the temple, chasing after those who would violate his god. I convinced him to help." But there was no satisfaction in the photographer's voice; his face was ashen.

Norman's eyes flicked toward Denal. The photographer wore a look of shame. But the boy crossed to Norman and hugged him tightly. "You saved us," he mumbled into the tall man's chest.

As Norman returned the boy's embrace, tears rose in his eyes.

Off to the side, Pachacutec groaned. He switched back to his native tongue as he bowed before the temple, rocking back and forth, praying. He was beyond consolation. Blood ran from under his robes and trailed into the golden chamber. He looked near death himself.

Henry crossed closer to the king. If Maggie's story was true, here knelt one of the founders of the Incan empire. As an archaeologist who had devoted his entire lifetime to the study of the Incas, Henry found himself suddenly speechless. A living Incan king whose memories were worth a thousand caverns of gold. Henry turned to Sam, his eyes beseeching. This king must not die.

Sam seemed to understand. He knelt beside Pachacutec and touched the king's robe. "Sapa Inca," he said, bowing his head. "The temple saved my life, as it once saved yours. Use it again."

Pachacutec stopped rocking, but his head still hung in sorrow. "My people gone." He raised his face toward Sam and the others. "Maybe it be right. We do not belong in your world."

"No, heal yourself. Let me show you our world."

Henry stepped forward, placing a hand on Sam's shoulder, adding his support. "There is much you could share, Inca Pachacutec. So much you can teach us."

Pachacutec pushed slowly to his feet and faced Henry. He reached a hand to the professor's cheek and traced a wrinkle. He then dropped his arm and turned away. "Your face be old. But not as old as my heart." He stared into the temple, his face shining. "Inti now leads my people to *janan pacha*. I wish to go with them."

Henry stared over the king's shoulder to Sam. What could they say? The man had lost his entire tribe.

Tears ran down Pachacutec's cheeks as he slid a gold dagger from inside his robe. "I go to join my people."

Henry reached toward the Sapa Inca. "No!" But he was too late.

Pachacutec plunged the dagger into his breast, bending over the blade like a clenched fist. Then he relaxed; a sigh of relief escaped his throat. He slowly straightened, and his fingers fell away from the blade's hilt.

Henry gasped, stumbling back, as flames jetted out from around the dagger impaled in the king's chest. "What the hell . . . ?"

Pachacutec stumbled into the temple's chamber. "I go to Inti."

"Spontaneous combustion," Sam whispered, stunned. "Like the cavern beasts."

Maggie nodded. "His body's the same as the creatures'."

"What's happening?" Henry asked, staring at the flames.

Maggie explained hurriedly, "The gold sets off some chain reaction." She pointed to Pachacutec. Flames now wound out from the dagger and coursed over his torso. "Self-immolation."

Henry suddenly recalled Joan's urgent message to him in the helicopter. She had warned him of a way to destroy Substance Z. The gift stolen by Prometheus. *Fire!*

Turning, Henry saw Pachacutec fall to his knees, his arms lifted. Flames climbed his raised limbs.

Oh, God!

Henry grabbed Sam and Maggie and shoved them toward the tunnel's exit. "Run!" he yelled. He kicked the kneeling guard. "Go!"

"What? Why?" Sam asked.

"No time!" Henry herded them all onward. Denal and Norman ran ahead, while Henry and Maggie helped Sam on his wobbly legs. As they fled, Henry recalled Joan's final warning: *Prometheus packs a vicious punch! Like plastic explosive!*

Her words proved too true. As they reached the tunnel's end, a massive explosion rocked the ground under their feet. A blast of superheated air rocketed the entire group down the path, tumbling, bruising. The passage behind them coughed out smoke and debris.

"On your feet!" Henry called as he bumped to a stop. "Keep going!"

The group obeyed with groaned complaints, limping and racing onward. The trail continued to tremble under their heels. "Don't stop!" Henry called.

Boulders crashed down from the volcanic heights. The shaking in the ground grew even worse. Below, hundreds of parrots screeched and flew out of the jungle canopy.

What was happening?

As Henry reached the escarpment below the cliffs, he risked a glance back up. A monstrous crack in the rock face trailed from the tunnel straight up the side of the cone.

Sam leaned on Maggie, both catching their breath. The others hovered nearby. Sam's eyes suddenly grew wide. "Oh, God!" he yelled. "Look!" He pointed across the valley.

Henry stared. The original steam vents had become spewing geysers of scalding water. New cracks appeared throughout the valley, belching more foggy steam and water into the sky. One section of the volcanic cone fell away with a grinding roar. "It's coming apart!" Henry realized.

Maggie pointed behind them, toward the volcanic peak to the south. Black smoke billowed skyward. The scent of sulfur and burning rock filled the valley.

Sam straightened. "The explosion must have triggered a fault. A chain reaction. Hurry! To the helicopter!"

Norman chimed in with even more good news. "We've got company, folks!" He pointed to the smoking tunnel.

From the heart of the enveloping blackness, pale shapes leaped forth like demons from hell. The creatures piled and writhed from the opening, screeching, bellowing. Claws scrabbled on rock.

"The explosions must have panicked them," Maggie said. "Overcoming their fear of the tunnel."

From the heights, black eyes swung in their direction. The keening wail changed in pitch.

"Run!" Henry bellowed, terrified at the sight. "Now!"

The group fled across the rough terrain. Chunks of basalt now rattled upon the quaking ground, sounding like the chatter of teeth. It made running difficult. Henry fell, scraping his palms on the jagged stone. Then Sam was there, pulling him to his feet.

"Can you make it, Uncle Hank?" he asked, puffing himself.

"I'm gonna have to, aren't I?" Henry took off again, but black spots swam across his vision.

Sam lent him an arm, and Maggie suddenly appeared on his other side. Together, they helped Henry across the rough terrain to the flat meadow. Ahead, Norman was already pulling Denal and the abbey guardsman into the belly of the chopper. The photographer's eyes met theirs across the meadow. "Hurry! They're at your heels!"

Henry made the mistake of looking back. The quicker of the pale creatures already flanked them. Not far behind, larger creatures bearing clubs and stones bore down upon them.

Henry suddenly tripped and almost brought them all down. But as a group, they managed to keep their feet and continued running. Henry found himself beginning to black out here and there. Soon he was being carried between Sam and Maggie.

"Let me go . . . save yourselves."

"Yeah, right," Sam answered.

"Who does he think we are?" Maggie added with forced indifference.

Everything went black for a few seconds.

Then hands were pulling Henry into the helicopter. He felt the rush of wind and realized the helicopter's rotors were already twirling. A loud metallic crash sounded near his head.

"They're lobbing boulders," Norman called out.

"But they're not coming any closer," Maggie added from the doorway. "The helicopter has them spooked."

A second ringing jolt struck the helicopter's fuselage. The whole vehicle shuddered.

"Well, they're damn close enough!" Norman turned and hollered to the pilot. "Get this bird off the ground!"

Henry struggled to sit as the door slammed shut. "Sam . . . ?"

He felt a pat on his shoulder as he was hauled into his seat and strapped in. "I'm here." He turned to see Sam smiling at him, Maggie at his shoulder.

"Thank God," Henry sighed.

"God? Which one?" Norman asked with a grin, settling into his seat.

The helicopter suddenly shuddered again—not from the bombardment of boulders, but from a hurried liftoff. The bird tilted, then rose slowly. A final crash on the underside rocked the chopper.

"A parting kiss," Norman said, staring out the window at the cavorting and gamboling throng down below.

The helicopter then climbed faster, beyond the reach of their stones.

Henry joined the photographer in staring over the valley. Below, the jungle was on fire. Smoke and steam almost entirely obscured the view. Fires lit up patches of the dense fog. A view of Dante's Hell.

As Henry stared, relief mixed with sorrow in his heart. So much had been lost.

Then they were over the cone's lip and sweeping down and away.

They had made it!

As the helicopter dived between the neighboring peaks, Henry stared behind them. Suddenly a loud roar exploded through the cabin; the helicopter jumped, rotors screamed. Henry flew backward. For a few harrowing moments, the bird spun and twisted wildly.

The pilot swore, struggling with his controls. Everyone else clutched straps in white-knuckled grips.

Then the bird righted itself and flew steady again.

Henry dragged himself up and returned to his observation post. As he looked out, he gasped, not in fright but in wonder. "You all need to come see this."

The others joined him at the window. Sam leaned over, a palm resting on his uncle's shoulder. Henry patted his nephew's hand, squeezing his fingers for a moment.

"It's strangely beautiful," Maggie said, staring out.

Behind the helicopter, two twin spires of molten rock lit up the afternoon skies, one from each volcano. It was a humbling sight.

Henry finally leaned back in his seat. Closing his eyes, he thought back to Friar de Almagro and all his warnings. The man had given his own life to stop the evil here.

Henry whispered softly to the flaming skies, "Your dying prayer has been answered, my friend. Rest in peace."

DAY SEVEN

Cuzco

Sunday, August 26, 3:45 P.M.
Cuzco International Airport
Peru

The small, single-engine plane, an old Piper Saratoga, dipped toward the tarmac. The city of Cuzco spread below the wings in a tangle of streets, a mix of gleaming high-rises and old adobe homes. Though it was a welcome sight, Sam turned from the window. It had been a long day of flights and plans.

En route from the volcanic caldera, his uncle had used the helicopter's radio to alert the authorities and to warn the base camp of the erupting volcanoes. Philip had sounded panicked over the radio. It seemed the Quechan Indians were already evacuating. Henry had ordered the Harvard graduate to go with them; their helicopter's fuel was too low for another landing and takeoff. Almost crying, Philip had begged for rescue, but Henry had been adamant about getting back to Cuzco as soon as possible.

His uncle had then arranged for a change of aircraft at a small commercial airfield near Machu Picchu, hiring the single-engine plane and pilot for the hop to Cuzco.

Still, for all the expedient planning, the flight there had taken almost an entire day.

As the plane shed altitude for its final approach, Sam sat up straighter in the cramped cabin, careful not to disturb Maggie, who leaned on his shoulder, asleep like everyone else on board. Sam envied their ability to rest. Slumber had been impossible for him. His mind still dwelt on the last twenty-four hours.

He had died.

It was a concept that he could not yet fully grasp. As much as he had struggled, he could not recall anything from that missing hour of his life. He recalled no white light nor heavenly choir. All he remembered was blacking out in the field of quinoa, a bullet wound in his chest, then waking atop the gold altar. The rest was a big blank.

Sam frowned. He could not begrudge the fates for this small mental lapse. He was alive—and moreover, he had a gorgeous redheaded Irish archaeologist sleeping beside him. He glanced over and gently fingered a loose curl from Maggie's face as she slept. He should wake her. They were about to land. But he hated to do it. It was nice to have her this close to him. Even if he was just a convenient pillow. He let his fingers drop from her hair, dismissing any further thoughts. From here, there was no telling where any of them would end up.

The small plane landed with a bump onto the tarmac of the airport.

The jostling and the whine of the hydraulic brakes had the cabin passengers startling awake. Bleary-eyed faces bent to peer out tiny windows.

"We're already here?" Maggie said, stifling a yawn. "I would swear I just fell asleep."

Sam rolled his eyes. The flight had been interminable for him. "Yep. Welcome to Cuzco."

The mumble of the pilot to the tower could be heard as they taxied toward the tiny terminal. Uncle Hank unbuckled from his seat, stretched a kink, and worked his way forward between the press of seats.

More plans and arrangements, Sam thought.

Earlier, Sam had questioned his uncle's urgency in getting to Cuzco, but Sam had been gently rebuked. When he had tried to persist, Maggie had warned him away with a shake of her head. "Leave him be."

Sam glanced to Maggie now. She stared at his uncle with pained eyes. What was wrong? What was being left unsaid?

"Who are all those people out there?" Norman asked behind them.

Sam leaned back to the window. Beside the terminal walkway, a small crowd had gathered. Half wore the khaki uniforms of local police, rifles at their shoulders. A few news cameras were carried on other shoulders, microphones ready. The others were a mixture of locals and men wearing suits too warm for the climate. These last had the stamp of government officials.

It seemed his uncle's calls had stirred up a hornet's nest of activity.

The plane pulled near, and the pilot unhooked himself from the cockpit, then crossed to the door. Henry bent his head in discussion with the pilot, then the slender fellow cranked the door open and kicked the latch to release the stairs.

Even from here, Sam heard the machine-gun clicks of camera shutters and the chatter of voices.

His uncle paused at the opening and turned back to them. "Time to face the press, folks. Remember what we discussed . . . how to answer any questions for now."

"No comment," Norman quipped.

"*Sin comentario*," Denal echoed in Spanish.

"Exactly," Henry said. "Until we get things cleared up, we speak only to those in authority."

Nods passed all around. Especially Sam. He had no desire to discuss his resurrection with the international press.

"Then let's go." Henry bowed his head, and the others all followed.

As Henry stepped from the plane, he winced. Even in the brightness of the afternoon, the splash of video lights and the strobe of flashbulbs were near blinding. Voices called to them: English, Spanish, Portuguese, and French. The throng was held in check by a line of police.

Henry stumbled forward, eyes searching the crowd. *Joan.* A part of him had secretly hoped his frantic call to the authorities in Cuzco might have been in time. He had only heard scraps of reports over the radio during the flight there, but they had been sketchy: the military raid on the Abbey, followed by an intense firefight. Many had died, but the details afterward were muddled.

Henry held his hands in clenched fists as he crossed the tarmac. He continued to scan the crowd of reporters, government officials, and onlookers. Not one familiar face.

Henry forced back tears. *Please. Not again.* As he searched futilely for Joan, an ache grew in his chest, a burn of bile and guilt. It was a familiar pain. He had felt it before—when Elizabeth had died. He had thought he had reconciled his wife's death long ago, but his fear for Joan had awakened it all again. In truth, it had never gone away. He had just walled it off, cemented and bricked it over with his need to care for Sam.

But what now?

His heart was ash and cinder.

Joan was not there.

A man in a conservative grey suit stepped forward, blocking his view, hand held out. "Professor Conklin, I am Edward Gerant, protocol officer with the U.S. embassy. We have much to discuss."

Henry forced his fist to relax and raised his hand.

Then a voice rose from the throng, cutting through the background chatter: "Henry?"

He froze.

Edward Gerant reached for the professor's hand, but Henry pulled away, stepping to the side. He saw a slender figure push through the barricade of police.

Henry's voice cracked. "Joan . . . ?"

She smiled and approached, slowly at first, then as tears flowed, more hurriedly. Henry met her with open arms. They fell into each other, lost in their embrace.

Never thinking to feel such joy again Henry murmured, "Oh, God, Joan . . . I thought you had been killed. But I had prayed . . . hoped . . ."

"Uncle Hank?" a voice said behind him. It was Sam. His nephew knew nothing about Joan. Henry had been too guilty to discuss aloud the choice he'd been forced to make earlier. Guilt and fear had kept him silent until he could discover Joan's fate himself.

As Sam came up to them, Joan and Henry pulled slightly apart, but Henry would not take his eyes from her . . . never again. Without turning away, he introduced his nephew to Dr. Joan Engel. She smiled warmly and gripped Sam's hand. Once they had shaken hands, Henry again laid claim to her palm. "But what about you?" Henry asked. "What happened?"

Joan's smile faded a few degrees. "I escaped just as the police raid began. And lucky I did. As the authorities breached the Abbey, the monks triggered a fail-safe mechanism built into their laboratory. The entire facility was incinerated, including the vault of *el Sangre*." She pointed toward the distant horizon.

Henry stared along with Sam. Smoke as thick as that of another volcano climbed into the sky.

"The resulting explosion took out the entire Abbey. It's still smoldering. All that remains are the Incan ruins beneath."

"Amazing," Sam commented.

Henry leaned closer to Joan. "But thank God, you escaped. I don't know if I could have lived with—"

Joan snuggled into his embrace. "I'm not going anywhere, Henry. You drifted away from me once in my life. I won't let that happen again."

Henry grinned and tugged her tighter to him. "Neither will I."

Sam stepped away, smiling sadly, giving them their privacy. He had never seen his uncle lose himself so fully in someone else—and clearly the feeling was mutual. While he was happy for his uncle, Sam felt oddly hollow as he backed away from the couple.

Nearby, Norman was talking to the jilted embassy official, relating some part of their story. The photographer's boyish laugh carried far over the tarmac. To the side, Denal hung in Norman's shadow. Norman had offered to sponsor the boy as an intern for the *National Geographic*—and with the death of his mother, Denal had nothing holding him here but a life of poverty. The two had already made plans to return to New York together.

Across the tarmac, cameras continued to flash.

Sam wandered farther back, near the wing of the plane, away from the crowds. He needed a moment to think. Ever since his folks had died, he and Uncle Hank had been inseparable. Their grief had forged bonds that had tied their two hearts together, allowing no one else inside. Sam glanced over to his uncle. That is, until now.

And Sam was not sure how he felt about it. Too much had happened. He felt unfettered, loosed from a mooring that had kept him safe. Adrift. Old memories intruded: the screech of tires, crumpled metal, breaking glass, sirens, his mother, one arm dangling, being hauled from the wreckage on an ambulance's backboard.

Tears suddenly sprang up in his eyes. Why was he dredging all this up now? He could not stop his tears.

Then he sensed a presence behind him.

He turned. Maggie stood there, staring up at him.

Where he expected ridicule or some scathing retort at his reaction, he found only concern. One of the paramedics had given her a bright yellow rescue blanket. Maggie stood wrapped in it against the cool afternoon breeze. She spoke softly. "It's your uncle and that woman, isn't it? You feel like you're losing him."

He smiled at her and wiped roughly at his eyes. "I know it's stupid," he said, his throat constricted. "But it's not just Uncle Hank. It's more than that. It's also my parents, it's Ralph ... it's everything death steals."

Sam struggled to put into words what he was feeling, staring up at the sky. He needed someone to listen. "Why was I allowed to live?" He waved an arm toward the distant Andes. "Up there . . . and back with my parents in the car wreck . . ."

Maggie now stood before him, almost touching toes. "And me in a ditch in Belfast."

He leaned into her and knew that Maggie could understand his pain more than anyone. "Wh . . . why?" he asked quietly, choking back a sob. "You know what I'm talking about. What's the answer? I even goddamn died and was resurrected! And I still don't have a clue!"

"Some questions have no answers." Maggie reached up and touched his cheek. "But in truth, Sam, you didn't escape death. None of us can. It's still out there. Not even the Incas could escape it in the end." She drew Sam closer. "For years, I've tried to run from it, while you stood back-to-back with your uncle against it. But neither way is healthy, because Death always wins in the end. We end up the worse for trying."

"Then what do we do?" He begged her with his eyes.

Maggie sighed sadly. "We strive to live as fully as we can." She stared up into his face. "We simply live, Sam."

He felt new tears. "But I don't understand. How—?"

"Sam," Maggie interrupted, reaching a finger to his lips. The rescue blanket fell from her shoulder with a soft rustle.

"What?"

"Just shut up and kiss me."

He blinked at her words, then found himself leaning down. Guided by her hands, he discovered her lips. He sank into the softness and heat of her, and he began to understand.

Here is the reason we live.

He kissed her tenderly at first, then more passionately. His blood rang in his ears. He found his arms pulling her closer to him, while she reached hands to the back of his neck, tangling in his hair and tumbling his Stetson from atop his head. They struggled toward one another, leaving no space between them.

And in that moment, Sam's heart soared as he understood.

In this kiss, there was *no grief . . . no guilt . . . no death.*

Only life—and that was enough for anyone.

Epilogue

Two years later
Thursday, October 19, 10:45 P.M.
Institute of Genetic Studies
Stanford, California

Three floors beneath the main research facility, a man wearing a long white lab coat approached the palm pad to a suite of private laboratories. He pressed his hand flat on the blue pad and watched the pressure-sensitive reader flash across his fingers. The light on the panel changed to green. His name appeared in small green letters on the reader: DR. DALE KIRKPATRICK.

The sound of tumbled bolts announced his acceptance by the computerized monitoring station. He removed his palm and pulled the handle. The vacuum seal cracked with a slight *whoosh* of air, like a short inhaled breath. The middle-aged scientist had to tug harder to pull the door open against the slight negative pressure of the neighboring rooms, a built-in safeguard to keep biologic contaminants from possibly escaping the lab. No expense had been spared on this project. A government think tank, backed by the Pentagon, had invested close to a billion dollars in this project. A good portion of which, he thought with a wry smile, went directly into his personal salary.

His shoulder protested with a sharp twinge as he pulled the door fully open. Wincing, he entered the lab and let the door reseal behind him. He rubbed the tender spot alongside his rotator cuff. The bullet wound he had suffered in the halls of Johns Hopkins had required four surgeries to repair. Though he still had occasional pain, he could hardly complain—not only had he survived the attack, he had come away with a small quantity of Substance Z, the test samples used in the electron microscope assay.

Once word of his find reached the right circles, Dr. Kirkpatrick was allowed to vanish. His death was reported, and he was whisked to the West Coast, to the Institute of Genetic Studies at Stanford. He was granted the lab, and a staff of fourteen with the highest government clearance.

Dale continued down to his office, past the rows of laboratories. As he passed the computer suite, he heard the whir of the four in-line Cray computers as they crunched the day's data collected by the gene sequencer. The Human Genome Project was a child's puzzle compared to what his lab was attempting. He estimated it would take four more years to figure out the exact code, but he had the time. Whistling to break the silence of the empty lab, Dale used a keycard to unlock the door and enter his personal office.

Shrugging out of his lab coat, he hooked the garment on a coat rack, then loosened his tie and rolled up his sleeves. He crossed to his desk and settled into the leather chair with a sigh.

He wanted to dictate the last of his annual review, so Marcy could type it up tomorrow for his inspection. He opened a drawer and removed his personal dictation device. Thumbing it on, he brought the microphone to his lips.

"Status Report. Conclusions and Assessments," he dictated, then cleared his throat. "Nanotechnology has always been a theoretical science, more a field of conjecture than hard science. But with the discovery of Substance Z, we are now prepared to bring the manipulation of atoms into the practical sphere of science and manufacturing. For the past two years, we have studied the effects of the 'nanobiotic' units found in Substance Z on early embryonic tissue. We have discovered the manipulation has proven most effective at the blastula stage of the human zygote, during which time the cells are the most undifferentiated and pliable. By observing these nanobots at work, and through a process of reverse engineering, we hope to be able to construct the first prototypes in the near future. But for now, we have made a significant discovery of our own, the first step in making nanotechnology a reality: We now know the programmed goal of the nanobots found in Substance Z."

Frowning, Dale switched off the recorder and stretched a kink from his neck. He was proud of his research, but a nagging doubt still itched at his conscience. Carrying the dictation device, he crossed to the sealed window.

Once there, he pressed a button and louvered blinds swung open, revealing the contents of the incubation chamber in the next lab. A yellowish broth bubbled and swirled. Small sparks of gilt floated like fireflies in the mix. Flakes of nanobot colonies. Substance Z.

But it was not the special nutrient broth that had drawn Dale here.

Hanging from two racks were the twelve developing human fetuses. He leaned slightly forward, studying them. The pair in the second trimester were already developing their wing buds. Heads, bulbous and too large for the tiny frames, seemed to swing in his direction. Large black eyes stared back at him, lidless for now. Small arms, doubly jointed, slowly moved. One of the fetuses sucked its tiny thumb. Dale spotted the glint of sharp teeth.

He raised the recorder again and switched it on. "I have come to believe that the gold meteors discovered by the Incas were, in fact, some form of extraterrestrial spore. Unable to transport themselves physically, an alien civilization seeded these nanobot probes throughout the stars. Like a dandelion gone to seed, the probes spread through space, hoping to find fertile ground among the countless planets. Responsive to the patterns of sentient life, the gold probes would attract the curious with their shapeshifting nature and lure in their prey. Once caught, the nanobots would manipulate this 'raw material' at the molecular level, ultimately consuming a planet's sentient biomass and rebuilding their own alien race from it, thus spreading their civilization among the stars."

Dale clicked off the recorder. "But not here," he muttered.

Leaning forward, Dale studied the largest of the developing fetuses. It seemed to sense his attention and reached tiny clawed fists toward him. Sighing, Dale rested his forehead against the glass tank. *What will we learn from each other? What will we discover?* The lips of the tiny figure pulled back in a silent hiss, exposing its row of sharp teeth. Dale ignored the infantile display of aggression, content with the success of his handiwork. He rested one palm on the glass.

"Welcome," he whispered to the newcomers. "Welcome to Earth."

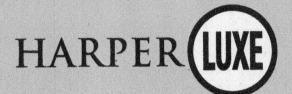

HARPER LUXE

THE NEW LUXURY IN READING

We hope you enjoyed reading
our new, comfortable print size and found it
an experience you would like to repeat.

Well – you're in luck!

HarperLuxe offers the finest in fiction and
nonfiction books in this same larger print size and
paperback format. Light and easy to read, HarperLuxe
paperbacks are for book lovers who want to see
what they are reading without the strain.

For a full listing of titles and
new releases to come, please visit our website:

www.HarperLuxe.com